TONINO

The Adventures of a Boy/Cricket from Boston's North End

JOHN G. STOFFOLANO JR.

Illustrated by William Griffin

iUniverse, Inc.
Bloomington

Tonino
The Adventures of a Boy/Cricket from Boston's North End

iUniverse books may be ordered through booksellers or by contacting:

iUniverse
1663 Liberty Drive
Bloomington, IN 47403
www.iuniverse.com
1-800-Authors (1-800-288-4677)

Because of the dynamic nature of the Internet, any web addresses or links contained in this book may have changed since publication and may no longer be valid. The views expressed in this work are solely those of the author and do not necessarily reflect the views of the publisher, and the publisher hereby disclaims any responsibility for them.

Any people depicted in stock imagery provided by Thinkstock are models, and such images are being used for illustrative purposes only.

Certain stock imagery © Thinkstock.

ISBN: 978-1-4502-9927-5 (sc)
ISBN: 978-1-4502-9929-9 (hc)
ISBN: 978-1-4502-9928-2 (ebk)

Printed in the United States of America

iUniverse rev. date: 12/02/2011

Dedication

The story that follows is dedicated to the elderly of the world, especially the spirits of those who have left us. Thanks for providing us with hope, wisdom, and vision. They serve as the conscience of those inhabiting the sphere we call "Mother Earth."

It is also dedicated to the youth of the world for providing new ideas and vital energy, which are so essential in helping shape tomorrow.

Only by understanding and appreciating other cultures, our natural environment, and the organisms that inhabit the world will we be in a position to preserve it.

Contents

Preface

Sabbatical in Siena, Italy

The fall sky was crispy clear in 1988, and the visibility seemed endless. Standing on the balcony of our apartment at the *Certosa di Pontignano, Collegio Mario i Bracci,* which is owned by the University of Siena, we could see the patchwork quilt of all the surrounding farms. The *Certosa,* about ten kilometers northwest of Siena, was previously the home of the Carthusian monks, a strict order of the Benedictine order. Every monk received his food through a small door in each of the individual cells, one of which we now called home. All the monks were sworn to silence, and silence we had at this wonderful place set amidst the best Chianti country of Tuscany. The only sounds at night were the insects, usually crickets, and the rustling and snorting of the wild boar outside the walls of the *Certosa.*

As we looked out over the Tuscan hills from the balcony that early morning, several prominent features of the landscape were obvious: the parallel rows of the grapevines, the tall green cypress trees lining the roads leading to the farmhouses, and the stone farmhouses with siena-colored roof tiles. One other distinct feature was evident: smoke rising from the various fields. It was as if Native Americans were trying to signal one another in the fields. The only difference was that it was a steady stream of smoke and not punctuated or puffing in a coherent message. What was the message, if any, and what was going on? My wife, Susan, asked me what they were burning. After some investigation and checking with Signore Lozzi, *contadino e proprietario* of the Quarciavalle vineyard, which was the first farm adjacent to the *Certosa*, I found out that at the end of the harvest, they burned all plant material and clippings throughout Italy and other European countries. This practice has been mainly abandoned in the United States, even though it is a nonchemical way of getting rid of pathogens and pests of the grapes, and whatever other infested plant material they burn.

Being an entomologist, I couldn't help but think of the nursery rhyme that depicted what we were looking at.

> Ladybug, ladybug, fly away home,
> Your house is on fire,
> your children do roam,
> Except little Nan, who sits in a pan,
> Weaving gold laces as fast as she can.

Ladybugs in Europe are considered good luck, and many a farmer's crop was saved from aphid outbreaks by the arrival of the ladybug, best known as a true beetle and not a true bug. The people of the time often called upon the Virgin Mary to save them, and their prayers were sometimes answered, thus the name "Beetle of Our Lady." Later, the names ladybug and ladybird, which came from "Our Lady's bird," were used. In this nursery rhyme, the farmers are calling out to the adult beetles to leave, because their house is on fire. They are essentially saying, "Please don't die; we need your help." Also, they are telling the adult beetles that their children, or larvae, are roaming and trying to get away from the fire and smoke. Unfortunately, they cannot fly and are destroyed along with the pupa. The pupa, called "Nan" in the nursery rhyme, is attached to the leaf, thus unable to move. Besides remembering the poem, something inside of me was awakened by the sight of the rising smoke.

One couldn't ask for a better place to spend a sabbatical. I was a visiting scholar in the Department of Zoology with entomology professors Massimo Mazzini and Romano Dallai. Massimo's mentor was Professor Baccio Baccetti, previously of Siena University, who is Italy's authority on the Orthoptera, which includes crickets.

A Small Book, but What a Treasure

Antiquing in Tuscany was a great treat. Arezzo, famous for its outdoor antique stalls of furniture and books, was one of our special places. Susan and I would arrive, have a cappuccino, and then set out to see what treasures we could find. The lira was very strong against the dollar at that time (1,200 lire to one dollar), so we had a little money to spend. As soon as we arrived, Susan would head toward the furniture stalls while I would start on the books.

It was May, and the weather was really not great. Today, instead of going to Arezzo, we went to Florence. The sky was dark, and rain was predicted. Even the cappuccino, along with the pastry *sfogliatella*, didn't brighten things up. I did make Susan smile because, as always, I got confectionary sugar all over my face and shirt. It was my choice where we would go first. Of course, I picked a very old bookstore known as Piatti. Unknown to me at the time, this is the same bookstore where Carlo Collodi, the author of *Pinocchio*, had worked when he was younger. As I pawed through the old but beautifully bound books, I happened to notice a very, very small book. It was exceedingly small for a book: only about one inch by one inch in dimension and about one eighth of an inch in thickness. Because of its size, this small treasure had been overlooked by those shuffling through the used books. I picked it up and looked at the title. It was a miniature Bible. "*Quanto costa?*" I asked the vendor.

"Twenty-four hundred lire," he replied.

I reached into my wallet and handed the man the money. I put it into my pocket and continued looking over other books. I saw many versions of *Pinocchio*. This was not coincidental. The province of Tuscany, especially the village of Collodi and city of

Florence, are well known as *Pinocchio* domains. Soon it was time for *pranzo,* or lunch.

For lunch, we spotted *saltimbocca* on the menu. Susan explained to me that this word comes from the Latin *saltare,* which is a verb that means "to jump," while *bocca* means "mouth." Thus, the dish is so good that it literally jumps into your mouth. I explained to her that early classification schemes of insects put all the jumping Orthoptera into a similar group, called Saltatoria.

After great deliberation, both of us decided to order the same thing. "*Saltimbocca per due.*"

"*Vino?*" the waiter asked.

"*Si, vino bianco per due, per favore.*"

Once the wine came, we toasted the day, "*Salute,*" and using my other hand, I reached into my pocket and pulled out my small gem.

Susan looked at it and said, "How are you going to read it? The print is so small, and it is in Italian."

"Don't worry," I said. "I can use the microscope in the laboratory, and Massimo can help me translate it."

Susan saw that this purchase had brightened up my day. Thus, she was content. Regardless of the weather, it was a good day all around.

Translating the Small Bible

The next day, I arrived at work very early. Massimo was already preparing to examine the sex-specific, modified orbital setae on the male Mediterranean fruit fly using the scanning electron microscope. I was patient but could hardly wait until he was done. When he finished, I shared my find with him. "Let's look at it under the microscope," I suggested.

Starting with the front of the book, we took turns looking at the various pages. One by one we would turn them. The writing was only about one tenth of a centimeter in height.

Massimo, who was a specialist in grasshoppers, crickets, and katydids, stated, "The way the Bible is written, and the way the verses are arranged, suggests that this is not a book for humans."

"What do you mean?" I said.

"It's a Bible for crickets," he said. "That's right. In fact, look here! Notice the spine from one of the prothoracic legs stuck on this page. It definitely is from a cricket."

"Whoever heard of insects writing anything?" I said to Massimo.

Massimo looked at me and responded, "You should be ashamed of yourself."

"What do you mean?"

Massimo assumed the posture of the professor, which he really was, and said, "You are an American, but you don't know about Archy the cockroach and Mehitabel the cat?"

"No, I never heard of them."

Massimo explained all about Archy and his friend Mehitabel. Archy used to use the typewriter in Don Marquis's office at the *New York Sun* after everyone left. The only way he could depress the key was to dive onto the letter from a key above. Because he couldn't depress two keys at once, all his writings were in lowercase and lacked punctuation. The two of them wrote stories about spiders, cockroaches, and even a lightning bug.

"Well, that solves that," I said. "Insects can write."

When we reached the twelfth page, Massimo found something else. He looked up with excitement and asked for his number five stainless steel forceps. Number five forceps have very fine tips and are used to pick up small things or do dissections on very small insects. Carefully, he used the fine tips to pull out a very tiny piece of folded paper. It was tucked between pages 12 and 13. Using the forceps, Massimo opened it and laid it flat on the glass stage of the dissecting microscope.

"What does it say?" I repeatedly asked him. "What does it say?"

He said, "It says, '*Il lignaggio della famiglia di Cricchetti*,' and it is signed 'Rolando Cricket, 1960.'"

I told Massimo that we could look at it after work. For the next three evenings after work, Massimo would translate from the Italian while I wrote in English what he said.

Just two days before Susan and I returned to the States, Massimo finished the translation. Our stay in Tuscany had been very productive. Massimo and I jointly published a paper in the Italian journal *Redia* on the structure of the modified orbital setae of the male Mediterranean fruit fly. I learned a lot about Tuscany and its food, culture, and people, and I was returning with a small gem of a book. More importantly, I had found a paper tucked into this small Bible, which most scholars of *Pinocchio*—even the late Collodi himself—would have loved to have found.

Grillo-Parlante's Progeny

I was greatly pleased to return with such a treasure to Amherst, Massachusetts, during the summer of 1989. It pleased me so much that I decided to share it with you. Below is information that has escaped the general public and *Pinocchio* scholars for years. It is about an important cricket lineage that started with the Talking Cricket, Grillo-parlante, in the original story *Pinocchio,* which was written by Carlo Lorenzini, better known as Carlo Collodi. Grillo-parlante, as he is always known in the literature, was really Grillo-parlante Cricchetti (1881–1921). He was the grandfather of Jiminy Cricket. You, the readers, are the first to know about this. Now, and only now, can one really understand more about the famous cricket, Jiminy Cricket, who was made popular by Walt Disney, but whose lineage was unknown until now.

Later, I discovered an interesting book by Harold Segel, *Pinocchio's Progeny* (1995), in which Segel discusses the history of our fascination with puppets and marionettes, and the important role *Pinocchio* played in the modernist movement of the theater. Thus, it was only appropriate that the conscience of Pinocchio— Grillo-parlante, or the Talking Cricket—be given equal time and have his lineage brought to light.

The lineage of this cricket continues, even after Rolando Cricket unknowingly lost the small piece of paper containing the family lineage he had carefully tucked into the family Bible. No one knows how it got into the chest of household items he and his wife Carmella sold in 1965, one year prior to leaving for America.

In 1982, Tonino, the great-great-great-grandson of Grillo-parlante Cricchetti, emerged from his eggshell in the North End of Boston. His character, his world adventures, and his experiences are laid before you in this wonderful story. As you read this story, no matter where you are in the world, or whatever you are doing, there are crickets around you. Look for them, watch them, learn about their behaviors, and most importantly, listen to them carefully. They may be telling you something important.

(The following is the lineage of the Cricchetti family as translated from the Italian by Professor Massimo Mazzini and transcribed by Professor Stoffolano, both entomologists. Both Mazzini and Stoffolano felt it was necessary for them to add some information to this lineage to help you better understand what is happening. In addition, both Stoffolano and Mazzini have done extensive research concerning Grillo-parlante's lineage. Thus, you are given a more detailed account of his family tree than was recorded on the sheet of paper found in the small Bible discovered by Dr. Stoffolano in Florence.)

Lineage of the Cricchetti Family

Grillo-parlante Cricchetti (1881-1921)

Hatched on July 4 in the small country village of Collodi, Italy, which is about thirty-five miles northeast of Florence, and near the town of Pescia, Grillo entered the world alone. This is not unusual since most insects enter the world without parents. Only a few insects have parental care. The majority of insects follow two main reproductive strategies. They either lay a lot of eggs, hoping that some will survive, or they develop only a few eggs, but retain them inside their body and deposit them in more fully developed stages, such as nymphs or larvae. Crickets follow the "lay a lot of eggs" strategy. It was a chilly July. The owners of the house where Grillo's mother lived had a fire in the fireplace. Because of the excessive heat, only one out of fifty eggs survived, and that one became Grillo-parlante.

Once he chewed his way out of the eggshell, Grillo waited until his exoskeleton had hardened and darkened. All arthropods (insects are arthropods) must shed their exoskeletons to grow. Prior to sclerotization (the process that gives the exoskeleton its hardness), however, they are white and very vulnerable to predation because the exoskeleton is soft. Have you ever eaten soft-shelled crabs? These are crabs that have just molted and their exoskeleton has not yet hardened.

Was Grillo a field cricket or house cricket?

The announcement of Grillo's hatching was published in the *Giornale per i bambini*. It was standard practice of the journal to publish hatchings of crickets whose parents were not known. This way, cricket couples that could not have offspring could adopt them. Unfortunately, Grillo was not adopted, but he was blessed with a special godmother: the Blue Fairy. The Blue Fairy often adopted young nymphs, young marionettes, and sometimes even boys. It was through this special relationship with the Blue Fairy that all the male descendents of the Cricchetti family were given three special wishes. These wishes, however, were not automatically granted. The receiver had to show the Blue Fairy that they were deserving of their wishes. Unfortunately, Grillo only had an opportunity to use one of them.

Early on in his life, Grillo developed an ability to fantasize. This helps explain why he told Pinocchio he had been in the same room for over a hundred years. He did this when Pinocchio discovered him. No cricket can live that long, and Pinocchio knew it. Grillo was pulling Pinocchio's wooden leg. In his rage, mischievous Pinocchio crushed Grillo on the wall with a hammer. Grillo was only trying to give Pinocchio some helpful advice.

> "Careful, ugly Cricket!" … At these last words, Pinocchio jumped up in a fury, took a hammer from the bench, and threw it with all his strength at the Talking Cricket. Perhaps he did not think he would strike it, but sad to relate he did hit the Cricket, straight on its head. With a last weak "cri-cri-cri" the poor Cricket fell from the wall, dead![1]

Illustration of Carlo Chiostri (1901)

Pinocchio not only questioned how old Grillo was, but he must have known that this cricket was a transformer.

> On reaching home, he found the house door half open. He slipped into the room, locked the door, and threw himself on the floor happy at his escape. But his happiness lasted only a short time, for just then he heard someone saying: "Cri-cri-cri!"[2]

Certainly Pinocchio had heard the sounds of crickets before and must have recognized the sound of an insect, not a human. So why did he address the sound as coming from "someone" rather than "something"? This is important because it establishes that all the progeny of Grillo-parlante were able to transform from cricket to human form. Why Collodi, who also knew the sound crickets make, never revealed Grillo-parlante in human form is not known.

Most important, however, is that humans and crickets think that Grillo died as a result of that accident. His hard exoskeleton, which is composed of chitin and a special protein called sclerotin, saved him from death. Chitin gives the exoskeleton strength, while sclerotin gives it hardness. It was the protein sclerotin that saved his life.

Slowly he slid down the wall, being held only by the surface tension of the life-giving fluid known as hemolymph in insects, which was oozing from the ruptured joints of his left foreleg. Pinocchio did not have enough education to realize that the hemolymph oozing from Grillo's foreleg was not red, as in most vertebrates. The red color of vertebrate blood is due to the hemoglobin molecule that attaches to oxygen, which is then carried to all the cells in the body. Probably 99 percent of insects lack hemoglobin. As you will learn later in this story, insects obtain oxygen in a different way than vertebrates.

Before hitting the floor, Grillo still had enough strength to ask the Blue Fairy to spare him such a humiliating death. She did, and his twisted body was rushed to an insect hospital by a special emergency ambulance owned by the local mice. Here he was tended to immediately. After two months of intensive care and therapy, Grillo was released. Insects have a very different immune system than humans, and blood transfusions can be given from one insect to another with no problem of rejection.

If you read the original *Avventure di Pinocchio* (1883) by Collodi, which was illustrated by Enrico Mazzanti, you will notice a drawing of Grillo holding a cane in his left foreleg.

In the original Collodi story, Pinocchio is hanged by assassins but is rescued by the "Little Girl" with blue hair. In order to determine if Pinocchio is dead or alive, she calls the three most prominent physicians in the area. One of these doctors is the "Talking Cricket." The other two physicians cannot decide whether Pinocchio is alive or dead. Finally, the Talking Cricket is asked for an opinion.

"And have you nothing to say?" the Fairy asked the Talking Cricket. "I say that the best thing the prudent doctor can do when he doesn't know what he's talking about is to keep quiet. Besides, that puppet's face is not new to me, I have known him for some time."[3]

Surely, the individual sitting in the chair at the scene of Pinocchio's bed using the cane is Grillo-parlante. Mazzanti drew Grillo-parlante with a cane, proving that Grillo did not die but suffered major trauma as a result of being hit by the hammer. Because his left prothoracic leg was severely damaged by the hammer, Grillo would be off balance when hopping and would fall forward if he didn't use a cane. In the early editions of *Pinocchio*, this famous cricket was known as Grillo-parlante. *Grillo* in Italian means "cricket," while *parlante* is from the Italian verb *parlare*, which means "to talk."

Illustration by Enrico Mazzanti (1883)

Because most of the drawings of Grillo-parlante are in black and white, he appears as a black cricket (as seen above in Mazzanti's drawing). Even in Chiostri's drawing (see below), the cricket is black.

Illustration by Carlo Chiostri (1901)

Unfortunately, Grillo is a house or domestic cricket and is normally yellowish-brown and not black.

Unknown to most people, including Pinocchio, Grillo had a mate. Grillo tried desperately to keep it a secret. Not even Collodi knew. In 1898, eight years after the death of Collodi, Grillo married Filomena Norelli (1882–1922), also a domestic house cricket, but from the south of Italy. She came from the small village of Squille, which is just northeast of Caserta. During their lifetime, they had only one offspring. In 1899, Pierangelo was hatched. At the time, Grillo was only eighteen years old.

Grillo never held any animosity toward anyone. In fact, he lived a satisfying and rewarding life of service. He spent most of his life as the conscience of Pinocchio, the marionette/boy who had tried to kill him with a hammer. On October 26, 1921, at forty years of age, Grillo died of normal aging with no visible signs of outward bodily damage (other than his dependency on using a cane and some arthritis in the joints of his foreleg).

Most male crickets show signs of age in that their wings are frayed and their antennae are often missing segments. This is due to fighting other males for territory and females. Grillo was lucky his body was found because the owners of the house in Collodi where Grillo lived saw him on the kitchen floor and threw his body away. His stiff body was swept up and thrown onto the compost pile with other organic leftovers. Grillo's wife, Filomena, with the help of her niece Annuciata, retrieved the body from the compost pile and prepared a proper burial. Filomena and Annuciata knew that Grillo wanted to be buried next to Collodi (a.k.a. Lorenzini). They also retrieved his cane. Thus, Grillo was buried in Lorenzini's family chapel in Florence, right next to Carlo (Collodi) Lorenzini.

Pierangelo-parlante Cricchetti (1899-1939)

Pierangelo was hatched in Collodi, Italy, on February 11, in the same house and under the same hearth as his father Grillo. Pierangelo became a talented musician and enthusiast of things that flew. Crickets are not great flyers, so anything that could fly better than a cricket, such as butterflies, birds, and even the new flying machines called airplanes, amazed Pierangelo. Pierangelo was well aware that on December 17, 1903, Orville Wright flew for twelve seconds, covering 120 feet, with a four-cycle, twelve-horsepower engine. This flying machine intrigued Pierangelo; he was aware that the Italian inventor and genius Leonardo DaVinci had plans for such a similar contraption, and now here it was, flying over the Tuscan landscape. As a young nymph, Pierangelo would hop onto an airplane, without being detected, and get a wonderful bird's-eye view of the Tuscan landscape, one that most crickets never saw. To black field crickets, the visual landscape was mostly vineyards, fields of sunflowers, olive trees, a little green grass with some taller plants, and a few scattered rocks. For house crickets like Pierangelo, the hearth was a favorite spot. Being able to see new sights, like the airplane view of the Tuscan countryside, was a treat.

Pierangelo and his family moved to Pavia, Italy, in 1915, six years before the death of his father. Pavia is known for its culinary fondness for *zampe di rana* (frog's legs). To a cricket, frogs represented a dangerous enemy and something to avoid. Many a cricket has served as a tasty meal for a hungry frog. Pavia is also well known because it is where two rivers, the Ticino and the Po, unite. As a young nymph, Pierangelo and his friend, Luigi Vidali Cricchetto, used to hop onto floating sticks to see how far they could go without getting wet. Luigi's mother continually warned them that if they fell in, they would become dinner for some hungry fish. Regardless of these constant warnings, Pierangelo never feared the water and continued, throughout his life, to jump onto anything floating in the various fountains of Pavia's piazzas. To help maintain his balance, he would often use the cane his father had used, the one Filomena and Annunciata had found and saved.

In 1917, when he was only eighteen, and in search of a better life following World War I, Pierangelo emigrated from Italy to Hollywood, California. Pierangelo, as many other Italian immigrants did, changed his last name. Rather than Cricchetti, he changed his name and became Pierangelo Cricket. In 1919, he met the young Italian-American actress Nancy Grimaldi (1900–1942), who was born in Northampton, Massachusetts, and they were married on June 18, 1920. Two years later, 1922, their only son, Jiminy Cricket, was hatched.

In the United States, Pierangelo found work as a musician while Nancy continued her work as an actress. This combination of parental involvement, plus the love for music and the theater, had a major impact on Jiminy. In later life, Pierangelo studied philosophy and psychology. He often would read and discuss with his son various ideas about cricket and human behavior.

In 1939, while attending the funeral of Luigi, Pierangelo died in Italy at the Certosa di Pavia. Luigi, who had not abandoned his love for the river, had fallen off a log and drowned in the cold, swift current. A fisherman recovered his stiff body. Pierangelo was buried next to his father in the Cricchetti family plot in Florence.

Jiminy Cricket (1922-1963)

Jiminy was hatched in Hollywood, California, on September 28, 1922, in the basement of a modest ranch house. Unlike most insects, which come into the world alone and without parents, Jiminy was lucky to have both of his parents. Pierangelo was in the musical side of the entertainment business, so he got to know a lot of writers who came to the jazz bars where he played the saxophone. Here, Pierangelo met Dave Hand, who was directing the upcoming Disney movie, *Snow White and the Seven Dwarfs*. Dave was telling Pierangelo something about the overall plot, and when the waitress accidentally spilled a drink on him, Dave abruptly shouted, "Jiminy Crickets!"

"What does that mean?" Pierangelo asked.

It is a phrase that means you are surprised, and it was used by one of the dwarfs who had just returned from the diamond mine in the Snow White movie. Pierangelo liked the name *Jiminy* so much that he gave it to his only son.

In 1938, at the age of sixteen, Jiminy began his acting career, appearing in several high school plays. At seventeen, he won a role in Disney's *Pinocchio*. This launched his acting career, and he became an instant star. The outfits he wore in the movie were designed by

Ward Kimball with the assistance of Walt Disney. Jiminy took voice lessons from Cliff "Ukulele Ike" Edwards, who was a radio actor. Cliff noted, however, that Jiminy had a natural voice and felt he really added little to launching his career as a singer.

Cricket "song" is hardwired from birth, unlike most birds and humans that learn from their parents. In fact, we must note here that crickets and other insects really do not sing. Singing involves air passing from the lungs over the vocal cords. Because crickets lack both, and instead produce their chirping with their forewings, it is really incorrect to say that crickets and other insects sing. It is interesting to note, however, that crickets of the same species, but from different countries or geographically isolated areas, do have different dialects.

Hollywood movie stars are generally manipulated by their agents who convince them they must change their image. Thus, Jiminy was forced to retire the wooden cane used by both his grandfather Grillo and Pierangelo, his father. Instead, he sported a red umbrella.

When he was twenty-three, on December 28, 1945, Jiminy married Mara Stoffolano (1924–1967). She was born in Big Bend, Texas. The following year, on April 1, 1946, in the small village of Montefegatesi, which is in the Apennine Mountains of Italy, their son Rolando was hatched.

On September 27, 1947, Jiminy became the announcer in the movie *Fun & Fancy Free.* Later, during the infancy of television, he had various roles. He also gave permission to let his image be used in numerous comic book series. The one image he enjoyed the most portrayed him as a great traveler. Michael Sragow, in his 1993 *Bazaar* magazine article, wrote that Jiminy was "a most simpatico conscience, dry and droll." He also wrote that he was "transformed from Collodi's didactic insect into a sprightly cracker-barrel philosopher, a hopped-up Will Rogers." Jiminy had a wonderful voice and proved this when he sang (or should we say chirped) *When You Wish Upon a Star,* in Disney's *Pinocchio.*

Jiminy never forgot his family's rural roots, which were in the Tuscan countryside. This grounded him to the area around the fireplace and gave him solace. His movie career had citified him, but he still loved getting back to nature. "That's where crickets really belong," he would say.

He worked hard and finally lost his Italian accent. This, his agent told him, was essential if he wanted to succeed in the entertainment industry. One of his favorite hobbies, and a strange one for a cricket because crickets dislike water, was watching the various sea life inhabiting the coastal waters of California, especially the mammals, such as seals and whales. Jiminy drowned at forty-one while whale watching off the coast of the Baja Peninsula in California. His body and kayak were never found. Disney in the movie *Pinocchio* portrayed Geppetto as swallowed by a whale (or was it really some other sea monster?). Some think a shark swallowed Jiminy because from the bottom, kayaks look like seals, which are sharks' favorite food. The latter belief seems more in keeping with the Crichetti family, because all the main characters in *Pinocchio* were swallowed, not by a whale, but by a *pesce cane* (dog shark).

Rolando Cricket (1946-1968)

Roland was hatched in the Italian Apennine Mountain village of Montefegatesi while his mother was visiting her aunt Elvenus Stoffolano. Thus, he had dual citizenship. Rolando immediately became a leader in local politics and a student of geography and Italian history. Montefegatesi is southeast of the village of Collodi. Rolando spent his early nymphal life in Hollywood but moved back to Montefegatesi in 1956 at the age of ten. At the early age of seventeen, Rolando married Carmella Pietra from Pavia, Italy. In 1964, at the age of eighteen, he and Carmella produced their only offspring. Giovanni was born on December 31, 1964. Carmella had a passion for family history and kept a detailed album of all the family photos.

Anticipating a departure to the United States in the coming year, Rolando and Carmella had to carefully plan what they would take to their new home in America. Space was a limiting factor. Rolando suggested to Carmella that they sell whatever items they couldn't bring with them. They did this and made enough money to pay for Carmella's ticket to the States.

The following year (1966), Rolando, Carmella, and their son Giovanni (then two years old) moved to the Italian section of Boston, Massachusetts, better known as the North End.

The small piece of paper placed in the family Bible and accidentally placed in the chest, which was sold by Rolando and Carmella in 1965, somehow made its way to Piatti, the bookstore in Florence where Collodi once worked. Purchased by Dr. Stoffolano during his sabbatical in Siena, and translated by Dr. Mazzini, this important document helps fill in the unknown paternal relationships of Jiminy Cricket, both prior to and after his hatching in 1922. The story continues.

Introduction

How many of us as adults ever get a chance to reread those wonderful children's stories? I did! In *Writing and Publishing Books for Children in the 1990s*, Olga Litowinsky states that we do not need another children's book about a talking animal, especially an insect. Since she is a successful editor, I assume she is correct; yet, being a scientist, I also know that truisms are ephemeral. If what she said is true, new discoveries would not be made and new literature would not be produced. I consider the creative process of writing as a type of science, with discovery as a major component, and view what she said only as a challenge to test her hypothesis (i.e., new children's books about talking animals, especially insects, are not needed). In order to appreciate the importance of insects in today's culture, one must only consider the overall popularity of insects in the movies (*Microcosmos, Antz, A Bug's Life,* and *Bee Movie*).

The following story represents a new discovery—at least a discovery in the author's mind. It gradually developed over a lifetime of learning and teaching about insects. It is not just an ordinary story about an insect, but it represents a synthesis and integration of ideas about life, culture, environmental issues, and history as seen through the life experiences of Tonino the cricket.

Tonino is an exceptional cricket. As you will soon see, he possesses special powers that make him different from any other living cricket (or, in fact, any human being, because he is both!). Humans are warned not to be anthropomorphic, yet this type of

John G. Stoffolano Jr.

thinking has helped us understand animal behavior. Tonino, the main character in this story, has also been warned by other insects not to be entopomorphic when it comes to dealing with humans. Being able to think like a human, however, greatly adds to his life. Like his parents, Maria and Giovanni, he is not only able to communicate with other insects and animals, but in his transformed state, he communicates and mingles with humans.

This is not unusual, especially since his great-great-great-grandfather, Grillo-parlante Cricchetti, was also able to do this. Since this ability to communicate with humans was linked to his Y-chromosome, all of Grillo's male offspring were able to do the same thing. Tonino, the great-grandson of Jiminy Cricket, was born in Boston's Italian-American section, also called the North End.

The cricket in George Selden's *The Cricket in Times Square* was named Chester Cricket. Why did Selden pick the name Chester, and how does one go about naming a cricket? My passion for the children's story *Le Avventure di Pinocchio* and the cricket in this story, Grillo-parlante, or the Talking Cricket, enticed me to learn more about the characters and the author of the story more commonly known to us as *Pinocchio*. When elementary school children visit the Department of Entomology at the University of Massachusetts in Amherst, I would always ask them about the insect character in *Pinocchio*. Of course, they all think that his name is Jiminy Cricket, and that the author is Walt Disney. In fact, *Pinocchio* was written by Carlo Collodi (the pseudonym of Carlo Lorenzini). Lorenzini was born in Florence, Italy, on November 24, 1826, and took the pen name Collodi based on the birthplace of his mother, the Italian village of Collodi, near the village of Pescia in Tuscany. He died on October 26, 1890, and is buried in Florence. His story was originally published in a weekly periodical for children, *Giornale per i bambini*, as a series of articles that appeared between July 1881 and January 1883. The story first appeared in book form in February 1883, and it wasn't until 1892 that its first translation into English appeared.

In the original story, the cricket's name is Grillo-parlante, not Jiminy Cricket. The cricket is a male because the original drawings by Mazzanti show a cricket lacking the female ovipositor. Why Disney made Jiminy green, rather than yellowish-brown, like most house crickets, is not known. I would encourage you to read the essay on *Pinocchio* in Perella's wonderful bilingual edition published in 1991. Pinocchio was created in the workshop of Antonio, an old cabinetmaker who sold the wood containing the wooden puppet to Geppetto, who was a maker of wooden puppets.

The name Antonio in this context recalls the popular pizzeria Antonio's in Amherst, Massachusetts. In addition, I grew up watching the TV commercial by the Prince Spaghetti Company, where the Italian mother in the North End of Boston comes out and yells to her son, Anthony, that it is Wednesday, Prince Spaghetti day. Thus, I initially was going to call this story *Anthony the Cricket.* I later changed the title (and the name of the lead character) after discussing the book with Dr. William Cooley, an ophthalmologist and Italophyle from Northampton, Massachusetts. Dr. Cooley sent me a short novel by an Italian author named Rodari about a young boy, Tonino, who tries to become invisible so that he could avoid problems with his teacher. Rodari (1920–1980) was one of Italy's best-known writers of children's books and the recipient of the Hans Christian Andersen Medal for children's literature.

Tonino means "little Anthony," and like Tonino the cricket, Rodari's Tonino had the power of becoming invisible. Also, something happens in the story that warrants calling him Tonino and not Anthony, the name he was originally given at his baptism.

I decided to provide information about how I named the cricket after going to an art opening at Hampshire College in Amherst in 1999. The Italian sculptor, Luigi Russo Papotto, showed a model of his proposed work and gave a detailed account of the thought process that went into its conception. His *Five Sculptures* has to do with our five fingers, the five human senses, the five continents, and the five colleges in the Amherst area. Unfortunately, this thought process is not normally shared when art forms like books, paintings, and sculptures are read or viewed. Viewers are left with their own interpretation, which could be thousands of miles away from the creator's original intention.

A good example of this is why Collodi chose a cricket to be the conscience of Pinocchio. As far as I know, no one really knows why he chose an insect, especially a cricket. There is little doubt that the cricket in the original story was a house cricket, *Gryllus Acheta domesticus*, thus Collodi named the cricket *Grillo-parlante* (*Grillo* = cricket and *parlante* = to talk). The only reference to the species of cricket in the original story comes from Baccetti's 1991 paper on the Orthoptera of central Italy, which includes Tuscany. Being a house cricket, and not a field cricket, Grillo-parlante's experience in the original story mainly centered on urban life. In personal correspondence, Professor Baccetti pointed out that in Italy, *Acheta domesticus* is known as *Grillo del Focolare*, which means "the cricket of the hearth, fireplace, or house." Baccetti also said that Geppetto, the father of Pinocchio, was so poor that he had no wood or fireplace. Instead, Geppetto painted a fireplace on the wall, and as Baccetti also said, "Evidently Grillo-parlante was influenced by the art of Geppetto, and was climbing the wall in the correct place."

In describing Geppetto's home, Perella writes, "At the back wall you could see a fireplace with a fire burning; but it was a painted fire, and along with the fire there was painted a kettle that boiled merrily and sent up a cloud of steam that really looked like steam."

I was intrigued with the idea of Collodi using a drawing of a fireplace and kettle as a place for Grillo the cricket to hang out. I did remember that Charles Dickens wrote *The Cricket on the Hearth* in 1845. I then began to research whether Collodi knew anything about Dickens, or if Dickens had been in Italy. To my surprise, I found that Dickens had spent time in Italy, and in 1846 he wrote *Pictures from Italy*. I continued to search for any connection between the two writers until (thanks to the Internet) I found an article by Maria Stella, "Pip and Pinocchio: Dickensian Motifs in Carlo Collodi," which was published in 2000 and is from a symposium held in Florence on *The Craft of Fiction and the Challenges of Reading by Carlo Dickens*. In that article, Stella convincingly presents the case that Collodi knew about Dickens's writings; based on her analysis, Collodi drew heavily on *Great Expectations,* in which Dickens developed the character of Pip. She then draws parallels between *Great Expectations* and *Pinocchio*, and suggests that Collodi obtained some of his ideas from Dickens and developed his own similar character.

Also, Stella notes that *The Cricket on the Hearth* was translated into Italian in 1856. Collodi didn't start writing *Pinocchio* until 1881. Thus, it is highly likely that Collodi read the translation of *The Cricket on the Hearth* and thus knew about the painting of the hearth and kettle. Being so poor, Geppetto couldn't afford a real hearth, and the painting tricked Grillo. But how is it that such a "wise" cricket could be fooled when, in fact, Collodi notes that Grillo-parlante was "a wise old philosopher"? Below, I will discuss my theory about why Collodi picked a cricket, instead of a wise old owl, to be the conscience of Pinocchio.

In August 1996, I visited the Pinocchio Foundation in Pescia, which is about thirty-five miles from Florence. I met Isabella Bellacari from the foundation, who took me to the Fondazione Nazionale Carlo Collodi in Collodi. At the foundation, we spoke about whether anyone knew why a cricket was chosen to represent the conscience of Pinocchio. I also had a wonderful visit to Pinocchio Park, where I was fortunate to watch a puppet show and observe all the children. During the show, one small boy continually ran up to the stage and tried to grab the puppets. Finally, his father grabbed him, picked him up, and walked away with the boy screaming and kicking. I guess things don't change, but why did Collodi select a cricket and not another animal to be the conscience of Pinocchio?

Entering into the world of crickets was a totally new adventure for me. I normally study flies. For over thirty years, I have devoted my life to studying the morphology, physiology, and behavior of flies: how they solve their everyday problems of feeding, mating, and producing eggs. I selected a cricket as the major character in this story, which was probably as scientific a choice as it was for Carlo Collodi when he selected Grillo-parlante to be the conscience of Pinocchio. In afterthought, however, I couldn't have made a better choice. As Tonino finds out while doing his history term paper, crickets have been major players in the lives of humans throughout history. For the writer, this adventure, as perceived through the mind of a cricket, has been a totally refreshing experience. I only hope that after reading this story, you will feel the same.

Chapter 1.

Growth and Metamorphosis

The North End and Pace's Grocery Store

Every summer evening Maria and her husband, Giovanni, would sit outside their cozy home. This was one of their favorite pastimes. The Italian music coming from the restaurant around the corner was enchanting. It also provided the smell of garlic to them, as well as lots of tourists visiting the Italian section of Boston called the North End. All this made each evening memorable. The tourists help make this a very special place to live because normal cricket food is difficult to get in the city. Most crickets living in the city get their food from tourists. If you happened to live in Chinatown, you'd get Chinese scraps; if you lived in the Puerto Rican section, you'd get lots of beans and fried plantains.

Tourists always provided lots of scraps that ended up on the sidewalks or in the trash cans. Giovanni was especially fond of the cannoli scraps, while Maria preferred the marzipan. Marzipan is a special candy of Sicilian origin, which is made out of almond paste, sugar, and egg whites, and is usually shaped and colored to look like different fruits.

Giovanni would say to Maria, "You know, if you eat too much of that marzipan, you'll get so fat you won't be able to jump up the curb to get to Joe's Deli."

Joe's Deli is a wonderful Italian grocery store in the North End. Maria and Giovanni wanted to be near it when they were looking for a permanent place to settle in Boston. Both of them agreed this was the place for them to live, raise a family, and get the Italian food they grew up eating and loving.

Joe Pace was a heavy-set, extremely lively, and jovial man. For twenty-five years, his last chore before closing the store was to sweep the front sidewalk. Joe would grab the broom and dance out the door singing an old Italian song to finish his day's work. Everything—paper, dirt, and old cans—was swept out into the cobblestone street and then collected into a long-handled dustpan.

One day, there were lots of empty soda cans on the sidewalk. When Joe's broom hit one of the cans, out came a small brown insect. Immediately, Joe trapped the insect by putting the head of the broom over it. He then knelt down, lifted up the broom head very carefully, and picked up the insect. Joe was surprised! As he opened his hand, the insect didn't try to get away. *It's a cricket,* he said to himself.

At that moment, the cricket tried to chirp but was so nervous it was unable to make a sound. Joe didn't know anything about crickets—he didn't even know that this cricket was a male.

Joe was unaware of the large, brown female cricket that was watching his every move. She was peering out of a neatly kept hole between the cobblestones in the street. Carefully returning the cricket to the curb, Joe watched as the small cricket hopped off the curb, stopped, turned around, and looked at him. Joe was again surprised because, as the cricket approached the hole, the larger brown cricket came out to greet the smaller cricket. They approached one another, touched antennae, and both disappeared into the hole.

Maria, the larger cricket that came out to greet the smaller one, was happy that Joe didn't kill Giovanni, her husband, because she knew she was expecting; she hoped it would happen before winter came. She wished this because they were currently living underneath the cobblestones in front of Joe's grocery store, and in winter it was very cold—in fact, it often snowed.

These cobblestones were another reason why Maria and Giovanni selected this place as a house. They both appreciated historical landmarks. The Bostonian Society had declared streets paved with cobblestones as historic sites because these stones once played such an important role in the settling of New England, especially Boston. To this day, many of the streets in Boston are still paved with cobblestones.

Wednesday evenings were very special to both Maria and Giovanni. This was the evening when everyone in the North End ate spaghetti. It was such a special event that the Prince Spaghetti Company even made several television commercials about this. Maria loved these commercials, which showed her neighborhood. Where they were living, they could see the television in Joe's store. This was another reason they chose to live there. They did not have enough money to buy their own television. They both knew if they worked hard and saved, someday they would be able to have the things they wanted. Giovanni kept saying to Maria, "This is America, and if you work hard, you can have a good life."

Maria always had the mental picture of the Italian mother in the commercial coming out onto the balcony of her North End apartment and shouting, "Anthony, Anthony! Come to dinner. Remember, it's Prince Spaghetti night." In fact, she loved these commercials so much that she told Giovanni, "If we have a boy, I want to call him Anthony."

In order to fit into their new life in the United States, many immigrants tried desperately to control the number of offspring in their family. This, however, wasn't necessary because Maria had a female problem and could only produce one egg at a time, unlike most other crickets. Maria told everyone about this wonderful TV ad. Because of this, everyone always referred to the expected baby as Anthony. Maria liked this name so much she would chirp out, "Anthony, Anthony!"

Giovanni would ask her, "What if it is a girl? Do you also have a girl's name picked?"

Maria was positive that it would be a boy. She even told her cousins in New York and Connecticut that Anthony would hatch in the fall.

The only worry Maria had was whether Giovanni would be there when Anthony hatched out of the egg. Every weekday evening, at 11:30, she would prepare and pack two panini, some fruit, and an Aranciata for him before he hopped onto the bus, always carrying his red umbrella and brown cloth satchel. Bus number 71 would take him directly to work. Giovanni knew Maria was worried that she would be alone when the baby came. In order to help solve this problem, he invited Maria's cousin Anna from Connecticut, to come and stay with them. Since Anna's daughter, Giulia, was old enough to stay alone, she could help Maria. Besides, Maria and Giovanni had an extra bedroom. This would be Anthony's bedroom after he was born.

Giovanni would repeatedly say to Maria, "If you can't count on family, who can you count on?" Also, Anna's husband, Marino, was continually traveling to Italy to make new contacts for his import/export business. Sometimes he would be gone for months at a time; he was now at a big trade show in Florence, so this was ideal timing. This would give Maria and Anna time to recall how their two families used to get together for all the big holidays and Italian festivals.

Anna and Marino lived in Manchester, Connecticut, a small town outside of Hartford. Anna always arrived in Boston by bus from Hartford. Because she could get to the country a lot easier than Giovanni and Maria, she brought them fresh vegetables from the farms. Giovanni would pick her up at the bus station. She always carried the vegetables in a woven cloth bag that had been her grandmother's. Giovanni knew if she had this bag, he would have a fresh salad for dinner that evening.

Anna arrived on Friday, October 5, 1982, three days before Columbus Day. She liked to be in Boston that day because of the parade and all of the festive spirit. Manchester didn't have enough Italian people to put on such a wonderful celebration.

That evening at dinner, Giovanni made a toast to the arrival of the new baby. He did this, however, only after tasting the wonderful salad Anna had brought them. In typical fashion, he would take a bite, sit back in his chair, and chew for a long time. Only then did he swallow. After dinner, Giovanni left to play bocce at Our Lady of Mount Carmel's Club House with his *pisani* (friends). Anna and Maria cleaned the table, washed the dishes, and talked about old times. Maria knew the baby would be born soon. She said to Anna, "What if he is born on Columbus Day? Will I have to call him Cristoforo?"

"Of course not," Anna replied. "We are all so used to the name Anthony by now, call him Anthony."

5

That pleased Maria very much. Maria and Anna were having a wonderful time. Not only did they talk about old times, they started to crochet a blue blanket for Anthony. Giovanni was also happy. When Anna came to visit, she also made him a special soup he liked: *pasta fagioli* (pasta and bean soup). The days went by very quickly. Giovanni had given Maria strict instructions to call him at work if she felt the baby was coming.

A New Generation Arrives

On Monday, October 8, 1982, five minutes after midnight, Maria felt the baby was going to be born. Since Giovanni had just left for work, she knew that even if she reached him by telephone, he would not be able to get home. At five minutes past midnight, the egg was laid and the nymph was hatched. Maria was so excited. She was especially excited because it was a male. She knew this because he lacked the ovipositor or long-median structure coming off the posterior portion of the abdomen. Only females have this, for laying eggs. Holding the nymph all wrapped up in the warm, blue blanket they had just crocheted, Maria looked at Anna and said, "Won't Giovanni be surprised to see Anthony when he comes home?"

Giovanni always came home at eight o'clock in the morning. He would stop and get a paper at the neighborhood newsstand and also buy some fresh Italian bread from the bakery. He knew when he got home Maria would have a fresh pot of espresso ready. Plus, she would also be frying some red peppers. He couldn't resist the wonderful aroma of the olive oil, the red peppers, and of course, the garlic. As Giovanni got off the bus that morning, he hopped along rather briskly. Not only was it Columbus Day, but he felt exceptionally happy.

He would always crack the door to the house a little and shout, "Maria, Maria, guess who has come to see you?"

Maria always played along with him and would reply, "I have no idea, who is it?"

Giovanni would then burst into the house and shout, "It's only me!"

Today, the reply from Maria was different. "Guess who has come to see *you*, Giovanni?"

Giovanni was confused by this unusual reply from Maria.

I wonder what's going on? he asked himself. As Giovanni opened the door, there was Maria, sitting in a chair, holding something all bundled up in the blue blanket she had made. He knew by the smile on her face that she had the baby. Before going any closer, he stopped and asked, "Is it our long awaited Anthony?"

"Yes," she replied with a smile.

And so it was; Anthony was born on this wonderful day of celebration of the adventurous Italian explorer who, most believe, discovered the New World.

Anthony Gets His Name

On October 18, the new infant was baptized at Our Lady of Mount Carmel Church and given the name Anthony. His aunt and uncle, Anna and Marino, were his godparents. From then on, life was very different for Maria and Giovanni. They both had to work harder and save for the day Anthony would go to college. Even before he was old enough to understand, Giovanni would put Anthony on his lap so he was facing him and look him straight into the eyes. Once he had his attention, he would then say, "You must study and work hard in school. It is important for you to go to college someday. I remember my father Rolando telling me each generation should try to do better."

It's Time for the Family Albums

Because his mother spent so much time with him, Anthony learned a lot about his family's history from her. Almost every evening, Maria would sit in the corner of the living room with Anthony on her lap and the family album on his abdomen. It was almost humorous to see this nymph with this huge album on his lap. Page by page they would go through the album. Once Anthony went to sleep, his mother would put a bookmark where they left off. This didn't matter because the next time, Anthony would insist his mother start from the beginning. These were favorite times for Anthony because he was very close to his mother, and he liked to hear about family history.

Anthony grew rapidly and went through several molts, shedding his old exoskeleton, getting a new one that fit better, and becoming more independent. Like any growing child, Anthony ate a lot and kept outgrowing his old exoskeleton. As he got older, his interests changed. He took on new hobbies and made new friends. When he went into junior high school, he became more focused on his academics.

Giovanni Passes on His Interests to Anthony

One of Giovanni's passions in life was geography. "This is the only way to preserve history and get to know something about the world we live in," he would tell Maria. Above the sofa in the living room was a huge *National Geographic* map he rescued from the trash bin at work. The map looked beautiful. Giovanni even bought colored pins to mark the places he and his relatives had lived or visited. His love for family history was obtained from his mother, Carmella, while his passion for geography came from his father, Rolando.

In fact, one of the first things to go into Anthony's bedroom was the *National Geographic* world map. "I want our son to know all about the world," he said to Maria. He then reminded her, "Being born on the same day as Christopher Columbus, Anthony will, without a doubt, be a world traveler when he grows up."

When you think about it, this belief was not unusual. Most parents want their children to have things they didn't have or to travel to places they were unable to visit. Another way to foster knowledge about the world is to visit museums, and Giovanni certainly had a passion for them; he eventually worked at one. He would say to Maria, "Museums are treasures that give visitors a unique opportunity to come face to face with things they would never have had an opportunity to see." Thus, one of Giovanni's favorite things to do with Anthony was to visit various museums on the weekend.

While in his human form, Anthony saw a lot of young children playing with funny-looking plastic toys called Transformers. They even called the changing from one form to another *morphing*. Anthony learned in school about the different kinds of insect metamorphosis. He learned there was gradual metamorphosis, where the stage that hatched out of the egg was called the nymphal stage, which then went through several molts (i.e., shedding of the exoskeleton) before becoming an adult. In this type of metamorphosis, exhibited by crickets, the nymphs look like the adults, except they lack functional and fully developed wings capable of flying. Instead, they have winglike structures called wing-pads.

As a nymphal cricket, Anthony knew all about these structures. Young crickets can't wait to go through a type of puberty, in which they obtain the fully functional wings of adulthood. For males this is important. It is almost like the change that occurs in the human male voice during puberty. Prior to becoming an adult, male crickets should be able to make sounds, but they cannot because they lack functional wings, which have the file and scraper on them that produces the stridulating sounds, or chirps. However, they can hear.

In his human form, Anthony knew the kinds of metamorphosis people go through, even though it is not usually as dramatic as that for insects. He also learned that butterflies undergo complete metamorphosis, where the stage hatching out of the egg is called a caterpillar (or larva for other insects), then comes the pupal stage (called the chrysalis for butterflies), and finally the adult. In this type of metamorphosis, the larva and adult usually eat entirely different types of foods, thus avoiding competition for a possibly limited food supply. In order to go through these different stages and grow, insects have to molt or shed their old exoskeleton. It is like a child who grows too fast. The parents must constantly buy them new clothes. Thus, while growing up, Anthony was well aware of both insect metamorphosis and the process in humans we call maturation. Being as young as he was, Anthony didn't realize that both processes, whether in humans or insects, are very similar and are regulated by biochemicals called hormones.

The other type of transformation present in Anthony's life was his ability to morph from a cricket to a human and back again. Anthony and his family actually took this for granted, and none of them really gave special attention to it. When he did think of it, one thing that he wondered was whether other animals were able to do this. Days and years went by so fast that before everyone knew it, Anthony graduated from middle school and entered high school. He was a teenager (or a last nymphal instar). Not only had he grown, he had also changed so much from when he was born.

Chapter 2.
Having Friends!

High School in the North End and Being Small

Going to high school in the North End of Boston was truly a multicultural experience for Anthony. This was an area of the city where immigrants first settled, found a job and place to live, got established, got married, and raised a family. This is exactly what his father and mother had done. Anthony knew all about the history of his family since his grandfather, Rolando, came to the United States in 1966, when Anthony's father, Giovanni, was only two years old. Anthony even knew all the jobs where his father had worked. His father was only eighteen when he started working on construction of the overpass that was going over the North End. He worked there for two years and then got a job as a security guard in a bank.

Maria hadn't liked this and worried for Giovanni's life. "What if the bank is robbed?" she would say to him.

Being a brave warrior, as all male crickets are, he would reply, "Don't worry, Maria, I can take care of myself. Haven't I taken good care of you since we got married?" He would reach down and give her a big kiss by touching his antennae to hers to reassure and comfort her.

This always made her feel very safe and content. About one year before Anthony was born, his father got a wonderful job as a guard at Harvard's Museum of Comparative Zoology. Maria felt better about this, but she still worried about her husband's safety. For a cricket, being a night guard is not a difficult problem because this is when crickets prefer to be active anyway. She remembered how the guard at the Isabella Stewart Gardner Museum in Boston was tied up and had his mouth sealed with duct tape. She didn't want this to happen to her Giovanni. The guard was blamed for the loss of an important Rembrandt painting, which was stolen and has never been recovered.

Unlike his mother and father, Anthony was not always able to eat Italian cricket-food. When Anna, his godmother, came from Manchester, she would bring cricket-food from the fields and gardens of rural Connecticut. Anthony knew all about the phenomenon of each generation eating slightly different foods from the parents until eventually no one could recognize their culture's original foods. Giovanni and Maria were very concerned about Anthony just eating people-food, such as French fries and hamburgers, and drinking only soda. They felt they could keep his diet somewhat under control by living in the North End, because none of the major fast food chains were located there. Anthony could see this diet shift happening with all his friends. Most of them did not get the same foods their parents ate when they were young. Instead, he ate a lot of Italian human-food. Because of this, Anthony was not growing as fast as a normal cricket would grow.

By the time he entered high school, Anthony was much smaller than his classmates. This did not bother him at all. In fact, it was because of his small size that he got the nickname Tonino, which means "little Anthony" in Italian. Anthony spent a lot of time in Joe's grocery store. Every night after school and on the weekends, he worked for Joe stocking shelves. Anthony not only had to work, but he liked to work. This gave him money to buy the things he liked and also do what he wanted to do. Because Giovanni didn't make much money, Tonino also had to give part of what he earned at Joe's to his father. This was the custom of many immigrant families.

In his home, music was very important. His father loved to sing and listen to opera. Every Sunday morning he would listen to classical operas on the radio. Giovanni's favorites were the Great Caruso and Tito Schipa. I guess he could attribute a lot of his likes and dislikes to Carmella and Rolando. Anyway, Anthony had quite a collection of CDs of great operas. In addition, he had developed a special interest in museums, geography, and the origin of words (etymology). Anthony had a good ear for when people incorrectly used a word. Ruby, a good friend of his father, overheard a conversation between two elderly women. The one woman said that her husband was going to a new "gastroentomologist." Not everyone knew what was wrong with this, but both Anthony and Ruby knew that an entomologist is someone who studies insects, while a gastroenterologist studies the digestive tract.

Tonino Gets His Nickname

One day, Anthony had to help Joe unload a truck full of canned goods. Isabella happened to be watching. Joe would get a case of canned goods from the rear of the trunk, swing around, and hand them to Anthony. The truck driver slid a large case of sardines in tomato sauce forward. Joe picked it up and realized it was very heavy even before he swung around. Regardless, he passed it to Anthony, who grabbed it and instantly felt his arms and knees giving way. Of course, he dropped it. Joe laughed and said to Anthony, "You'll have to eat more pasta." Isabella, however, didn't think this was very funny. She liked Anthony and didn't want him to get hurt. Besides, how would she explain it to Maria, Anthony's mother?

Afterward, when she and Joe were alone, she said, "Joe, that was too heavy for Anthony; he could have gotten hurt. After all, he is just a little Anthony."

Joe laughed and said, "I like that name, little Anthony. Let's call him Tonino."

And so it was from that time on that Anthony was always called Tonino. His friends Pete Barbosa and Chih also had nicknames. Pete was called Pedro, while Chih was called Ming Ming. Tonino was very lucky to have such good friends. His life experiences to date always included the two of them in some way or another. The only thing they hadn't done together was to take a trip. "Maybe someday!" Tonino would say to them, "Maybe someday!"

Tonino was reaching the age when he wanted to spend more time with his friends. He also started spending more time with one friend than any other. This is a common trait of people in general, not just young people. Pedro was currently his best friend.

Tonino Goes to Puerto Rico

When school was almost over for the academic year, Pedro invited Tonino to spend one week with him in Puerto Rico. Because

Pedro's mother, Magdalena, was going with them, Maria didn't worry. Giovanni knew he had to give Tonino some freedom and independence in order for him to grow up into a confident and well-rounded adult. Unlike most crickets, which receive no parental care, Tonino in his cricket morph was well cared for by his parents. Maria had talked to Magdalena so she knew exactly what he would need for the trip to Puerto Rico. It was easy: shorts, cap, sneakers, bathing suit, some underwear, a couple of T-shirts, and his toiletries. He would also bring fifty dollars of his own savings. This was money he earned from working at Joe's store. Giovanni always told Tonino it is important for young people to work, to learn how to save the money they earned, to develop a sense of satisfaction and a good work ethic. Joe would say, "If you have these traits, you are ready for life's adventures. If you don't, you are in trouble."

When Tonino was packed and ready to go, Giovanni called him aside and gave him ten dollars extra. His father often did this, and regardless of the amount, Tonino knew this was a special gesture of love. The money was only a symbol of his father's affection for him. He knew this and so did all his friends. What Tonino and his friends didn't like to see, however, was when some of their classmates took advantage of their parents and accepted money only as a tangible item and not as a symbol of love. "Some of my friends only care about the money," Pedro would tell Ming Ming and Tonino.

Because they didn't have a car, they all took the bus to Logan Airport. The flight to San Juan was only two hours and fifty-five minutes. They left promptly at half past eight, and before they knew it, they were landing in San Juan, the capital of Puerto Rico. This was Tonino's first trip out of continental United States.

Tonino Goes to a Cockfight

They spent the first afternoon at the beach, enjoying the sun and swimming. Magdalena wanted Pedro to have some cultural experiences during this trip so she arranged for them to go to the Galleria that evening in a small, nearby mountain village. The Galleria is a special place where roosters fight in combat. Magdalena and the boys arrived at the cockfights early. This way they could watch the birds being weighed and also get the best seats. It was a wonderful cultural event. People were talking about politics, their gardens, and which birds would win. Each bird was weighed using an old-fashioned balance hanging from the ceiling. Using the weights, birds were paired in an attempt to make the fights more even. Once in the ring, the birds were handled very carefully. Just prior to the fight, someone came around and washed the breast feathers and the spurs of each bird.

Tonino asked Pedro what that was all about, but he did not know.

The fight was uneventful to Tonino and Pedro, but not to the locals who had placed a lot of money on their favorite rooster. Since most owners only had a few special roosters, they couldn't afford to let them get killed. In fact, few cockfights in Puerto Rico end with a bird being killed. After the fights, everyone left for home.

Tonino still wanted to know what was going on when the person washed the bird's feathers and spurs. Tonino asked Pedro to find out why they did this. At lunch, Tonino finally asked Pedro's mother. She said she didn't know either, but would ask her brother, Franco.

For lunch they had rice, black beans, plantanos, pork, and breadfruit. This was the first time Tonino had eaten this fruit. It had the consistency of a potato, but tasted more like an artichoke. Tonino liked this because his parents often gave him artichokes. He not only loved the taste, he also loved the way you eat them. His father taught him how to do this when he was very little. Tonino wanted to share this with everyone at the table so he carefully described it.

"You must realize that you are eating the bud or flower of the plant. First you individually pull off a bract, dip it in melted butter with some lemon and spices, place the bract into your mouth, bring your upper and lower teeth together, and slowly pull it out. As it comes out, your teeth will scrape off the soft part of the bract. You then swallow what you have scraped off."

Little did Tonino know that the feeding behavior of baleen whales was somewhat similar to this way of eating an artichoke. Not until his trip to Hawai'i would he realize this. Also, on that same trip to Hawai'i, he would re-encounter breadfruit.

Unfortunately, Franco did not know why they washed the rooster's spurs and breast feathers.

After lunch, they went to see Pedro's oldest uncle, Jesús, who was 101 years old. He was a great old man. He was bent over, completely gray, with a beard and a weather-worn look because of his leathery brown face and piercing, coal-black eyes. Tonino had a sense that if anyone knew about this washing behavior of the roosters, Jesús would.

Jesús didn't speak English, so Pedro translated the conversation to Tonino. The way Jesús used his hands told Tonino something was being caught and something was being pulled out. "In the past," Pedro said, "some owners of the birds wanted to win so badly they cheated. To do this they went into the forest and carefully caught the giant centipede. Then, they carefully pulled out the jaws, which have the poison glands attached to them. These glands contain a potent poison, which if it gets into your blood by a puncture, such as that made by a spur, it could kill the opponent. This is why they washed the spurs with alcohol. Not only did the owners put the poison on the spurs, but they also rubbed it onto the breast feathers. When a rooster grabs the breast feathers of its opponent, its own saliva could pick up the poison on the opponent's feathers. Once people knew how some owners were winning all the fights, they decided to make it mandatory to wash, not only the spurs, but also the breast feathers with alcohol. The alcohol destroys the poison. That's why they do that."

What a great bit of culture that no one seems to know anything about, Tonino said to himself. The washing of the feathers had become a standard procedure, but the reason behind doing it had been lost. As Tonino would find out later, this was something that was happening all over the world. Customs, culture, and even languages are being lost. *Before we know it, everyone will look like Americans: blue jeans, T-shirts, and sneakers,* thought Tonino to himself. *Unfortunately, they will all be eating the same food.*

Tonino Learns Something about Pedro's Roots and Culture

Tonino asked Magdalena if they could go shopping. "Sure!" she said. "Where would you like to go?"

"I would like to go somewhere featuring the arts and crafts of this enchanting Caribbean Island."

"Okay, we will go to a place that specializes in local artisans."

So, off they went to *Calle Cristo*, where they looked for *Centro Nacional De Artes Populares y Artesanías*. "There it is," Pedro shouted.

Crossing the street, they entered the store. Tonino looked around. He saw some beautiful bobbin lace (a.k.a. *mundillo*, which stands for "little world" and which has been a specialty of the island since Spanish rule).

Tonino bought a small sample because he knew Isabella would love it. She had a special fondness for lace because she had been born in an Italian village that specialized in making Burano lace. Because it is so expensive, he can only afford a small sampler.

"I know she will love it. Don't you think so, Magdalena?"

"Yes, she will treasure it."

After searching around, Tonino asked if there was another store they could visit.

"Yes, we can go to the Puerto Rican Art and Crafts store."

Magdalena told the boys, "You only have twenty minutes in the store before we go to the Puerto Rican Museum of History, Archeology, and Anthropology."

They both rushed into the museum to see who could find the best treasures. Tonino entered an area with carved wooden figures. They were beautifully painted. "Pedro, come here! What are these?"

"These are called *santos*."

"What are they for?" Tonino asked.

"Each village or city has its own patron saint, and each one of these represents a different saint. It is believed that before the Spanish came, each small village or tribe had some sort of statue that they worshiped. The individuals carving them are called *santeros*. Today's *santeros* have strayed somewhat from the original type of carvings in that they often use different colors, paints, and even material to clothe the carving."

Tonino left the room of the *santos* and entered an even more interesting room. Hanging all over the walls were grotesque, horned masks painted black, yellow, and red. Some looked like devils, while others resembled humans and animals. Tonino quickly left the room to find Pedro, who had gone in the opposite direction. Grabbing him by the shirt, he pulled Pedro into the room of the "monsters."

"What in the devil's name are these?"

"They are called *caretas* and are papier-mâché masks, usually worn at carnival time. The city of Ponce is the center for this type of craft."

"What was the original purpose of these masks?"

"I believe it was to terrify those considered sinners, especially young children. Apparently, they believed, and some still do today, that the thought of going to hell would bring them back into the church."

"Are they expensive?"

"They can be," replied Pedro.

"Well, I don't think I will buy one. It would look great, however, hanging in Joe's store amongst the hanging prosciutto."

"Don't even go there," Pedro said emphatically. This time Pedro grabbed Tonino by the shirt. "Come on, my mom is waiting to go to the museum."

Away they went.

"This is the first time I have ever been here," Pedro told Tonino.

Magdalena said, "We will meet in an hour at the bookstore."

"Okay!" they answered, and off they went.

In the history section of the museum, there was one room devoted to music. Since Tonino was also an insect musician, he entered. The one item that interested him the most was something he had seen on *Scientific American*, the TV program hosted by Alan Alda. One episode focused on how humans often made instruments that looked like something used by an animal. Here, right in front of him in the glass case, was the instrument. The sign read "Qüiro."

The description stated, "This is an ancient musical instrument made from a gourd that is hollowed out and then a sound-hole cut in one side while the other side has numerous striations cut into the gourd's surface. One plays it by placing one's hand in the sound-hole and holding onto the gourd while scraping the parallel grooves with a scraper, which usually has a wooden handle with metal, forklike tines called a pua."

Tonino looked at Pedro and said, "That's just how crickets do it. They pull the scraper (similar to the pua) of one wing over the file of the other wing, which is just like the grooves of the qüiro."

"How do you know so much about crickets?" asked Pedro.

"I just like them," Tonino said. "What's really interesting, however, are the special papillaelike structures on the head of the lycaenid butterfly caterpillar, which look just like the qüiro itself. The caterpillar moves these over rough and raised portions of its head to produce a sound that attracts ants."

"Why would they want to do that?" asked Pedro.

"Because the ants protect the caterpillars from predators, and in turn, the caterpillars give them a honeylike liquid they produce from special structures."

"Wow! That's so interesting."

"I think so," replied Tonino. "When I get back home, I'll ask Dr. Wilson which types of ants do this."

In another room labeled "The Taínos," Tonino saw some wonderful stone artifacts called "Zemis." Tonino had no idea what these were. He read on. This was the general name given to both the deities and the statues of the deities the Taínos worshiped. Originally, the Puerto Rico natives called themselves *Borinquen.* Later, ethno-historians grouped those having a similar language and culture living on the various islands (Cuba, Bahama Islands, Jamaica, Hispaniola—now Haiti and Dominican Republic—and Puerto Rico) into one group called the Taínos, which means "good" or "noble." Zemis were made from stone, wood, or bones of their ancestors and kept in their homes and worshiped. The figures of the zemis were often tattooed on their bodies or carved into stones as petroglyphs. There were two main deities or zemis: Yúcahu (the lord of cassava and sea) and Atabey (the goddess of fresh water and human fertility), who is also Yúcahu's mother.

The Taínos hid zemis in caves so the Spaniards would not destroy them (they were considered heathen idols). Also present were beautifully carved three-pointed stones. They are probably the most numerous remaining artifacts of the Taínos.

Tonino moved on to the next glass case. There in front of him was an object that made Tonino gag and take a deep breath as he thought how easy it was for him to communicate with the Blue Fairy (the same Blue Fairy that Grillo-parlante communicated with). In the case was a vomit stick. In order to communicate with zemis, the Taíno had to either fast from eating or use a stick to induce vomiting. Only when they were purged was it possible to make contact with the spirit. There was even a male zemis known as Baibrama who assisted the Taínos, in not only growing cassava, but in curing people poisoned by the juice of the cassava. Both men and woman painted their bodies for ceremonial purposes with the juice while the men going into battle used it as a sort of "war paint." Often they used the color red, which was probably from the achiote plant, which is also called the lipstick tree because of the red color from the seeds, which the Taíno women used as lipstick.

The Taínos ate many things. Most important was their staple, which was cassava. The roots of wild cassava, however, contain a poisonous juice.

Wow! Tonino thought. *I wonder how many people became sick or poisoned before this was known. Apparently agriculturists have bred a variety that is not poisonous. I wonder if any insect eats the plant and whether they can avoid the toxic poison if eaten?*

Tonino moved to another room. Above the door was a sign that said, "Taíno Ball Courts."

"I must find Pedro. I am sure he will love this room."

Tonino hurried, found Pedro, and grabbed him by the shirt before looking at the next exhibit. He knew Pedro loved ball games. Pedro pushed Tonino's hand away. "Hey! That's my new Michael Jordan T-shirt you are stretching. Be careful."

"Come with me. I believe you will like this next exhibit."

They entered a room containing many photographs and a glass case housing what looked like heavy stone collars. They moved over to a wall with photos of what looked like large oversized bocce courts. The ball courts, known as *bateyes*, were rectangular in shape and often contained large stone carvings (petroglyphs) surrounding the court. Underneath the photo it said, "Photo of a Ball Court at Caguana."

These petroglyphs sometimes had figures of important zemis. Rouse (1992) noted, "Only the Mayas, their neighbors—including the Hohokam peoples in the southwestern United States—and the central Ostionoids built artificial courts for that purpose." Rouse also suggests that these ball courts may not represent independent invention, but parallel development from earlier peoples who played a similar game.

Tonino returned to the glass case and pointed to the stone collars, which were really belts worn by the ball players. Since the ball was never touched by hand and was supposed to be kept in the air, the stone belt would have given players strength to hit or deflect the ball. Similar stone devices were important in the Mayan ball game, while they used heavier belts only for ceremonial purpose.

"I just can't imagine playing with something so heavy around my waist," Pedro remarked.

"The way different cultures treat games is very interesting," Tonino said.

The two boys looked at a couple of other rooms and noticed that they only had ten minutes at the bookstore. Tonino rapidly scanned the bookshelves. Two books caught his eye: *Columbus's Outpost Among the Taínos* by Kathleen Deagan and Jose Maria Cruxent, and *The Indigenous People of the Caribbean* by Samuel M. Wilson. Quickly he wrote the titles and authors down. The boys found Magdalena and returned to their apartment. Soon it was time for dinner, and Magdalena suggested a restaurant she always liked. She told the boys, "Whenever I want a quiet dinner, I always come to this restaurant."

Coqui and Noise Pollution

At dinner in the small restaurant that evening, Magdalena quizzed the boys about the day's events. Both boys had to shout for her to hear them. This was not because she is deaf. Everyone in the restaurant was doing the same thing. It was like a shouting match.

Finally, Tonino asked, "What is that constant noise?"

Pedro looked at Tonino. "You don't know? I thought you knew everything."

"No, I don't know."

"It is a coqui, which is a very tiny, tiny frog. For its size, its sound is deafening."

Magdalena told the boys, "I am sorry, but it never used to be this noisy."

Soon they realize it was impossible to have a conversation, so they finished their meal and left.

It was dark outside, and all of a sudden a large batlike or birdlike thing landed on Tonino's shoulder. Not being afraid of situations like this, he asked Pedro, "What's this?"

"It's the black witch moth. They are really large, aren't they?"

"They sure are," responded Tonino as the moth took off.

Extinction in Puerto Rico

Not only did Tonino learn about the almost complete extinction of the Taíno people, but he was about to learn that the hunting and gathering activity of the early peoples caused many living organisms to go extinct. This is contrary to what Tonino grew up learning. He was told over and over again that modern humans were the major cause of many living organisms going extinct. This is not true, although the rate of extinction has certainly been accelerated by modern man. That evening the boys went on the Internet to learn something about extinct animals in Puerto Rico (www.answers. com/topic/list-of-extinct-animals-of-the-united-states). Tonino was surprised to see the following list of extinct animals:

Web-footed coqui, 1980s
Golden coqui, 1980s
Virgin Islands screech owl, 1980
Mauge's parakeet, 1892
Culebra Puerto Rican parrot, 1899
Puerto Rican long-nosed bat, 1900?
Puerto Rican long-tongued bat, 1900?
Puerto Rican ground sloth, 1500
Puerto Rican hutia, 1500
Puerto Rican paca, 1500
Lesser Puerto Rican agouti, 1500
Greater Puerto Rican agouti, 1500
Puerto Rican shrew, 1500

Tonino also read that the rail, a large flightless bird, was hunted to extinction by the Taínos. Tonino looked at Pedro, waving his arms as if flying, and said, "Wings make sense for both birds and insects."

"What do you mean?" Pedro responded.

"If you are flightless, like the extinct rail, you are unable to escape from predators."

Tonino will later learn that flightlessness is a common trait of many island animals.

Tonino Returns Home from Puerto Rico

When they returned to Boston, Pedro's mother decided to have Tonino and Ming Ming over for spaghetti. Even though they were not Italians, the Barbosa family, like everyone else in the North End, ate spaghetti on Wednesday nights. While they were eating, Ming Ming asked Tonino what he liked best about his trip to Puerto Rico.

"Before I tell you, let me tell you what I learned that I didn't like. You may not know, but the Taíno Indians were the first native people to contact Christopher Columbus and his crew. Unfortunately, this contact led to almost complete extinction of the Taínos within only two decades. With that off my mind, I can tell you what I liked. I enjoyed learning something about Pedro's heritage. I now can understand him and other Puerto Ricans much better," replied Tonino.

"Be more specific," said Ming Ming.

"Like going to the cockfights and watching all the detail that accompanies such an event." Tonino went on to explain the whole story to everyone at the table, even the part about the poison from the giant centipede.

"Tonino, what do you think about the cockfights?" Pedro's mother asked.

"I personally don't approve of using animals to fight against one another."

Pedro immediately stepped in to defend his culture. "This is part of our culture and tradition."

Tonino replied, "Yes, but I am sure no other culture does this."

"That's not true," interjected Ming Ming. "The Chinese have bred crickets for fighting since AD 690."

Pedro and Tonino looked at one another with amazement. "I didn't know that," they said in unison.

Tonino, with a surprised look on his face, said, "I thought I knew a lot about crickets, but I didn't know that."

Tonino was growing up and realizing that having friends of many different ethnicities was not only fun, but it also would give him a broader and richer outlook on life. He would become better prepared for what people say is the "shrinking world" or what Thomas Friedman champions in his book, *The World is Flat*. Friedman cleverly demonstrates how modern technology and communications has flattened the world. In other words, it has put people and diverse cultures throughout the world in touch with one another. A good example of this is outsourcing. He also discusses what this means to companies, countries, and individuals.

Chapter 3.
Tonino in Massachusetts

Boston—A Wonderful Melting Pot

Boston was a wonderful place for Tonino to grow up. Because of its cultural diversity, he had many friends of different ethnic backgrounds, plus he got to taste many wonderful and unusual foods. It was interesting to Tonino that, even though many cultures are very different, they often have many things in common. An example of this is the use of garlic. Remember, Tonino's parents, Giovanni and Maria, loved sitting outside the apartment and savoring the smell of garlic coming from the various kitchens of the North End. At the same time, Tonino liked to go to his friend Ming Ming's house for dinner because his mother would stir-fry lamb with garlic. Tonino often thought about various cultures: how they were different, and how they were the same.

Anyway, America certainly was everything his father always said it was. Tonino could hear him saying, "Remember, America is a melting pot of different cultures. The one thing everyone must remember is we are first of all Americans. It is important, however, for all groups to celebrate their individual cultures, but this must not interfere with keeping America united." Tonino agreed with his father on this point. He also felt it was essential for everyone to know something about different cultures and to respect cultural differences. Because of this, Tonino was liked, not only by his friends, but also by their parents.

One of Tonino's favorite pastimes was to go to the different museums in Boston. He liked the Boston Children's Museum; however, his favorite was the Museum of Comparative Zoology. This is where his father worked, and on Sundays, when he wasn't working, Giovanni would take Tonino to see the laboratory of Professor E. O. Wilson. Tonino liked to watch the leaf-cutting ants walking around, carrying pieces of leaves in their mandibles as they marched to their nest. Later, his father would show him all the different ant species from all over the world.

As Tonino got older, he would ask his father, "How many different kinds of insects are there in the world?"

Giovanni would reply, "Maybe eight hundred thousand."

Tonino always thought his father knew everything. Little did Tonino know his father kept getting an update from Professor Wilson about the current number of living species. This is because new species are continually being found.

Pedro and Basketball

Many of the young boys in Tonino's neighborhood liked to play basketball, especially Pedro, who was obsessed with the sport. After all, basketball is one thing that is truly American, and in Boston, the Boston Celtics are legendary. As Tonino would find out later, Dr. James Naismith invented basketball in 1891 in Springfield, Massachusetts. Every time Tonino saw Pedro, he had a basketball in his hand. Pedro was going to go to a basketball clinic at the Boston Garden. Both he and Tonino had watched many of the Boston Celtics home games on television, but never in person.

Pedro invited Tonino to go with him the first evening of the clinic. "You don't have to play, you can just sit on the bleachers," he told Tonino. "The first evening is going to be just demonstrations."

Tonino wasn't quite sure if he would like it. Since he was a cricket, Tonino was a great jumper, but not a good shooter. When Pedro told him Michael Jordan and Shaquille O'Neal were going to be at the clinic, Tonino said, "I'd love to go."

Pedro had reserved seats so they went right in. Both boys were very excited to see these players in person. The demonstrations were outstanding. Tonino was particularly impressed with Michael Jordan's ability to jump, and Shaquille O'Neal could not only jump, he was *big*. Tonino was a fairly good judge of character and somehow felt some kinship with these two sports heroes.

After the demonstration, both players answered questions from the audience. Someone asked what they ate that helped them jump so well. Everyone thought they ate hamburgers and French fries all the time because both players did so many commercials for large fast food hamburger chains. They avoided giving a direct answer to this and only mentioned how important proper nutrition was.

Tonino became more and more interested in this topic; at the same time, he kept feeling this strong bond with them based on their jumping ability.

Finding the Truth

Following the question-and-answer period, some of the participants played a short game. Pedro was selected to be one of the forwards for the North End's team. He preferred, however, to play center. His coach always said he would have to improve his ability to jump if he planned to be a center. After Pedro left to get ready for the game, Tonino morphed to a cricket. This way he could enter Michael and Shaq's dressing room without being seen by anyone. He squeezed under the door and hopped into the dressing room. Both players had towels around them and were heading for the showers. Tonino decided to check out their lockers. As he hopped into Michael's gym bag, he couldn't believe what he saw. There, before his compound eyes, was a metal container, about the size of a can of soda, with a label that read, "Cricket Food—Fluker's Cricket Farm, Louisiana. Take one spoonful three times a day." Tonino couldn't believe what he was seeing. He hopped out of Michael's bag and into Shaq's. In his gym bag was a much bigger container. The label on his can said, "Grasshopper Food—Connecticut Valley Biological Supply House, Easthampton, Massachusetts. Take two spoonfuls three times a day." Just as he finished reading the label, he heard the two players returning from the shower.

Oh boy, now I am going to get caught, Tonino thought to himself.

The next thing Tonino knew, Shaq grabbed his gym bag and pulled it out of the locker. This shook everything up in the bag, including Tonino. As he looked up, Tonino could see this big hand coming straight at him. Most humans believe that insects see many images of whatever they are looking at. This is because insects have compound eyes and each facet, called an ommatidium, is believed to see the same, identical image. Not so. Instead, insects see a mosaic, so Tonino saw a big hand made up of many dots. Tonino quickly turned to the side and began to jump. This startled Shaq, but he wasn't afraid of insects. He carefully grabbed Tonino in his palm, closed those big fingers, and sort of shook him like dice.

"Guess what I found?" he said to Michael.

"No idea," was the reply.

Shaq then held out his hand to Michael and carefully opened his closed fist by slowly pulling his huge fingers, one by one, away from the palm. It was like being in a cage, Tonino thought. Even though he was now free to move, he was so scared that he couldn't jump. You can imagine! Here was this tiny cricket in the palm of this giant basketball player's hand. Tonino wondered what would happen to him. He was so scared that he didn't even move an antenna. Shaq then said to Michael, "You know how much I love grasshoppers and you love crickets; we should let him go."

As soon as Tonino's legs touched the floor, he didn't waste any time in hopping out of there. After he left the dressing room, Tonino immediately morphed.

The game had already started, and Pedro had been looking for his friend. Every time Pedro scored a point and ran by where Tonino had been sitting, he looked for Tonino, but didn't see him. After Tonino returned from the locker room, Pedro saw him sitting there. During the game, Tonino noticed that Pedro couldn't jump very high. He was a good forward only because he was tall. He would have to improve a lot to play center.

After the game, Pedro asked, "Where were you? I kept looking for you and you weren't there."

"You would never believe it even if I told you," Tonino replied.

On the way home, Pedro kept pestering Tonino about his absence at the game. Finally, Tonino said, "Sit down! Let me tell you what happened."

Pedro knew that when Tonino said, "Sit down," he was serious. Tonino told him the whole story. He said, "I had to find out what these two guys ate." He then went on to tell Pedro about the cricket and grasshopper food. "Since you are big like Shaq, I think you should try grasshopper food rather than the cricket food. As soon as I can, I am going to order you some."

"You're crazy," replied Pedro.

"Why not try it? It can't hurt you, and it might even help."

That evening, after Pedro went home, Tonino couldn't help but think that maybe these two super athletes were really jumping insects. If they were, it would explain a lot of things.

The Great Experiment Begins

The next day, Tonino called the Connecticut Valley Biological Supply Company and ordered two cases of grasshopper food. Without thinking, he had them ship it to Joe's grocery store. That week Tonino was very anxious. He was afraid he had made a big mistake by having the food shipped to Joe's, and he hoped that Joe would not be angry. In order to avoid any problems, Tonino planned to intercept the order before Joe or Isabella saw it.

One evening, Tonino was fifteen minutes late for work. As he entered the store, Joe looked at him with a big scowl. Tonino knew the grasshopper food had arrived. As he went into the back room, Joe walked over to him. He started to ask, "Did you order these two cases ...?"

Before he even finished, Tonino said, "Yes."

"Get them out of here immediately," Joe said. "You know that many salespeople and workmen come in through the back door and could easily see these cases. Can you imagine what my customers would think if the word got out that I had ordered two cases of grasshopper food? I don't even want to know what you ordered them for. Just get them out of here."

Tonino took them over to Pedro, who immediately hid them in his closet. Thus, Tonino and Pedro's great nutrition experiment would start the next day.

Italian Music

Giovanni had passed on to Tonino the love of music. As Tonino grew up, his own collection of music got bigger and more diverse. Once or twice Giovanni had taken him to hear the Boston Symphony at Symphony Hall. He marveled at the conductor, Seiji Ozawa. His long hair, the dynamic and enthusiastic way he conducted the orchestra, and the way the audience responded to him all made Tonino love this conductor.

Even though Tonino liked being a human, he spent more time as an insect. This ability to move in and out of the lives of humans was a special gift he inherited from his great-great-great-grandfather, Grillo-parlante. Because of his strong connection with his insect roots, Tonino wanted to see insects and other animal musicians succeed in the music profession. Many of his friends were great musicians. There was Julius the katydid, Matt the fiddling cricket, and Marilyn the buzzing honeybee. In addition to insects, many of his other animal friends were great singers or musicians. The wonderful three tenor bullfrog vocalists, Adamo, Massimo, and Roberto; several of his bird friends, including Suzanne Nightingale; and other animals made great music. Charles the drumming partridge was truly exceptional. Roberta the trumpeter swan was an exquisite soloist. Bradley the fiddler crab would make an exceptional first violinist. Tonino felt obligated to all his friends and hoped he could ask Seiji Ozawa to give these animals an opportunity to be in one of his performances.

Tonino and His Animal Friends at Tanglewood

Giovanni's friend, Antonio Nappi, was a guard at Symphony Hall and told Giovanni if he brought Tonino over some time, he might get a chance to meet Ozawa. Tonino liked this idea. In fact, he even sat down and wrote a long letter to Ozawa describing all the talents of his friends. He concluded the letter by saying that the animal musicians could audition for him.

Tonino gave the letter to his father to give to Antonio. That week, Antonio put the letter on Ozawa's desk. The following Monday, all Tonino's friends were invited to Symphony Hall for a rehearsal. Ozawa had picked the six-movement *Insect Symphony* by Kalevi Aho. This was appropriate because each of the six movements represented a different insect.

Because none of the animals were conductors, it was up to Ozawa to conduct this unusual and eclectic group of musicians. The rehearsal went so well that Ozawa invited them to play at the opening summer concert on July 4 at Tanglewood, which is in the Berkshire Mountains in western Massachusetts. Ozawa asked Tonino to help him plan the concert. Tonino liked this idea and immediately began to make plans. Tonino talked Ozawa into using fireflies as ushers, for general lighting around the grounds, to light the stage, and even in some of the fireworks displays.

Tonino told Joe he would be traveling to western Massachusetts. Joe was very helpful. "You know, Tonino, I have two *pisani* in Amherst. Their names are Mauro Aniello, who owns *La Cucina de Pinocchio*, and Bruno Mattarazzo, who has a very popular pizzeria called Antonio's. When you are in Amherst, stop to see them."

Tonino was excited about this, especially since Grillo-parlante had been the conscience of Pinocchio. At the same time, Tonino had animal friends to consult with before going to Amherst. Early one morning he happened to meet David the mouse at a newsstand near his house. Tonino told him about his plans to go to Amherst and asked him if he knew anyone there.

David replied, "Yes! I have a cousin named Emmaline. She is a white mouse and lives in Emily Dickinson's house on Main Street. I haven't seen her in a long time. Please contact her when you are there."

"I surely will," replied Tonino.

June 30, exactly four days before the Fourth of July opening concert at Tanglewood, Tonino headed off to Amherst. Tonino had promised to take a trip with Pedro and Ming Ming. He already had taken a trip to Puerto Rico with Pedro, but now he would be with both of them. They all hopped onto the Peter Pan bus with their backpacks and headsets and waved good-bye to their parents.

Tonino Meets Dr. Stoffolano and His Friends

Within less than two hours, they were pulling into the Amherst Town Common. Joe had written to Mauro that his friend Tonino and two other teenagers would be arriving on the five o'clock bus. Tonino recognized Mauro without ever having seen him because Joe so accurately described him. Mauro was wearing black-and-white checked chef's pants. Tonino could easily see Mauro because he was the only one dressed like that. Mauro greeted the three teenagers and took them over to his restaurant for dinner. After dinner they went to Antonio's pizzeria. They crossed the parking lot and went up a very narrow alley sandwiched between two buildings. By then it was about ten o'clock and all the college students from UMass were lining up for pizza. Because the crowd was so big, Mauro said, "Let's go through the back door."

On the way around the building, Pedro saw a sign that said, "Calipari's Closet." He asked Mauro if that was the same Calipari who coached the UMass basketball team. Mauro said, "Yes. In fact, maybe you will get a chance to meet him before you leave for Tanglewood. He's Italian, you know. Also, if you have time you should stop and visit the home of the Basketball Hall of Fame."

Tonino looked at Pedro and gave him a hopeful nudge.

When they finally got into Antonio's, Mauro saw Bruno sitting at one of the tables talking to someone. Mauro introduced Tonino and his friends to Bruno and then said, "I would like you to meet *Professore* Stoffolano." Mauro always called him *Professore* rather than just *Professor*. Professor Stoffolano taught about the *insecti* at UMass.

Professor Stoffolano extended his hand and greeted all three teenagers. Mauro had forgotten to mention that Tonino was a good friend of Joe Pace. After Professor Stoffolano mentioned that he always stopped at Joe's Deli to get *baccala* and other Italian foods when he was in Boston, everyone agreed that the world today was really a small place. Like a spider's web, there were many strands connecting the people of the world.

Tonino wanted to take front stage, so he mentioned that his father was a guard in the MCZ at Harvard and said how much he enjoyed going to Professor Wilson's laboratory to watch the leaf-cutting ants. As a consequence of this small bit of conversation, Professor Stoffolano asked the young boys if they had read Wilson's book *The Diversity of Life*. None of them had, so Professor Stoffolano gave them a quick sketch of what it was about. "Wilson presents the current situation concerning biological diversity in our world today and tells how the intervention of humans is having a major impact on both plant and animal diversity. The more diverse an ecosystem, the more stable it is. By reducing diversity, we are creating unstable ecosystems. This book is a must for those interested in maintaining both a healthy and stable planet for us and future generations. This is certainly something you should read."

"Are there any good examples of where people are trying to preserve the natural habitat to prevent certain insects from becoming extinct?" Tonino asked.

"Yes," replied Stoffolano. "One of the best examples is that of preserving the overwintering sites, called *refugia*, for the monarch butterfly in Mexico. In fact, Professor Lincoln Brower, who is spearheading this project, taught at Amherst College when I first came to UMass in 1969. He is now at the University of Florida, but spends a lot of his time in Mexico."

Tonino plugged all this information into his own "little computer." Joe always told him, "Now don't forget! Remember what people tell you; you never know when you will need that information again." Tonino was well aware he not only received good advice from his parents and relatives, but his older friends and mentors also gave him very sound advice.

Professor Stoffolano interjected, "When you boys are ready to go to Springfield, I will give you a ride. Let's leave early so we can stop at the Italian section to see my friends at Mom and Rico's."

Tonino Meets Emmaline the Mouse

Before leaving, Tonino asked where the Emily Dickinson house was on Main Street.

"Why do you want to know that?" everyone asked.

Tonino didn't want to let anyone know that he wanted to visit Emmaline, David's cousin, so he made up a long and complicated story. He couldn't help but think about what had happened to Pinocchio whenever he told a lie. He wondered if that would ever happen to him.

Dr. Stoffolano interjected, "We go very close to it on our way to your bed and breakfast. You are staying at the Allen House Victorian

Inn, which is at 599 Main Street, while the Dickinson house is at 280 Main Street."

Once they checked in to their bed and breakfast, they made arrangements for Dr. Stoffolano to pick them up the next day.

As soon as Pedro and Ming Ming were asleep, Tonino fixed his pillows so it would look like he was still in bed and quietly left the room. He did not want to transform too soon because he wanted to walk down Main Street to the Dickinson House as fast as he could. Once he reached 280 Main Street, he walked up to the back of the yellow house and transformed. Squeezing under the door was difficult because his hind legs got in the way. He made his way to the kitchen; even though it was dark, he could see a white mouse eating something underneath the table. "Are you Emmaline?" Tonino asked.

"Yes," the petite mouse responded. "Who are you?"

"I am Tonino, a good friend of your cousin David in Boston."

After much conversation, Emmaline[4] began to tell Tonino about Emily Dickinson. "Would you like a piece of this gingerbread while I tell you more about the Dickinson household?"

"No thank you, I ate a lot of pizza at Antonio's."

Tonino knew nothing about poetry, but he was always ready to learn. Just before he left, Emmaline told Tonino that Emily Dickinson had written a poem titled *"The Cricket Sang."*

"I didn't know that," he replied. "What kind of cricket was it about?" Tonino asked.

"You know, I really don't know," Emmaline responded. "However, I do know that she included crickets in several of her poems. Where are you going next?"

"We are going to the Berkshire Mountains."

"What are you going to do there?"

"Well, we have a meeting with Seiji Ozawa."

Emmaline responded, "You mean the famous conductor?"

"Yes, I have convinced him that the Fourth of July concert at Tanglewood should be performed by animals."

"What a great idea. Of course, you should know better than others what beautiful music animals make."

"True."

"Have you read the wonderful book by Vincent Dethier? He lives in Amherst and was the first director of the neuroscience program at the University of Massachusetts."

"No, what's the title of the book?"

"*Crickets and Katydids, Concerts and Solos*," Emmaline responded.

Tonino said, "I must read it because I personally know crickets are great musicians." Tonino thanked her, crawled under the door, and quickly ran back to the Allen House after transforming.

When he was back in bed, he felt very lucky that Pedro and Ming Ming were sound sleepers; he wondered what type of cricket Emily wrote about. Was it a field cricket, a house cricket, or a tree cricket? Tonino also made a mental note to read Dethier's book.

Leaving for Springfield

Tonino and his friends were up early because Dr. Stoffolano was taking them to Mom and Rico's before they went to the bus station in Springfield. It was a short trip; there was absolutely no traffic. They drove down Interstate 91, and just before the turn to go to Mom and Rico's, they saw a huge basketball sphere on their right. As they got closer, they read a sign that said, "The Basketball Hall of Fame." Dr. Stoffolano told them that they did not have time to visit this spectacular tribute to America's number one sport. Regardless, Pedro still got really excited and told Tonino and Ming Ming all about the origin of basketball in Springfield and how James Naismith invented the sport in 1891. Pedro liked telling the story about how the first hoop really was a peach basket.

Ming Ming, who loved to read, responded with, "Yeah, I'd like to see the size of the basket needed to fit the peach in *James and the Giant Peach*."

Everyone laughed since they had not only read the story, but also saw the movie distributed by Disney Pictures.

As they came down Main Street, they spotted a statue. "Who is that?" they asked Dr. Stoffolano.

"That is Cristoforo Colombo. This is the beginning of the South End, which is the original Italian neighborhood. Now, Puerto Ricans and African Americans also live here."

As they approached Mom and Rico's, they saw a sign for *La Fiorentina's Pasticcieria*. Next to that was Mom and Rico's. Loud music was emanating from the speakers; signs and photos covered the windows, and there was a plaque showing the famous Italian boxer, Rocky Marciano, on the left side before you entered the parking lot. As they entered the store, Rico Danielle greeted everyone and shook Professor Stoffolano's hand.

"I'm on my way to New York City," Dr. Stoffolano said, "so I am dropping the boys off one hour early. They need to catch the bus to Tanglewood at nine o'clock."

"I will make sure they get there." Rico showed the boys around the store and then took them over to Our Lady of Mount Carmel to show them the bocce courts. It was now half past eight, and Rico said they needed to leave for the bus station.

Rico drove the three teenagers to the bus station. They hopped on, but now they had a new item of luggage. Rico, who is president of Bocce World International, had given them all T-shirts with "Bocce World" across the back, plus he gave Tonino a set of bocce balls. As Tonino skipped along, the string bag holding the balls together kept swinging and hitting his legs. This didn't bother him. Besides, he now owned his own set of bocce balls. Wouldn't his father be proud of him? He could just hear his father going down to play bocce at the club telling his *pisani* his son now had his own set of bocce balls.

Playing the Quiz Game on the Way to the Berkshires

Not long after the bus left Springfield, the three boys began to test one another's knowledge. They were really into trivia and quiz shows. Ming Ming knew Tonino was interested in etymology, so he asked Tonino, "What does the word *Massachusetts* mean?"

Tonino didn't know the answer, but young boys like to think they know everything. After Ming Ming stumped him, Tonino wondered what question he would ask. As they rode the bus, Tonino noticed the rooster weather vanes on the top of many old barns.

This led to his question, "Why do so many of the barns here in Massachusetts use a rooster as the symbol for the weather vane?"

Pedro and Ming Ming looked at one another, hoping that the other would answer the question. Just then Tonino said, "Look, over there on top of the beautiful, red weathered barn. See? It's a rooster."

Pedro thought Tonino was picking on him because of the cockfight they saw in Puerto Rico; he admitted, "I don't know."

Tonino laughed and responded, "I don't know either," and together, they both laughed.

A little later, Pedro asked Tonino what the word *bocce* meant. He didn't know that Tonino had secretly been studying Italian.

Tonino had ordered *Italian Made Easy* CDs and listened to them for one hour each night before going to sleep; he answered Pedro confidently, "'To kiss.' When the large balls are rolled, they often smack into the other balls, or kiss them."

Pedro was impressed with Tonino's new knowledge of Italian; Pedro could speak fluent Spanish and always told Tonino he should learn Italian.

Tonino hadn't told his friends that he was leaving two weeks after the Fourth of July for Italy. *Will they be surprised when I tell them,* he kept thinking.

There is no regular bus service to Tanglewood from Springfield, so the boys had to take a chartered bus. The trip from Boston to Amherst, and now the trip on the Massachusetts Turnpike from Springfield to Tanglewood, had presented a new dimension for the boys. They were surprised to see that so much of Massachusetts was still forest.

At ten o'clock, they pulled into the parking lot of Tanglewood. Several tour buses were letting people off. Tonino gave the guard at the entrance the letter he had from Ozawa. After a brief telephone call, the guard led everyone to the building where Ozawa was; Tonino's excitement grew. Seiji greeted the boys and sat them down for a short briefing.

Tonino Meets Susan

Seiji mapped out the days prior to the July 4 concert. He also told them that their animal friends were arriving in a small chartered van from Boston at one o'clock. Seiji, Pedro, and Ming Ming didn't know that Tonino was a cricket. It might seem strange to some that Tonino's best human friends didn't know he was also a cricket, but just think about your own situation. Do you know everything about your best friends? I don't think so. Seiji just thought that Tonino had a special gift for dealing with animals; he never said any more about Tonino's relationship with these animals.

Following lunch, Tonino went to the parking lot to wait for the van while Ming Ming and Pedro went to explore the grounds and buildings of Tanglewood. On his way to the parking lot, Tonino had to go to the bathroom, so he morphed. He finished what he had to do when he saw a beautiful young girl coming his way. Quickly, he hopped behind a rock. To his amazement, the young girl morphed into a cricket and also went to the bathroom. Tonino was in total amazement.

He waited awhile until she morphed. He then also morphed and hurried up to catch her. "Excuse me," he said. "My name is Tonino; what is yours?"

"My name is Susan."

"What are you doing here?" Tonino asked.

"I am in an apprentice program for young violin students. What are you doing here?" Susan asked.

"I am helping Seiji prepare for the upcoming concert."

"How interesting," Susan replied.

Tonino politely asked, "Could you tell me where the parking lot is?"

"Just turn around and you will see it."

Tonino turned around and was totally embarrassed because the parking lot was right in front of him. As Susan left, Tonino couldn't help but think that she was a very special female cricket. He was also experiencing some special feelings, feelings he had never experienced before.

Promptly at one o'clock, the van arrived. All the humans stopped what they were doing and crowded around the animals as they left the van. "What is going on here?" they all asked Tonino.

"These are the musicians that will perform at the Fourth of July concert. Make sure you attend. It will be very special," Tonino told everyone.

One of the guards then escorted Tonino and all the animals to a special building where they would stay. Being at Tanglewood was a special treat; all the animals could get their meals on the grounds or in the adjacent forest, fields, or ponds.

Moby-Dick Out of Water

That evening before going to sleep, Pedro gave Tonino a brochure about points of interest near Tanglewood. The one that captured Tonino's fancy was Arrowhead, which was the home of Herman Melville from 1850 until 1862. It was here, and with the view of Mount Greylock appearing as a large white object in winter, that he wrote *Moby-Dick*, the great story of a white whale. "If we have time, I would like to visit Arrowhead," Tonino said.

Instead of visiting Arrowhead, Tonino went on a bus trip to visit the home of another writer, Nathaniel Hawthorne. The one thing that stuck in his mind was when the docent took them upstairs to the bedroom and showed them the rope springs on the bed. She then told them the old saying, "Sleep tight, don't let the bedbugs bite," and went on to explain that "sleep tight" meant that a special wooden device was used to tighten the ropes for a good night's rest.

They were busy the next two days rehearsing for the upcoming concert. The amateur musicians could barely read music, and with all the organizational stage arrangements, everyone was exhausted by the evening of July 3.

The day of the concert, things began to get extremely busy. Busloads of people from everywhere converged on Tanglewood. Tonino was extremely nervous because he had been the one who convinced Seiji to do this concert with the animals. Tonino was especially exhausted because he had been morphing back and forth so that he could keep the communication between everyone in order. At 7:15 p.m. sharp, everyone was ready for the concert to start.

The animals were introduced and came out to take their seats and warm up. The crowd was "abuzz" with conversation about this unusual event. Finally, Bradley the fiddler crab, the first violinist, came out and introduced the conductor. Everyone clapped and clapped as Seiji came out on the stage, and then silence overtook the audience. The great conductor finally began. The trees and bushes were full of birds, while other animals that had heard about the concert looked on. There were so many animal friends that some had to share blankets with humans, who had set up elegant meals with fancy tablecloths; some even had candles. The humans did not mind because they knew most of these animals had traveled a long distance to hear their friends perform. It was the chance of a lifetime.

The best musical piece was *Insect Symphony*. Immediately following was the grand finale, "The Star Spangled Banner," which was accompanied by fireworks and cannons going off.

The next day was both exciting and depressing. Tonino saw Susan and she told him how much she liked the concert. "I especially liked the insects that produce music with their wings. It is almost like me playing the violin," she said.

Tonino knew she was Japanese and had read that the people of Japan ate a lot of dolphin and whale meat. "Is it true that the Japanese eat a lot of whale and dolphin meat?" Tonino asked.

"Well, being brought up in the United States, I never did."

Tonino scratched his head and said to himself, *I will have to find out more about this.* He shook Susan's hand and said, "Let's e-mail one another."

"Okay," she said and turned around slowly and left.

It was also depressing because everyone had made new friends and they all liked the Berkshires. Some of the animals liked it so much that they decided to stay. This made room in the van for the boys. The trip back to Boston was uneventful, and the boys talked about their stay at Tanglewood. One discussion centered on the visit to Nathaniel Hawthorne's homestead.

"Tell me again what the docent said about the rope bed?" Ming Ming said.

Pedro loved the saying since his mother often used it. "Sleep tight, don't let the bedbugs bite." The docent had told them that to make the bed firm, people would use a wooden device to tighten the ropes because they didn't have modern spring mattresses. Also, bedbugs often inhabited the old mattresses and would come out at night and bite the sleeping occupant.

Another incident they talked about centered on Tonino reading an old *International Wildlife* magazine at the cottage he was staying in. Tonino explained that the colorful red in the American flag originally came from an insect.

"Explain that to me?" Pedro asked Tonino.

"In this article, it talks about how this small insect, called a scale insect, sucks the juices of the prickly pear cactus, which is actually farmed in many Central and South American countries. The Aztecs and the Incas based a major part of their agriculture on farming this insect; they used the red dye from it to color their wool. The red color, called cochineal, comes from the female's body fluid or hemolymph. At one time, it was as valuable as gold."

"What does this have to do with the American flag?" Ming Ming asked.

"Well, this article said that the color for the red stripes on the first American flag probably came from this scale insect."

Both Pedro and Ming Ming always remarked how Tonino loved detailed trivia about insects and culture. After about forty-five minutes, all the boys and other animals went to sleep. Before they knew it, they had arrived in South Boston. Everyone exchanged good-byes and waited to be picked up at the bus station. Tonino was too tired to discuss the trip with his parents; when he got home, he immediately went to bed.

Tonino was very busy over the next twelve days, practicing his Italian and making sure he was packed for his trip to Italy. The night before he was to leave, Tonino, Pedro, and Ming Ming went out for pizza. Everyone was discussing what to do for the rest of the summer.

Ming Ming turned to Tonino, who wasn't saying anything, and asked, "Why are you so silent?"

Pedro asked, "Well, other than working at Joe's, what are you going to do this summer?"

Tonino puffed himself up and said, "Tomorrow, I leave for Italy."

"Come on!" was the response. "You really don't mean it."

"Of course I do. Here are my tickets."

Tonino had been waiting for the best opportunity to tell his friends about his trip and to show off. This moment was perfect, and he knew it. He hadn't said anything to them before about this trip. As he did in Tanglewood, Tonino had now taken the front stage. He spent about an hour telling his friends about his trip.

Before departing, both Pedro and Ming Ming said to him, "Now don't forget, drop us a postcard."

"Of course I will." As he was leaving, Tonino turned around and said to Pedro, "Don't forget, let me know how the great nutrition experiment is going when I return."

Pedro and Ming Ming just looked at one another; both said at the same time, "Can you imagine, we are supposed to be his best friends and he didn't even tell us he was taking this trip."

"Yeah," said Ming Ming. "By the way, what's this experiment Tonino was talking about?"

"Oh, it's nothing."

Ming Ming now felt he maybe wasn't really a good friend of either Tonino or Pedro because neither one would confide in him about their experiment.

Chapter 4.
Finding One's Roots: Italy

Tonino's First Big Trip

Saying good-bye to his parents at Logan Airport was both sad and exciting for Tonino. It was sad because he was going away from home. It was exciting because he was going to find his roots.

"Of course you will fly Alitalia," his father said. "You must start hearing Italian spoken right away."

This was fine for his father, who could still speak Italian, but it was not the same for Tonino. He spoke very little Italian because neither of his parents spoke Italian at home (only when they didn't want him to know what they were talking about). Tonino had learned a few words from Joe, but his mother scolded him whenever she heard him using them. This was the same for most of Tonino's friends. Pedro was born in Puerto Rico and could speak Spanish because his parents hadn't moved to Boston until he was twelve years old. Ming Ming's parents, and his older sister Lucy, spoke Chinese, but he didn't. Tonino, however, always had a great desire to be multilingual. "Maybe someday," he always said to himself. "Maybe someday." The day finally came for the good-byes and the excitement of boarding the nonstop flight to Milan.

Arachnophobia

The captain said the flight would be about seven hours long. Except for watching the movie, Tonino slept for most of the trip. He sat next to Nicoletta, a five-year-old girl from Sardinia, a small island of Italy. She spoke no English and continually spoke to Tonino in Italian. Tonino didn't understand anything, but it didn't seem to matter to her that he didn't reply to any of her questions. When the flight attendants announced the movie was going to be shown, Nicoletta quieted down. She put her earphones on and settled into her seat. The movie was *Arachnophobia*. Since Tonino had friends that were arachnids, he already knew something about this movie. He put on his headset and became engrossed in the movie. It must have been extremely frightening for a young Italian girl who didn't speak any English.

What a ridiculous movie, Tonino thought to himself. *There are so many wonderful, exciting, and educational topics about arthropods to make movies about. I don't understand why movie producers focus on the scary, dangerous, or bad things in life.*

After the movie, Tonino often heard people ask the attendants, "*Che ora?*" The flight attendant would then look at his or her watch and say something back in Italian. Tonino figured out that "*Che ora?*" meant, "What time is it?" Being adventurous and bold, he stopped the attendant and proudly asked, "*Che ora?*"

The attendant looked at her watch and replied, "*Sette e mezza.*"

This stopped Tonino in his tracks, because he didn't expect to be answered in Italian. He quickly pulled out his Radio Shack translator and typed in the Italian words he just heard. "Seven thirty" came up on the screen of the hand-held translator, which Tonino had purchased with the money he made working at Joe's.

Tonino's thoughts drifted to thinking about Joe. Joe always teased him about being the "technological kid" of the North End. Joe knew Tonino had a Sony Walkman, a CD player, and even a Dell computer. The only things he still wanted were a DVD player, an iPod, and a digital TV. Joe was proud that he could help this teenager make it in life and attain the goals he had set for himself. Tonino continually tried to get Joe to use e-mail. Joe would always say, "Why would I want to do that? All my friends are here in Boston." Joe's whole family now lived in Boston; all his relatives had come over from Italy and were now citizens of the United States. "No one is left over there for me," he would say to Tonino.

Finally, Tonino fell asleep, and the next thing he knew, the pilot was saying they were beginning their descent into Milan's Malpensa Airport.

His uncle Marino, husband of his aunt Anna, was going to pick him up. Marino and Anna had an apartment in Florence, and Tonino was going to spend two weeks with them. Anna had joined Marino on vacation from her new job in the municipal library in Manchester, Connecticut. Guilia had remained in Connecticut to work.

As he exited the 747, Tonino spotted Anna and Marino. Simultaneously, all three began to wave. When he reached them, however, Tonino was not quite sure what to do. He was now seventeen years old and felt he was too grown up to hug his godparents. Once he was within a step (or hop) of them, he yielded to his childish ways and gave them both a big hug and kiss. Anna explained, "Italians kiss each other on both cheeks, so be ready." Tonino paid attention to all these details because he knew it was important to know different ethnic customs and follow them correctly.

Anna and Marino were glad to be with Tonino at this time in his life. They were his godparents and wanted him to find out about his lineage. For several days, they took Tonino to see such important things as the Uffizi Art Gallery, which was founded in 1581 by the Medici family, and the world-renowned *Ponte Vecchio*. On the fifth day, Anna decided it was time for Tonino to visit the grave of his great-great-great-grandfather, Grillo-parlante.

They arrived at the cemetery at San Miniato al Monte, the same place Carlo Lorenzini is buried. Even though he didn't know exactly where he was going, Anna let Tonino lead the way. Anna gently held onto his sweater and carefully guided him. Tonino seemed to instinctively know where he was going. Finally, Tonino stopped. Right in front of him was Carlo Lorenzini's mausoleum.

Tonino and Anna couldn't see very much because of the glass windows protecting the graves, so they morphed. As they crawled beneath a crack and entered the protected area, they could see just next to Carlo's tomb was a very small stone that said, "Grillo-parlante Cricchetti" on the top of the stone, and below it were the dates 1881–1921. Next to this grave was another stone that read "Pierangelo-parlante Cricket" (1899–1939). This was confusing to Tonino because, as long as he had known, his family name was Cricket. Tonino tried not to appear surprised. After all, he was seventeen and should know these things. He said to himself, *Why didn't my parents ever tell me about this?* In fact, he didn't say anything to Anna until they returned to the apartment.

That evening, Anna explained to him that many Italians changed their names when they came to America so they could integrate easier and not always be looked upon as immigrants. "You will notice that when anyone spells your great-great-great-grandfather's first name, they anglicize it as 'Gryllo' rather than its original 'Grillo.' Other ethnic groups did the same. In fact," she said, "did you know that Bob Hope convinced the great singer Tony Bennett to change his name from Anthony Benedetto because he said, 'That's too long for the marquee. We'll call you Tony Bennett.' People often changed names for professional reasons. Would you like to see a brief lineage from your father's side of the family?" Anna asked.

"Sure, I would like that."

Anna went to the family Bible, pulled out a piece of paper, and handed it to Tonino. As he read down the list, he saw that his great-great-grandfather Pierangelo had changed the family name to Cricket when he immigrated to the United States.

> *Grillo-parlante Cricchetti* (1881–1921). Hatched in Collodi, Italy, on July 4. Had one son, Pierangelo, in 1899; wife's name Filomena Norelli from Squille, Italy.
>
> *Pierangelo-parlante Cricket* (1899–1939). Hatched in Collodi and moved to Pavia in 1915. Emigrated to Hollywood, California, in 1917 and changed his name to Cricket. Married Nancy Grimaldi, an Italian American, in 1920 and had a son, Jiminy Cricket, in 1922 who became a movie star in Hollywood. Died in Italy while attending the funeral of his close friend Luigi.
>
> *Jiminy Cricket* (1922–1963). Hatched in Hollywood, California. In 1940, he became a star in the Disney movie *Pinocchio*. Married Mara Stoffolano in 1945

and in 1946 had a son, Rolando. Jiminy drowned while at sea watching whales off the coast of the Baja Peninsula.

Rolando Cricket (1946–1968). Hatched in Italy while his pregnant mother Carmella was visiting her aunt in Collodi. Thus, he had dual citizenship. In 1964, he and Carmella had a son named Giovanni.

Giovanni Cricket (1964–). Hatched in Italy, he married Maria in 1982. They had a son, Tonino, in 1982.

Tonino Cricket (1982–). Hatched in Boston on Columbus Day in the North End or the Italian section of Boston.

It was getting late and Anna said it was time for everyone to go to bed. "Pleasant dreams," she said to Tonino.

Marino then said, "Sleep tight, don't let the bedbugs bite." Tonino smiled as he remembered the wonderful visit to Nathaniel Hawthorne's house, the Tanglewood concert, and the Berkshires in general.

The next day, Tonino, Anna, and Marino took the train to see the sites of Rome. They spent two days there before returning to Florence. Tonino was feeling very Italian after his trip to Rome. He was greatly impressed by all he had seen, especially the Roman Coliseum, where his imagination took over, sitting there, hearing the great roar of the crowd, and watching the combat of the gladiators. It was hard for him to believe that humans were forced to fight humans and sometimes even animals, such as lions. These were not free men, but were usually slaves, prisoners captured during battle, or criminals. Initially, these sacrificial combats were waged to honor the spirits of the dead with offerings of blood. Blood has played a significant role in various cultures. His thoughts returned to the cockfight he saw in Puerto Rico. He also remembered Ming Ming telling him that for centuries, the Chinese forced crickets to fight other crickets. He wondered, "Could I ever be a cricket warrior?"

Following a good bowl of *pasta alla cecca*, Tonino excused himself and went out into the garden. It was dark, and the crickets had started to perform their evening concert. To get a better look at the musicians, and not to disturb them, Tonino transformed and set off into the garden. He heard chirping off to his left. He headed that way when all of a sudden another cricket jumped out and landed on him. It was a big surprise, and this cricket was much bigger and heavier than Tonino.

"What are you doing?" he shouted. "Get off me!"

The other cricket responded, "I thought you were the one singing."

"No, it wasn't me."

"Excuse me," the other cricket said, and he went in search of the one singing to claim his territory. Tonino followed the larger cricket and witnessed a fierce fight between the two crickets.

Tonino had never seen a cricket fight. He had witnessed some gang-fights by humans and even saw someone get shot, but city crickets chirped only to find a mate. There wasn't good territory to fight over in Boston, so crickets never fought. Tonino had heard that studies were being conducted on what is called "male weaponry" in fighting crickets. He heard about how his male ancestors had evolved larger heads and mandibles than females, and these traits favored males fighting for territory. He carefully watched the fight and tried to judge which male had the larger head and mandibles. The fighting was so intense and fast that he was not able to see. Later, however, he looked in the mirror and sized up his own mandibles. Tonino continued to watch very intently as the two crickets battled. Finally, the one cricket that had landed on him turned and hopped away. Its right antenna and left cerci had been badly damaged.

Tonino hopped over. "Are you okay?"

"Yes, but I am sore and a little ashamed."

"Don't be," responded Tonino. "What is your name?"

"My name is Tito Schipa, Jr."

Even though it was dark, Tonino could see that this cricket species was black while the species he belonged to was usually yellowish-brown. "Why are you embarrassed?" Tonino asked.

"Well, my father was the great Italian tenor, yet I can hardly carry a note."

"Your father would still be proud of you. Don't worry about that."

"Thanks for your kind words, but I must go now." Tito turned and hopped away.

Tonino hopped to the edge of the garden and transformed.

The night before he returned to Boston, just before it was dark, Tonino said to his aunt Anna, "I would like to visit the grave again, but I prefer to go alone."

"That's fine, but do take some flowers for the graves."

Tonino picked some beautiful flowers from the garden and set off to pay his last respects to both his great-great-great and great-

great-grandfathers. By the time he reached the graves, evening was approaching.

Something was magical about this evening. Tonino felt very mature, he felt he had connected with his roots, and he just felt good. Walking down the path to the graves was very beautiful. Even though it was night, there was just enough light from *la luna*, as Tonino now called the moon, to see the way. The smell of the flowers was almost overpowering. Just on the horizon, he saw a star that seemed to be shining brighter than all the others. Quietly approaching the graves, Tonino immediately morphed; at the same time, the flowers he was carrying also became the appropriate size. He knelt down and put the flowers on the graves, first on his great-great-great-grandfather's and then on his great-great-grandfather's. Small tears appeared in his eyes, forming little pools that streamed down his cheeks.

This was a very unusual behavior. You see, insects do not have tear ducts. They also do not have eyelids to protect their eyes or to keep them moist, or even to remove dust or debris that lands on their lenses. Insect eyes are covered with the same cuticle that covers the rest of the body, except it is clear. Why Tonino could produce tears in his insect form remains a mystery to this day. Could he be moving in the direction of that awful marionette Pinocchio, who ultimately became a real boy? He hadn't cried for a long time, but he knew it was important to not only live life, but to feel it in his heart. How often his parents told him that. Joe would say, "Tonino, you can judge a person, not by their words, but by what is in their heart. It's good to cry every so often. A person that doesn't cry has no heart."

At that instant, there was a bright light all around the graves. It was as if someone had put white Christmas tree lights all around the gravestones. Grillo's grave was lit up as if it had a halo around the smoothly polished marble. This surprised Tonino, and he sat back on his hind jumping legs.

As he saw this overpowering light, he heard a soft voice say, "Tonino." Tonino looked around to see if anyone else was there. He bit his left antenna to make sure he wasn't imagining this. He had heard about jetlag, but he had been in Italy too long for this to explain what was happening. Again, the voice said, "Tonino."

This time, Tonino responded. "Yes, I am Tonino."

The voice then said, "I am the Blue Fairy, spiritual guardian of your great-great-great-grandfather and all the males of the Cricchetti family."

"What do you want from me?" Tonino said.

"I want to discuss your future," the Blue Fairy replied. "Because Grillo-parlante did such a wonderful job as the conscience of Pinocchio, I have come here to ask you to become the environmental conscience of the world. This world is in great need of a conscience. With overpopulation, pollution, and global warming, someone must come forward to advocate for our silent sphere. At this particular moment, many of the earth's numerous habitats are rapidly being destroyed, along with many plants and animals. Since this is a worldwide problem, I have chosen you to remind humans when they are committing a grave sin against Mother Nature. You have been selected to do this important task because you are interested in all cultures and eventually will have traveled extensively. Only someone with this background can accept such a responsibility. I have come here to grant you three wishes if you are willing to accept this task. Before you can get the three wishes, however, you must truly understand the meaning of friendship. This is the only condition your great-great-great-grandfather placed upon those receiving this special privilege. You may remember, Pinocchio had trouble knowing who his true friends were."

Tonino knew that Grillo-parlante was the conscience of Pinocchio, but he had never been told why he was chosen to do this important job. *Why was a cricket like me*, he asked himself, *chosen to be Pinocchio's conscience, and not a bird or some other animal? Why not another human?*

Tonino also knew Pinocchio didn't always listen to his conscience, and this often got him into serious trouble. Tonino was aware that everyone's conscience is very important and can help them if they are heading for trouble; however, many ignore the warning.

Tonino didn't reply to the Blue Fairy. Instead, he put his foretarsi to his head, scratched it, and thought to himself. This is exactly the way his father behaved when thinking about something important. Finally, after a short deliberation, Tonino said out loud, "First of all, I would like to be able to speak and understand every language. Second, I would like to be able to be invisible when necessary. Last of all, I would like to be able to transform from a cricket to a human and vice versa."

The Blue Fairy said, "Your three wishes are granted. Go now, but remember, before you can use these magical powers, you must not only realize the true meaning of friendship, but you must prove your friendship."

Tonino crawled out of the mausoleum, transformed, and started back to Anna and Marino's apartment. Little did he know that any member of the Cricchetti lineage, or anyone marrying into that lineage, could readily transform without asking permission of the Blue Fairy. Thus, he had wasted a wish. He didn't realize this because he had never seen his father morph. After he returned home and told his parents about what happened, his father told him about the Cricchetti family's ability to do this.

As he turned the corner to his godparents' apartment, he could see them both anxiously awaiting his safe return. His aunt and uncle greeted him outside in the garden entrance to the apartment. They were just getting ready to look for him.

Anna noticed that somehow Tonino looked different. She couldn't put her tarsus on it, but she was sure he had changed somehow. Before going to bed, she asked him, "Do you feel okay, or are you just nervous about your flight tomorrow?"

"That's it," he replied. "I am nervous about the flight."

It was difficult for Tonino to fall asleep that evening. Not only did he keep thinking about the trip the next day, but his bedroom seemed to be exceptionally bright. He got up to close the blinds and saw the light wasn't coming from *la luna*, but from that same very special star he had seen at the cemetery. While falling asleep, he couldn't help but think how fortunate he was to have such wonderful parents, kind and dedicated friends, and now a good guardian, the Blue Fairy, plus a great opportunity to travel. Tonino suddenly realized that he had forgotten to send Pedro and Ming Ming a postcard.

Thinking about home and his friends, and trying to go to sleep, he recalled telling Pedro many times, "I just don't dream." Tonino remembered how surprised Pedro was at this statement. He would always tell Tonino, "Everyone dreams, you just don't remember them." Talking aloud to himself, Tonino said, "I guess if you have pleasant dreams it is nice to remember them, but I imagine having scary dreams must not be too pleasant." With those thoughts, Tonino went to sleep. The next day, his aunt and uncle took him to the airport in Milan, where he boarded the nonstop flight to Boston's Logan Airport.

At the airport, he had a cappuccino and *sfogliatella*. He now felt very integrated into Italian life. He kissed his godparents on each cheek, hugged them, and quickly boarded the plane. As the plane taxied onto the runway, Tonino could see his aunt and uncle waving good-bye. He waved, but knew they really couldn't see him. How could he ever forget this trip?

The flight from Italy was uneventful, which gave Tonino a chance to read many of the magazines available on the plane. Because his family didn't have a lot of money, the only literature available in his house was the *Boston Globe*, which his father would pick up every day from the local newsstand. Giovanni's friend, Harold, had run the newsstand for twenty-five years.

Tonino's favorite magazines were those about science. He happened to pick up the December 1994 issue of *Popular Science*. As he flipped the pages, he came to an interesting article, "The World According to Dan Janzen." Janzen got his PhD in entomology from the University of Kansas. His specialty within entomology is ecology. Tonino was totally captured by this article. It told how Janzen helped lead the crusade to identify all the living organisms within a given area of Costa Rica before human activity destroyed their natural habitats. A chart showed that there were only 45,000 known species of vertebrates, while there were 950,000 species of insects (and possibly 8 to 100 million still remained undiscovered).

"Wow," Tonino said, "this is a lot more than the 800,000 my father told me." The article went on to explain how a new breed of prospectors are not looking for gold or diamonds, but instead are looking for new chemicals that are present in plants and animals. Tonino didn't know anything about where a lot of our medicines originally come from. This whole new area of "chemical prospecting" was something even the large pharmaceutical companies, like Merck, were actively becoming involved in. In fact, Merck's most recent venture into this area is a $2.5 million collaboration among Janzen, several drug companies, and the National Institutes of Health. Collaboratively, they are exploring the tropical rainforests for new chemicals that may have a practical and medicinal use for humans. After Tonino read this article, he relaxed into his seat and thought to himself, *Wow, what a wonderful and exciting thing to do.* Tonino knew one of his major problems in life was learning to focus on something he really liked doing. He could just hear his father and Joe saying to him, "Don't forget, Tonino, you can't do everything."

This important topic of what to do with one's life was something Tonino often discussed with Pedro and Ming Ming. He had eaten the meal the attendant gave him, read this wonderful article about chemical prospecting, and now was getting tired. Since he had already seen the movie on the way over, he didn't want to watch it again. *Anyway,* Tonino said to himself, *it is one of those Hollywood spectaculars made to excite and scare people.*

Unfortunately, *Arachnophobia* not only made humans afraid of all spiders, it also made people afraid of all arthropods, which could develop into entomophobia. Since insects are arthropods, the movie really stereotyped all arthropods as being dangerous and evil. Tonino knew from tenth grade biology class that he, all his insect friends, and his spider friends belonged to this large phylum of animals called Arthropoda.

Tonino had a special ability of taking words apart and trying to understand their origins. He remembered breaking the Latin word *Arthropoda* into the prefix *Arthros-*, which means "jointed," and *poda-*, which means "foot or leg." Thus, he would tell his vertebrate friends, "I belong to the phylum of animals with jointed legs or appendages."

It had been a very exciting but emotionally tiring evening the night before. Just before Tonino fell asleep, he realized that he had just been given a very special assignment. Like Grillo-parlante, he was also given the charge of being a conscience. Unlike his great-great-great-grandfather, however, his was a much bigger responsibility. He kept thinking, *How can I be the conscience of the world when it comes to saving the environment?* This was a huge task for such a young person. The Blue Fairy knew, however, that it would take someone who had a multicultural flair to do a good job. Tonino thought to himself, *In addition to physically finding one's roots, maybe accepting responsibilities and understanding traditions handed down from one's family is also part of finding one's roots.*

A short while after reading the article and thinking about his new assignment in life, Tonino fell asleep. It was a deep and sound sleep. The next thing he remembered, he was being awakened by the pilot coming on the intercom and stating that they had started their descent into Boston's Logan Airport. He had slept so soundly that he even missed breakfast.

Not having a lot of luggage, Tonino was able to exit customs without any delay. Pedro and Ming Ming were waiting for him and holding a big sign saying, "*Benvenuto* Tonino." His parents were also there, but Giovanni was in a wheelchair. Tonino was worried something serious had happened. Following the traditional hugs and kisses—now on both cheeks—they headed back to the North End. Everyone was happy, but nothing was said about Giovanni. After returning home, Tonino said good-bye to Pedro and Ming Ming. As the two boys left, he called out to Pedro to come back a minute.

When Pedro returned, Tonino said quietly, "How is the experiment going?"

Pedro's eyes lit up. "You will never believe it," he said to Tonino. "I am now the starting center rather than one of the forwards. It is because of you and your idea about this new diet that I have this opportunity. Thanks again for all your help. I have increased my jumping ability by three feet. I guess it works."

That evening, Tonino couldn't stop thinking there was more to this insect food and the two star athletes.

Tonino kept asking everyone what had happened to his father, but no one, not even his mother, would tell him. Finally, his father told him he just stepped on a bocce ball, slipped, and had a bad fall.

Joe agreed, "That's the way it happened. It's all over. I don't ever want to discuss it again."

Giovanni had made everyone promise they would never tell Tonino what really happened. This secret would be kept for a long time. Only because Giovanni was such a powerful personality and everyone loved him so much did they agree to make such a promise. Everyone except Joe! When Giovanni said to Joe, "You must promise me never to tell Tonino the true story," Joe agreed; however, at that moment he crossed his fingers behind his back, releasing him of his promise.

Fall was coming and everyone was getting ready for school to start (everyone, that is, except Tonino's animal friends). What would they do during the winter? Tonino liked the fall because of all the colors of the trees. He also liked jumping in raked-up leaves, even when he was transformed into a cricket. Boston has wonderful parks, and on weekends or after school, all his friends loved to go to the park and play before dinner. The common true katydid annually announces the coming of fall and the school year. Its mating call can be heard each evening as other males participate in a group concert. Tonino had read and loved the book Emmaline had recommended, *Crickets and Katydids, Concerts and Solos,* by Vincent Dethier.

Chapter 5.
Flying with the Monarchs and Sledding with the Whales

Tonino's Seventeenth Birthday

Only a few weeks remained before school started. Tonino was looking forward to this school year because he now felt he had a more mature outlook on life. Because Tonino's family, as crickets, lived in an area where they could easily get scraps of people food, they spent less time foraging for food than rural crickets. This gave Tonino an opportunity to go to school. Tonino, Pedro, and Ming Ming would be going into eleventh grade. Even though he was getting older, Tonino still had trouble talking to his parents about personal things. It took Tonino a long time, and a lot of serious thinking, before he told his parents about the Blue Fairy. He was afraid they would say he made it all up or was just using his imagination.

Little did Tonino know that other young people had doubts about communicating with adults just for the same reason. It all depended on your parents, as Tonino was soon to find out.

Tonino was getting ready to celebrate his seventeenth birthday. His parents wanted to have a party for him, but he felt he was too old for that. "Regardless," stated Giovanni, "we will have the relatives and Joe and Ann Maria for some cake and ice cream."

Luckily, Joe offered to have the party at his store. Twenty relatives showed up. Joe had put red-and-white checked tablecloths on the tables and made a special effort to have all the foods Tonino liked:

salami, prosciutto and melon, and many more wonderful Italian foods.

Giovanni couldn't wait until Tonino opened his presents. Giovanni knew Tonino would like the special book he and Maria bought for him. He wanted this to be the last present Tonino opened. Tonino was very thankful for all his gifts. Regardless of the gift, he sincerely thanked everyone. He could hear his mother saying, "Now Tonino, it is the thought that counts, not the gift itself. Be thankful for every gift you are given."

Only two presents remained: one from Joe and Isabella and one from his parents.

Giovanni lifted the present from the Paces, looked at it, mentally weighed it, and said to himself, *This is obviously a book; is it the same book we got him?* This could happen because they all knew Tonino's likes and dislikes. Crossing his fingers, he handed Tonino the Pace's present. Tonino started to open it. Giovanni stood right over him, looking very carefully at what emerged from the wrapper. The back of the book came up first. Giovanni was beside himself because he couldn't see the front cover. Slowly, Tonino turned it over. While trying to read the title out loud to everyone, he had to push his father away. Giovanni sighed with relief as he saw the title: *Milkweed Butterflies: Their Cladistics and Biology,* by Ackery and Vane-Wright. On the inside cover, Joe and Isabella had written something.

Tonino read it out loud:

> *To our technology boy from the North End. Remember!*
> *Before there were computers, there were butterflies.*
>
> *Love, your dear friends,* Joe and Isabella.

As he leafed through the book before passing it on for other people to see, Tonino tried to understand what Joe and Isabella really meant by the statement, "Before there were computers, there were butterflies." Either Tonino was missing the subtle meaning of this statement or he was too tired to understand its real meaning. Regardless, he stored it into his mental computer for later reference and recall.

Giovanni proudly took the last present from the table. Unlike the previous present, which had been wrapped with butterfly paper, this gift was wrapped with colorful paper showing a tropical scene. The paper showed plants and tropical animals like parrots, toucans, bird wing butterflies, large katydids, and other beautiful insects. Tonino went through the same weighing motions as with previous gifts. Because it was the same size and weight as the Paces' present, he was worried it was going to be the same book. He certainly didn't want his parents to be embarrassed.

To show some enthusiasm, and to take the attention away from the possibility it could be the same book, he rapidly tore off the beautiful wrapping paper and threw it into the air. It landed on Joe's head, and everyone laughed. *Whew*, he thought to himself. *That simple act really reduced the tension.* Again, the book was the wrong side up. He quickly turned it over and breathed a deep sigh of relief. It was *The Diversity of Life* by E. O. Wilson. Tonino read the title to everyone and then read the passage his parents had written:

> *To our loving son Tonino. Someday you will be an important citizen of the world, and this topic is something you should know about.*
>
> *Love, Mom and Dad*

That wasn't all; another person had written something inside the book. Before reading this, however, Tonino read it to himself. He then paused and read it aloud,

> *To one of my favorite visitors. I always enjoy watching you when you come to my laboratory to see the leaf-cutting ants. I remember watching you ever since you were three years old. Your father had to hold you up and let you stand on his knees because you were too small to see the ants. You and your father would then sing the song, "The ants go marching one by one." As a young boy growing up in Alabama, I also enjoyed entering the world of insects, but for some reason, which I can't explain, you seem to naturally understand the*

> *ants and other insects in my laboratory better than I*
> *do. I wish you well in becoming an entomologist.*

E. O. Wilson

Giovanni knew Tonino was pleased with the book by the expression on his face when he saw it and after reading what Dr. Wilson had written. Giovanni told Tonino, "Dr. Wilson wanted to come to the party; however, he is in Costa Rica with Dr. Janzen."

Of all the presents, Tonino valued the books the most. This was his way to see the world and to know how other people think. The party continued for another half hour. Everyone constantly chatted and even sang a few Italian songs. At six o'clock, Giovanni thanked everyone for coming and told them to be careful going home.

All of those attending gave Tonino a hug before leaving and said, "*Arrivederci,*" to Giovanni and Maria, and "*Mille grazie,*" to Joe and Isabella for hosting the party.

Tonino's Revelation

Tonino and his parents returned home with all the gifts. It was a lovely evening. Not one cloud in the sky. Before entering their house, something happened that Tonino had never noticed before. Either it was too commonplace to notice or now he could see it because he had a better sense of who he was. His father was carrying all the presents. At Joe's store everything was people size. Previously, it never occurred to Tonino that these presents wouldn't fit into their small, cricket-sized apartment. As soon as his mother and father stepped onto the mat in front of the door, everything became cricket size, even the presents. Tonino didn't say anything to his parents, but he thought to himself, *Why hadn't I ever observed this before?*

It was strange because he wasn't even aware that when he left the house to go to school or to work at Joe's store, he became human and people size. At the same time, when he returned home, he again automatically became an insect and cricket size. All this time he had taken this for granted. He didn't want to seem foolish, especially since he was now seventeen. Instead, he waited until his father said, "Well, I must go outside to check the stars before going to bed."

Tonino knew his father only went out if there was a clear sky and you could see all the stars. Giovanni loved looking at the stars. Maybe it was something he inherited from Jiminy Cricket, who sang *When You Wish Upon a Star* in the Disney movie. After Tonino heard the door close, he hopped up the stairs to join him. The sky was clear and beautiful. Every star seemed to be trying to outshine the others.

Again, the author believes it is essential to remind readers how insect vision works, otherwise they might expect Giovanni to see more stars in the sky than there really are. Humans often think that each single unit of an insect's compound eye transmits a separate and identical image to the visual area of the insect's brain. In other words, people think that insects see hundreds or thousands of the same images. The truth of the matter is that this is not how the arthropod eye works. Instead, each individual unit sees a portion of the visual field, and this is transmitted to the visual cortex and integrated into an image. Insect vision is similar to how our computer and television screens function. All the individual units or pixels are integrated by our visual system to form one image.

Tonino moved beside his father and turned the same direction his father was looking. His father put his hand on Tonino's shoulder, turned, and looked him straight into the eyes. Tonino got a lump in his throat and felt uneasy. His father's eyes then turned away from him and looked straight at the horizon. Tonino did the same thing. To Tonino's amazement, he found himself looking at the same bright star he had seen in Italy while standing in front of the grave of Grillo-parlante. His father didn't say anything. Instead, he just took a deep breath, sighed, and started back to the house. Tonino took special notice. His father had come out of the house, but didn't become human and people size. *Wait a minute*, Tonino said to himself. *What's going on here?* He called to his father, "Dad, wait! I want to talk to you." Giovanni turned around and walked toward Tonino. "Let's sit down," Tonino said.

Giovanni jumped up on a rock and started to sit down, but Tonino interrupted his movements by saying, "No, sit over here." Tonino was pointing to the small wooden bench Giovanni had made. Normally,

Tonino would never sit on this bench because, as a boy, he had gotten a long, wooden sliver in his abdomen, and he remembered how painful it was when his mother took it out. How vividly he recalled her lighting a match to sterilize the sewing needle before digging and prying out the splinter. Not only did taking the sliver out hurt, but he experienced additional pain when his mother put mercurochrome on it. Unlike alcohol, a drop of mercurochrome always left a reddish-brown spot where it was applied, which lasted for several days. It was your badge of courage for undergoing this awful treatment. Tonino could now sympathize with all those dolls, like Raggedy Anne and Andy, who must have felt pain when those sharp needles used to put them together missed and jabbed them. Thinking about how any instrument used to injure one's skin must hurt caused Tonino to think about how Pinocchio must have hurt when Geppetto carved him out of wood.

His father knew something was up because Tonino never wanted to sit on that bench. In fact, it was sort of his father's place to sit. Giovanni sat down and Tonino joined him. "I want to talk to you about something," Tonino said.

"That's fine, go ahead." Giovanni was especially careful not to embarrass Tonino so that he wouldn't tell him his personal feelings.

Tonino started, "Did you know …," but then suddenly stopped. He then started again, "Did you know that when I was in Italy, I went to the grave of your great-great-grandfather?"

Because Tonino was presenting it as a question, his father replied, "Yes! Your Aunt Anna told me."

"But there is so much more to the story," replied Tonino, who was being very serious. Tonino didn't really know where to start. *Well, why not start from the beginning?* he asked himself. Not to bore his father, he focused only on the main highlights and left out a lot of the details, like placing the flowers on the grave. Tonino turned away from his father and, at that moment, focused his eyes on the bright star on the horizon. This seemed to give him some confidence. He then turned to his father and said, "Did you know that our family's original name was Cricchetti?"

Giovanni took a few seconds before responding. "Yes," Giovanni replied.

You did? Tonino said to himself, and he then said in a loud voice, "Did you also know that I was given three special wishes while I stood at the grave?"

"Yes. I was also given the same opportunity to have three wishes when I was about your age. It was also my first trip to Italy." Tonino and his father were talking as if, for the first time ever, they really understood one another.

Tonino then said to his father, "Why don't you use the special powers?"

Giovanni paused, looked at the star, and turned back to face Tonino. "Many of these powers are used only by young people. As you get older, you no longer need these things to survive." The intense conversation continued.

"Why have you and mother chosen to live as crickets here in this small, cricket-sized house when you could live in a large, people-sized apartment as humans?"

"When your mother and I started dating here in Boston, we knew we couldn't afford to have a big human apartment. Being able to change sizes and forms was only beneficial when we wanted to interact with humans. Besides," he noted, "another benefit of being small is that we need less food."

Tonino thought for a moment and agreed this all made perfect sense. There was only one thing still troubling him; he asked himself, *Why did my father say most of these powers were for young people?*

Because he felt good about having a positive conversation with his father, and rather than change subjects, Tonino completely dropped the topic. He looked at his father, gave him a kiss by touching both antennae to his father's, and said, "I'll bet that you are a lot like your great-great-grandfather." Tonino turned and started into the house. On the way, he kept repeating, like most teenagers, to himself, over and over, *I'm nothing like my father. I'm nothing like my father.* This may be a universal truth, but Tonino felt that his father did not go to school, knew nothing about modern technology, such as computers, and hardly travelled outside his neighborhood, while he did all of these.

Life went better for Tonino after he and his father had talked. His mother noticed a marked difference in the way the two of them interacted. Tonino, for the first time in his life, shared with his father what was happening in school. He told him how the library was such a different place than probably he remembered. Little did he know, his father never went to the library. He was too busy working and helping the family make it in America.

"Now it is all computerized," Tonino said. "You don't have to use the card file. You can enter the subject, author, or title of any book you want. Anyone of these techniques will pull up the reference on the screen if it is in the system. If the book is owned by the library, it will even tell you whether someone has already signed it out. If it is not in the library, it may tell you what other library has it and how to get it on an interlibrary loan."

All of this was beyond belief for Giovanni, who had seen some major technological changes during his lifetime (e.g., the telephone, automobile, television), but what about these things called computers? Tonino often told his father that computers, especially being able to use e-mail, unite people throughout the world because they are interactive. His father agreed even though he didn't know anything about e-mail.

Planning for Thanksgiving on Nantucket with Relatives

One day, Maria and Giovanni received a letter from one of Maria's cousins. Daniela Marcheschi, who now lived in San Juan, Puerto Rico, wanted to spend Thanksgiving vacation in Boston. Maria's side of the family were not true crickets; they were short-horned grasshoppers. Daniela and her husband, Angelo, had moved to Puerto Rico five years ago, where he started his own law firm. Angelo specializes in international law, especially environmental issues. Their son, Carlo, who was now twenty-one, was at the U.S. Air Force Academy in Colorado Springs. Daniela and Angelo wanted to come to the mainland for Thanksgiving vacation. Carlo, who had his small pilot's license, would meet them at Logan Airport. Daniela also mentioned that if Tonino was interested, Carlo would take him up for a ride. Maria checked with Giovanni and Tonino, and everyone agreed this would be a nice time to get the family members together. Maria telephoned Anna in Connecticut to see if she and Marino could join them. "We would love to," Anna replied. As in most families, this fall holiday was a special occasion.

Maria told Tonino about Carlo's offer to take him for a ride in his plane during the vacation break. This sounded like a great idea to Tonino, because he had often heard stories about how Pierangelo loved to fly over the Tuscan countryside. Tonino had seen a television program about William Lishman, a.k.a. Father Goose, who in the 1980s trained Canada geese to fly south by using a small ultralight airplane. In 1993, Lishman took eighteen Canada geese from Toronto to Virginia, a distance of four hundred miles, to help the geese learn their migratory route south. Many of these geese had been born in Toronto but never left because the winters were mild and there was plenty of food available. Thus, they never learned the route south from experienced birds that made the trip the year before. By training them to fly behind the ultralight airplane, Lishman would show them the route the way they'd learn it from other geese.

What a great idea! Tonino said to himself. *Humans helping other animals.* Maria always encouraged Tonino's interest in environmental issues. Later in his life, Tonino would learn more about how humans are helping other living organisms through captive breeding programs, which raise them in captivity and then release them into their natural environments.

Maria often gave Tonino articles from the *Boston Globe* about science, especially about insects; she would say, "Being an insect, you must learn as much as you can about your ethnicity." One Sunday, she showed him a feature article about the monarch butterfly migration, which had already started in Canada and was headed south. The author predicted the northern monarchs would pass through Nantucket Island, off the coast of Massachusetts, about two to three days after Thanksgiving. This was a natural stopover because they would have been flying over the ocean for quite a while and would need to rest and refuel on nectar.

As a youngster, Tonino remembered his parents celebrating Thanksgiving every other year on Nantucket with their friends, Ginni and Howie. Ginni worked in the public schools and Howie was a house painter. The thing Tonino liked best about Howie is that he always took him around the island to see the birds, plants, insects, and other life forms. Even though he isn't trained as a scientist, Howie is an amateur naturalist. Howie tried to mirror his life after E. O. Wilson. After reading Wilson's book, *Naturalist,* Howie changed how he thought about and treated other living organisms. Howie is also an excellent artist. He often made very detailed colored pencil drawings of all the wildlife and flowers he saw on the island. Tonino remembered Howie telling him about a saying by the African ecologist, Baba Dinn, who loved nature and wrote the following: "In the end, we will conserve only what we love, we will love only what we understand, we will understand only what we are taught."

Tonino also recalled one vacation when Howie took him to one end of the island to see the local monarchs getting ready to join their monarch relatives coming down from the north. Howie explained to Tonino that all the monarchs throughout the eastern corridor of the United States and Canada would fly along the Atlantic coast to Florida and then on to Mexico, where they would spend the winter. In the spring, the overwintering population would migrate back to the United States.

Two unrelated events Tonino had stored in his own little computer brain now seemed to give him an idea. If William Lishman could teach the geese their migratory route using an ultralight airplane, why couldn't someone use an ultralight airplane to follow the monarchs during their migration to Mexico? *What a brilliant idea*, he said to himself. Tonino really liked moments like this, when the words, ideas, and events in his brain created something new. It was the type of discovery he enjoyed. *I must talk to my cousin Carlo about this over Thanksgiving vacation*, he thought. The next morning, he presented the idea to his parents, who agreed to the idea, as did Carlo's parents in Puerto Rico.

Planning to Save the Monarchs and a Trip to Mexico

Tonino purchased maps from the airport and sent them to Colorado for Carlo to study before arriving. Giovanni knew Lloyd Kirley at Logan Airport, who arranged for them to rent an ultralight plane. Giovanni talked to Lloyd over the telephone. The only thing that Giovanni thought was out of the ordinary was that Lloyd kept asking him what color plane he wanted. Giovanni finally said, "Green, red, and white: the Italian colors, of course."

Lloyd replied, "That won't be any problem because Prince Spaghetti, one of our local pasta companies, owns the plane and leases it out. In fact, we have a plane with those identical colors."

That's perfect, thought Giovanni. *What a great adventure for two young boys. They will love it!*

Tonino never really knew how he came to be named Anthony. This was the time for Giovanni to tell him. "You know, your mother absolutely loved the name Anthony because of the commercial Prince

Spaghetti put on television; we had to call you Anthony, and now, here you are going to fly in their plane."

The day before Thanksgiving, Tonino and his parents went to Logan Airport to meet Carlo coming in from Colorado and Angelo and Daniela flying up from Puerto Rico. The weather was perfect and everyone arrived on time. Dinner that night was like being in a busy beehive. Everyone was talking at the same time, and it sounded just like a bunch of excited worker bees buzzing over a newly discovered source of nectar.

Somehow, everything, even the food for this great celebration, was overshadowed by conversation about the boys leaving for Nantucket the next day. Everyone went to the airport to see them off. Even Joe and Isabella went. The weather was clear, the winds just right, and Carlo felt confident all would go well. Both boys looked great in the two-seater ultralight. Giovanni was the first to notice the inscription on the side of the plane; he shouted out loud, "Go, *Farfalla*, go! Let's thank Prince Spaghetti for sponsoring this plane."

Carlo was in the cockpit, with Tonino behind him. Both had their pilot's caps on, which included goggles. Goggles were only needed when they were in their human form because insect eyes have a hard cuticle over them, they also lack eyelids, and they cannot close their eyes. They needed the goggles, however, in case they had to rapidly transform. Excitement only increased as they headed down the runway and took off. Carlo knew enough about navigation and safety that he made sure the small craft had everything, even a radio. It was a great takeoff. As they cleared the runway, both boys looked down over the side to see the water of the Atlantic below them. About forty minutes later, they were landing at Nantucket Memorial Airport.

Arriving in Nantucket

As Tonino and Carlo came in for the landing, they could see Howie and Ginni waving. They taxied and got out of the plane. Howie was very excited and said, "The population of monarchs on the island had peaked, and all we need to do is wait for those arriving from the north. I hear from the website on monarchs and their migration that they will arrive here in two days."

After preparing the ultralight and securing it, they went to Howie and Ginni's house for something to eat and to catch up on what had been happening in everyone's life. After dinner, and before retiring for the evening, Howie gave Tonino a present. It was a book wrapped in hand-painted paper that Howie had made. The paper showed the life cycle of the monarch. The yellow, black, and white colors gave the caterpillar a striped look. The prolegs had a white marking making each false-leg appear as if the caterpillar was wearing spats. The gold on the chrysalis, and the orange, black, and white markings of the adult were accurate to the small scales on the butterfly's wings. Tonino was surprised. Unlike when he opened his parents' present, he carefully dissected the package, making sure not to destroy Howie's artwork. When he finished, he removed the book, whose title was *Butterflies Through Binoculars: A Field Guide to Butterflies in the Boston-New York-Washington Region* by J. Glassberg. Tonino opened the book, and on the inside of the front cover, Ginni and Howie had written something.

To Tonino, our budding naturalist. Remember! Computers are tools and can help you find information, but you must observe nature first hand to appreciate the place all life forms have in nature.

Best wishes, Ginni and Howie, *2000.*

For Tonino, this saying was very similar to the one his parents had written in the butterfly book they gave him. *Maybe there is something to this if two sets of adults independently reached the same conclusion,* he thought to himself. *I will have to think more about this.*

After dinner, they all drove out to see the aggregation of monarchs. Carlo had never seen it before; it is one of the most spectacular natural events. The leaves on the trees were orange and yellow, with just a little green at this time of the fall. Some trees had completely lost their leaves because of the winds on the island. As they drove up, everyone could see the beautiful shimmering of the orange and black markings of the wings, not just hundreds, but thousands of butterflies draped on the trees.

Howie went on to say, "On windy days, large numbers can be found hunkered down in kettle holes in the moors, mobbing various species of goldenrod for nectar, along with painted ladies, American coppers, crescent spots, Leonard's skippers, various hairstreaks, and other native butterflies."

Everyone sat there passing around the binoculars, looking at the butterflies for about an hour and continuously referring to Tonino's new book to identify them.

The Northern Monarchs Arrive

The sun had started to set. Just then, Howie noticed something in the distance. He was like a young kid, jumping up and down and shouting, "They're here! They have arrived earlier than predicted."

It was difficult to determine the size of the cloud of butterflies that was about to land. The sky was almost completely darkened. All of a sudden, as if someone told them to, they all landed at once. What a spectacular event.

"Now they will feed for about two days," Howie told the boys. "They must refuel after their long flight over the ocean. They have a storage sac in their digestive tract that is used, like a gas tank, to store nectar for later use. They get most of their nectar from the various goldenrods."

"What species of milkweed does the larva feed on here in Nantucket?" Tonino asked.

Being the naturalist he is, Howie rattled off the scientific names: *"Asclepias syriaca, A. incarnata, A. amplexicaulis, A. tuberosa,* and *A. purpurascens.* The last one is rare. I will show you some tomorrow."

The next day, everyone returned to make sure the butterflies hadn't taken off. Sure enough, Howie was right. All the monarchs were busy feeding on the goldenrods and the purple blazing stars, which Howie said "brightens the sandplain grasslands on the south shore." Howie then took time to show them several species of milkweed inhabiting the island. Following this, they went to the Atlantic Café on South Water Street for lunch. After everyone ordered, Tonino asked the waitress about the fish on the menu.

"What is scrod?" he asked.

"In some places, it is the young of a haddock or pollack, but here in Nantucket, it is the young of a cod," the waitress replied.

Tonino ordered the scrod.

Howie picked up on the cod focus. "You know, the Atlantic cod is considered a species at risk or endangered. At one time cod were so abundant that Bartholomew Gosnold, an English explorer, visited the Cape around 1602 and gave Cape Cod its name. If you like to read, I recommend Henry Thoreau's book, *Cape Cod*."

Carlo raised his hand and asked, "Where did Nantucket get its name?"

Howie responded, "Let me think about it."

During lunch, their conversation focused on two things: insects in trouble on the islands and the flight route the boys would take with the monarchs.

Howie told them that three insects on the island were in danger of extinction: the chain spotted geometer moth, which lives in the Miacomet sandplain grasslands and is a pest of blueberries; the rare regal fritillary; and the American burying beetle. He then said, "The Roger Williams Zoo in Rhode Island is involved in a captive breeding and release program of the American burying beetle. They have already raised sufficient adults and released a new colony, which has been successfully established on Nantucket."

Other than being chased by predators or stepped on by humans, Tonino never thought about insects being in trouble. These monarchs could be in trouble if they didn't make it to the mainland, where they would follow the coastline to Florida. Because of its significance, it was crucial for the boys to know their route. They had to make sure everything was ready for an early takeoff the next morning. They were to fly to the mainland, just below Boston, and follow the coast to Florida. From there they would refuel, adjust flight plans, and make the rest of the trip to Mexico. That afternoon, however, Howie wanted the boys to learn something about the history of Nantucket and the occupations of its early inhabitants.

Tonino said to Howie, "You said you would tell us the origin of the name *Nantucket*, and you haven't done that."

"Well, I thought about it a lot and I am embarrassed to say, I really don't know."

Nantucket Sleigh Ride

As they drove down India Street, Tonino noticed a sign above a store that said "Nantucket Sleigh Ride." It had a picture of a boat with two men being pulled by a white whale.

"What's that sign all about?" Tonino asked Howie.

"Well, that's a very good question because it pertains to something we will talk about today. That shop sells Christmas ornaments and decorations. What the owners did was to take ideas from different places and put them together for their store logo. The white whale represents Moby-Dick, while the so-called 'sleigh ride' represents the whaling industry here in Nantucket. Originally, whalers would go out in whaling ships and harpoon a whale. Once the whale was harpooned, the harpooner and one other man would stay in a small boat that was literally pulled around like a sleigh. Once the whale died, this boat would remain with the whale until the larger ship found them. Thus, this boat ride of whalers following a harpooned whale became known as the Nantucket Sleigh Ride."

How interesting, Tonino thought to himself. Tonino could not, however, put his tarsus on why whales had cropped up twice now in his life.

Refining Flight Plans

That evening, Howie and the boys refined their flight plan. The plan was to go to Memorial Airport early in the morning and wait until they saw the huge cloud of monarchs in the sky heading toward the airport. Howie knew they would fly directly over the airport. He had been keeping records of their arrival and departure for fifteen years.

At about nine thirty in the morning, the huge cloud of monarchs was seen heading toward them. Just as the leading edge of the "monarch cloud" reached the boys, the small ultralight took off. What a sight!

Howie shouted excitedly, "Look Ginni! Look at that beautiful green, red, and white ultralight amongst all that bright orange and black."

As the huge cloud of butterflies passed overhead, Howie and Ginni were unable to see a very special event. The normal-sized ultralight they saw take off suddenly changed into a tiny ultralight, just large enough to hold a cricket and a grasshopper. This was the only way Tonino could feel assured that none of the monarchs would get injured or killed by the larger ultralight.

Originally, Tonino and Carlo had planned to make the entire trip to Mexico with the monarchs. Carlo knew, however, you always have to be ready to adjust your flight plans when flying long distances. Bad weather, low fuel, problems with the plane, and other unexpected events could change your original plans.

Carlo kept in touch with all the airports along their coastal route. The word had gotten out that two young boys were leading the monarch migration, which now included an estimated 250,000 butterflies. Radio announcers, television newscasters, and newspaper reporters were picking up this special event.

One announcer contacted them in flight and said, "What is the name of your plane?"

Carlo turned to Tonino and said, "What is the name for 'butterfly' in Italian?"

"*Farfalla*," Tonino replied.

Carlo then responded to the announcer on his radio and said, "Our plane, which has the Italian colors, is called *Farfalla*. That means 'butterfly' in Italian."

The amazing thing was nobody was able to see anything flying with the monarchs. The ultralight, including Tonino and Carlo, was actually no bigger than two monarchs. Thus, they didn't show up as anything special amongst all the butterflies.

By the evening of the second day, Tonino and Carlo could see the monarchs were getting tired and knew that the one-mile-long flock of butterflies would have to land in Georgia. The landing went well. Before the airport came into sight, the plane and boys changed back into human size and normal ultralight size. Many people came out to see the monarchs, but other curious folks wanted to see these two adventurous boys flying with the monarch migration in a green, red, and white ultralight plane called *Farfalla*.

The next day, after the butterflies fed on flower nectar, they were ready to take off again. The monarchs and the ultralight both had a chance to refuel and were ready to make the next big flight to Florida.

A Major Plane Crash

Tonino and Carlo knew when they were approaching Florida. They could see the Everglades with all its shimmering waterways in the distance. Their landmark, however, was Cape Canaveral, NASA's Kennedy Space Center. As the "cloud" approached the ground, the plane, including its occupants, morphed back to people and normal ultralight size again. In order to avoid killing any monarchs, the ultralight had to go ahead of the huge flock by about a hundred yards. Everything was going fine. Even though Carlo had radio contact with the air traffic control tower, it was impossible for them to warn the boys of the oncoming squadron of brown pelicans. They had just taken off and were picked up by the radar, which showed them heading directly toward the ultralight and cloud of monarchs. The next thing the boys remembered was a big crashing sound; all they saw was a lot of flying feathers.

When they woke up, they were in the hospital. They were not seriously hurt, only a broken arm for Carlo and a broken left leg for Tonino. They looked at one another and simultaneously said, "Well, it could have been worse!" Tonino's first concern, however, was not with himself or Carlo, but was for the safety of the monarchs.

Lying on the table was the *Miami Herald*. On the front page was a picture of the damaged ultralight, two bodies lying beside the fragmented flying machine, and millions of monarchs covering everything, even the boys. The article was "Two survive pelican crash after safely bringing in one of America's most valued treasures: several hundred thousand monarchs! Not one monarch injured." Of course, both sets of parents were very concerned once they were contacted by the hospital. They were worried but were told that in two days the boys would be flown to Boston aboard a U.S. Air Force jet.

Dr. Brower Visits the Boys in the Hospital

That evening, while Tonino and Carlo were eating their dinners in bed, someone they did not recognize appeared at their door.

"May I come in?" the person said. "I am Dr. Lincoln Brower, from the University of Florida in Gainesville. I have been following your flight with the monarchs. I planned to meet you both in Mexico. When I heard you crashed, I decided to return to Florida and personally thank you both for being concerned about the well-being of the monarchs. I have been very active in Mexico trying to preserve their overwintering habitat or *refugia*. I also know that the life of every monarch is extremely important."

Dr. Brower stayed for about twenty minutes, discussing the boys' trip and answering some questions about monarchs. As he got up to leave, he turned and said, "I know neither of you is thinking about flying for a while, but I hope to see you both in Mexico in the near future. In fact, you can stay with my research group at the overwintering site. I would be glad to have you join us."

As he closed the door, both boys just looked at one another; neither said anything. The two days of notoriety went fast. Before they knew it, they were ready to go home.

Flying Home in Style

Boarding the air force jet for the flight to Logan Airport was exciting. Neither of them had been on a military plane, even though Carlo was at the Air Force Academy. Once on board, they taxied onto the runway, where they had to wait for clearance from the flight tower. They were told they would have to wait about twenty minutes for a huge "cloud" of unknown objects to fly over. Probably only Tonino and Carlo knew what the cloud was. Looking out the side window, Tonino and Carlo could barely recognize the elliptical cloud of monarchs because they were too far away to see individual butterflies. Just then, the cloud broke up into several different patterns. It was just like a synchronous air team.

"Look," Carlo said to Tonino. "They're spelling something."

As both boys pressed their faces to the window, the sun lit the letters being spelled. There in shiny orange letters were the words, "Thank you!"

Here were two youngsters, in reality one cricket and one grasshopper, being flown back to Boston on a military plane. The flight was difficult for Tonino because it was the first time he had a plaster cast of any kind, and he hoped it would be the last time he used crutches. The Florida TV and news media were there to see the boys off. Maria, Daniela, Angelo, and Giovanni were at Joe and Isabella's house to see their youngsters on *The Today Show* with Matt Lauer. It was a reassuring sight for all of them to see that the boys were really okay. Both boys slept the entire trip. The pilot announcing their descent into Logan awakened them. As they descended, they could see a crowd of people waiting outside where they were to exit the plane. As they taxied to their arrival area, Tonino could see his parents and friends.

Departing the jet, Tonino could see a young woman pushing a wheelchair. *I hope that's not for me*, he said to himself, but it was. As he left the plane, he was told to get into the wheelchair. It was a short distance to the crowd and not a problem for him to hold onto his crutches. Tonino couldn't help but think how surprised he had been to see his father in a wheelchair when he returned from Italy. Now the situation was reversed. The boys had lots of pictures taken, they talked to reporters, but they were anxious to get home. Everyone kept trying to draw on their casts. Both boys kept saying, "We'll have lots of time for that later."

That evening, both Tonino and Carlo told everyone how Dr. Brower came to see them in the hospital and invited them to join his research crew in Mexico during Christmas vacation. They knew this was not exactly true. Dr. Brower had said, "I hope to see you both in the near future." Because they were so excited to be home, they had completely forgotten about their accident. Like most youngsters, all they could think about was their next adventure. They never even inquired about the fate of the brown pelicans. Something in Tonino's head kept reminding him, *Don't forget your friends; don't forget your friends.*

Planning a Christmas Vacation Trip to Mexico

School after the Thanksgiving vacation was less eventful but provided Tonino with more time to think because he could not work at Joe's until his cast was removed. During the rest of the school semester, Tonino kept in touch with Dr. Brower on e-mail and planned to join his research group during the Christmas vacation.

This time, however, they planned to take a commercial airplane to Mexico. Dr. Brower told Tonino it would be okay if he brought two friends with them.

Pedro would be an asset because he spoke Spanish. Ming Ming could also help because he was interested in engineering. Thus, his technology skills would be useful in fixing things. Everything centered on the trip to Mexico to see the monarchs. It was wonderful for all the parents and teachers to see how involved youngsters could be about learning things they were interested in.

Chapter 6.
Conservation Biology: Mexico

Going to the Library

Tonino was interested in both butterflies and computers. Normally, his activities fluctuated between studying about his favorite butterfly, the monarch, and sitting at his computer. Now, however, he had two new areas of interests: biodiversity and conservation biology. One day, while on the Internet, he entered the keyword *cricket* and found several books that he had not seen before. One of them was *A Cricket in Times Square*, by George Selden. The next day he went to the library to see if they had the book.

The Boston Public Library was founded in 1848 and was the first library to allow people to take out books and written materials. Every time Tonino went to the main branch of the library, however, he felt like he was going on a safari in Africa. It was impossible to keep his eyes on both of the lions guarding the entrance, but he tried. In fact, he would always increase his pace when walking between them. It wouldn't be until he was a mature cricket and realized that young people often exaggerate the things in their world that he would feel comfortable walking past these large stone lions. This exaggeration not only took the form of large statues of lions, it also applied to personal things, such as how much your friends hurt you.

At the library, Tonino sat down in front of the computer. It seemed like the computer was taking a more important role in his life. Just like the automobile, telephone, and television did in his parents' lives. The screen menu allowed him to select a book's author, title, or subject. He typed in *Subject*. He then entered *Cricket*. He pushed Enter and the following came up on the screen:

HSPLS CATALOG is the database you are currently searching.
Your search: S=CRICKET
LINE # of
titles ------------------Subjects------------------------------------
1 5 Cricket
2 1 Cricket -- Australia.
3 2 Cricket -- History.
4 1 Cricket -- Rules.
5 1 Cricket -- Terminology.
6 1 Cricket -- West Indies.
7 5 Crickets.
8 17 Crickets -- Fiction.
9 1 Crickets -- Folklore.
10 1 Crickets -- Hawai'i -- Vocalization
(More)

----AVAILABLE COMMANDS--------------------------------------
　　1,2,3,...(line #) for more information N=Next screen; ST=to start over; P=Previous screen; EXIT to exit

He decided to look at #1, so he typed in a 1 and pushed Enter. Up came the following on the screen:

Your search: S=CRICKET
LINE
------Author---------- ----------------Title---------------------- Date
1 BRADSHAW, IAN ABC OF CRICKET THE HISTORY, THE LAWS, 1985
2 COWDREY, COLIN TACKLE CRICKET THIS WAY, 1964
3 EASTAWAY, ROBERT CRICKET EXPLAINED/ROBERT EASTAWAY; ILLUS, 1933
4 GREIG, TONY CRICKET THE MEN AND THE GAME. 2ND ED. 1977
5 PARKER, ERIC THE HISTORY OF CRICKET, 1950

```
----AVAILABLE COMMANDS-------------------------------------
1,2,3,...(line #) for more information N=Next screen ; ST=to start over;
P=Previous screen; EXIT to exit
```

He decided this wasn't what he wanted, so he returned to the previous menu and typed 8. Up came seventeen references. The only ones he was interested in were as follows:

```
LINE
# -------Author-------------------------Title---------------------- Date
10 Selden, George Chester Cricket's New Home. 1983
11 Selden, George Chester Cricket's Pigeon Ride. 1981
12 Selden, George The Cricket in Times Square. 1960
13 Selden, George Tucker's Countryside. 1969
```

He then examined line items 10 through 13 and pushed "PRINT" on the menu so he would have a hard copy. He also went back to the previous screens and printed everything out. He remembered his father saying, "You must pay attention to detail and keep good written records of everything." *The computer certainly has made this easy,* he said to himself.

He got up, took his printout, and used the call numbers for *The Cricket in Times Square* to find the book. The computer had shown that it was available. He easily found the book and proceeded to the checkout desk, where he gave the librarian his identification card. She scanned his card, cancelled the magnetic security along the book's binding, and handed the book to Tonino. As he left, he had to go through the security check. Since his book was already checked out, he had no problems in exiting.

Regardless of how much homework he had, Tonino kept thinking about Dr. Brower's invitation to visit him at the monarch *refugia* in Mexico. Tonino liked to daydream, and currently it took him to Mexico.

Visiting the Monarch *Refugia* in Mexico

The fall term of the school year went exceedingly slow following the Thanksgiving vacation. The one thing that kept Tonino interested, however, was planning for the Christmas vacation break in Mexico. He was very excited about visiting the monarch refuge and seeing Dr. Brower again. Tonino, Ming Ming, and Pedro would get together at the library once a week and talk about what they were going to do once they got there. As he had done previously, Tonino asked Dr. Stoffolano if he had any contacts in Mexico. He sent back an e-mail saying, "Fly into Mexico's Carretero Airport from Phoenix and take a van to *San Miguel de Allende*. This is a very nice town that has become inhabited by people from the United States and Canada. Here is the e-mail address for Greg Johnson and Murray Friedman, the owners of several wonderful private *casas* within *Las Terrazas San Miguel*: contact@TerrazasSanMiguel.com. Once there, Greg and Murray will assist you in contacting Arturo Morales Tirado, who will be your tour guide to the monarch refuge."

As soon as he could, Tonino went to the travel agency near his home and made reservations for everyone. They would fly directly from Boston's Logan Airport to Phoenix and then on to Carretero Airport. Tonino also went online to the website for Las Terrazas. He was very surprised to see the names of the four units available: *Casa Grillo* (cricket), *Casa Mariposa* (butterfly), *Casita Colíbri* (hummingbird), and *Casa Aquila* (eagle). It was hard deciding where to stay, but Tonino selected Mariposa in honor of the monarch. This, however, was not the main reason for making his selection. He really didn't want Ming Ming and Pedro to think that all he could think about were crickets.

It was difficult traveling in December because of the cold weather in Boston versus the warm weather in Mexico.

"What do we wear?" Ming Ming and Pedro asked Tonino.

"We will dress real warm for going to the airport with my parents, but we will have summer clothes once we are in Mexico. However, we will need sweaters because we will be high in the mountains, where it can get cold."

On December 22, the boys left Logan Airport. It was a long trip, and finally they landed in Carretero. The van was there just as Dr. Stoffolano had said. The trip to San Miguel was about an hour. Driving up the steep, cobblestone hill, they were finally dropped off in front of *Las Terrazas*. They rang the bell and were greeted by Murray, who took them to *Casa Mariposa*. Without eating, they went directly to bed. The next morning, they were awakened by small donkeys going past the *casa* carrying firewood for people in the city. Following breakfast, they went on the Internet to find out more about the monarch refuge (www.tasma.info). Murray telephoned Arturo, who would be their naturalist and guide for the day. They made reservations for three and then went into the center of town for the rest of the day. They loved walking around this wonderful city of about 70,000 people. They spent a lot of time in *El Jardin*, which is the city's main plaza. Knowing they had to get up early, the boys decided to retire early.

A knock at their door at 6:00 a.m. reminded them that they must get ready because the van would be there at 7:00 a.m. sharp. They brushed their teeth, packed a few things for the trip, and ate a quick breakfast, which took fifty-five minutes. Greg escorted them out the door as the van was just pulling in. Arturo exited the van and shook everyone's hand. He was short in stature with a rugged build. He helped everyone get into the van, and soon they were off to see the monarchs. Arturo told them the trip to the monarch site would take about two hours.

As soon as they reached the outskirts of San Miguel, Arturo began his guided tour. They soon crossed the mountain range of the *Sierra de Agustinos*. The ride was exceptional, and before they realized it, they started climbing until they reached *Sierra Chincua*, which is at 3,000 meters (9,000 feet). It was spectacular! The forest was made up mostly of evergreen trees. Arturo made it a point to tell everyone that these trees created a microclimate for the overwintering monarchs, and if they were removed for timber or firewood, the monarchs would not be able to survive the cold winters at the site (e.g., temperatures fell below zero and sometimes even snow blanketed the area and the monarchs).

Young boys and girls surrounded Arturo as soon as he exited the van. They were the children of the people working at this wonderful ecotourism site. Tonino had read about ecotourism and liked the idea; however, he realized that it also had its problems when it came to the environment and the living organisms of that area. The children were eagerly waiting for Arturo to hand out the fresh doughnuts he purchased in San Miguel.

Everyone got out of the van and headed toward a small tourist area composed of wooden buildings with tin roofs. There were gift shops selling crafts from the region and trinkets related to the monarch. A few buildings also served food of the region.

"After our trip, we will have a sit-down meal," announced Arturo. "The next part of the trip we will ride on horses. It is the best way to get to the site."

This was a great experience for the boys because none of them had ever been on a horse. Tonino, Pedro, and Ming Ming started to joke around once they were mounted up. They made believe they were cowboys of the Wild West, but soon the guides grabbed the reins and they were off up the mountain.

The path leading to where the monarchs were resting was very dusty, and the boys had to cover their faces with a handkerchief, just like real cowboys.

"Look," Tonino shouted to his friends. "There are two monarchs over to the right!"

Sure enough, they began to see one or two monarchs flying in the beautiful, clear blue sky as they followed the path toward their destination. Finally, Arturo stopped, and everyone got off their horses.

Arturo again assumed his tour guide responsibility. "Before we go into the site, let me tell you a few things about the monarchs. These monarchs come from the Great Lakes region and the northeastern part of North America. They begin leaving those areas around the end of September and usually show up over San Miguel between November 8 and 12. In this area they usually fly between ten and fifty meters over the surface of the ground.

"At the site, both males and females are present. Toward the end of winter, around March, the males mate with the females, and within three days, all the males die, leaving only the females to make the trip back north. By the end of March, females lay eggs and die. These caterpillars eat milkweed leaves and molt several times; the females leave Mexico and return to the central plains of the United States. Here they find milkweed, and the cycle repeats itself. Once the adults emerge from their chrysalides, they feed on flowers, mate, and fly further north. This happens several times until some actually reach the northern United States and Canada. Here the cycle starts over again with several generations until the fall, when the emerging adults enter a diapause and prepare for the trip back to Mexico. Are there any questions?"

Ming Ming raised his hand. "How do they know where they are going?"

"That's a good question," Tonino said, but he dropped it at that. Ming Ming looked on in bewilderment but didn't push the issue.

Tonino and his friends looked at one another in amazement when Arturo told the tour group, "There is a record of one monarch that was tagged in Campbell, Minnesota, and it flew 1,844 miles to a site in El Rosario, Mexico."

"Wow!" said Pedro. "Can you believe these small butterflies can fly that long distance?"

"I know," Tonino responded.

"Well, if there are no more questions, let's go into the site."

Everyone at the site, even including Arturo, who had seen this phenomenon over and over, was totally amazed at the extraordinary number of butterflies. He noted, "It is estimated that in total there are around a hundred million monarchs here. Be careful when you are walking because many of them fly to the ground to drink. It is easy to step on one if you are not careful. Take time to walk around and look at the monarchs flying in the sky and those resting on trees."

Tonino was anxious to show Pedro and Ming Ming how much he knew and pointed to two monarchs resting on a branch; he said, "Can you tell me which one is the male?"

Ming Ming and Pedro looked at them and turned to Tonino. "It's almost impossible," Ming Ming said.

"I can't see any difference," Pedro added.

Tonino responded, "It is true that it is difficult for you to tell the difference because most people, like you, do not take the time to carefully examine the minute details of life forms. More importantly, however, is that most people spend little time in the wild."

"Well, what about you? You are always at the computer."

Tonino was silent and thought about what Joe and his wife wrote on the book they gave him about milkweed butterflies: "To our technology boy from the North End. Remember! Before there were computers, there were butterflies." He looked at his friends and said, "Maybe I do, but I shouldn't."

"Come on, Tonino. Tell us how to tell the difference."

"The males have a scent pouch on the hind wings, while the female lacks it. Can you see it?"

The boys moved real close. They were able to do this because the monarchs were in diapause, and when it is cold, they do not fly very much. All of a sudden one of the males left the tree and kept flying around Tonino's face. In fact, its wings often brushed up against Tonino's face. Tonino kept trying to gently brush the male away with his hands, but the butterfly persisted.

"He is trying to kiss you," Pedro said.

"Yes," Tonino responded. "Let's call him Bacio."

Both boys were very excited. Tonino realized that if one has never been real close to an animal in nature, the experience is exhilarating. In fact, Tonino told the boys that they should read the book, *The Last Child in the Woods: Saving our Children from Nature-deficit Disorder*, by Richard Louv.

While the three boys carefully examined the male and female monarchs, someone quietly walked up behind Tonino and tapped him on his left shoulder. As Tonino turned, a voice said, "Hi, Tonino! Do you remember me?"

Seeing who it was, Tonino said, "Of course, Dr. Brower! How could I forget? You were so kind to visit me in Florida after the accident."

"How's your tour going?"

"Great," all three boys resounded in unison. "'Arturo is a great guide. He loves nature and believes more people should get out and view it. He says, 'How can anyone appreciate a delicious burrito by just looking at a picture of one? You must eat it and smell it. At the same time, you must see living things in what naturalists call their habitat.'"

"Do you have any questions?"

Ming Ming responded, "Yes. How do the monarchs know where they are going?"

"I will try to encapsulate what we know. Just think about a desert ant that has to leave the nest in search of food and safely return to that same nest. There are no trees, no landmarks, and the sands are always shifting so it can't put down a chemical trail to follow. What's left in the environment it could use as a cue?"

Brower paused and the boys put on their thinking caps.

Pedro was the first to answer. He suggested, "What about something in the sky?"

"That's close. Remember, it's not night so they can't use the stars. Desert ants use the polarized pattern caused by the ultraviolet, or UV, light from the sun. This pattern changes as the sun's position changes depending on where you are on the earth's surface. Thus, desert ants use this for their navigation; so do honeybees. Two theories have been proposed for monarch migration. Chip Taylor at the University of Kansas says they use the earth's magnetic fields as cues, and a group in Boston proposes they use the sun's UV polarized light patterns. There are doubts about Taylor's experiments, and scientists tend to support the latter mechanism."

"You mean that scientists don't always agree?" asked Ming Ming.

"That's for sure. Often they get involved in such heated debates, each one taking a different view. What usually happens is that the answer is somewhere between the two groups. Whether that will be the case here, I am not sure."

Tonino asked Dr. Brower, "What is your latest research on?"

"Well, at first we thought that there was only one overwintering site or *refugia*, but now we believe there may be twelve or more pockets scattered throughout the forested mountains (usually above 9,000 feet) in Mexico. To better understand the population size, how many sites there are, and where they are located, we are using Global Positioning Satellites. We need to know that information if we are going to preserve these important habitats."

"That's great," Ming Ming responded.

Tonino chimed in, "Technology and engineering have come a long way to help biologists."

Brower agreed and said, "I must be going, and you had better get back to Arturo." Brower turned and headed into the huge bowl containing the majority of the overwintering population, while the boys returned to the tour group.

"We now have to leave this area and return for a short dinner. Let's get on our horses."

The ride back seemed much shorter than Tonino imagined. It was difficult for Tonino to erase the image he had of so many butterflies hanging on the trees. Tonino thought to himself, *How can I ever look at a regular Christmas tree and not compare it to what I have just seen? These trees are so much more beautiful and are naturally decorated.*

At the ecotourist campsite, everyone entered one of the sheds that were crudely constructed of wood with tin roofs. Picnic tables were arranged to accommodate the entire tour group. Women whose husbands worked as guides were preparing a wonderful dinner. The noisy dinner conversation prevented Tonino from reflecting on his visit.

"We must load up and get back to San Miguel," Arturo told the group after they finished eating.

They stopped on the way back to see a church and to watch how pottery was made. The descent from the mountain seemed rather abrupt. The moon was full, and Arturo told everyone to look at the moon. "What do you see?" The boys giggled because they thought of the moon as being made of cheese. "Look carefully. Can you see the rabbit?"

"Yes, now we can," everyone in the van responded.

Arturo told them about the Mayan myth of the rabbit on the moon. Soon after this story, and because of the high altitude, everyone riding in the van took a short nap.

Arturo's van returned to San Miguel; the sleeping tourists awoke because of the noise of the tires on the cobblestones. Tonino and his friends were the first to be dropped off. "I hope you had a great time," Arturo said as he helped them out of the van.

"We did."

When Murray let them in, he asked, "What do you think?"

Only Tonino responded, "It was the chance of a lifetime. The image of all those butterflies will be imprinted in my memory forever. It is truly one of nature's, and the world's, most spectacular events."

Tonino and His Friends Return Home

They ate dinner, took a short walk to the central plaza, and had a sound sleep. After saying good-bye to Greg and Murray, they took the hour ride to Carretero, boarded the various planes, and finally landed in Logan. It happened so fast that Tonino had little time to collect his thoughts. He was pleased, however, that he had been able to see the monarchs in Mexico. His parents met them at the airport and hurried the three tired boys home to their own beds.

Tonino gave his parents a detailed account of his trip, including meeting with Dr. Brower. His parents were pleased with the monarch gifts Tonino had purchased for them.

"Buying these small gifts gives the Mexican people money and supports their lifestyle, which in turn makes them less dependent on logging. Thus, ecotourism works," Tonino told his parents.

Vacation ended and the boys found themselves thrust into all those things young people seem to dislike. Each one of them had recounted their trip to see the monarch *refugia* several times. They hoped that telling their friends about their trip would bring more focus to the plight of the monarch and help Dr. Brower save their fragile habitat.

Chapter 7.
Tonino in New York City and the American Museum of Natural History

Tonino Thinks about College

Tonino was now eighteen years old; it was his senior year in high school, and he had to study extra hard. He wanted to do well on his SATs so he could get into a good college. Tonino had become even more interested in insects, biodiversity, and conservation biology. He decided to apply to the University of Massachusetts in Amherst, where he wanted to major in entomology. This choice made sense to him. He reasoned that if three fourths of all known animals are insects, and one wanted to investigate animal biodiversity, knowing the insects present in a given habitat was essential. Tonino thought back and remembered what Dr. Wilson had written in the book his parents had given him for his seventeenth birthday: "I wish you well in becoming an entomologist." *How did Wilson know I would want to become an entomologist?* he wondered. *I didn't even know myself what I wanted to do at that time.*

After meeting Professor Stoffolano in Amherst on his way to Tanglewood, Tonino had kept in contact with him. He had selected UMass for several reasons: it had an excellent entomology department, he could easily get home to visit his parents, and Pedro was also planning to go there to play basketball. It was also a university his parents could afford. He remembered Joe saying, "Tonino, you can get a good college education wherever you go. It is up to you. The professors and the library are there to help you, but if you don't do the work, you will come away with nothing."

Etymology

Tonino found that his computer was more useful and essential. He loved accessing the Internet. He was interested not only in his own personal roots, but the whole family of crickets known as Gryllidae; he would sit for hours at his computer interacting with different people around the world. One person's name that kept coming up on the screen in conjunction with crickets was Dr. Dan Otte.

Tonino liked to share with Joe some of the new information he found on the Internet. He read that crickets, grasshoppers, and katydids were related and belonged to the insect order Orthoptera, whose members had legs modified for jumping (this order was previously called Saltatoria). Tonino explained the derivation of these two words to Joe. "*Orthoptera* can be broken down into the Latin prefix *orthos*, which means 'straight,' and the suffix *pteron*, which means 'wing.' You know, the doctor that children go to in order to get their teeth straightened is called an orthodontist."

Joe, who had never finished high school, was always interested in what Tonino said. He had to leave to get a job and to contribute to supporting his family. This was very common for new immigrants. In order to survive, all members of the family had to work and pool their incomes to make it in their new country.

"So Joe," Tonino said, "*Saltatoria* comes from the Latin and means 'to jump,' while the Italian verb *saltare* also means 'to jump.'"

These conversations greatly enriched Joe's life. He would never have these conversations with an adult because he didn't want to admit his lack of formal schooling. Joe would say to Tonino, "You know, I went to the college of HK's."

"What's that?" Tonino would always politely reply.

"It's the College of Hard Knocks," he'd say, and they both would laugh.

Let's return to the etymology of the word *Saltatoria*. After explaining all this to Joe, Tonino waited to see if Joe was listening.

"It now makes sense to me," said Joe.

"What makes sense?" responded Tonino.

"One of my favorite customers just gave me a book, *Italy, the Beautiful Cookbook*, by Lorenza De'Medici. There was a recipe for *saltimbocca*. I know what *bocca* means, because my grandfather would always say to the kids when they got noisy, '*Chiuso la bocca.*' If what you told me is correct, *saltimbocca* must mean 'jump into your mouth.'"

"I think that's right, but let me check with my Aunt Anna. You know she is now a librarian."

The next day when Tonino went to work, he told Joe he was correct in his translation of saltimbocca. Tonino went on to say, "The literal translation is 'jump in your mouth,' just as you said, but the meaning is, 'It's so good that it jumps into your mouth.'"

Why Not Visit the Big Apple?

Giovanni and Joe were not the only people interested in Tonino's education. His mother, Maria, was always there if he needed help. Maria had left high school her junior year to work and helped contribute to her family's income, but she went to night school and passed the high school equivalence exam with an outstanding score. She was continually pointing out various articles in the newspaper to Tonino. She pointed out one article that seemed most appropriate. It was about the new insect zoo at the American Museum of Natural History in New York.

"Why don't you go to the Big Apple on the bus," she suggested to Tonino. "You could stay with your cousin Vincenzo and visit the museum. You haven't seen him since your birthday party."

This seemed like a good idea to Tonino, and he could do it on a weekend so he wouldn't miss any school.

Maria knew Tonino enjoyed reading the book *The Cricket in Times Square*, so she also said, "While you are in New York, why not check to see if any relatives of Chester Cricket are still alive? Vincenzo certainly knows how to get to Times Square."

"That's a great idea." He was always amazed at the great ideas his mother came up with.

Planning for His Trip

When Tonino went on any trip, he didn't take it lightly. Instead, he made extensive plans. This was a trademark of Tonino's behavior. *It would be nice to have a contact at the museum*, he said to himself. *This way I could get behind the scenes of the museum and even talk to the entomologists.* The only thing standing in his way, however, was he didn't know anyone there. *Ah-hah, I know, I'll e-mail Dr. Stoffolano. Maybe he knows some of the entomologists there.*

He sat down at the computer and sent Dr. Stoffolano an e-mail, asking, "Do you know any entomologists at the American Museum of Natural History I might talk to when I visit?"

All he had to do now was wait for a reply.

Maria, Giovanni, and Tonino were friends of other animals living in the city. Several weeks earlier, Tonino had a conversation about Vincenzo with David the mouse. David knew mice all over the East Coast. He had told Tonino about his cousin, Emmaline, who lived in the Emily Dickinson house. David told him that he had another cousin, named Bruce, who lived in Times Square. Tonino e-mailed David and asked him, "Do you think I could contact Bruce when I am in New York to see if we can find any relatives of Chester Cricket?"

The reply came back, "I am sure he will help you. I have attached his address. I hope you have a good trip."

Tonino Gets the Names of Three Entomologists

That evening, Dr. Stoffolano replied, giving Tonino the names of three people to contact: Dr. Randall Shuh, Dr. Andrew Brower, and Dr. David Grimaldi. Tonino looked at the names again. Dr. Grimaldi sounded like an Italian name. Tonino realized that he now knew two entomologists with Italian names: Stoffolano and

Grimaldi. Maybe someday his name would also be listed in the Directory of the Entomological Society of America. *First of all,* he thought, *I must change my family name back to Cricchetti.*

Many young people subconsciously take on mentors who are of the same culture and ethnicity. They may think, *If he can do it, I can also do it.* They fail to realize the subtleties of what a mentor really represents. It is not the personal traits of the mentor one wants to emulate, it is usually their profession or lifestyle. In other words, you want to do what they are doing, you don't want to take on their character.

Even though this was slightly what Tonino was doing, it was a little different. It is true that these two entomologists had Italian last names, which he identified with, but Tonino was making an additional comparison. He was being entopomorphic. He was giving humans insect qualities and making the assumption that if these two human entomologists could study insects, why couldn't he? Tonino knew someday he also wanted to change his family name back to Cricchetti. He wondered what his parents would think about it.

Tonino recognized the other name Dr. Stoffolano sent him: Dr. Andrew Brower. He wondered if he was related to Dr. Lincoln Brower, the scientist he met at the hospital in Florida, and then again at the monarch wintering *refugia* in Mexico.

Tonino knew it was poor manners to just drop in on someone without letting them know you were coming, but Dr. Stoffolano had made it easy because he also included their telephone numbers in his e-mail message. Tonino contacted all three and made appointments to see them on the Saturday he and his cousin Vincenzo would visit the museum. Tonino had been to New York before, but he had never visited the museum.

On Friday, Vincenzo met him at the bus station, and they spent that evening catching up on things they had both done since they last saw one another. The next morning, they took the subway to the museum.

Meeting Drs. Shuh, Grimaldi, and Brower

Dr. Shuh had told Tonino to go to the guard at the front desk of the museum, who would then call him. Dr. Shuh, a tall, slender man, came down, greeted them, and took them to his office. Even though Tonino was not that excited about Dr. Shuh's area of research, which was the taxonomy of the Hemiptera or true bugs, he respected his choice of specialization. Unlike most insects, which usually specialize in doing one type of job, Tonino liked the fact that humans have a wider choice of what they could do with their lives. Tonino was impressed that Dr. Shuh had gone to graduate school with Dr. Stoffolano at the University of Connecticut. Tonino told Dr. Shuh that he was interested in monarch butterflies, and Dr. Shuh asked him if he knew Dr. Orley Taylor.

"No, I don't," replied Tonino.

"Well, he was a graduate student at the same time that Dr. Stoffolano and I were at the University of Connecticut. He also started the website, *Monarch Watch*. You should check it out sometime."

"I will," Tonino responded as he entered the website name in his notebook.

Rather than taking the boys over to Dr. Brower's office, Dr. Shuh escorted them to his laboratory. They knocked and entered. It was like a tropical garden, with adult butterflies flying all over the place. They were introduced to Dr. Brower, and Dr. Shuh said good-bye and left.

This was a very interesting laboratory; Dr. Brower was a lot younger than Lincoln Brower, and he was even younger than Dr. Shuh. Dr. Brower told the boys to call him "Andy," but they still addressed him as "Dr. Brower." Andy proceeded to tell them about his research.

"I am trying to study butterfly speciation using molecular techniques involving mitochondrial DNA. This is an extremely important topic because it gets at the heart of how some butterflies may be able to survive while others become extinct."

This was pretty heavy stuff for two eighteen-year-old boys. They did, however, know what DNA was from high school biology.

Tonino was dying to know if this Dr. Brower was any relation to Dr. Lincoln Brower. When Dr. Brower asked them if there were any other questions, Tonino responded with an emphatic "Yes."

"What is it you want to know?"

Tonino politely asked, "Are you any relation to the monarch butterfly man?"

Andy replied, "Yes, he is my father."

Tonino liked this because it made him feel that somehow he was making connections within the field of entomology. He also thought it was nice that a son had chosen the profession of his father. He wondered if his father had ever wanted to do what Rolando had done for a living.

Dr. Brower asked Tonino why he wanted to know if he was related to Lincoln Brower. Tonino explained how he had met Dr. Stoffolano at Amherst while in Antonio's pizzeria, and he told him how Dr. Stoffolano had mentioned that Lincoln Brower was working to preserve the monarch's habitat in Mexico.

Tonino continued, "Your father came to see me and my cousin Carlo in the hospital in Florida following the crash of our ultralight plane."

"I read about that," Andy commented. "Didn't your ultralight plane crash into a squadron of brown pelicans while you were bringing in a large group of monarchs for a landing at Cape Canaveral?"

"Yes," Tonino replied. Tonino let Andy know that he still kept in touch with his father because of his interest in monarchs.

Andy was pleased to see other young people, beside himself, had an interest in insects, biodiversity, and conservation biology. He knew from the newspaper article about the crash that Tonino had grown up in Boston, but was curious how a city boy became so interested in insects.

Tonino told him about the relationship he had with Dr. Wilson and also that his father had always taken him to natural history museums. A lot of naturalists come from inner cities. They get their experience in natural history from museums, nature centers, and sometimes even TV programs like *Nature* or *Nova* or the Discovery Channel. Tonino knew how important museums and nature centers are. Even though he didn't make a lot of money working at Joe's, he always made it a point to donate part of his earnings to the Children's Museum in Boston every year.

After answering many questions, Dr. Brower took the boys to meet with Dr. Grimaldi.

Tonino Gets to Peer into the Past

As they approached Dr. Grimaldi's office, Tonino and Vincenzo noticed a large poster tacked on his door. It was a poster advertising the movie, *Jurassic Park*. They both looked at one another and wondered why Dr. Grimaldi was interested in *Jurassic Park*. Dr. Brower knocked and a voice from inside said, "Come in." As they entered the room, they saw someone sitting at a large table with what looked like yellow, translucent rocks strewn over the top of the table. In front of him was a dissecting microscope with one of the yellow objects on its stage. Dr. Brower introduced the boys and told them, "Dr. Grimaldi is one of the leading authorities on the insects found in amber from the Dominican Republic. He also is a specialist on fruit flies of the genus *Drosophila* and has recently written a book on insect evolution."

Both boys knew what *Drosophila* is, because they studied fruit flies in biology class. But they didn't know what amber was. They also did not know where the Dominican Republic was. However, they did not ask these questions. Of course, they didn't want to appear stupid. Tonino was trying to get over the feeling that if he asked a question he didn't know the answer to, that he would be considered stupid. However, when Dr. Grimaldi asked the boys if they knew how to use a microscope, Tonino, who had used one once in biology class, said, "Yes, I know how."

While Tonino was looking through the microscope, Vincenzo began to browse Dr. Grimaldi's bookshelves, which contained hundreds of books. Vincenzo, who was interested in becoming a lawyer, had little interest in science or entomology. Tonino didn't want Dr. Grimaldi to think he was a novice entomologist, which he was, so he acted like he knew everything. Tonino leaned forward and took a good look at the clear yellow material through the microscope. Most people mistakenly use only one eye when using a binocular, dissecting microscope. Well, Tonino had no trouble using both eyes. His eyes seemed to get bigger and bigger as he looked at this object. Grimaldi commented on how, unlike most teenagers, Tonino was having no trouble keeping both eyes open. "That's unusual," Dr. Grimaldi said.

Trapped inside the clear, yellow material was an insect. Dr. Grimaldi leaned over Tonino's shoulder and said, "You know, you are looking at the oldest member of the true crickets, which is the family Gryllidae. The specimen is *Micromacula gracilis* and is from the Lower Jurassic, which is about 199 million years ago. The specimen was sent to me by Dr. Sam Heads, who is an authority in this area."

Tonino didn't want to appear uninformed, so he replied, "Oh yes, I know." He asked Dr. Grimaldi, "Are there other members of the cricket family that are ancient?"

Before answering the question, however, Dr. Grimaldi felt Tonino needed some other information. He explained, "You know crickets belong to the insect family Gryllidae. In that family are the following subfamilies: Oecanthinae or the tree crickets, Encopterinae or bush crickets, Trigonidiinae or sword-bearing crickets, Mogoplistinae or short-winged crickets, Myrmecophilinae or ant-loving crickets, Nemodiinae or ground crickets, Brachytrupinae or short-tailed crickets, Grillotalpinae or mole crickets, and last of all the Gryllinae or house and field crickets."

Tonino eyes were bulging. He could hardly utter a word and when he did, he said, "That's a lot of different crickets."

"Now that you know that," Dr. Grimaldi went on to say, "I can tell you about one of the oldest known members of the cricket family. In the June 17, 1999, issue of the noted science journal *Nature*, a German research team reported finding a fossil cricket from Denmark; this is the oldest known bush cricket. Its name is

Pseudotettigonia amoena and it provided evidence that about fifty-five million years ago, or during the Tertiary period, male crickets produced sound or chirps the same way modern crickets do."

Meanwhile, Vincenzo was anxiously hopping from one foot to the other, trying to get Dr. Grimaldi's attention. Finally, he rudely interrupted and said very excitedly, "Excuse me! Excuse me!"

"Yes," replied Dr. Grimaldi.

"What is this book about?"

Grimaldi walked over to see what Vincenzo was pointing to; it was Kenneth Smith's 1986 book, *A Manual of Forensic Entomology*.

"It's a new and exciting area of study where entomologists use insects to help solve murder cases."

Vincenzo also didn't want to appear stupid, so he replied with just, "Oh!"

"Is there anything else I can help you boys with?"

"Yes," replied Tonino. "I would like to speak to someone about birds."

Tonino was thinking about the question Pedro had asked him in Puerto Rico, "Do any vertebrates produce sound like crickets do?" Tonino had been thinking about this for a long time and had reached the conclusion that if any vertebrate could produce sound in a manner similar to crickets, it would have to be birds. Of course, they have wings as crickets do, he said to himself.

"I'll take you to see Dr. Joel Cracraft, who is curator in charge of our ornithology section." Dr. Grimaldi took them to meet Dr. Cracraft. "I would like you to meet Tonino and his cousin Vincenzo. Tonino had a question about birds, so I figured you were the person to ask."

"Well! I hope I can. What is your question?"

"Do any vertebrates produce sound in a manner similar to that of crickets?"

Dr. Cracraft responded, "Great question and very timely. Kimberly Bostwick of Cornell University and Richard Prum of Yale University just published an article in the journal *Science* on how manakins produce sound using a similar mechanism used by crickets. To date, this is the only known case of a vertebrate being able to do this."

Visiting the Insect Zoo

As they were leaving, Dr. Grimaldi asked, "Do you have anything else I can help you with?"

Vincenzo said, "If you could just direct us to the Orkin Insect Zoo, that would be very helpful."

Dr. Grimaldi took them into the hallway and pointed the direction to the zoo. Both boys thanked him and shook his hand. They turned and walked toward the zoo. They were so excited and full of questions, they started to talk at the same time.

"You go first," Tonino replied.

"No, you," said Vincenzo.

"Since this is your city, and I am the visitor, you go first," replied Tonino.

Vincenzo, who is usually not so animated, threw his arms into the air and said, "Can you believe they use insects to help solve murder cases?"

Tonino could hardly contain himself until Vincenzo finished. "I can't believe the cricket family is as ancient as scientists report. They were around when the dinosaurs were roaming the earth."

Both boys were beside themselves. This truly had been an exciting visit. They were so excited about the new information they had obtained, they only spent about ten minutes in the zoo.

During those ten minutes, however, they didn't even get to see one insect. Instead, they focused on a young father who was taking his daughter through the zoo; she looked like she was about four years old. What a wonderful thing for a father to do. This reminded Tonino of all the Sundays his father took him to various museums and zoos. Soon, however, they drastically changed their minds about the intentions of this father.

In one large aquarium, labeled "Insect Relatives," was a large, brown, and hairy tarantula. There was a little step stool for the little girl to climb upon to get a better view. As she did this and was in position to get an excellent view of the tarantula, she called to her father, "Dad, come and see this beautiful spider."

She turned around to get a real close look. Her face was pressed against the glass. Slowly her father silently crept up behind her, grabbed her by the waist, and shouted, "It's gonna get you!"

This ruined Tonino's visit to the zoo. He said to Vincenzo, "This is why so many people have fear of arthropods. You know, they even have a name for it."

"What is it?" replied Vincenzo.

"It is called entomophobia or arachnophobia. When I get home, I'll write a letter to Dr. Shuh about this. I believe that before you enter any museum or zoo, they should make you watch a video about how to behave in a museum and show sensitivity toward the animals and plants you are going to see; but they should also make you learn something about people's attitudes toward arthropods and how to present and develop a good image. We could call it a sensitization area."

Vincenzo agreed. He told Tonino, "You know, I have a fear of insects and spiders. That's because my friends put a Madagascan hissing cockroach in my sleeping bag one night when we had a sleepover at our house. I was terrified. I've never liked insects or spiders since."

"That's too bad because they represent over three fourths of all known animals on this planet. Since they are so numerous, one must learn to share the earth with them and enjoy them for whatever their function is in life. You must remember this incident so that when you have children, or are dealing with other people, you don't do the same to them."

"Don't worry, I won't."

Leaving the museum much more informed than when they arrived, but still with a few unanswered questions, they got onto the subway home.

Looking for Chester Cricket's Relatives

At dinner, Vincenzo and Tonino had a lot of things to share with everyone at the table. Around eight o'clock, just a short time after dinner, Vincenzo said, "Come on Tonino, let's go to Times Square."

On the way, Tonino told Vincenzo his friend had a cousin named Bruce who lived in Times Square. "We probably won't find him until after dark," Tonino said. "My friend told me to go to the subway station and look for an abandoned drainpipe. That is where he said we could find Bruce."

It took some looking, but they did find the old drainpipe. They morphed, went to the entrance, and tapped on the pipe. Soon, a brown mouse greeted them and invited them in. "My name is Bruce," the mouse said.

Tonino introduced himself, and Vincenzo did the same. The drainpipe had a hole in it that was covered with a piece of plastic. It was positioned just right so that the streetlight above provided enough light for everyone to see.

"May I interest you in a snack?"

"Sure," they replied.

"All I have is some liverwurst."

"That's fine," Tonino replied. "But I have never eaten liverwurst."

"Well, it's a food that my father always ate, and I have coveted it ever since. Where are you guys from?" Bruce asked.

"I am from Boston and my cousin Vincenzo lives here in the city."

"Well, why are you here? Why did you knock on my drainpipe?"

"I know your cousin David in Boston. I told him we were coming to New York and that I wanted to see if I could find any relatives of Chester Cricket. He said maybe you could help us. He also sends his regards and says he would see you later this year."

"Well, Chester was a good friend of my father, Tucker. Unfortunately, Chester never married and left no offspring."

"That's too bad," replied Tonino.

Bruce responded, "Maybe so. Did you know Chester was really from Connecticut?"

"I wonder if he knew my Aunt Anna and Uncle Marino. They live in Manchester."

"Probably not. Chester was from Canaan, which is farther south." Bruce went on, "I believe it was difficult for Chester to live in the city."

"What do you mean?" asked Vincenzo.

"Well, he had trouble finding the kind of food a field cricket would get in the country, plus there are many cats and rats here. They consider crickets a great delicacy."

"I find those same problems living in Boston. Well, I guess you can't help us," Tonino continued.

"I am sorry, but do come back anytime. You are always welcome," said Bruce as he walked the two out to the end of the pipe.

As they hopped out, they turned around and waved to Bruce. Both said, "Thanks for the snack."

As soon as Bruce went back into the pipe, they morphed and headed back to Vincenzo's apartment. On the way, Tonino said to Vincenzo, "It's amazing how many family names disappear because no offspring are left to carry on the name."

"That's for sure," replied Vincenzo.

They went to bed. In the morning, they had a quick breakfast. Soon it was time to go, and Vincenzo took Tonino to the bus station.

"Come again when you can stay longer," Vincenzo said.

"Thanks for a great visit," Tonino responded as he hopped onto the bus for his trip back to Boston.

During the trip he kept thinking about the cricket he had seen trapped in amber and the movie poster on Dr. Grimaldi's door for *Jurassic Park*. When he got home, he knew he would have to learn something about amber and try to rent the video *Jurassic Park*. He still didn't know why Dr. Grimaldi had the poster on his door, but again, he didn't want to ask a stupid question. *I must get over this feeling of not asking a question, especially when I don't know the answer, just because I don't want to appear stupid. I will get over this*, he kept repeating to himself.

Tonino Returns Home

When he got home late Sunday night, Tonino had a lot to do. He had to finish his homework for the next day and be prepared to tell his history teacher what his term paper was going to be about. He really didn't have any time to talk to his parents about his trip, other than to say, "It was neat."

Before going to sleep, his thoughts kept returning to the 199 million-year-old cricket he saw preserved in amber. *Maybe this would make a good term paper*, he thought to himself. He didn't sleep well and was tired the next morning. For some reason, he continued to think about the cricket in amber.

Tonino Selects a Topic for His Term Paper

On the way to school, Pedro kept bugging him about what topic he had chosen for his term paper. Tonino didn't want to let on that he had just decided. "I'm not sure," he replied. "What are you going to write about?"

"I might do something about Puerto Rico; maybe the plight of the Taínos."

"Sounds good to me," replied Tonino.

Tonino had a study hall just before his history class with Mr. George Waddington. Mr. Waddington was an excellent teacher and coached the tennis team. Even though Tonino didn't go out for the team, he liked tennis. He liked the machine used to collect all the tennis balls after team practice. Tonino's mind wandered. All he could think about was summertime and being with his father. He could still see young children at Our Lady of Mount Carmel's Italian festival jumping up and down amongst thousands of different colored tennis balls. He wasn't really sure why his mind sometimes wandered like this, but he knew that it also happened to Pedro and Ming Ming.

Taking his seat in study hall, Tonino looked out the window and continued to daydream. First, he again saw children jumping up and down amidst millions of tennis balls. He then started to think about the cricket in amber, his interest in searching the Internet looking for cricket topics, and his trip to Italy. He knew he was daydreaming, but he remembered Mr. Grant, principal of the middle school, saying daydreaming was both constructive and creative. "You should always be curious and learn how to use daydreaming to become a regular part of your creative thinking," he would say.

Tonino started to jot down some notes for his term paper. He then turned the rough notes into a nice outline. As the bell rang to go to history class, Tonino felt that he had accomplished something during study hall.

Mr. Waddington went around the class asking everyone what topics they had chosen for their term papers. When he came to Tonino, he hesitated a moment, looked around until he saw his friends, and said, "I would like to do something on the importance of crickets in history."

Pedro and Ming Ming couldn't believe what they were hearing. They just looked at one another and whispered, "What is the connection between Tonino and crickets?"

Many of the students began to laugh. However, Pedro and Ming Ming didn't. You see, no one knew Tonino was really also a cricket, and they also didn't know that crickets have played an important role in many cultures throughout history. This didn't bother Tonino. Now that he had selected his topic, Tonino had a lot of work to do.

Thanking Those Who Helped Him

That night, he wrote thank you notes to his aunt and uncle in New York for letting him stay with them. He also thanked Drs. Shuh, Brower, and Grimaldi. In the note to Dr. Grimaldi, he asked him if he had any information about how old crickets really were compared to some other animals, like dinosaurs. In his thank you note to Dr. Shuh, Tonino mentioned that zoos should have some way to sensitize people visiting the living exhibits. His last sentence went like this: "The father's behavior I just described and his daughter's response is exactly what the movie producers depend upon to keep producing movies like *Arachnophobia*."

Tonino Starts His Term Paper

That week Tonino knew he had to start collecting information for his term paper. He realized the computer would be very helpful. Before going to bed, Tonino went onto the Internet. He typed in the word *Cricket*, and here are some of the things that showed up:

Cricinfo.com: The Home of **Cricket**

Welcome to the home of **cricket** on the Internet. Cricinfo offers users the most comprehensive live coverage of international and domestic **cricket** available ...

www.cricinfo.com/

Cricket-Online: Live scores, stats, news and more!

Includes scores, articles, software, emerging players and information on international **cricket**. WAP access.

www.**cricket**-online.org

BBC SPORT | **Cricket**

Offers news and results for all levels of **cricket** with interviews, video and audio clips. UK.

news.bbc.co.uk/sport1/hi/**cricket**/default.stm

www.baggygreen.com.au

Cricinfo Australia: The home of www.baggygreen.com.au. The very latest news on Australian **cricket**, live scores from around the world and much more.

www.baggygreen.com.au/

Cricket news, fixtures & results, live coverage and features

Cricket news, scorecards, live coverage and features from Cricket365.com.

www.**cricket**365.com/

Cricket Communications

Wireless phone and service provider in the Midwest. Includes coverage areas, pricing plans, where to buy, and employment opportunities.

www.**cricket**communications.com/

Cricket World

Quarterly magazine offers news and features, links to club and school news, postcards, online shopping, games and forum.

www.**cricket**world.com/

Cricket Home

Cricket is MRTG on Steroids. If you need a high customizable tool in a large enterprise, **Cricket** is for you.

cricket.sourceforge.net/

It was a long and difficult week. Not only did he have to start his term paper, but he also had to work after school. Staying up late in the evenings, he started to put together a rough outline of his paper. Some of the references he used came from going to the library and typing "cricket" in the Subject area. He also tried pairing "cricket" with "history" and "culture." Following is a quick look at his rough outline. You will notice that there are blanks within the text. This is information Tonino still has to research.

THE IMPORTANCE OF CRICKETS
IN HISTORY AND CULTURE
by Tonino Cricket

I. Introduction
II. Crickets in history
III. Crickets in culture
   A. Folklore
   B. Mythology and legend
IV. Crickets in literature and movies
   A. Children's literature
   B. Adult literature
   C. Movies

I. INTRODUCTION

Crickets belong to the insect family Gryllidae and the insect order Orthoptera. This order also includes relatives of the cricket, such as the katydids and grasshoppers. True crickets are found worldwide and in a variety of habitats. They are only found associated with land. There are no aquatic crickets. Crickets are found in deserts, high mountains, and fields; in caves; on trees; and even in houses (e.g., the house cricket or *Acheta domestica*). Currently, there are about ___ species of crickets known worldwide. Just in the United States alone, there are _____ recorded species. They vary in size from the smallest (___ inches and found in ___) to the largest (___ inches and are found in ___). All true crickets lay eggs and require both male and female for reproduction. The adult female can be distinguished from the male because she has a long and single, terminal filament known as the ovipositor. She uses this to deposit her eggs in the soil or whatever medium she lays them in. In addition, she has two long and paired filaments called cerci at the tip of her abdomen. Males lack the ovipositor, but have the two cerci. The cerci are used for perception of touch and wind vibrations. They have long, segmented antennae that function mainly in olfaction or smell and recognition of species, and sex by contact.

If they are sound producers, and most crickets are, they have their "ears" or tympanum located on the inside section (i.e., the tibia) of their front legs. Only adult males are able to produce sound. They do this by rubbing the scraper of one forewing over the file of the other forewing. On these forewings they also have a structure called the mirror, which acts as an amplifier of the sound. The life expectancy of crickets varies from ___ for males to ___ for females. Crickets are usually plant feeders while some are omnivorous or eat many types of foods.

No cricket is dangerous or acts as a vector of organisms that cause diseases of humans or domestic or wild animals. They do, however, serve as food for birds, snakes, lizards, frogs, and insectivorous mammals. Thus, crickets are important in the food webs of most terrestrial habitats. Recently, the demand for crickets as food for pets has resulted in the establishment of several farms, such as Fluker's Cricket Farm in Louisiana, that raise crickets on a large scale. In addition to being important as food for many animals, crickets have a long history of association with humans. It is because of this association with humans that crickets have come to play important roles in the history and culture of people everywhere. Because of the enormity of this topic, I will not be able to provide a comprehensive coverage, but will be selective in the information included.

The house cricket, *Acheta domestica,* is the same cricket as the Talking Cricket, Grillo-parlante, in the famous story Pinocchio. Following is information I received by e-mail from Dr. Sam Heads in England about the house cricket.

"In response to your other question: *Acheta domesticus* is originally a native of North Africa and the Middle East but today has an almost cosmopolitan distribution. In Europe, the species rarely survives outside of heated buildings and rubbish-tips and sewage-plants where fermenting organic matter provides a heat source. The species has long been established in Europe and is thought to have been introduced by European armies returning from the crusades in the thirteenth century. Here in Britain, *A. domesticus* was widespread up until the late 1940s and early 1950s; prior to that time most towns and large villages had at least one bakery which provided ideal habitat for this species. Hospitals, factories, large private houses and many other premises were fuelled by coal fires, and the ash and rubbish-tips would have also provided ideal habitats. From the 1950s many of these sites disappeared: baking became industrialised, gas-fuelled heating replaced coal and numerous rubbish-tips were bulldozed for redevelopment. At the same time insecticides (particularly chlorinated hydrocarbons, such as DDT) entered widespread usage and *A. domesticus* declined rapidly. Today, *A. domesticus* is still well represented in the UK, but is generally restricted to the southern half of England and Wales, with very few post-1960 records from the northern Watsonian vice-counties."

Quote taken from e-mail from Dr. Heads.

II. CRICKETS IN HISTORY

A misinterpretation of information shows up in the book, *Insects and History* by Cloudsley-Thompson when he discussed how the "Mormon cricket" devastated the food and forage crops of the Mormons in 1848 in Utah. The California seagull that arrived in numbers and ate the crickets saved the crops. In its honor, a statue to the seagull was erected in Salt Lake City. Unfortunately, this was not really a cricket, but a shield-backed katydid. This is why one must not take common names of plants and insects too serious. It is better to use the scientific name. The insect in question, *Anabrus simplex*, is not even a cricket, but in the family Tettigoniidae, or more commonly known as the katydids and long-horned grasshoppers. Like the monarch butterfly, it is one of the well-established migratory insects in North America. It is also surprising that this is the only mention that the author makes of the importance of crickets in history.

III. CRICKETS IN CULTURE

    A. FOLKLORE
    B. MYTHOLOGY AND LEGEND

IV. CRICKETS IN LITERATURE AND MOVIES

    A. CHILDREN'S LITERATURE
    B. ADULT LITERATURE

Probably the best-known story involving a cricket is Charles Dickens's (1812–1870) short novel, *The Cricket on the Hearth*, which was published in 1846. This story uses the cricket as a fairy-tale device to intervene in the affairs of the human characters. The title comes from the competition or singing match that takes place between the kettle on Dot Perrybingle's hearth and a house cricket. This story was later (1859) put into play form by Dion Bouccault and titled *The Cricket on the Hearth as Dot?* Still later (1896) it was made into an opera, *Das Heimchen am Herd*, by the Viennese composer Karl Goldmark.

    C. MOVIES
    Pinocchio and Jiminy Cricket

Tonino Watches the Movie *Jurassic Park*

Tonino had a wonderful childhood. His parents, his relatives, and family friends like Joe, who was like another father, always supported what he did and gave him good advice. "If you want something in life, Tonino, you will have to work for it. Nothing good is given away free," they would all say. After a hard week at school, Tonino looked forward to Friday night and the weekend.

It was raining Friday, so he, Pedro, and Ming Ming decided to rent a video and watch it at Ming Ming's house. Tonino knew the entire Yin family would watch it with them. They had done it before, and he always enjoyed their company. All of them went to Blockbuster Video to see what they could find.

"What should we watch?" asked Pedro.

"Ever since going to Dr. Grimaldi's office and seeing the fossils in the amber at the American Museum of Natural History, I have wanted to see *Jurassic Park*," replied Tonino.

With the *Jurassic Park* cassette under Tonino's arm, they left for Ming Ming's house.

Snacks were always a part of video night. When the boys got there, they made popcorn. Then they grabbed their drinks and settled in to watch *Jurassic Park*. Tonino could still see the poster on Dr. Grimaldi's door. He could perfectly re-create in his mind the scene when they first entered the room: A scientist sits at a table with lots of amber on the table, and one piece under the microscope.

I guess I will find out tonight what the connection is, Tonino said to himself.

Everyone was excited about the action in the video. Tonino really focused on the screen. As he watched, scientists were drilling a hole through the amber to get down to the mosquito to collect blood from its midgut using a syringe. Immediately, Tonino made the connection with Dr. Grimaldi's poster and the movie. Tonino just relaxed after making the connection. Only when the station in Costa Rica lost its power did he again start to get tense.

This was almost a repeat of watching *Arachnophobia* on his way to Italy. He could still vividly remember how scared the little Italian was. Instead of spiders, the moviemakers had chosen dinosaurs to be the bad guys in *Jurassic Park*. Even though Tonino knew that this was a fictitious story, he didn't realize how subconsciously he was affected.

The movie had some very realistic and extremely scary scenes: *Tyrannosaurus rex* trying to get at and eat the children in the smashed car, eating not only humans, but other dinosaurs like velociraptors, and then the velociraptors trying to get the children in the kitchen. The last part of the movie, with everyone flying away in the helicopter, reminded Tonino of landing the ultralight plane in Florida. Instead of the beautiful squadron of pelicans flying in the movie, Tonino remembered crashing the ultralight plane into the brown pelicans.

At the end of the movie, everyone cleaned up and put their popcorn bowls and glasses in the sink. Tonino said good-bye and thanked the Yins. He ran home, because he was still scared by the movie, and immediately jumped into bed.

Tonino and His Scary Dream

It was late and Tonino had to work on his term paper the next day. He already told Joe he couldn't work on Saturday. Joe understood and told Tonino, "Always finish your homework and hand it in on time." As you will recall, Tonino usually wasn't disturbed by his dreams; in fact, he seldom remembered them.

Two hours after falling asleep, Tonino dreamt he was normal cricket size and was actually in *Jurassic Park*. Why not? He knew that crickets had been around during the Jurassic period, when dinosaurs were the dominant form of life on earth. Tonino found himself being chased and almost eaten by several different types of insectivorous dinosaurs. The most harrowing experience was when he was being chased. To avoid being eaten, he jumped up onto the side of a big tree. Now he was in an even worse predicament. Just like the crickets that had been trapped in amber, Tonino had landed into the resin of a huge tree. He had escaped being eaten, but was now facing an even more gruesome death: suffocation. Every time he moved to escape, he sank deeper into the resin. He could actually feel something tightening around his body. Even though his head was not covered with pitch, he could still suffocate because his abdomen is where the spiracles or "breathing holes" are located.

117

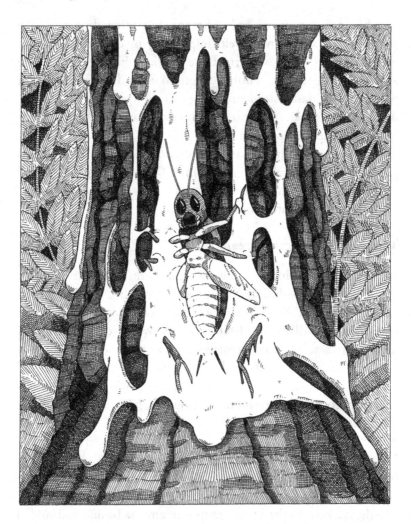

Just before his head went under, he woke up. He was sweating and completely wrapped up in his sheets and blankets. No wonder it felt like he was getting trapped. He went to the bathroom, washed his face, and went back to sleep. When he woke up in the morning, he said, "I now know what the saying 'look before you leap' means."

In his dream, Tonino didn't think ahead, or even fast enough. That type of behavior gets most people in trouble. Surprisingly, we know that Tonino usually planned ahead and listened to advice given to him by others.

Working on the Term Paper

Tonino spent most of Saturday working on his term paper. During lunch, he e-mailed Dr. Grimaldi to get some references on fossils in amber and any entomologists who might specialize in crickets. Dr. Grimaldi listed three references: Poinar and Poinar's *The Amber Forest: A Reconstruction of a Vanished World*, and two of his own books: *Amber: Window to the Past* and *Studies on Fossils in Amber, with Particular Reference to the Cretaceous of New Jersey*. He also gave Tonino the name of Dr. Dan Otte, a specialist on crickets.

Planning Another Trip

On Sunday, Tonino convinced Pedro and Ming Ming to take a trip across the United States. "Let's do it during the summer vacation," he said, "before going to college." Ming Ming had won an academic scholarship to go to MIT, while Pedro was joining Tonino at UMass Amherst. Pedro was now an excellent basketball player, and the summer he met Coach Calipari in Amherst had been a very important turning point in his life. Coach Calipari had been scouting him for one year prior to them meeting, but didn't want the youngster to know about it. Pedro's basketball mentor was Julius Irving, who had also played basketball at UMass.

Tonino and Native Americans

Tonino finished his term paper, handed it in early, and received an "A." Mr. Waddington told the class it was the best term paper he had read in a long time. This pleased Tonino because he remembered how the students in the class had laughed when he said he would do his paper on the importance of crickets in history. As the semester progressed, the focus in the history class shifted to Native Americans.

Two weeks later, during a short visit to Amherst, Tonino went with Professor Stoffolano to a meeting of the Five-College Native American Studies Program. Here he met Professor Peter d'Errico, who taught law at the university. Professor d'Errico was very committed to helping the Native American communities throughout the United

States solve many of their legal problems, such as land rights. Tonino was very curious, however, about why Dr. Stoffolano, obviously an Italian American, was a member of this committee. He asked Dr. d'Errico and his response was that Dr. Stoffolano's mother was part Mohawk Indian.

It now was beginning to occur to Tonino that this country he lived in was truly made up of a mixture of people, and that you really couldn't tell anyone's ethnicity by their name. He also met Dr. Welburn, a Cherokee in the English department, who taught poetry and wrote a book of selected poems, *Coming Through Smoke and the Dreaming.* At the Josephine White Eagle Cultural Center, he met the director, Joyce White Deer Vincent. Tonino told Joyce that he was planning a trip this summer across the country. "Why not visit some reservations?" Joyce asked.

"Why not?" Tonino replied.

After completing all their business in Amherst, they returned to Boston.

During their return trip, the boys began planning their trip across the continental United States. They would fly from Logan Airport to the Albuquerque Airport in New Mexico and then drive on to Arizona to see various Native American tribes. From there they would go on to California, where Tonino wanted to catch the monarch festival that is held every year in Pacific Grove. Tonino wrote to Dr. Stoffolano to ask if he had any suggestions where they should go in New Mexico. An e-mail came back stating that they should look up his friend, Sue Sturtevant, director of Statewide Partnerships for the New Mexico Department of Cultural Affairs in Santa Fe.

Chapter 8.

Tonino Goes to the American Southwest: New Mexico and Arizona

Albuquerque, Gathering of Nations Powwow, and Coronado State Monument

Being teenagers with lots of enthusiasm and energy, but little money, Tonino, Pedro, and Ming Ming thought that most of their travels in New Mexico and Arizona would be done by bus or hitchhiking. Even though their parents had vehemently advised them against hitchhiking, they felt safe together. They arrived in Albuquerque, a city of about 465,640 and the site of the largest meeting of Native American tribes in North America, called the Gathering of Nations. Every spring, people come together for this annual powwow to renew old friendships, to share in the history of the past, to discuss the future of their respective tribes, and to tell their stories in the traditional ways of dance. Over 3,000 dancers perform from all over the Americas.

The boys took a bus to the central part of the city and made arrangements to stay in an inexpensive motel within walking distance of the convention center, where the powwow was taking place. After grabbing a quick meal at the local McDonald's, they retired early. It seemed like they had just fallen asleep when the alarm clock went off. They ate a quick breakfast at the motel and headed off to the convention center. Ming Ming picked up their tickets and programs, and everyone found a place to sit in the large hall. The sounds of the various drum groups filled the air with vibrations like a heartbeat.

It was also extremely colorful with so many native people dressed in traditional clothing.

Tonino liked this very much and commented to Pedro and Ming Ming, "You know, I wish more people would dress in traditional clothing. Today, we all look alike—blue jeans and T-shirts."

It was a full day of dancing and storytelling. Soon it was time to eat.

Coronado State Monument

Tonino and his friends met some native teenagers at the convention center and were invited to join them for dinner. At dinner, which consisted of white corn bread, beans, squash, and venison burgers, they learned that the next morning there would be a bus trip to the Coronado State Monument, just outside of Albuquerque, to see the kiva murals. Tonino was excited about doing this because he overheard someone at the powwow telling how the local Indians from the Sandia and Santa Ana Pueblos wanted to take their murals back from the state, and this might be the last time for any non-Indian to see them. This was a great incentive for Tonino. He didn't want to miss seeing them. It took a lot of encouragement on his part to convince Pedro and Ming Ming to go with him.

He said, "I don't know anything about kivas, especially kiva murals, but I am willing to learn. You guys should feel the same way. This might be the last time any non-Indian gets a chance to see them."

"All right," they both said reluctantly.

After dinner they returned to their motel, and Tonino went to bed, anxiously awaiting the next day's adventure. The night was too short, and before they knew it, the alarm was again ringing in a new day. Everyone ate a quick breakfast and hurried over to the convention center to catch the bus. They loaded the bus, and before they knew it, they were at the Coronado Monument.

The main building was small but provided exhibits that were very informative. This building and its exhibits, however, were not the main feature of the visit. It was the kiva murals. Excavations showed that originally there were six kivas, four rectilinear in shape and two circular. Tonino learned that kivas were special rooms below ground and only accessible via a ladder and an opening in the roof. Here kachina dancers performed dances and conducted religious ceremonies in attempts to bring rain or to secure a good hunt.

At the bottom of the ladder, and about one foot in front of the ladder, but away from the opening that let smoke from the fire leave the kiva, was a deflecting piece of adobe about two feet high and three feet wide. Inside the kivas were murals, or wall paintings. These were painted very much like the frescoes Tonino had seen in Italian churches. Instead of plaster, these were painted on an adobe wash. Tonino read to Pedro and Ming Ming from a brochure he picked up at the entrance of the museum: "These pictures around here, they are everything that we believe. They show us how to live. To us, these paintings are everything to live for."

Tonino and the others now made their way outside and followed the meandering path that many natives must have followed in the past. As they wandered along, they saw the remains of several kivas. At one point, they could see the Rio Grande, which at one time provided the essential water for the pueblo. Soon they arrived at a kiva they could enter. Tonino climbed onto the roof and looked down the three-foot-square hole into the kiva. He had to turn around to descend the wooden ladder. When he arrived at the bottom, Tonino was surprised at how big it was. It was difficult to see much of the murals since many forms of erosion and destruction had taken place. It was dark, cold, and lonely. He couldn't wait to climb the ladder to enter the world of sunshine, just like the original peoples did when they left the underworld. He then moved onto a separate building housing many of the preserved murals. What Tonino saw was just a small portion of the kiva murals, which had been taken from their original owners, physically removed, and stored in archives away from the people they were painted for. Tonino couldn't believe that this could happen.

He asked Ming Ming, "Can you imagine what the world would do if someone went into the Sistine Chapel in Italy, removed most of the frescoes, and then put them somewhere accessible to only a few people?"

"I can't imagine that. Unfortunately, it has happened throughout history, and unless people are sensitive to this issue it will continue to happen. Just think of what recently happened when the Al Qaeda blew up the beautiful Buddha statue in Afghanistan. It is our generation that has to try to make a difference."

"We will do it!" both Tonino and Pedro said.

All three of them put their hands together in agreement and gave high fives.

"Well, let's go, the bus is ready," Pedro said to his friends.

They returned to the convention center by noon and were able to watch more dancing, look at the art of the various vendors, and listen to some more stories.

Pedro had some important information for Ming Ming and Tonino. He was carrying a notice that told about a trip to Petroglyph National Monument the next afternoon.

"Let's go," Pedro said. "It's less than twenty-five minutes from here, and who knows if we will ever get back to this area again?"

Tonino and Ming Ming couldn't say no because they knew Pedro had become interested in petroglyphs during his trip to Puerto Rico.

"Go sign us up; we would be glad to go."

Petroglyph National Monument

It was here that the boys met Dave Tyroler, Park Law Enforcement Officer. Dave agreed to take them on the trail to see what he considered the best petroglyphs. It was a short walk on a dusty, sandy path. As they were walking, Tonino noticed antlike insects emerging from holes in the path and darting around to do their business. While they were walking amongst the petroglyphs, they came upon a man who appeared to be drawing many of the petroglyphs. They all watched at a distance as the man skillfully reproduced the petroglyph images on paper. When he realized someone was watching, he stopped, stood up, and walked over to the group.

Dave introduced him. "This is Ron Rivera, who is one of our most famous gourd painters. His gourds are sold in many galleries in northern New Mexico. He is gathering images to start a new line of gourds designed with petroglyph images."

In conversation, Ron told the boys he was mainly here in Albuquerque for the powwow.

"So are we," Tonino replied.

"Would you like to get together for dinner this evening?" Ron asked.

"Sure," the boys responded.

"Let's meet around seven at the main entrance of the stadium."

The boys continued on with Dave while Ron finished his drawing. The sun was beginning to set and Dave had found his favorite petroglyph. As they sat there looking at it, a beautiful hawk came and circled above them.

"That's a good sign," Dave said.

The walk back seemed shorter, and they had to hurry so they didn't miss the van back to the powwow. "Thank you very much," all the boys said to Dave as they shook his hand and boarded the van.

The boys had just enough time to return to the motel and drop off materials they had picked up on the trip to Petroglyph National Monument. Returning to the convention center, they met Ron. His van was something spectacular. It almost looked like a gourd and was beautifully painted, black on white with stylized designs of various animals, even insects, all over it. During dinner, Tonino told Ron about his various adventures, such as flying with the monarchs and visiting the monarch refuge in Mexico.

"Sounds like you guys have had some great trips," Ron said. "Where are you going next?"

"We are going to Santa Fe tomorrow," Ming Ming responded.

"How are you getting there?"

"We don't know," they all chimed in at once.

Ron replied, "I have to go that way to drop off some gourds in Santa Fe, and it's on my way home. I would be glad to give you a ride."

"That would be super," Pedro quickly responded.

After dinner Ron gave the boys a ride back to their motel and told them he would pick them up after the powwow closing ceremony.

Going to Pueblo Country to See Sue Sturtevant in Santa Fe

Following the powwow, they left with Ron for the land of the Pueblos: Sandia Pueblo, San Filipe Pueblo, Santo Domingo Pueblo, Cochiti Pueblo, Tesuque Pueblo, Nambe Pueblo, Pojoaque Pueblo, Santa Clara Pueblo, San Juan Pueblo, Picuris Pueblo, and Taos Pueblo. The boys remembered from their history class that Pueblo Indians of the American Southwest lived in the mountain and semi-desert regions of northern New Mexico and Arizona in houses with flat roofs made of stone or adobe. The houses were usually built in groups and often were built on top of one another. They were called *pueblos*, which is the Spanish word for "towns." They were the condominiums of the Pueblo world. Thus, the people living in these pueblos came to be known as the Pueblo Indians. Most Pueblo Indians live in the Rio Grande Valley, which is near Albuquerque and Santa Fe. Their villages, however, extend to the west and across into three mesas in northeastern Arizona. This is where the Hopi Indians live, and just beyond, to the north, live the Navajos. It is reported that when Francisco Vazques de Coronado led an expedition into the Southwest in 1540, there were eighty-five pueblos, while today there are only nineteen.

The boys left Albuquerque and traveled on to Santa Fe with Ron. Here they met Sue Sturtevant, who is director of Statewide Partnerships for the Department of Cultural Affairs for New Mexico. She got her doctorate in museum education at UMass Amherst and has worked in Santa Fe for five years. She is also a good friend of Dr. Stoffolano. By the time Ron delivered all his gourds, it was close to six o'clock. "Well, let's find your friend's house," Ron said. They arrived at Sue's house. Tonino was very excited to meet Sue because he loved museums and knew she was involved in museum work.

Tonino's Problem at the Mexican Restaurant

Ron knocked on the door. Sue was surprised to see Ron when she opened the door. She couldn't see the boys behind him and said, "Aren't you Ron Rivera? What are you doing here?"

"Yes, I am. I delivered some young men who say that you are expecting them."

"Yes, I am."

Ron turned around and introduced the boys to Sue, who invited them in and told them to relax while she changed from her work clothes. After having some snacks and conversation, Sue invited everyone to join her at Tomasita's, an excellent Mexican restaurant. "Do you boys like hot Mexican food?"

"Of course we do."

Sue and Ron look at one another and shrugged their shoulders. Living in Boston, the boys only knew Mexican food from eating at Taco Bell or Chili's. Sometimes they had spicy hot food at Ming Ming's house, but they hadn't experienced anything yet. Sue forgot to tell them to keep their fingers out of their eyes when eating Mexican food. Unluckily for him, Tonino got hot pepper in his eyes.

The only way to solve the problem was to be excused and quickly go to the bathroom. Tonino excused himself and rapidly made his way to the men's room. His next problem was that it didn't say "Men's Room," it said "*Caballeros,*" and he didn't understand Spanish. He waited until a man emerged before going in. Once inside, he quickly morphed into cricket form, thus avoiding the action of the chemical causing the burning sensation in his human eye. By doing this, all the hot pepper substance, called capsaicin, would be on the outside of his compound eye and not between his eyelid and eyeball, where chemicals can easily penetrate the soft membranes.

For those of you who have forgotten, there is a thin layer of cuticle covering an insect's body, or exoskeleton. On the surface of this layer is a waxy coat that helps prevent water-soluble substances penetrating into the body. Thus, by letting water run over his compound eye, and drying it with a piece of paper towel, Tonino could get rid of it. This was exactly what he did. Well, not exactly. Today, the faucets in most public restrooms are run by a light sensor, which creates a problem for a small cricket. To solve this, Tonino morphed and remained people size just long enough to partly close the sink stopper so he wouldn't get washed down the drain when he morphed back to cricket size. He transformed, solved the problem of turning the sensor on by jumping in front of the light beam, which started the water, hopped down into the bowl, washed his eyes, and hopped out.

Of course, he got water all over his body, but because of the outer waxy epicuticle of his exoskeleton, the water beaded up and didn't penetrate like it would on regular clothing. In fact, most of it slid off his body. Only a few small beads remained. He then found a small piece of paper towel someone had left on the counter and rubbed his compound eye on the paper.

Just as he finished, someone came in, went to the bathroom, washed his hands, and turned on the air dryer. Tonino hid behind the soap dispenser to avoid being seen. The dryer remained on long enough for Tonino to jump in and out of the hot air stream. Having solved this problem, he transformed and returned to the table. After a wonderful meal and great conversation, they returned to Sue's house. Ron thanked Sue for dinner and left to return to Ocate, where his home is.

That evening everyone discussed some of the things they could do in Santa Fe. Since Ming Ming and Pedro had come along mainly to accompany Tonino, they let him decide. Tonino said he really wanted to visit the Museum of Indian Arts & Culture. This wonderful museum is located on top of Museum Hill, which is also the site of the Museum of International Folk Art and the Wheelright Museum (home of the largest collection of Navajo sand paintings), plus the Laboratory of Anthropology. Pedro and Ming Ming went to bed early, but Tonino continued to talk to Sue.

"Why do you think we are so tired today?" Tonino asked Sue.

Sue said it might have something to do with the high elevation, which was about 6,345 feet above sea level, resulting in lower oxygen content in the air. She explained how initially she had trouble adapting to the high elevation of Santa Fe; she would often get dizzy. "Once I was at a meeting and had to go to the car to get some papers. On the way to the car, I fainted and fell into the bushes. It was awhile before anyone at the meeting came to find me. This condition is called high altitude sickness," she told Tonino.

It should be noted here that altitude hypoxia (high altitude dizziness) is caused by the lack of oxygen. This is not due to a decrease in the amount of oxygen as one goes higher in altitude, but a decrease in barometric pressure. Our atmosphere contains about 21 percent oxygen. What changes in this situation is how much air we can get into our lungs. Thus, the less the amount of air we get into our lungs, the less oxygen in our lungs. Humans acclimatize (or adapt) to this by breathing faster; the heart rate also increases. Within a ten-day period, people should be about 80 percent acclimatized, and after six weeks, they should be 95 percent. Over the long term, humans adapt to this by producing more red blood cells, thus more cells with hemoglobin to carry the oxygen to all the cells in the body, but how will Tonino adapt to this altitude if he transforms?

Insects don't have red blood cells, and 99.9 percent of them also lack hemoglobin. Only a few insects have hemoglobin, including the bloodworm or chironomid midge larva and the endoparasitic bot fly larva. Both insect larvae live in habitats low in oxygen, thus hemoglobin evolved to act as storage molecules for the life-giving gas oxygen. In these insects, hemoglobin serves as a storage molecule and is not transported by the circulatory system.

Remember, insects get their oxygen through the system of tubes called trachea and not through the circulatory system. As far as he knew, Tonino didn't think any insect would suffer from this problem of altitude sickness. Thus, being an insect at any altitude was better than being human.

As they sat on the sofa in her living room talking about various things, Tonino noticed a book on the coffee table titled *Distant Shores: The Odyssey of Rockwell Kent*. This interested him because he had gone to the Norman Rockwell Museum in Stockbridge, Massachusetts, when he was in the Berkshires. *I wonder if there is any connection*, he said to himself.

It was getting late, and Sue said she was retiring. "May I look at this book?" he asked.

"Sure, you will probably find it interesting. His grandson, who is also a painter, lives next door."

Tonino started to read the book and noted that in 2000, an exhibit of Rockwell Kent's art had been shown at the Norman Rockwell Museum. He also learned that the two artists, who were often confused by the general public, had corresponded, but never met. He read, "Kent is generally identified with his powerful and dramatic illustrations for Herman Melville's *Moby-Dick*." Tonino looked at two wonderful line drawings, *Moby-Dick Rising* and *The Spirit Spout*. Kent was labeled a Communist and was continually harassed; he left his collection to Russia in 1960. *Wow*, Tonino said to himself.

He put the book on the table, brushed his teeth, and went to sleep. His dream that evening was about Grillo-parlante being swallowed by the dog shark and his great-grandfather, Jiminy, being swallowed by the whale in Disney's movie *Pinocchio*. "I only hope this never happens to me," he said in his dreams.

He also recalled the drawing labeled *The Spirit Spout* and couldn't help but imagine that the spout looked just like smoke. At breakfast Tonino asked Sue about the importance of smoke in Native American cultures.

"I am sure you will learn about it during your visit here in the Southwest," she said. "Let's go to the museum."

Santa Fe's Museum of Indian Arts & Culture

The Museum of Indian Arts & Culture was very exciting. Tonino wanted to see the new exhibit, tracing the native cultures of the Southwest from ancestral to contemporary times. As they moved through this exhibit, the boys could see many wonderful ancient artifacts (e.g., beads, baskets, pottery, clothing). Tonino only wished his parents, especially his father, could be with him to share this experience. Tonino often remembered his father's willingness to take him to so many museums when he was little. Tonino was surprised to learn that the ancient peoples of this region included more than just the Anasazi (Ancient Ones). The Hohokam, Patayan, Mogollon, Sinagua, and Salado, as well as the Anasazi, made up the original peoples in the Southwest.

As the boys moved around the museum, they came to one section called the "Ancient Ones." "I wonder what this room is about?" Tonino said as he turned to his friends.

"I don't know," they responded in harmony. "Let's take a look!"

Inside were many intellectual treats. The boys learned that the Ancient Ones were descendants of the western Desert Culture who originally lived about 8,000 years ago; the Pueblo culture, especially Hopi, was rooted in the Anasazi culture of the Four Corners area, where New Mexico, Utah, Colorado, and Arizona meet. Later, during the seventh century AD, the Anasazi developed a type of pottery that had black designs on a white background. These Anasazi lived during the period known as Pueblo I. The word *Anasazi* really means "enemy ancestors" and is from the Navajo language, not the Pueblo language.

The Anasazi are also credited with developing the kiva. During the Classic Period (AD 1100–1275), the Anasazi began to build houses similar to modern pueblos. Then in the last quarter of the thirteenth century, something drastic happened that led to the complete collapse of the Anasazi peoples in this region. Like the

Taíno Indians in Puerto Rico, they had no written language. In fact, all that is known about them is based on some of the remains of their dwellings and some pottery sherds. Tonino remembered learning about the three-cornered stones known as zemis when he was in Puerto Rico. Like the pottery sherds of the Anasazi, the zemis were one of the few articles remaining of the Taínos. Why the Anasazi thrived for so many centuries and then mysteriously disappeared is not known. This was interesting, but it was a lot of information for them to remember.

"Our history teacher would be proud of us now," Ming Ming said with a giggle.

Pedro replied, "Yeah, too bad we didn't find early American colonial history as interesting as this."

"I agree," responded Tonino. "But remember, that was at least five years ago, and we have matured some, haven't we?"

They all puffed out their chests and said, "Yeah, that's right."

Tonino was the one most interested in museums, so he always went first, while his two buddies followed closely behind. They were moving along at a good clip when suddenly, Tonino stopped. Pedro and Ming Ming were not paying attention. They both kept walking and crashed into Tonino, causing everyone to fall down. They collected themselves, made sure no one was hurt, and picked up their pamphlets. Tonino got up first. He turned, walked over to a glass exhibit case, and looked into the case, waiting for Ming Ming and Pedro to follow. Tonino was completely mesmerized by what was in the case. Staring him in the face were pieces of pottery sherds. It was not the white pottery with the black designs he was interested in, but it was what was painted on them. "Look here," he said as he pointed to the case.

"What's so great about that?" said Ming Ming.

As you know, Ming Ming often went to the Boston Museum of Art to see the Chinese pottery collection, where he had seen whole vases, much bigger than any pots here, plus they were not broken pottery pieces like this. Instead, what he liked was the colorful and beautifully painted pottery with a shiny glaze. "Why such a fuss over some broken pieces of pottery?" he asked Tonino.

"It's not their beauty or colors, but their significance. This is all that remains of any communication between this vanished, ancient peoples and modern man. Also, the interesting thing to me is how they painted such beautiful and stylized figures of animals, including insects, on the sherds. This tells me that insects must have been an integral part of their life. Best of all, look here," Tonino said. Pedro and Ming Ming lined up behind Tonino to follow where his finger was pointing. "Can you see it? There's part of a cricket."

His friends never understood why Tonino was so focused on crickets. They never associated his last name, Cricket, with his interest in the insect. In fact, since he would never tell them why he was interested, they were tired of asking him why and agreed never to ask him again.

As they moved on, Tonino thought the following to himself: *Now, I have seen three bits of evidence showing that crickets were around for a long time: once in amber at Dr. Grimaldi's office, the report from Dr. Heads, and now here on the sherds of the Anasazi.*

As they moved to the next exhibit, Ming Ming asked Tonino, "I thought the term for broken pieces of pottery was spelled *shards.* Isn't that correct?"

"No! *Sherds* is the correct term for broken pieces of pottery, while *shards* is correct for broken pieces of glass."

"I never knew that," Ming Ming said.

Pedro checked his watch and said they must hurry because Sue was going to pick them up at the museum gift shop in fifteen minutes. Tonino couldn't get to the museum shop fast enough. His passion for books, and now Indian pottery of the Southwest, motivated him to find a book on ancient pottery. As he rapidly scoured the hundreds of books on the shelves, one stood out. He could only see the binding that read in black letters on a white background, *Mimbres Pottery: Ancient Art of the American Southwest.* He had no idea where this new acquisition would take him as he tucked it under his arm and headed to the cashier.

As Sue approached the boys, she said, "Well, what did you like the most?"

Rather than giving Tonino a chance to speak, the other two boys said in unison, "Tonino liked the pottery shards. Excuse me, I mean sherds, with the insects on them. He especially liked the one with the cricket."

"That's interesting," said Sue. "Coming from the city, I'll bet you don't get to see many crickets. Why the love for crickets, Tonino?"

"Don't even go there!" Pedro and Ming Ming said.

Tonino had learned how to skillfully evade certain questions. He had heard others say, "Oh, I just am!" And so, that's how he responded to Sue. Being as aware as she was about people's sensitivities, Sue didn't pursue the issue. She noticed that Tonino was clutching a new book and asked if she could see it.

"That's a great book," Sue said after looking at it. "I know Dr. Brody, who wrote one of the essays in that book. He is a specialist on Mimbres pottery and was former director of the Maxwell Museum in Albuquerque."

Not being bashful, Tonino said, "I would like to learn something more about the Mimbres people, or Mimbreñoes."

"Why are you interested in them?" Sue asked.

"I remember being enchanted by these bowls the first time I saw them. When I was younger, my father took me to the Peabody Museum in Boston. There I saw a large collection of Mimbres pottery. I was interested in the pottery because of all the animals that were painted on the bowls. Unfortunately, I didn't learn anything about the people who made the pottery."

Sue replied, "Maybe we will have a chance for you to learn more about these interesting people, only known to us by this wonderful pottery style. Well, it's getting late, and I am sure you are all hungry," Sue said as they walked to the car.

It was a short drive from the museum to Sue's house.

Sue took requests and ordered three pizzas for the boys because she had an important meeting that evening. Before she left, the pizza arrived. "I won't be home until late, so don't wait up for me," she said.

After eating the wonderful pizza, the boys cleaned up and went to the TV to watch a replay of last year's NCAA basketball tournament.

Soon, Tonino became bored and excused himself. He prepared for bed and pulled out his new book. The first thing he always did with a new book was to flip through the pages, just like when he was a boy sitting on his mother's lap, looking at the family photo album. He couldn't believe the wonderful designs on the pottery, especially those showing animals. Soon he was off to dream land, where all the animals he was just looking at jumped from the pots in the book and escaped by slithering out between the pages. Before he knew it, they had transformed from flat animals into three-dimensional, live animals. They were dancing all over his bed, just like Pinocchio did, but without strings. Tonino didn't remember much after that.

It was morning, and Pedro, Ming Ming, and Sue were up and about, getting breakfast. At breakfast the conversation focused on the evening's events. Pedro and Ming Ming recounted each basket of the game they had watched.

"Well, what did you do?" Sue asked Tonino.

"I looked through the book on Mimbres pottery."

"What do you think of it?"

"It's beyond imagination," Tonino responded. "The black on white pots with such wonderful stylistic designs of various objects, including animals, are wonderful. They are ancient yet very modern. Do you think I could go to the Maxwell Museum and meet Dr. Brody?"

"Well, I'll give him a call at nine o'clock."

While everyone was cleaning up and doing dishes, Tonino kept watching the clock. When it was nine, he reminded Sue to make the call.

"He will see you at eleven o'clock at the museum," Sue said after hanging up the phone, "so let's get organized so we can leave at ten." The boys agreed, and at ten they were in the car and on their way to Albuquerque. As they pulled into the parking lot on the side of the museum, Sue could see Dr. Brody waiting. Sue made the introductions, and everyone went into the museum.

Tonino at the Maxwell Museum

Dr. Brody told them they all had to sign in. After that, he said, "I want to take you downstairs to where the ancient pots are located. Follow me, and please don't touch any of the pots."

Everyone formed a single file, just like ants, and followed Dr. Brody to see the Mimbres pots. They entered a room containing many, many ancient pots sitting on wooden shelves. Dr. Brody put on his white gloves and carefully picked up a pot to show everyone. "Look here at this beautiful design." As he showed them the bowl, Dr. Brody rotated it, thus giving the inside design and figures a sense of movement. "Do you notice anything different about this bowl?" Dr. Brody asked.

Ming Ming raised his hand and said, "Being Chinese and knowing something about Chinese pottery, I am curious why they only painted and finished the inside of the bowls?"

"Great observation," Dr. Brody responded. "You must remember that these people had very little in their homes that resembled art or design. If they used the bowl to eat with, they would continually be looking into a picture that usually had elegant designs. Also, most of the bowls were not used for eating, but were placed over the head or face of the owner of the bowl when that person died." Ming Ming giggled. "What's so funny?" Dr. Brody asked.

"Well, when I was little I remember my father putting a bowl over my head and using it to cut my hair."

"I am sure many people had that same experience," Sue replied.

"Why do most of the bowls have a hole in the bottom?" Tonino asked.

Brody replied, "Another great question. Some people believe that this represents a 'kill hole' and may have provided a way for the dead person's spirit to leave the body. You must remember, however, that we have no record, other than the bowls, to obtain any information about either the bowls or the person who made the bowl. The body of knowledge that has been written is mainly the interpretation of the person writing the article. Now, let me show you a couple of other bowls."

Dr. Brody placed two different bowls on the table. To everyone's surprise, inside one bowl was a cricket, and inside the other was a grasshopper. Tonino and his friends were speechless.

Tonino thought to himself, *There is no way Dr. Brody could know I am a cricket and my cousin is a grasshopper.*

Even Sue was amazed because she knew Tonino was interested in crickets. "Any other questions?" Dr. Brody asked.

Pedro asked, "First, did the Indians of the Southwest pit animals against one another in combat like cockfighting or cricket fighting? Second, did they use boats? Third, is there any evidence that the Indians got the idea for making clay pots from insects, such as potter wasps? I ask the last question because Dr. Stoffolano told Tonino that there is good evidence that humans learned how to use wood fibers to make paper from paper wasps."

"The last question is very interesting; I didn't know that this is how we learned to make paper from wood. One would like to think that at that time, some inquisitive person watched a potter wasp make a clay pot and then tried to duplicate it, but unfortunately archaeological evidence shows that pots were first made in a basket form and then later on they used the basket to put clay on it. Sort of like a form. This then led to the making of clay pots without a basket intermediary."

"Now, for your second question. There is no evidence that any of the Southwestern tribes used boats. Your first question is one I have never thought about. Now that you posed it, however, I believe that most indigenous peoples, especially those that believed in human-to-animal transformation, would never fight animal against animal. All animals, and many plants, were considered equals on Mother Earth. You would never know if it is someone you knew or was related to you that you were fighting."

"That makes sense," Tonino said, as he looked at Pedro.

Dr. Brody didn't know anything about the controversy Tonino and Pedro were having about cockfighting. Tonino remembered when Pedro's mother took them to the cockfight in Puerto Rico. Tonino had objected to fighting one animal against the other. Pedro, however, had said that other cultures, like the Chinese, often fought cricket against cricket.

"One last question before we have to leave," Tonino said, raising his hand. "I noticed the painting on the back cover of the book you edited, *Mimbres Pottery*; does this picture really represent a fish swallowing a person?" Tonino was the only one who knew where he wanted the discussion to go. Remember, Pinocchio's father, Geppetto, had been swallowed by a dog shark, and Jiminy Cricket was believed to have been eaten by a shark. Also, in Disney's movie, Jiminy Cricket goes with Pinocchio into the stomach of the whale to find Geppetto.

"The painting on the book cover is believed to represent a myth involving one of the Hero Twins that is transforming into a fish; it is not a depiction of a fish swallowing a person."

With that response, Tonino could not continue on with the discussion. He just replied, "Oh!" and left it at that. Everyone thanked Dr. Brody for a wonderful experience and departed.

On the way back to Santa Fe, Tonino flipped through his book on Mimbres pottery. When he came to page 21, he stopped. Staring him in the face was a photo of a bowl depicting a man in a fetal position, possibly still inside the embryo or uterus, with two animals on each side of him. What interested Tonino the most about this picture were the two zigzag lines connecting the two animals with the embryo. The figure legend said that these lines represented the umbilical cord. Tonino wondered if this picture also represented the strong connection that existed in the minds of these people concerning transformation between humans and animals.

That Evening at Sue's House

At dinner that evening, Tonino brought up the topic of transformers, which is well represented in pictorial form in Mimbres pottery. He opened the discussion by saying, "Speaking about transformation between humans and animals, what about Smokey the Bear?"

"What do you mean?" Pedro said.

"Who do you think Smokey is in human form?"

"You have a great imagination," Ming Ming said to Tonino.

Sue picked up on the conversation and asked Tonino, "Would you like to visit the Capitan Mountains, where Smokey the Bear Historical State Park is located? It's not too far from here."

"Yes, I would," Tonino replied with great excitement.

"That sounds like a plan," responded Sue. She addressed Pedro, "What do you and Ming Ming want to do tomorrow?"

They looked at one another, and then Pedro said, "The Capitan Mountains are fine with us, but why does Tonino want to go there?"

"I want to see where Smokey the Bear is buried."

Ming Ming whispered into Pedro's ear, "First it's crickets and now it's bears. I can't figure this guy out."

"Is it the Capitan Mountains?" Sue asked.

Everyone nodded their heads yes. So the next day, off they went toward Las Cruces, where they would pick up Route 70 to Capitan and the Smokey the Bear Historical State Park. They took Route 25 out of Albuquerque and headed south to Route 380, which took them to Capitan.

Smokey the Bear Historical Site

Growing up in Boston, Tonino had little opportunity to personally experience forest fires, but he, like every other child in the United States, knew all about them because of Smokey the Bear. Tonino thought it was wonderful that a black bear had been given the charge to be the conscience of everyone in the United States for helping prevent forest fires. What he didn't know was that the origin of Smokey really went back to the late 1930s. The fear of forest fires peaked in 1942 because of World War II and the threat of sabotage to one of our essential natural resources, the forests. The life of Smokey really started in May 1950, following a forest fire in New Mexico's Lincoln National Forest. Little did the scared and badly burned four-pound black bear, found clinging to a tree following a major forest fire, know that he would be swept into such national recognition. The same thing happened to Tonino's great-great-great-grandfather, Grillo-parlante. The fame and responsibility thrust upon these animals was often too much. They only survived because

139

they were able to get away from the stress of the human world. Tonino's father had told him that, without being able to switch body forms, he probably would not have been able to accomplish all he did. Being able to transform was his way of dealing with the daily stress of the world. Tonino thought, *Children seem to survive pressure much better than adults. Maybe this is because they are able to daydream and transform themselves into more favorable situations.*

Tonino had previously read two magazine articles about Smokey, one in the *Conservationist* and the other in the *Smithsonian*. Neither of these mentioned Smokey's other life form. *Did he have one?* Tonino asked himself.

As Tonino and his friends drove up to the visitor's center at Smokey the Bear Historical State Park, the place where he was buried after his death in 1976, Tonino thought he might find an answer to his question, "Who was Smokey the Bear?"

Tonino read all the information at the center, asked rangers, and even asked some visitors if they knew. Since he had had a vision while alone at Grillo-parlante's grave in Florence, he thought if he went to Smokey's grave alone, maybe the answer would be revealed to him. He excused himself from Pedro and Ming Ming and walked up the path to the grave. No one was there. He stood there silently for about ten minutes. Nothing happened. He then sat quietly for another fifteen minutes. Still nothing happened. Thinking the "animal spirits" might be more willing to communicate with another animal and not a human, he transformed. Just then, he heard a voice say, "Tonino."

Tonino looked around but didn't see anyone. Suddenly, out from behind a tree stepped the Blue Fairy. Tonino was so surprised to see her he didn't know what to say. He kept grasping for words when she spoke: "I have come to tell you something that is bothering Smokey the Bear in his afterlife."

"What is it?" responded Tonino.

"He has expressed deep concern over the practice of bear farming in several Asian countries. This situation is making him very depressed, and he has asked for my help. What is happening is extremely cruel and potentially threatening to certain bear species. I can say no more, but you are the guardian of the world when it comes to problems of conservation biology. Sometime in your life you will be confronted with this issue, and I am sure you will do your best to deal with it."

As soon as she finished her sentence, she disappeared. *But I didn't even get to ask her who Smokey really was in human form,* Tonino said to himself.

He waited ten more minutes but nothing happened. Finally, he transformed again and returned to find his friends. He explained that he tried everything he could think of, but still had no answer as to who Smokey was.

Pedro, who loved sports, especially basketball said, "Maybe he was Julius Erving."

Ming Ming, however, thought he was one of the weekly guests on *Wall Street Week* with Louis Rukeyser. "Often while studying and doing my homework," he told Tonino and Pedro, "I overhear them saying something about a bear's market."

"Well, I guess we will never know," Ming Ming said as they prepared to depart the park.

As they left, they headed toward Silver City and the Mimbres Valley. Sue decided to go via Alamogordo and the White Sands National Monument. As they approached White Sands, they could see what looked just like snow.

White Sands National Monument

It was noon so they bought sandwiches and something to drink at the lodge. Taking along their lunches, they went to the picnic grounds just a short way from the lodge.

They spent about an hour and a half frolicking in the white sand before Sue ordered everyone into the car. Their next destination was Silver City. As they left, Tonino regretted not looking for crickets in this unusual habitat. Would the crickets be white in color, because cricket color often matches the environment? This was something he recorded in his notebook to look up when he returned home.

Silver City, Mimbreñoes, and Pottery

They arrived in Silver City and the Western New Mexico University Museum about an hour before closing.

"What are we doing here?" the boys all asked.

"This is a special treat for Tonino," Sue said.

"Why me?" Tonino asked.

"Because you love museums, and I said that you might get a chance to learn about something you knew little about."

As they entered the museum, Sue picked up three brochures and gave one to each one of the boys. Standing in the entrance hall they looked at the brochure. The cover showed pictures of some Mimbres pottery and read, "Most surprising and awe-inspiring about WNMU Museum in Silver City, NM, is that it houses the largest permanent display of Mimbres pottery and culture in the world."

Sue said to Tonino, "Now you will get to learn something about the people that made the pottery." They went to the gift shop and Sue asked, "Is Sue Berry here?"

"No, she isn't, but Jim Carlson is."

Sue Berry, the director of the museum, was a good friend of Sue Sturtevant, but she was not there so they spoke to Jim Carlson, who is the curator of the collections. Jim showed them what the museum had and said they would get more information over at the Museum of Western New Mexico University. He told Sue they should see Cynthia Battison, director of the museum. Jim called over, and unfortunately, Cynthia was also away at a meeting, but Karen Rossman agreed to see them.

It was a short drive over to the museum, which was located on a hill with a beautiful view. Sue introduced the boys to Karen and noted that Karen was very knowledgeable about the Mimbres; however, her specialty is gourds. From the exhibits and what Karen told them, below is some of the information they learned.

The Mimbres people lived from AD 200 to 1150. They got their name from the Mimbres River that starts from Cameron Creek, near Silver City, and flows into an endorheic basin in Southwest New Mexico. The word *Mimbres* means "willow" in Spanish and was the name given to the people who lived along the Mimbres River, a place where willows still grow. The Mimbres people were considered Mogollon and their stay in the region was divided into three periods: Early Pithouse, Late Pithouse, and Classic Mimbres. It is the latter that most people identify with the Mimbreñoes. This was the period when they learned how to use a white kaolin slip, giving the pottery of this region its distinctive white color. They were painted using an agave paintbrush. The black color, rather than red, however, occurred sometime after 750. Before that, the pots were kiln fired in an oxygen-rich atmosphere, but after 750, they were fired in an oxygen-poor atmosphere, which gave the pots the distinctive black on white because the hematite in the slip was reduced, producing a black color. They made these pots using a coil and scrape method.

Sue approached the boys and said, "See the rest of the exhibits and then go to the gift shop. We will meet there in thirty minutes."

When Tonino went to the gift shop, he saw a wonderful bowl with the design of a cricket. He purchased two books: *Treasured Earth* and *Mimbres Classic Mysteries*. The first book is about the life of Hattie Cosgrove, who provided important information on Mimbres archaeology. Her collection is now in the Peabody Museum at Harvard University and is the one Tonino had seen when he was young. As he flipped the pages of this new book, Tonino was surprised to find out that Richard Woodbury, who wrote the foreword to the book, was from Shutesbury, Massachusetts, which is just about one mile from the University of Massachusetts in Amherst. Woodbury came to the university to start an anthropology department.

Tonino also noted that both books had drawings of bowls featuring insects. The first one showed bowls having cricket designs painted on them, while the other had an elegant grasshopper and stated that during periods of drought, the Mimbreñoes, like the Pueblos, might have eaten grasshoppers. Tonino was interested in reading that the designs and figures in the petroglyphs in the Mimbres region also showed up on their pottery. His reading also told him that they supplemented their diets by using bows and arrows to kill deer and rabbits. It is interesting to note that the bow and arrow were independently invented by people in the Mediterranean area around the time of Christ and by the Native Americans between AD 500 and 700.

The Mimbreñoes were mainly subsistence farmers, cultivating corn, beans, and squash. Also, the stylistic images of people on some bowls suggest that the Mimbreñoes either tattooed their faces or wore masks. The absence of any masks at the sites, however, indicates that they probably tattooed their faces. The painting of men's bodies, especially the head, arms, and legs, that were attached to various animals on bowls strongly suggested to Tonino that they, like most early human cultures, believed in transformation between humans and animal forms.

One statement that meant a lot to Tonino was from the Mimbres pottery book that Tonino purchased in Santa Fe. Tony Berlant wrote, "For the Mimbres, humanity is not master of the world, but rather an inseparable part of it." This statement sums up the belief of most indigenous peoples: one cannot separate humans from the rest of the living world. Tonino also found it interesting that the painters of these bowls often did not depict what we consider nonliving entities of the world (e.g., lightning, sun, sky, fire, water).

Around AD 1150, the Mimbres society collapsed or disappeared, not unlike the Anasazi. The main identifier of the Mimbres culture has been their distinctive black on white bowls. Yet no evidence has been uncovered showing that this aspect of their culture was transported or moved to another area. Where did they go? It is speculated that they were assimilated into adjacent cultures and that their pottery was not practiced once they left the area of their origin, or else it would have surfaced somewhere else in the American Southwest. Tonino was surprised to learn that the emerging society in the region of the Mimbres Valley was south and in Mexico. Here *Casa Grandes* was built and flourished. It was a large town and appears to have been built using a different adobe technique than the other *Casa Grandes* in Arizona.

They had learned so much; Tonino was surprised that both of his friends also found the museum interesting.

Sue and Karen returned, and Karen asked, "Does anyone have any questions before you leave?"

Tonino raised his hand and didn't wait to be recognized, "Where are we going next?" Sue replied, "To Arizona."

Pedro raised his hand. "I noticed that all the bowls in the museum had round bottoms. How would they fit on a table?"

Karen replied, "Great observation. Think about it! They did not have tables, and a round bottom would permit them to sit the bowl in the sand or dirt without it tipping over."

Sue got to ask a question. "Tonino is interested in crickets. Are there good examples of cricket designs on the Mimbres pottery?"

"The only one I am familiar with is discussed in a book by Fred Kabotie on designs from the Ancient Mimbreñoes. The book shows a young chief riding on the back of a cricket. Apparently, Kabotie's interpretation is that, like the Hopi legend where the frog with its jumping legs is able to get the chief to where he is going, the cricket is able to do this." Karen continued, "Let me ask you a question. Besides our museum, where are some other collections of Mimbres pottery found?"

Karen was sure the boys didn't know. "The Peabody Museum in Boston," Tonino quickly answered.

"Now, how did you know that?" responded Karen.

"When I was little, my father took me to the museum and I remember how different this black on white pottery was from anything I had ever seen. Also, I was enchanted by the animal designs on the bowls. In fact, I am even more enchanted by this pottery now that I learned that this is all that we know about these ancient peoples."

Sue looked at Tonino and said, "Tonino, you amaze me. You know so much about so many different things. I only hope other young people have the same enthusiasm for learning that you do."

"Thank you for the compliment," Tonino replied.

Pedro raised his hand. "At the Museum of Indian Arts & Culture in Santa Fe, we saw examples of ancient pottery. One exhibit showed a collection of mugs, just like coffee mugs used today. Could this be why those people were called Mugollons?"

Tonino and Ming Ming started laughing, and Karen and Sue also found it very difficult to contain themselves. Neither Karen nor Sue wanted to embarrass Pedro.

Sue responded, "The word is spelled *Mogollon* and not *Mugollon*. It was the name of the mountains where these people came from (the Mogollon Mountains of New Mexico), which were named after the Spanish Colonial Governor, Juan Ignacio Flores Mogloon."

"Thanks," Pedro responded.

"If there are no other questions," Sue said, "we must hurry because we have a long drive to Tucson."

Everyone thanked Karen and piled into Sue's car.

Driving to Tucson and Native Stories about Insects

The drive to Tucson was a long one. Tonino sat in front with Sue while Pedro and Ming Ming slept most of the time in the back seat.

Tonino mentioned how multicultural New Mexico was.

Sue replied, "It certainly is, and that is why I love my new job. Do you have any questions about our trip so far?"

"The only thing I can think of is how is Kokopeli related to insects? Is he just another example of a transformer?"

"I believe the answer to that question will be provided when we get to Arizona."

Just before they arrived in Wilcox and the Cochise Visitor Center and Museum of the Southwest, Pedro and Ming Ming woke up. "Let's have dinner and visit the museum," Sue said.

"Sounds great," the boys responded.

Sue checked to see if there were any programs and was excited that there would be storytelling that evening around a campfire. That sounded great to three boys from Boston who never had this experience. In fact, they had always been instructed not to play with matches or start fires. They always remembered the words of Smokey the Bear: "Only you can prevent forest fires." After dinner, they returned to the museum, where a good size crowd was gathering around the fire.

As they sat around the fire, Joe Hayes, the great Southwestern storyteller from New Mexico, told a story about the involvement of two insects in native culture. These were not written stories, as most of us know; they had been passed down orally from one generation to the next. It was a coincidence that he was visiting the museum and was going to be the storyteller that evening. Joe Hayes heard from Sue that Tonino liked butterflies, especially monarchs, so one of the stories was about the woman and the butterflies. She didn't tell Joe how Tonino and his cousin helped rescue a flock of monarchs and how Tonino had visited the monarch's overwintering site in Mexico.

The temperature outside was cool because the lack of clouds in the desert permits the radiant heat of the ground to dissipate rapidly. The heat from the fire felt good. The sky was crystal clear, and every star was doing its best to be seen. The sparks from the fire looked like fireflies being swept up to the sky as the warm air forced its way upward. When everyone was quiet, Joe began the story.

"There was a woman who was discontented with life as it was in the community. One day, she decided to take her small child and go outside the village to gather roots and seeds. As she came upon a manzanita bush, she put the baby down and rested a moment. As she did, a beautiful butterfly came by and flew around the head of the baby. The butterfly flew away as the baby reached for it. The woman decided she would try to catch it for the baby. The butterfly's erratic flight made it impossible for her to catch. She had gone a long distance from her baby. She was tired and laid down to rest."

"The next thing she knew, a gentle hand awakened her. It was a beautiful young man. He told her he was the butterfly she was trying to catch, and if she would follow him always, he would take her to his village, but they would pass through the land of the butterflies. During that time, he told her she must not take her eyes off the ground to look at any of the butterflies. She agreed, and off they went. It was impossible not to look at all these beautiful butterflies landing on her and even gently brushing her face with their wings. Being unable to resist such a temptation, she looked up and saw these beautiful creatures of the air. Immediately, she tried to catch one. She chased one this way and another one that way. Before she knew it, the handsome man was out of sight. She became so tired and exhausted she had to lay down to rest. For many days she unsuccessfully tried to catch a butterfly. After several days, she became so worn out and tired that she lay down and died alone among the butterflies."

This was a very powerful story, and Tonino knew the lesson being taught very well. As one goes through life, one should be happy with what they have and not chase nonessential things; here, butterflies are the metaphor. He had a flashback to his ultralight plane crash in Florida while trying to save the monarchs. Even though completely unrelated to the story, he remembered seeing the picture in the newspaper of himself, Vincenzo, the injured pelicans, and the destroyed ultralight completely covered with thousands of butterflies.

Tonino listened carefully as Joe said, "That story was for you, Tonino. I heard you liked butterflies. This next story is also for you. It is about how the opossum got its bare tail."

How could this story apply to me? thought Tonino. *I have never even seen a real opossum.*

Rather than sitting for this story, Joe stood up and acted out much of the story. Joe began, "Mister Opossum was a real bore. He always was bragging about how beautiful his fluffy tail was. He would prance around and say to all the other animals, 'Just look at this beautiful, fluffy white and gray tail of mine. None of you have such a beautiful tail.' Mr. Opossum did this so often the other animals were getting rather tired of listening to him. In two days, all the animals were going to gather for a great dance to celebrate the coming of spring. Mr. Coyote thought he had a great idea to make Mr. Opossum feel more humble. He called aside Mr. Cricket and discussed with him their plan."

"The morning of the dance, Mr. Cricket went over to Mr. Opossum's house to make his tail beautiful. 'Now, just lay back,' he said, 'and I will make your tail very beautiful for tonight's dance.' Mr. Opossum laid back and dozed off. During that time,

Mr. Cricket, using his powerful mandibles, cut off all the hair on Mr. Opossum's tail. He cut it so short that nothing but a bare tail was showing. He then carefully wrapped it in a red ribbon and cleaned up all the hair. As soon as he finished, Mr. Opossum awoke. He turned around and saw the beautiful red ribbon. Mr. Cricket immediately told him the red ribbon was to keep all the hair clean and in place. 'Now don't take off the ribbon until you start dancing,'" Mr. Cricket said.

"That evening, all the animals were gathered. There was lots of food, and the music was spectacular. The Moonlighters were playing. All the musical animals in the band were warming up while they waited for the other animals to arrive. Mr. Opossum was the last to enter. As he entered, all the animals politely greeted him, looked at the red ribbon, and gave a small smile. They all knew about the plan."

"As the music started, Mr. Opossum was the first to get up. Rather than walking onto the floor, Mr. Opossum strutted onto the dance floor, too proud for any animal. Slowly he started to dance. At the same time, he slowly unwound the red ribbon Mr. Cricket had carefully wound around his tail. When it was completely off, he held the ribbon in his left hand and used it to wave around as he showed off his beautiful tail. No one but Mr. Opossum was on the dance floor. Of course, he had not even looked at his tail. As the music became faster, Mr. Opossum danced faster and faster. All the time he had a big smile on his face, as if to say, 'See my beautiful tail.' All the animals were actively clapping."

"The next thing Mr. Opossum knew, everyone was standing up and clapping even louder. The more they clapped, the faster Mr. Opossum danced. Mr. Opossum was so vain he had overlooked that, in addition to clapping, no one else was dancing and all the animals were laughing. Were they laughing at him? As soon as he realized this, he turned around and saw his ugly and bare tail. He was so mortified and embarrassed, he immediately fell to the ground on his back, pulled his front paws up to his face, and gave that funny grin that opossums now always give when disturbed."

Being so tired from dancing and animating the story, Joe could hardly get out the final words, "And that's how the opossum got his naked tail."

Tonino loved it. He clapped and clapped, and jumped with laughter over the story. All the little children just looked at this overly enthusiastic teenager, who liked this story even more than they did. Everyone slowly left the area and headed their own directions. It wasn't too late, so Sue and the boys drove to Tucson, where Sue had made motel reservations.

"Tomorrow we will meet Dr. Davis and his wife, Shirley. They will be your companions for most of your stay in Arizona," Sue said.

Everyone went to their room and immediately went to sleep, and an early morning breakfast was followed by a short drive to the Davises' house.

Sue and the Boys Go to the Sonoran Desert Museum

After arriving at the Davis home and meeting them, Sue decided she would join everyone for a visit to the Sonoran Desert Museum, which is located just outside of Tucson.

"The Sonoran Desert Museum," Dr. Davis told the boys, "will give you an excellent opportunity to see the plant and animal life of a desert community."

On the way, Tonino remembered how Sue, having been involved most of her adult life with various museums, maintained that museums are one of the best ways to learn a lot about a specific topic. Tonino certainly shared this belief, which was just one thing that helped make a strong bond between the two. Before they knew it, they arrived at the museum.

The Sonoran Desert Museum Gift Shop

The boys were excited about seeing more of the desert. Pedro, however, was picking cactus spines out of his rear since he inadvertently backed into a saguaro cactus. They waited in the parking lot while Sue and the Davises went into the gift shop. When Sue returned, she had three packages in her hand.

"Here are gifts for each of you. I hope you will enjoy them."

It was a race to see which one would unwrap their package first. Pedro won and proudly displayed his book, *Basketball: Its Origin and Development* by James Naismith and W. J. Baker. Ming Ming was second and thanked Sue for his book on technological discoveries. Tonino was the last because he wanted to preserve the wonderful wrapping paper, which showed stylized images of the Southwest. These included Kokopeli, dragonflies, grasshoppers, and of course crickets. Tonino was excited about his book by Edgar Malotki entitled *The Making of an Icon*, which is about Kokopeli. The boys laid down their books, grasped hands, and made a big circle around Sue. They danced around her and said in unison, "Thank you, Sue, for a wonderful experience and thoughtful gifts."

"You're welcome," she replied.

The boys were surprised how attached they had grown to Sue, who had to return to Santa Fe. Each of them had trouble hiding the tears that raced down their cheeks, which they immediately wiped up with their sleeves. None of them looked at one another. Dr. Davis, being a very sensitive person himself, made no comment about this show of emotion.

"Well," he said, "we must move on and see what Arizona has to offer."

Sue got into her car and headed off. As she looked into her rear view mirror, she thought she saw Pedro and Ming Ming, but where was Tonino? She squinted because of the desert sun's brightness and again looked into the mirror. Maybe it was her imagination, but she was convinced she saw the two boys standing next to a cricket. *Must be the heat,* she thought to herself, *or maybe the tears that are streaming down my cheeks.*

Casa Grande Near Phoenix

Leaving Tucson, Norm and Shirley drove to their next destination, *Casa Grande* Ruins National Monument. They felt it was important for the boys to see this ruin since it was our nation's first archaeological site to be set aside as a national treasure. This was the home of the Akimel O'otham, or ancient ones. They are also known by the Pima name, Hohokam, which means "those who have gone." Like many of the other peoples of the Southwest, the Hohokam were considered masters of the desert. It is recorded that the peoples in this area started about 5500 BC as hunter/gatherers. Around AD 300, when they developed an intricate canal system and began to irrigate their crops, they became known as Hohokam. Anthropologists divide the Hohokam period into four major phases: Pioneer Period (AD 300–750), when they were farmers and drew water from the Gila River; Colonial Period (AD 750–950); Sedentary Period (AD 950–1175); and Classic Period (AD 1175–1450). Between 1200 and 1350, the irrigation system of the Hohokam failed because of the river's fluctuations, and by 1450 they had abandoned the area.

It was about ten o'clock, and they were going to hear a talk by Dave Witherspoon, a national park ranger. On the way to the talk, Norm reminded the boys not to touch the cactus; Pedro was still sore from his spiny encounter at the Sonoran Desert Museum. The audience was seated under a ramada, a structure commonly used by the Southwest Indians as a place of shade. Dave told the audience that Casa Grande had been built around AD 1350. "Its Indian name is Hothai Kih, but in 1694, a Jesuit priest gave it the Spanish name, *Casa Grande*."

Tonino recalled Dr. Stoffolano talking about an entomologist at the University of Rhode Island named Richard Casagrande, but he was Italian, not Native American. As Dave finished his talk, Tonino noticed the large ruin behind him.

Finally, Dave finished and asked the audience, "Are there any questions?"

Tonino raised his hand. "How much mud did it take to make this large house?"

Dave replied, "It is estimated that around 3,000 tons of mud were needed. Any other questions?" he asked.

No one raised their hands, so off the group went to explore the ruins. Dave had explained that there were specific holes in the four- to five-foot walls of the large house that aligned with the summer solstice, thus permitting the sun to enter. After exploring the ruins, the boys returned to the museum while Norm and Shirley decided to see what birds they could find, especially their favorite hummingbirds.

Tonino went to the gift shop, where he purchased the book, *How Indians Used Desert Plants*. He then joined Pedro and Ming Ming in the museum. Pedro normally wasn't so animated and excited, but this time Ming Ming and Tonino could not ignore his enthusiasm; he insisted that they come and see what he had found. "You must see this. You won't believe it," he kept saying over and over.

"Okay," they both replied as he led them over to a glass case.

As they looked in, they could see the title of the display, "Ancient Ball Courts." "Just like the ones we saw in Puerto Rico," Pedro said.

As they read down, they learned that this sport probably originated with the Mayans and later spread to the land of the Taínos.

"That may not be correct," Tonino told the boys. He remembered reading a book by Rouse (1992), who questions whether the ball courts of the Taínos really originated in Mesoamerica. Rouse proposes that it was a parallel development, and not a migration of ideas, that resulted in the similarity of the courts and game proper. The Mayan ball court was rectangular, as was the Taínos', while the Hohokam courts were oblong. For both the Mayan and Hohokam game, twelve players were used, while there is no record of the number of players for the Taíno game, which was played by both women and men.

What interested Tonino was that the Hohokam got the rubber material to make the balls from the plant known as Guayule, which is found in the Mexican deserts. It is a natural rubber source and was discovered around 1550 by the Spanish.

Tonino had to show his knowledge about insects so he remarked, "Insects have a special rubber protein called resilin that is even more elastic than natural rubber from plants. It is found at the joints like the legs of fleas and wing base of flying insects. It is also found in the muscles controlling the rapid movement of cicadas tymbal."

Pedro and Ming Ming looked at each other and wondered how he knew so much about insects.

They continued on with their reading; at the end, the written narrative read, "Now, go outside to the ball courts." The boys ran as fast as they could, swerving between people and being careful not to knock anyone over. As they stood on the platform and peered onto the court, they imagined a real live game was going on. Soon, twelve Gambel's quails came running onto the court. They ate something and quickly flew away in different directions. As they looked into the parking lot, Tonino could see Norm and Shirley waiting.

"I'll race you to the car," Pedro said as he got a head start.

Once they piled into the car, Norm said, "Let's get rolling."

On the way to Apache Junction, Shirley asked each boy what he liked about the ruins. Of course, Pedro talked about the similarity of the sport and ball fields of the different groups of people. Ming Ming talked about how he had read that the Hohokams tattooed their bodies.

"Do you have any ideas what the tattoos meant?" Tonino asked.

"No," Ming Ming replied.

Tonino had two things to talk about. First, he noted that the Hohokams made tools from volcanic obsidian, which is as sharp as a surgeon's knife. Second, he was greatly impressed that the Hohokams had developed a system of using canals, very similar to those used by the Romans.

Tonino asked Shirley, "Did you see any hummingbirds?"

"No, I didn't see one, but I did see a cricket."

Tonino asked, "Do you know what kind of cricket it was?"

Shirley responded, "No, I don't know one cricket from another."

Tonino continued, "But you know the names of all the birds. Why not crickets?"

"I guess I just haven't taken the time, plus most crickets are active at night and not so easy to see," Shirley replied.

"Well, sounds like you had a great time and also learned something new," Norm said. "Try to rest. We have about a one-hour ride to Apache Junction."

They arrived an hour later in Apache Junction, gateway to the Superstition Mountains. Sue had arranged for them to stay at a rustic ten-acre ranch. Driving up the private road to the ranch, known as "Meanwhile Back at the Ranch," they saw many cactus and other desert plants along both sides of the bumpy dirt road.

The owner, Joy Bishop, greeted them. Joy is a pleasant, laid-back, charming lady. She made the boys immediately feel comfortable. The ranch backed up to government land next to the Superstition Mountains. They planned to stay here for a couple of days. Tonino was tired and wanted to remain at the cabin, while Ming Ming and Pedro decided to take a short walk.

Tonino, who knew both Pedro and Ming Ming were scared to death of snakes, jokingly said, "Stay on the road because there are lots of rattlesnakes here."

Both boys responded, "Don't worry, we will." They left to explore the surroundings of the ranch.

Norm and Shirley stayed in the old part of the ranch in a spectacular, well-preserved ranch home that looked like a museum. The boys stayed in a small, rustic cabin about fifty feet away from the main ranch home. The large picture glass window of the cabin's bedroom/living room provided a picturesque view of the wonderful desert habitat. The beautiful, rugged, multicolored Superstition Mountains provided the backdrop.

Joy had placed a small birdfeeder just outside the window. She told the boys this attracted a great diversity of birds, desert cottontail, and white-tailed antelope squirrels. Just beyond the window, and the bird feeder, was a mesquite tree. There were also lots of palo verde trees and creosote bushes. Tonino had seen small cactus plants in stores in Boston, but this view gave him an opportunity to see barrel cactus, cholla cactus (twenty species in the genus *Opuntia*), and the magnificent and stately giant saguaro cactus. It was about five o'clock and time for most desert birds to feed, thus avoiding the heat of the desert, which can reach 110 degrees Fahrenheit. Joy had left the book, *50 Common Birds of the Southwest*, on the windowsill for them to use.

First to arrive at the feeder were a male and female black-throated sparrow. Tonino knew from high school biology class that most birds, as some insects, show sexual dimorphism: males are more striking in pattern and color than females. The next to show

157

up was a large curve-billed thrasher. Normally this bird is a ground feeder, but to get to the seed, it landed on the small plastic feeder; its weight and jerky motions caused a lot of the seed to fall to the ground. Then, two cactus wrens, the state bird of Arizona, alighted on another feeder. The weight of the two birds again scattered seed from the feeder onto the ground below.

Tonino's eyes remained focused on the feeder and the two cactus wrens. Suddenly, his eyes were drawn to the ground. In an instant, from out of nowhere, came twelve stocky bluish-gray birds. They almost looked like walking gourds, but to Tonino they looked like little Indians. You don't see them and then all of a sudden they are there. As with many birds, only the males were wearing "war paint." Their faces were black with two white facial stripes, one going from the ear on one side and across the forehead to the other ear, while the other one went from just behind the eye on one side down under the throat and up to just behind the other eye. Just above the white stripe, and above the eyes and across the forehead, was another black line that seemed to support a wonderful, rusty brown cap. To top it off, they had a magnificent black feather, about one inch long, that was central to the head, emerging in front of their cap and curving forward. The central, lone feather drooped down between their eyes. When looking forward, it was out in front and perpendicular to the ground.

Tonino quickly recalled just seeing the black-throated sparrow. It also had facial war paint. In both cases, only the males sported war paint. In addition to the simple, but wonderful headdress, the male Gambel's quail also wore a white apron, kilt, or breechcloth that featured a large black spot. Its wings were beautifully colored brown and spattered with white. As Tonino watched these wonderful little Indians of the desert, he could almost see them dancing as they moved with their rapid leg and feet movements, and their heads going up and down as they fed on the scattered seed.

As the quails kept on dancing, Tonino's mind wandered to the term paper he had written. After writing his term paper on crickets and human culture, Tonino had continued his search for information concerning the involvement of crickets in various cultures. In the cabin, he looked up the word *cricket* in the index of *The Facts on File Encyclopedia of World Mythology and Legend* that was on the shelf.[5] He read the following:

> Tawiskaron (Flint). In North American Indian mythology (Mohawk), an evil being who attempts to build a bridge to allow wild animals to travel so that they can prey on humans. He is foiled in his evil design by Sapling, who sends a blue jay with a cricket's hind legs stuck in its mouth to frighten Tawiskaron. When Tawiskaron sees the sight, he believes it is human legs; he flees, and his bridge disappears.

After visiting *Casa Grande*, everyone had gone to the O'odham Tash, which is the powwow for this group of people. Here Tonino had seen some spectacular hoop, basket, and social dancing. Everyone, including Ming Ming, who doesn't like to dance, participated in the social dance. Tonino remembered this and wanted to join the Gambel's quails in celebrating their finding food. Tonino put down the book, morphed, and squeezed between a small opening at the base of the picture window. He waited a few seconds and hopped down to the ground. At first the quails were startled and dispersed, but then they regrouped under the feeder. *What fun this is*, Tonino thought to himself. He felt safe because he assumed the birds coming to the feeder were seed feeders and not insectivores.

Tonino decided the dancers needed music, so he stopped dancing and began to chirp. Bringing attention to oneself is not the thing to do during the daytime for any cricket. A gray-breasted jay flew down from out of the sky; Tonino did not see it because he was concentrating on chirping. The quails scattered again, and the jay caught Tonino by the hind legs. There was nothing else for him to do but to morph. Quickly, Tonino morphed. This disturbed the gray-breasted jay, who found his pants distasteful and flew away. At that moment, Shirley, who dearly loves birds, came around the corner and saw Tonino on the ground.

"What are you doing lying down there?" she asked.

Before responding to Shirley's question, Tonino looked over his shoulder and saw a large bird land on the forty-foot saguaro cactus, only twenty feet from the cabin. "I wanted to get a ground-eye view of that big bird," he said.

Shirley put her binoculars up to her eyes, looked at the bird, and said, "It's a red-tailed hawk."

Just then, a hummingbird whizzed by within a few inches of Shirley's head, to feed on the bright red flowers of the ocotillo. This plant is not a cactus. Its stems are stuck into the ground, where they root and can be used to make a living fence.

"What kind of hummingbird is that?" Tonino asked Shirley.

"I believe it is a Costa's hummer," Shirley responded. "I just wanted to let you know I am heading up toward Superstition Mountain to go bird watching for a while."

Tonino got up and returned to the cabin, this time through the door. He again took his seat to watch those wonderful little Indians, thinking that his legs could have been left behind in the mouth of the gray-breasted jay. Just as things quieted down, the birds that had returned to the feeder all flew away.

The covey of quail dispersed in different directions like warriors fleeing to confuse an attacker. Here, however, the "attacker" turned out to be Pedro and Ming Ming returning from their walk. Like most city people, they were none too quiet. They threw open the door, came into the room, and then slammed it shut.

"Could you be a little more quiet?" Tonino asked.

"Sure," Ming Ming said, "but what are you doing that requires such silence?"

"Well, I was just watching a small band of Indians dancing under this birdfeeder."

"You've got to be kidding," Pedro said.

"Come here by the window, be very quiet, and watch."

Soon the same band of Indians came out of hiding and began doing their ceremonial dance under the feeder.

"That's great," Ming Ming said.

Tonino couldn't contain himself. He was bursting with ideas. "Do you guys know about independent invention?"

"No, not really," they replied.

"It's when things produced by humans in one part of the world are also made in another part of the world, even though the two groups had no contact. This same principle of independent invention also applies to customs, such as painting or adorning the body. Look at these Gambel's quails. Don't they look like little Indians?" asked Tonino.

"Sort of," Ming Ming responded.

Tonino continued, "It must be through independent invention that the Indians of the American Southwest, and other peoples throughout the world, came up with the idea of body painting, adorning themselves with various materials, and tattooing, which was taken from birds. It is usually only the male bird that is brightly 'painted,' and only the male that engages in battle to defend territory or win a mate. Just like warriors of many cultures."

"I think you are right," replied Ming Ming.

It was getting close to supper so Norm and Shirley agreed to drive them into Apache Junction to eat. During supper Tonino unfolded the map and smoothed it out on the table. He loved geography, and this was his domain. "Where should we go tomorrow?" he asked.

Everyone looked at the map; Ming Ming pointed to a spot and said, "Let's go here!"

Tonino couldn't believe his eyes. Ming Ming's finger was pointing to Grasshopper Junction. Immediately, Tonino thought of his grasshopper cousin, Carlo.

Everyone agreed, "That sounds great."

Tonino thought to himself, *I wonder why they gave it the name 'Grasshopper'?*

After dinner they returned to the ranch. It was a full moon and very light out. As they drove up the road to the cabin, Pedro shouted, "Look, there are four dogs in the road."

"Be quiet, you idiot!" Tonino said. "Those are coyotes, not dogs, but they won't hurt you."

Norm stopped the car and everyone watched as the four coyotes headed off into the desert. When they got back to the ranch, they all went to bed; everyone said at the same time, "Good night."

As usual, Tonino couldn't get to sleep until he read something. He pulled his recently purchased book out of his backpack. Of all the plants listed, Tonino was surprised to learn that the yucca was the most important plant for most of the Native Americans of the Southwest; the yucca contains fifteen different species and is widely distributed. Its roots contained saponin, which has soaplike qualities; when mixed with water, saponin produces a liquid that natives used to wash, not only themselves, but also their clothes. In addition, they consume the flower stalks, blossoms, and seeds of the yucca. Tonino smiled as he read, "The leaf mass was eaten like a giant artichoke." Immediately he remembered eating breadfruit in Puerto Rico with Pedro's family and how he told the story about how his father taught him how to eat artichokes. The yucca's leaves were also soaked in water and pounded to produce fibers that could be made into sandals, rope, or clothing.

He read further and learned that some Apache tribes used the juice from the young yucca flower stalks to make *pulque,* an intoxicating drink. Tonino also learned that distilling *pulque* makes tequila. Just before he fell asleep, he read about the mesquite shrub, which is very drought tolerant because of its deep penetrating roots. The natives collected seeds or seedpods, stored them for winter, and later pounded the seeds and mixed them with water to form a mush that was eaten as is or dried to form cakes that were easily transported for long trips.

White Mountain Apaches—Grasshopper Junction

Following a brief breakfast, everyone headed off to Grasshopper Junction. They entered the land of the White Mountain Apaches, whose economy was originally based on waging war. The word *Apache* is of Spanish origin but is believed to be a corruption of the Zuni word that means "enemy." The Apaches were great warriors and earned the name "enemy" because they raided the Pueblo people and Mexicans and took whatever they wanted. There are six subtribes of the Apache Nation, whose people settled the Southwest around AD 850. It is a matriarchal society. They also are transformers—they believe that coyotes, insects, and other animals were once human beings.

As they arrived on Apache land, Norm said, "I guess we should head up to the cultural center so that we can get back to Apache Junction before dark."

At the cultural center, Tonino found a book, Teiwes's *Western Apache Material Culture: The Goodwin and Guenther Collection,* and snuggled into a soft chair in a corner of the lodge. Shirley and Norm went off birding, while Pedro and Ming Ming explored the outdoors. Tonino was surprised to learn that the Apache and the Navajo speak the language of the Athapaskans, and that they both are related to the Alaskan, Western Canada, and Northwest Coast Indians. Unlike the Puebloan peoples, the Apaches and Navajos both arrived in the Southwest during the sixteenth century. The Apache were not agriculturists, but were hunters and gatherers. The men used bows and arrows to hunt local game.

One of the main plant foods was the ikaz (i.e., agave or mescal). They used a digging stick and a knife made of stone to harvest the agave. It was hard work and mainly carried on by men. They could harvest hundreds of mescal heads, stems, and leaves in a day. They look like trimmed artichokes, but much, much bigger. These would then be roasted in pits and eaten that day. They would pound the roasted agave root into cakes and sun-dry them for later consumption. Using a *metate* and *manos,* they ground various types of seeds, including corn (once it was introduced into the region).

They drank two types of intoxicating beverages, *pulque,* made from the young flower stalks, and corn beer, which they probably inherited from the Mexicans. And of course, they ate fry bread. Eating fry bread reminded Tonino of the festivals at Our Lady of Mount Carmel church. He and his friends loved the fried pizza dough with tomato sauce on top.

Tonino learned about the unique way the Apache carried water, using a saguaro "boot." The more commonly used water container, however, was the pitched basket. The water basket is made from squawberry or sumac. To make it waterproof, they first caulked it with ground juniper leaf paste and then sealed it with hot pine pitch using a paintbrush made from the frayed end of a yucca leaf. Since they were great warriors, and often traveled great distances, it was essential that they had both water and food.

To use a saguaro "boot," they had to find a dead cactus. Then they would look for the boot to use as a water or food container. Tonino wondered how this boot is made. He read on and found out that the gila woodpecker makes a hole for its nest in the giant saguaro. To form the boot, a cactus wren has to take over a nest the woodpecker has abandoned. In other words, it is a bird joint effort. The cactus, in turn, produces a callus, like a scar, around the wound so that bacteria and fungi don't attack the living plant tissue. This callus, often shaped like a gourd, becomes the boot. An Apache would carry water in these containers, and his food was dried mescal cakes.

The Apaches became masters at tanning hides and doing elaborate leatherwork. Tonino was pleased to learn that hummingbirds provided the link between the Apache's world and the supernatural. They guided the spirits of the dead to the upper world. The Apache *gaan* dancers served as intermediaries between the supernatural spirits.

Tonino knew time was drawing short so he decided to read something about the sports and musical instruments of the Apache. There were two games played by Apache that interested Tonino. One was called hoop-and-pole, and the other was Shinney ball. The latter game interested Tonino because it reminded him of hockey; he remembered how every winter in Boston, all the young boys carried hockey sticks to school. The ball was usually made of buckskin and stuffed with agave fibers. Their Shinney sticks were made of mesquite or mountain-mahogany. They were about three feet long and were crooked on the end.

Drums were used for both social and ceremonial events. The men made flutes out of reeds, and young men used them to court a woman. The flutes usually had a symbol of the butterfly cut and burned into it. This is because the butterfly and flutes have a long tradition in Apache courtship culture and mythology. Tonino read about how the Apache men played flutes decorated with hummingbirds to attract a woman. He recalled the myths surrounding Kokopeli, the hunchbacked flute player.

Apaches made bows with one to three strings, and fiddles were made out of the flower stalks of the agave or century plant. They used horsehair for the strings. As he started to close the book, Tonino saw pictures of Apache houses. These were called *gowas* or wikiups and were made of long branches covered with brush or hides. They were like a tent.

Time was running out, and Tonino had to stop reading. He returned the book to the shelf and made sure to record the reference. *When I get home I can order the book online,* he said to himself.

After all his reading, Tonino still didn't know why this area had been named after the grasshopper. When he returned the book he was reading to the shelf, he noticed another book, by Reid and Whittlesey, *Grasshopper Pueblo: A Story of Archaeology and Ancient*

Life.[6] He had little time so he skimmed it. He soon found his answer:

"Spring and camp on Fort Apache Indian Reservation, at head of Salt River Draw. So called as early as 1880 after a lame Apache woman whom the Indians call 'Naz-chug-gee' (Grasshopper) from her peculiar limp. She had one short leg which caused the limp."

The book also notes that many Apaches say that the name came from the numerous grasshoppers found in that area, but because they lacked a written language, no one will every really know. Tonino could accept either explanation. *Almost like the myths and legends of Kokopeli, who also had a body deformation or unusual way of walking,* Tonino thought to himself.

On his way to the car, Tonino silently made a note, *Don't forget the great Apache chiefs like Geronimo and Cochise.*

Before getting into the car, Norm asked the boys, "Do you have any questions?"

"I hate to dwell on grasshoppers, but they seem to be a problem in many parts of the world. I was wondering if any plants try to 'fight back,' so to speak, when grasshoppers try to eat them."

"Yes, there is a good example of that. You may have heard of Dr. Elizabeth Bernays from the University of Arizona in Tucson. Well, she studied the grasshopper and showed that one of the defenses of the cassava plant is that when the grasshopper bites into the leaves, a toxin in the cassava's cells is converted into hydrogen cyanide, a deadly poison."

Tonino couldn't contain himself. He was jumping around and couldn't wait to be recognized.

"Yes, Tonino, what is it?" said Shirley.

"When I was in Puerto Rico with Pedro, I learned that cassava was the main staple of food for the Taínos and that even today, people eating the cassava root have to be very careful to get rid of the toxin, otherwise they can be poisoned. Once they got rid of the poison, they would make cassava cakes or bread."

Phoenix and the Heard Museum

"Is there anything else you want to see in this area?" Norm asked the boys.

Tonino responded, "I would like to see the Heard Museum."

Pedro asked, "But why?"

"Because when we were at Sue's house, I noticed she had many dolls on a shelf, and when I asked her about them, she said they were kachina dolls, and we would learn more about them as our trip continued. Since then, I have gone online and learned that the Heard Museum in Phoenix has around 500 Hopi dolls, including many from the collection of Senator Barry Goldwater. Also, you know I love museums, and this is considered one of the best for Native American culture and art."

So, off they went to Phoenix. As they entered the parking lot, they noticed the beautiful Spanish architecture of the Heard. Once inside, and while waiting in line to pay, Tonino said, "I would like to get the self-guided narrative tour of gallery 6, Native Peoples of the Southwest."

Tonino and Pedro both decided on this gallery. Norm and Shirley went to gallery 8, which is the Jacobson gallery of Indian art, while Ming Ming went off alone to the Ullman Learning Center. They all agreed to meet in an hour at the gift shop and bookstore. Tonino and Pedro put the string supporting the self-guided narrative around their necks and headed off to gallery 6.

The first exhibit described the major types of Indians in the Southwest (e.g., Sonoran desert people, uplands people, and Colorado plateau people). As they moved along, they learned that the O'odham people were divided into the Tohono O'odham, the Akimel O'odham, and the Pima (River People). They also learned that the Mohave women tattooed their faces in the late 1800s, using a cactus needle to puncture the skin and charcoal from the mesquite as the pigment. The narrative explained how each clan had different tattoos and gave the example of the roadrunner and butterflies, but said other animals were also tattooed on men's faces.

To paint their bodies, they used various minerals mixed with deer fat. The paint also protected their faces against biting insects and the sun. Tonino enjoyed learning how the baskets woven of plant material were made waterproof by dipping them in boiled pine pitch. Of course, this reminded him of the amber experiences he dreamt about and the method used by the Apache men when making their water containers. Tonino didn't want to forget anything, so he made a list of things he wanted to remember to tell Shirley and Norm, and also his parents and Joe. To do this, he put the following facts into his diary:

The Navajo or Dine is the largest tribe in the United States. Spiderman taught these people how to make the tools for weaving (i.e., the loom and the shuttle). Spiderwoman taught these people how to weave. Four sacred mountains circle the Navajos, and the number 4, unlike 3 for Christians, is important to them.

The tape continued. "These people used the tips of the yucca leaves to make fiber paintbrushes. Once introduced, corn became an important food. It also became the cornerstone of their culture. The narrator in the tape then told Pedro and Tonino to go left and into the room housing the katsina (in Hopi) or tihu. Once there, they were told about the collection and the significance of the dolls. Pedro and Tonino walked in front of the large glass case of tihu. Tonino looked at several dolls and then abruptly stopped at the seventh. There it was! It was only about seven to nine inches tall, with a white face and head with three dark black spots, two for eyes and one for the mouth. The doll had branches of a small plant for its antenna, with a white feather between them. Around its neck was a scarf of white and black stripes. It had a yellow string around its right wrist and a green one around its left wrist. Tied around each thigh was some black yarn, and around each ankle was tied a cornhusk. The breechcloth was completely black, with one red stripe and one green stripe. In his right hand was a gourd rattle, while he held something in his left hand that Tonino couldn't identify. The sign said "Sösööpa, the cricket, circa 1939."

Pedro noticed that Tonino had stopped, so he went to see what his friend's eyes were fixed on in the case. He seemed mesmerized by what he was looking at. Tonino thought for a minute, scratched his head like his father always did, and said, "Go ahead, I'll be with you in a moment." As Pedro left the room, Tonino turned to look at the cricket tihu. The longer he stared at it, the more his imagination took over. He almost convinced himself that Sösööpa moved his eyes as he moved to his right. *This is spooky,* he said to himself. He gave his own eyes a hard blink to regain his composure. Then he quickly looked at the other tihu in the case. None of them seemed to move, so he moved to his right. Before him was a spectacular exhibit concerning the butterfly dance of the Hopis. Tonino learned that the butterfly dance was used in early August, and young men and unmarried women danced together. The women wore beautifully painted tabletas attached to their heads by string, made from agave fibers. The general term for tableta is kopatsoki, which means "that which sits on top of the head," while the specific name for the butterfly tableta is polikopatsoki. The next exhibit showed a Hopi wedding robe and the embroidered line that is supposed to represent the umbilical cord.

As he moved to the left, he came to a spot that was just across from Sösööpa. Again, Tonino had a funny feeling. He turned around quickly and was convinced that Sösööpa was waving his left hand at him. What was in his hand still remained a mystery. This was too much for Tonino. He hurried through the rest of the exhibits in the gallery.

Tonino reached the gift shop just in time. Everyone was waiting to leave. "Just one minute, please," he said. "I would like to buy something." He went to the shop and found the katsina section. He asked the clerk, "Do you have a cricket katsina?"

"Yes, I have some in the back room. I will get one if you want me to."

"Yes, please hurry, because my friends are anxious to leave."

Soon, she came back with a katsina. It didn't look anything like the one in the Goldwater collection. The price was $165, far too costly for Tonino. "Could you find out who carved it?"

"Sure!" When she returned, she had written down the name and location of the artist: Debbie Toopkewa from the First Mesa in northern Arizona.

As Tonino left to find the car, he wondered why the cricket katsinas were so different from one another. He got into the car and Norm drove off to their motel.

"Well, what did you like about the museum?" Norm asked.

Tonino was first to respond. "I really liked the Goldwater collection of katsina dolls."

"Did you like any special doll?"

"Yes, I really liked Sösööpa, the cricket katsina."

Pedro and Ming Ming looked at each other and grinned; they knew what Norm would ask next. As they predicted, Norm asked Tonino, "Why a cricket katsina and not something else?"

The boys also knew what Tonino's response would be. "Well, I just liked it, but there was something else about it. It was carved in 1939, and I believe that is the year Dr. Stoffolano was born." Norm was on Dr. Stoffolano's doctoral committee at the University of Connecticut in Storrs, so he knew who Tonino was talking about.

"Well, you should tell him about that when you see him," Norm said.

"I will," responded Tonino.

The Hopi

That evening, while sitting in the motel lobby, everyone said they wanted to visit a Hopi Indian reservation. The boys remembered the wonderful pictures of various Indian sites hanging on the living room walls at Sue's house. They especially remembered one particular doll. They did not see one like this at the Heard. Pedro had asked Sue at the time, "What is this type of doll?" and Sue responded, "That is a Hopi spotted corn kachina doll. You will learn more about kachinas when you go to Arizona."

Tonino also remembered having a dream the same evening he learned about the kachina doll. He dreamt his father was helping Pinocchio the marionette, a different type of doll that is manipulated by strings, dance over him while he was still in bed.

"Will we see kachina dolls at the reservations?" Ming Ming asked.

Shirley said, "We will see kachina dolls and possibly some kivas."

Tonino's ears (not his tympanum) perked up. He remembered going into the kiva at the Coronado Museum in New Mexico, and he really wanted to go into one that was still in use. They continued their discussion about their trip to Hopi country. Tonino had more questions about kivas and their significance. Norm and Shirley didn't ask Tonino why he was interested in them, but assumed it was his natural curiosity.

Norm explained that since 1900, most pueblos refused to let any non-Indians into the kivas. "These are sacred places," he said, "and because the Franciscan missionaries burned their baskets, dance masks, and other ritualistic items, they had to restrict entry to the kivas to Indians."

At one time, the Spanish forbade the Hopis from using the kivas, prevented them from practicing religious ceremonies, and forced them into slavery. Tonino was disappointed that he would not get to go into a kiva at the reservation, but he certainly understood why the Hopis restricted them. Again, the repression of one culture by another culture continued to trouble Tonino. He knew, however, his mission was to be concerned with environmental issues and not the social or cultural ones. Even though this was the charge given to him by the Blue Fairy, he felt the environmental issues should come after resolving the social issues.

Norm told the boys, "Well, get a good night's sleep because tomorrow we head off to the Second Mesa to learn more about the Hopi culture."

The next morning, after a good breakfast, they headed off to Hopi land.

Hopi and Katsinas

"Today," Shirley said, "we will go to the Hopi Cultural Center on the Second Mesa, where there is a museum and gift shop." She added, "A kachina (in English), or more correctly *katsina* (in Hopi), is a supernatural being that lives in high places. These supernatural beings usually represent a spirit of a plant or animal, or even inanimate objects." Tonino thought, *In other words, they are transformers.*

Tonino recalled another supporting bit of evidence that the idea of transformation or metamorphosis existed in the Mimbreño culture from the *Mimbres Pottery* book; Hopi consultants had been asked to comment on a bowl depicting a human with animal (possibly rabbit) traits. The picture caption says, "Some thought the picture was intended to demonstrate that animals were really humans inside who shed their animal skins at night and then lived as humans." Tonino liked this statement very much, especially the part about shedding skins. Remember, however, that arthropods shed their exoskeletons, not their skins. Their exoskeletons are very different from human skin even though they serve similar functions.

"In no way are these supernatural beings the same as their gods or deities," Shirley explained. "Only a few of their gods are ever represented by katsinas. One place where the supernatural katsinas live is the San Francisco Peaks near Flagstaff."

There are three basic forms of a katsina: the supernatural being, the masked impersonator of the supernatural being, and the small katsina dolls, which are made in the likeness of the masked impersonator. Each one of these forms serves a function in the lives of the Hopi. The supernatural being is like a god and has been created in the minds of the people. They usually represent significant things, such as animals or plants. During the year there are five major religious ceremonies that include katsinas: *Soyalang-eu,* or Winter Solstice Ceremony; *Pamuya*; *Powamuya,* or Bean Ceremony; *Palölökonti,* or Water Serpent Ceremony; and *Niman* Kachina, or Home Dance Ceremony. Following the Niman dance, the kachinas return to their mountain homes. In December, after the winter solstice, the kachina spirits live among the Hopis in their villages; during that time, kiva and plaza dances are performed by the kachina dancers. Each of the ceremonies lasts nine days and usually takes place in the kiva.

Tonino realized that of all the deities of the Hopis Shirley had talked about, he liked *Kokyang Wu-uti,* or Spider Woman, the best.

At the cultural center and museum, they learned a lot more about kivas than they did at the Coronado Museum. A kiva is a special underground room that is usually near the plaza of the Pueblo Indians. The only way to enter this religious room is through a trap door and down a wooden ladder. Tonino knew about this because he climbed down the ladder of one at the Coronado Monument. Their functions range from religious to ceremonial; they are also used for assembly. Each kiva differs as to what is found in it. Usually there is a fire pit, an ash pit, an altar, and niches in the walls for storing ceremonial materials or offerings. Many kivas also have elaborate wall paintings that depict religious ceremonies, mythical creatures, and legends. A *sipapu* or small hole is located in the floor and is believed to be the way the first people emerged from the underworld. The dancing katsinas often perform here during certain religious ceremonies.

The Hopis, Pueblo Indians who live on a high plateau in northern Arizona, get their name from a contraction of the Shoshonean *hopitu*, which means "peaceful." The earliest village, Oraibi, is located on the Third Mesa; based on tree ring dating, it is from about AD 1125. The Hopi people are agriculturists, irrigating lands and growing corn, beans, cotton, melons, and squash. They are known mainly for their colorful ceremonial dress and their katsina dolls.

Not all of the ceremonies involve masked, dancing katsinas. Depending on the ceremony, the dancing and masked katsinas can perform in the kiva or in the plaza for everyone to see. The major sound produced by the dancing katsinas comes from the tortoise shell rattles attached to their legs and the handheld rattles made from gourds. While they are dancing, they sing various songs that are appropriate to that ceremony. If the dance is in the plaza, the dancers distribute gifts to the children once they have completed their dance. During intermission, clown katsinas perform and entertain the children and the rest of the audience. Once a man—and only men can be katsinas—puts on the mask, body paint, and other apparel of a particular katsina, he assumes the spirit of the katsina he is representing and loses his own identity.

Tonino came to a wall display and read the narrative very, very carefully because it really applied to him. "In addition to wearing a mask, dancing katsinas usually cover their bodies by wearing a costume and body paint. Thus, the dancing katsina is transformed from the human form to the form of whatever the katsina represents. These dancing katsinas are believed to be intermediaries between the people and the god they represent."

"Oh, I get it," said Pedro, who is Catholic. "It's like our saints."

"That's correct," Shirley said.

"You said earlier there were three forms of katsinas, but you have only told us about the supernatural and masked or dancing form. What are the katsina dolls used for?" Ming Ming asked.

"The katsina dolls are given to the children during special ceremonies by a male relative who makes it for them. The doll usually looks like the dancing or masked katsina who is giving the gift. These dolls are not really toys but are used to help educate the children as to the type of spirit the katsina doll represents in their religion, and also to help them learn the different types of katsinas. Today, there are well over 300 different katsina dolls."

"Are there female katsinas?" asked Tonino.

Shirley responded, "Only in the supernatural form and the doll form. Remember, only the men can take the position of being a dancing masked katsina."

Shirley then launched into a lengthy discussion about making the dolls from the dried, gnarled roots of the cottonwood trees (also called the "water tree" because its roots are able to find water in very dry conditions).

For Tonino, the most interesting aspect of doll making was the place where the maker got the black paint. One source was the soot from corn smut, which is a fungus. In fact, just the day before Tonino had seen a can of corn smut in the grocery store.

When he asked about it, Shirley said, "It is commonly eaten by Mexicans. They also eat a lot of different kinds of insects."

Tonino was surprised to hear this and thought to himself, *I wonder if a lot of cultures eat insects?*

When they left the museum, Tonino had a flashback to when he was growing up. He had had a few dolls, but what he liked most of all was the puppet of Pinocchio his parents had given him. He never really was successful in getting it to work properly. He always got the strings all tangled up. His father, however, could make it dance and would even sing as the wooden doll danced. "I can't wait to see more katsina dolls," he told everyone.

Hopis, Plaza, Kiva, and Tourism

Since the Hopis rely on tourism, accommodations were available in the village, not far from the central plaza. Shirley and Norm went to their room to put their suitcases away while the boys removed their backpacks and put them in their room. They then assembled on the plaza, where they began their tour of the pueblo. Many things looked similar to the Taos and Picuran pueblos they had seen in New Mexico. Finally, they entered the main arts and crafts center. The boys immediately gravitated to the far wall that had shelf upon shelf of katsina dolls. These colorful dolls varied in size from a few inches high to several feet tall and took the form of very different spirits. There were so many different kinds that after a while they gave up trying to figure out what each one represented.

Tonino turned to Pedro and said, "Do you remember another type of carving that you and I saw together?"

Pedro thought a moment. "No, I don't."

"Well, let me give you some help. We were at the Puerto Rican Museum of History, Archeology, and Anthropology in San Juan."

"Oh, yes. Now I remember. The time I told you about the *santos.*"

"Correct," Tonino said. "It is interesting that, for both the Hopi and the Puerto Ricans, carvings serve as spiritual connections."

"True," replied Pedro.

Before long, Norm informed them they would be going to dinner. They ate at the lodge within the community, where they had a very interesting selection of native foods. Everyone loved the piki bread, which is made on a flat hot stone from blue corn meal. Full and tired, it was time to retire. It wasn't really late, but both of his friends were extremely tired.

"It could be the altitude," Tonino said. "Remember what I told you Sue said about Santa Fe and her altitude problem."

Because of his curious nature, Tonino couldn't wait until Pedro and Ming Ming went to sleep. He knew that under certain circumstances, it was best to explore a new area as a cricket. As soon as he was sure both Pedro and Ming Ming were asleep, Tonino arranged his bed and fluffed up his pillow so no one would suspect he wasn't there. Quietly, he transformed and headed toward the door of their room.

He crawled under the door; he could now hear faint sounds of chanting and drumming in the distance. To focus on where the sound was coming from, he would alternate lifting his left foreleg and then his right foreleg, each time exposing the inner portion of the tibia, which housed the tympanum or eardrum. By doing this, he could locate the source of a sound. The drumming was coming from the north corner of the plaza. As he hopped over to that area, the sound became louder.

Being in cricket form, what would be a small crack to a human became a big crevasse to him. He didn't realize it, but he also was feeling a little dizzy, possibly because of the altitude. As he got closer to the drumming, he became so excited to see what was going on he started to hop too fast. Before he knew it, he was falling, falling, falling down into a crack in the ground; he landed in a dimly lit room.

It was a long drop for a cricket, probably ten feet. Fortunately, he landed in a pot filled with dried bean seeds that was placed on the deflecting structure near the ladder. It was just like landing in two to three feet of tennis balls. It reminded him of the church festival every summer, where he had seen children jumping up and down and landing, not on beans, but different colored tennis balls.

Tonino just lay there for several minutes, collecting his thoughts, catching his breath, and figuring out where he was. As he looked around, he realized that he was in a kiva. The first thing that caught the attention of his compound eyes were the beautiful wall paintings.

He also knew that the light was dim in the kiva because his ocelli, or simple eyes, sent this message to his brain, or control center. The ocelli serve as detectors of light intensity. All that he could make out in the murals, as the light from the central fire flickered from bright to dim, were large animals like deer and sheep, stalks of corn, and a stylistic figure of a hunchbacked flute player. He could count about thirty people inside the kiva. Some of them were seated around the fire pit, a few were placing offerings in the special indentations of the wall, and about six were getting ready to dance. Tonino knew, based on what Shirley had told them about the masks the dancers wore, they would be dancing a mixed katsina dance. This is where each mask and costume is different. As the dancers took their places, Tonino became more excited. He shifted his weight back and forth a couple of times so that he would be more comfortable in the beautifully decorated bean pot. From this vantage point, he could see quite well. He said to himself, *Well, I finally made it into a functioning kiva.*

What was also exciting to him was that every dancer, except one, symbolized an insect. As they started dancing past him, he recognized the following katsinas: bee, hornet, cricket, cicada, butterfly, and dragonfly. He recognized the last dancer as *kokopölö*, or Kokopeli. He knew that Kokopeli was the legendary hunchbacked flute player, but why was he in with all these insects?

Time was flying, and Tonino figured they had been dancing for about an hour. The heat from the fire pit had since warmed up the kiva; it had also warmed up Tonino. This made him more active. Since he is cold-blooded, like all insects, his body temperature usually takes on that of the surrounding environment. Thus, when he landed in the pot, the temperature in the kiva was much cooler and his body metabolism was much slower. In fact, it was so warm now that he felt like chirping. Without thinking where he was, Tonino started to stridulate. Because it was very warm, the speed of his song was at its maximum. Just as he finished a few notes, he looked up and saw the cricket katsina standing in front of him. He knew it was Sösööpa because he had seen the doll rendition in the Heard Museum. Tonino realized this was going to be a repeat of when Shaquille O'Neal had grabbed him in the locker room at the Boston Garden. Down came the hand over his body, the fingers closed up, and he was gently being squeezed. This time, however, the hand was much smaller.

The next thing Tonino knew, he was thrown into a clay pot known as a seed-pot. It was a narrow pot, and the sides were too steep for him to crawl up or jump out. It was designed to keep mice from eating the seeds stored in the pot during the winter. There was no top, so he could hear everything. Because everything was being spoken in the Hopi language, he quickly asked the spirit of Grillo-parlante to make him fluent in Hopi. The Blue Fairy interceded and granted him his wish. It was late and she was not happy about being awakened at two o'clock in the morning.

What the cricket katsina was saying was that the great-spirit *Alosaka,* also known as *Muy-ingwa* or the germ-god, was sending them good spirits (or in some cultures, good mana). *Alosaka* lives in the underworld and is the god of reproduction for man, animals, and plants. It had been a week without rain, and rain was badly needed for the corn crop.

"This cricket was sent to us by *Alosaka* as a sign of good luck," the cricket katsina said.

Everyone in the kiva was excited and thankful for this good sign. Tonino's presence in cricket form also agreed with much of the mythology about crickets in other parts of the world. Because of his high school history project, Tonino knew that crickets represented different things to different cultures and fall into four major categories: crickets are deliverers of good or bad luck; they are forecasters of death or rain; they are used in folk medicine; and they are the personification of the house-spirit. In this particular situation, and in his cricket form, he was the deliverer of good luck because he was forecasting the coming of badly needed rain. Because of this, he knew he wouldn't be harmed, but how was he going to get back to his room? What Tonino didn't know was that when a cricket gets into the home of a Hopi, everyone tries to locate it and kill it once they hear its chirping. Because crickets like to hide in cracks, it is believed that they cause these undesirable cracks; because this was a kiva, and not a home, the men in the kiva would probably feel different about this cricket.

It was getting late, and Tonino wondered how he was going to get out of there. Suddenly, the dancing cricket katsina took the pot with Tonino inside and started climbing up the wooden ladder to the outside. Tonino could feel the movement as the dancer, whose name was David, climbed the ladder. Once outside, Tonino could see part of the sky with its great array of stars on display.

As the dancer entered his house, he said to his wife, Rena, "Look, *Alosaka* has sent us a good sign."

As Rena stared into the jar, Tonino stared right back. "You should put a stone over the opening," she said, "so the cricket doesn't get out."

"I will," David said, "but if a mouse can't get in, I doubt a cricket can get out."

Tonino figured that it was now around midnight. Little did he know that it was actually two in the morning. He knew he had to develop a quick plan to get out of this pot and back into bed before Pedro and Ming Ming woke up. *"One wish I have never used was to be invisible and walk through solid objects, such as walls or doors. I don't know what Grillo-parlante's spirit is going to think of my having two wishes in the same day, but here goes."*

Of course, Tonino had awakened the Blue Fairy now for the second time, and she was really grumpy. "In order to avoid this situation from happening again, I will also automatically grant you an extension on your first wish. I will make you completely multilingual. The only catch is that, if you abuse the language you have been given access to in any way, you will become a very silent cricket regardless of what form you are in. Also, if you abuse the ability of being invisible at any time, you will remain forever in the form you are in at the time of the wish."

These were strong words, and troublesome for Tonino. What if he was in his human form and he could never get back to being a cricket? He just couldn't think about that, because he would miss his mother and father in their cricket form too much even though he would see them once in a while as humans. We all know, Tonino preferred to be in cricket form. After giving Tonino a good scolding, the Blue Fairy said, "I grant you this wish."

Being invisible and able to walk through solid objects meant Tonino could hop right through the pot, which he proceeded to do. Once outside the pot, he could see he was at the foot of David and Rena's bed. He knew they were asleep because he could hear them breathing. Silently, he hopped to the door. In order to avoid another accident, like the one that happened earlier, he decided to transform. This would accomplish two things: first, it would prevent him from falling into holes or cracks in the plaza, and second, he could get back to his room faster. As he crawled under the door, however, he morphed too soon. The heel of his sneaker caught the bottom of the door, just enough to make a noise and wake up David.

David removed the stone and checked the pot. To his surprise, it was empty. He went to the open door and saw a young boy running across the plaza. David was sure he would recognize the boy the next day because the light from the full moon gave him a good look at Tonino's face every time Tonino turned to see if anyone was following him.

When Tonino reached the lodge, he jumped into bed, arranged his pillow, and tried to go to sleep. All he could say to himself before he went to sleep was, *That was close! Thanks, Blue Fairy! Everyone should have their own Blue Fairy.*

The next day following breakfast, everyone was called into the plaza. The elder, whose name was Joseph Sando, was standing next to David. Joseph spoke first and told everyone what had happened. He told them that *Alosaka* had given a sign, the presence of a cricket in the kiva, to announce the ending of the draught. He then turned to David, who told everyone how this cricket had vanished from the pot with a stone on top of it. "This is truly a good sign; this must be a very powerful cricket," he said to those gathered.

It was a custom of the Hopis to honor one of their guests at the plaza gathering. It was David's turn to pick out the guest and decide how he would be honored.

As David walked amongst the visitors seated on the plaza, he recognized the young boy he had seen fleeing across the plaza. He pointed to Tonino to come forward. All Tonino could think was, *This will blow my cover.*

He then realized Shirley, Norm, Pedro, and Ming Ming would never believe it. As Tonino walked up to David, they both looked at one another straight in the eyes. Tonino knew David was aware of his secret. David didn't say anything about what had happened. He knew in his heart this was a special boy who could transform from a cricket into a human and vice versa. In fact, they both had a lot in common. You see, no one in the village, not even David's wife, knew he was the dancing cricket katsina, and none of Tonino's friends knew he was really a cricket.

As David led Tonino into the center of the plaza, he said something to one of his Hopi friends, who left, but immediately returned with a katsina in his hands. David said something to everyone in Hopi, turned to Tonino, and handed him the katsina. Since Tonino could now understand all languages, he knew he was being given a Sösööpa *tihu*. The visitors did not realize the katsina represented the bringer of rain, but it was obvious to Tonino he was getting a cricket katsina doll.

Before Tonino left, David said to him, "Thank you for visiting me and my people and bringing us good luck. Your spirit will live long in my heart."

As they walked away from the plaza, Pedro asked Tonino, "What did he mean you brought his people good luck?"

"I have no idea," replied Tonino.

Everyone went back to the lodge to get their belongings. Tonino carefully wrapped up his new Sösööpa *tihu*, because dry cottonwood is very fragile.

Pedro noticed that something was wrong. "What is it?" he asked.

"It's a cricket katsina, but it's not exactly like the one I saw in the Heard Museum."

"What do you mean?" Pedro asked.

"This one is yellowish-brown, while that one was white."

"Why the difference?" asked Pedro.

"I am not quite sure," responded Tonino. "I will have to think about it."

Everyone met in the parking lot. In addition to Norm and Shirley, there was a woman Tonino didn't recognize. "This is Dr. Karen Oberhauser," Shirley said. "Karen is very active in monarch butterfly research and also in teaching teachers about ecology and behavior. Karen has agreed to take you to California to the monarch festival. She readily agreed to do this, especially when she heard that Tonino was one of the young boys who helped save the migrating monarch butterflies."

"Pleasure to meet you," the boys chimed in.

Sue had told Norm and Shirley that the boys loved books, so in the parking lot everyone received a book. "Now don't open them until you are on the road to California. It will give you something to do during the trip," Norm said.

The boys replied, "Thank you," to Norm and Shirley, and everyone exchanged hugs. Karen put their belongings into her van, the boys hopped in, and Norm and Shirley watched as they drove off.

Heading to Pacific Grove for the Monarch Festival

As they departed, the boys looked out the windows and saw Dr. Davis and Shirley waving good-bye. Tonino found the presence of Karen a good omen since she was interested in studying the monarch butterfly. It would be a long trip to Pacific Grove, and the boys were thankful for the books they received. Tonino, however, had been thinking about the different colors of the two cricket katsinas: one white, the other yellowish-brown.

"I think I know why the katsinas are different colors," Tonino said to Pedro.

"Well, tell me," responded Pedro as he gently poked Tonino.

"I think the white one in the Heard Museum is a cricket that has just molted. You know, when any arthropod molts, its cuticle or exoskeleton is white. Once it has molted, it takes awhile to darken, or what we call melanization. That explains it," responded Tonino.

"How do you know that?" Pedro asked.

"From practical experience," responded Tonino.

Pedro looked at Tonino in amazement and said, "I wonder about you sometimes."

Karen was not very talkative, so the boys had plenty of time to read. She was focusing on the meeting that was to take place when they arrived. She would be speaking about the genetically engineered corn plant and the effect on monarchs feeding on genetically altered pollen. Thus, the boys didn't wait too long to open their presents. They opened their packages and agreed that, as they read their books, each would share special things with the others when they encountered what they considered interesting information. Tonino's present was a book, *Chasing Monarchs: Migrating with the Butterflies of Passage,* by Robert Michael Pyle. Karen had read the book and told Tonino that he would enjoy reading it. As Tonino scanned the table of contents, he saw there was a chapter about the Pacific Coast overwintering site, which included information about Pacific Grove.

It was a long trip. The boys slept and read a lot. Finally, they reached California. It was the first time any of the boys had been on the West Coast.

Chapter 9.

The Monarch Parade and Old Acquaintances

As they entered the small community of Pacific Grove, population around 32,000, which is located on the Monterey Peninsula of California, Tonino noticed the granite sculpture of the monarch by sculptor Gordon Newell, which is located on the waterfront. It was the beginning of the annual Monarch Days Celebrations, which commemorate the return of the monarchs to their overwintering sites. Monarchs west of the Mississippi fly here to spend the winter months instead of to the Mexican *refugia*.

Karen stopped at the information booth to pick up a brochure listing all the events for this great celebration. Ming Ming liked parades and mentioned to the others that the annual Butterfly Parade would take place while they were there. Tonino, however, was more interested in the academic aspects of the celebration and read that there would be a series of lectures about monarchs. Two important scientists were listed as speakers: Dr. Brower would speak on conservation biology and the future of the Mexico *refugia*, and Dr. Orley Taylor was speaking on how the monarchs know where they are going during migration. He scanned down and noted that Karen was also giving a talk. "I can't wait to hear what you have to say," Tonino told her. Going to these talks was a must for Tonino.

Karen then drove to the Feather Bed Inn, which had a lovely room with a fireplace and Jacuzzi. Tonino liked the name, because of the fact that some bird, probably a goose or more likely several geese, gave their feathers to help make the comforters.

It was getting late and everyone was tired. After a small dinner, they all retired. The next day the weather was spectacular. It was crispy clear with great billowy, white clouds scattered on a brilliant blue background. Today they would go see where the monarchs were spending the winter.

As they approached the Monarch Butterfly Sanctuary, Tonino and the boys became very excited. They remembered the wonderful winter vacation they spent in Mexico with Dr. Brower. They entered the sanctuary and began the tour. Everyone was emphatically instructed not to touch the butterflies, even if they looked dead. The eucalyptus trees were covered with shimmering butterflies that looked like orange leaves during the fall in Massachusetts. The guidebook mentioned that originally the monarchs roosted on the branches of the Monterey pines, cypresses, and coastal redwoods, but these trees had been cut down for development, and now the Australian eucalyptus trees were their main resting site. Tonino reminded himself that this was just another example of a tree helping another living organism. He remembered how the cottonwood sacrificed its roots for the *tihu* and the Pacific yew tree gave its life for the important anti-cancer drug Taxol.

Even though the Pacific yew has given humans something desirable, he was discouraged, because he read that the riparian habitat in the desert areas of the American Southwest were declining because of human intervention affecting the normal water patterns. The southwestern willow flycatcher has even been put on the federal endangered subspecies list. One of the main problems for this beautiful bird is habitat destruction and loss of the willows along the streams and rivers. *I don't know what the Hopi will do without the cottonwood roots for their kachinas,* he said to himself.

The rest of the tour consisted of seeing more of the same, so the boys split up and went their separate ways. Tonino decided to continue down a shaded, unused path. About twenty feet down the path, he decided to morph. This gave him a better sense of what the real world of the monarch was like. As he hopped down the trail, he came upon an injured male monarch. Tonino knew it was a male because of the scent pouches on its hind wings; he noticed the frayed wings and the beak marks on its front and hind wings. Tonino knew from his Mexican experience that these marks were mainly due to bird attacks. He also knew that experienced birds knew the taste of the cardiac glycosides, and when they grabbed a monarch and tasted that bitter chemical, they would let the butterfly go. All that remained on the wings was the mark where the bird had grabbed the wing with its beak.

Tonino thought he knew this injured monarch. "May I help you?" Tonino politely asked.

"Yes," the male monarch responded.

"What is your name?"

The butterfly responded, "Baccio."

"Glad to meet you. I'm Tonino the cricket. Don't you remember me from Mexico? In fact, I gave you that name because you kept flying in my face and it felt sort of like a kiss."

"Yes, I do remember, but I didn't expect to see you way out here."

"You didn't expect to see me out here, but why are you out here? You shouldn't be overwintering here."

"I know that, but a huge storm blew a bunch of us off course and into this West Coast flyway for overwintering monarchs. All I need is for you to help me get up into a tree so that I don't get stepped on."

"That's easy," said Tonino. Tonino quickly transformed, gently put his small hand under Baccio, and put him onto a branch of the eucalyptus. Tonino did not want to transform again but knew Baccio was okay. Slowly he made his way to meet his friends. This was the second time Tonino had helped a monarch (the first time was when he and Carlo had guided the monarch cloud off the island of Nantucket). This wouldn't be the last time he helped out his favorite butterfly.

Tonino, like other youngsters, often did not watch where he was going. As he turned quickly to the right around a big tree, he crashed into someone, knocking them down. "Oh, I am so sorry," Tonino said apologetically.

As he looked down, he could see it was a girl. When she turned around he was extremely surprised.

"Tonino!" she said.

"Susan!" he replied.

"What are you doing out here?" Susan asked.

"I came with my friends to see the monarch parade and the overwintering site," he responded. "But why are you here?"

"Well, I must admit that I was taking a chance. I know you love monarchs, and I had a strong hunch that you might be here. In fact, I really missed you."

From that moment on, except for when he returned to the inn to sleep, Pedro and Ming Ming never saw Tonino.

The day of the conference, Tonino and Susan went to the plenary lectures. The lectures started at 7:00 p.m.; they arrived at 6:30 so they could sit up front. At 6:45 two men came walking into the conference hall. It was Dr. Lincoln Brower and someone Tonino had not yet met. As Dr. Brower approached the podium, he recognized Tonino. He waved him over and asked how he was doing. Tonino introduced Susan to Dr. Brower. "This is the professor who came to see me in Florida when my cousin Carlo and I crashed in our ultralight plane bringing in the migrating monarchs from Nantucket."

Dr. Brower interrupted, "I want to introduce you to Dr. Orley Taylor."

Tonino was very excited since he knew about Dr. Taylor's website called Monarch Watch. He also knew he had been in graduate school at the University of Connecticut with Dr. Stoffolano.

"It's a great pleasure to meet you," Dr. Taylor said. "Dr. Brower was telling me about this young adventurous teenager who is so interested in insects, especially monarchs, and here you are."

Tonino was very proud and said, "Well, I am only trying to do my part in preserving plants and animals. My real love, however, is crickets."

Brower looked at Tonino and said, "I didn't know that!"

Just then, Dr. Bill Calvert, who was chairing the program, told everyone they should sit down and get ready for the program to start.

Dr. Brower's talk was very informative, but Tonino already knew most of it. During the fifteen-minute recess, Tonino asked Susan about the Japanese killing whales. Susan, of course, kept trying to evade the discussion and instead talked about her upcoming trip to Hawai'i to see her aunt and uncle. "Tonino, I am going on a trip to Hawai'i and also to New Zealand and Japan. This would be a great opportunity for you to see some other parts of the world and to see for yourself whether Japanese eat a lot of dolphin and whale meat. Why don't you join me? It would also give us a chance to get to know one another better."

Tonino couldn't let go of the issue and Susan knew it. Finally, Susan was spared more questions by Tonino as the speaker called the session back to order.

Dr. Taylor was introduced and immediately captured Tonino's attention. He reported on how the monarchs had a built-in compass and used the earth's magnetic field to keep them on track during their southward migration. Dr. Taylor also spoke about how other animals, such as pigeons, have compass-orienting mechanisms. After his speech, many members of the audience had questions about Dr. Taylor's results.

"Why are so many people doubting his results?" Susan asked Tonino.

"I guess that is an important part of science and research," Tonino said to Susan.

Soon Dr. Calvert interrupted the questioning and introduced Karen Oberhauser. If you think Tonino was excited about Dr. Taylor's talk, you should have seen how enthusiastic he was about Karen's speech. Tonino didn't know that much about genetically modified organisms, but he could get the gist of what she was saying. Susan was not interested in science at all, so after Karen finished speaking, she asked Tonino to explain what the talk had been about.

"Scientists have now figured out ways to identify, isolate, and then take the genes from one organism and put them into another organism. It is called genetic engineering. In this case they have taken the gene from a bacterium, *Bacillus thuringiensis* (a.k.a. Bt), which produces a toxin that kills many insects, and put it into the genes of the corn plant. This gene then becomes incorporated into all the cells of the corn plant, even the pollen. Monarch caterpillars often eat the leaves of milkweed that sometimes contain pollen from the genetically modified corn plants in the vicinity; the caterpillars can die if they get enough pollen containing the Bt toxin."

Susan gasped, held her hand over her mouth, and said, "How awful."

Tonino immediately responded, "This is why I must sacrifice my life saving all plant and insect species."

"That's a big job," Susan replied.

Following Dr. Oberhauser's talk, as Tonino walked Susan back to her motel, he kept trying to discuss whaling in Japan. He even convinced her to go whale watching the next day. When he returned to the Feather Bed Inn, Tonino made arrangements to go on a whale watch.

Susan and Tonino arrived just before the boat departed. They were very excited and hoped to see gray, humpback, killer, and possibly blue whales. Unfortunately, the weather turned bad, and they had to return to dock. Tonino was extremely upset.

"Don't worry," Susan said. "You can go whale watching in Hawai'i."

Tonino could not get Susan to agree that the Japanese should ban killing whales, but Susan's persistence was paying off. *Maybe I can get Tonino to go to Hawai'i with me*, she thought.

In addition to persuading him about the benefits of going to Hawai'i, Susan tried "gift-giving." All insects know about gift-giving. Amongst certain species, this is a common practice used by males to entice a female into mating. It is also a way for females of certain species (including humans) to evaluate which males are best suited to sire their offspring. Remember, Susan was a special individual. As a cricket she could produce insect music, but in human form, she was exceptional at gift-giving and also buying gifts. As part of the sales pitch for Hawai'i, Susan gave Tonino a wonderful gift.

She had purchased a book, *The Monarch Butterfly,* by George Gibbs from Wellington, New Zealand. Professor Gibbs knew all about the monarch butterfly migrating to the South Pacific. The book had a map of the emigration route from California to the island of Hawai'i, where the monarch was first reported in 1840. It then moved to some of the other islands, reaching Australia in 1871 and New Zealand in 1873.

Tonino agreed to travel to Hawai'i with Susan; first they would go to San Francisco and visit Susan's parents, Linda and Joe Maki. They would be able to stay on the Big Island of Hawai'i with Susan's aunt and uncle, who had moved there from Japan fifty years ago and now owned a farm. Susan only had one living relative in Japan, Yorimoto Wada, her mother's brother, who lived in the Japanese village of Taiji. In fact, her aunt and uncle in Hawai'i suggested that they visit him if they went to Japan. They said, "He is old now and lives all alone. He never married, and I am sure he would love to see you."

Tonino's decision to extend his trip surprised and upset his parents. He wrote them a letter explaining his decision. He reminded them how he first met Susan at Tanglewood and said that her family originally came from Hokkaidō, Japan. Susan had been on an apprentice program at Tanglewood, studying the violin.

> Dear Mom and Dad,
>
> It is difficult to tell you this, but I have decided to postpone going to college for a while. I would like to travel and see more of the world. I believe this experience will only enhance my studies once I return to college. I have decided to travel with Susan to see her aunt and uncle in Hawai'i and then go on to New Zealand and Japan. I have already e-mailed Dr. Stoffolano and the admissions office at the university to explain that I wasn't coming back this spring but wanted to start in the fall. Dr. Stoffolano's response was that it sounded like a good idea. He also said that more students should

travel and see part of their own country and the world before they go to college. Travel makes one mature.

Also, in case you didn't know, in 1876 Dr. William Clark, then president of Massachusetts Agricultural College, was invited to be the vice president of Sapporo Agricultural College, which is now Hokkaidō University. This was the beginning of a long-standing relationship between Hokkaidō and the University of Massachusetts.

I am sure you will understand and remember what Dad said about geography and travel. Well, now is my chance. I will keep you posted and will share my experiences when I return.

Love, Tonino

Tonino's reconnection with Susan also made his friends think twice about their pisano. Susan was the same age as Tonino; she was a beautiful young Japanese-American woman who was also of cricket descent. Originally from Hokkaidō, Japan, her father was now a professor at the City College of San Francisco, and when Tonino first met them her father was on a sabbatical leave at the University of Massachusetts, Amherst campus, in the computer science department.

Tonino was so taken with Susan that Pedro and Ming Ming felt he was not behaving rationally. They had never seen him like this before. Both tried to talk him out of prolonging his vacation. Tonino gave the two boys a letter for his parents that explained everything. Neither one of them was very excited about doing this. Only because they really loved Tonino as a friend did they agree. The two boys were starting school in the fall, but Tonino was not scheduled to start until the following fall semester because he failed to get his application in on time.

Before leaving for San Francisco, Tonino and Susan decided what things they would bring with them. Certainly they needed their backpacks, CD player and headsets, and of course their personal things. Susan mentioned to Tonino, "Maybe it would be a good idea to buy an umbrella."

"What would we use it for?" Tonino asked.

"Many people use them in New Zealand because of the intensity of the sun."

Tonino didn't know that the ozone layer above New Zealand is being rapidly depleted. Because of this, dangerous ultraviolet rays, which are so detrimental to the skin, result in a lot of skin cancer on the island.

Since they were both fair skinned, it seemed like a good idea to buy an umbrella; they each went off to buy one. They decided on the type that collapses and takes up less space. Tonino, however, had not picked up on Susan's comment about going on to China. Could she persuade him to go with her?

Pedro, Ming Ming, Susan, and Tonino boarded the bus for San Francisco. Susan and Tonino had lots to talk about and to share. They were starting to get to know one another better. They discussed everything from likes to dislikes. Susan mentioned that she really didn't like to eat garlic just as Tonino saw a sign that said, "Exit for Gilroy." Tonino quickly turned his head as they passed the exit and said to Susan, "That city has a garlic festival every year in July."

"How do you know that?"

"I read an article in the *Smithsonian* magazine last year. It was something about how life without garlic would be just tasteless."

Tonino was surprised that Susan didn't like garlic. He recalled how his parents loved to sit out at night in Boston's North End. They loved the smell of garlic emanating from the various Italian restaurants. For Tonino, this same odor was now imprinted in his brain. During the bus ride, Susan convinced Tonino that they should stop in New Zealand and Australia after going to Hawai'i, and then go on to China. Tonino's reply was, "Why not?"

When Tonino and his friends arrived in San Francisco, Susan's parents picked them up at the bus station. The next day they telephoned Aunt Mary and Uncle John in Hawai'i and made all their plane reservations. Susan's parents were kind enough to take Ming Ming and Pedro to the airport.

Tonino gave Pedro and Ming Ming the letter he had written to his parents; he told them, "Don't forget to give this letter to my parents and reassure them that I am fine." He then said, "Good luck in college."

Before leaving the security area, Pedro whispered into Tonino's ear, "Are you sure you want to do this?"

Tonino pulled away and looked at him, saying, "I am sure. Make sure you give the letter to my parents."

Everyone hugged and off they went.

With all the plans completed, Susan and Tonino made sure they had their passports for New Zealand, Australia, and China. They didn't need passports in Hawai'i because on March 12, 1959, Congress passed the Hawai'ian State Bill, making Hawai'i the fiftieth state.

Susan's parents took them to Los Angeles International Airport. They caught their Aloha Airlines flight to Honolulu. Once the plane was in the air and they were settled into their seats, Susan gave Tonino a pamphlet to read about the Polynesian Cultural Center. She felt this would give him a wonderful introduction to the islands of the South Pacific. Professor Stoffolano had e-mailed Tonino with the name of Dennis Lapointe, a UMass graduate in entomology who was getting his PhD at the Manoa campus of the University of Hawai'i. Dennis had agreed to pick them up at the airport. Tonino made arrangements for Dennis to show them around the island of Oahu and take them to the Bishop Museum. Dennis knew Tonino was from Boston and planning to study for his bachelor's degree in entomology at UMass when he returned from the trip.

While researching their trip to Hawai'i, Tonino learned that of all the insects in Hawai'i, the fruit flies reigned supreme, not crickets. He also remembered that Dr. Grimaldi was a fruit fly specialist. He was curious if anyone had studied the crickets of Hawai'i. *"Well, I guess I will find out soon."*

Chapter 10.
Hawai'i

Meeting Dennis and Lisa

Dennis and Lisa Lapointe met Susan and Tonino at Honolulu's International Airport. They were holding a sign saying "Aloha, Tonino and Susan." Lisa placed a yellow and white lei around the necks of their guests while everyone shook hands. This necklace of flowers, "*lei 'a'i*," has become the typical Hawai'ian way of greeting people, while the head lei, "*lei po'o*," is mostly used by dancers. Susan lifted up the lei so she could smell it while Tonino launched into a discussion with Dennis.

Tonino asked Dennis, "What does *aloha* mean, and where did the name *Hawai'i* come from?"

"*Aloha* means 'hello' or 'good-bye,'" Dennis said, "and it can also mean 'love.' The word *Hawai'i* is more difficult to explain. It seems to mean the place from where the original peoples came. The beaches in Hawai'i have lots of lapping waves. These are believed to help cool the fiery revenge of Pele, the goddess of volcanoes, but one must remember that being a female, Pele could not make fire. The land we call Hawai'i was formed with the help of *Na-maka-o-Kaha'i*, Pele's older sister and goddess of the sea."

"Wow," Tonino responded. "I didn't know the volcanoes in Hawai'i were under the control of a woman. I wonder if that is the same belief in other countries with volcanoes, like Italy."

Since the flight from San Francisco had taken only five and a half hours, and Tonino and Susan were not tired, Dennis and

194

Lisa gave them a capsule view of Polynesian culture; they went directly to the Polynesian Cultural Center, which is about a forty-five-minute drive from the airport. On the way, they discussed various topics from traditional customs to the cost of living in Hawai'i. Dennis also told them about his research, which is studying the various ornithophilic (i.e., bird-loving) mosquitoes, to determine which species vectored the causative agent, *Plasmodium gallinaceum*, of bird malaria, and to examine the effect bird malaria was having on the indigenous bird species. This idea of an animal having a disease that was caused by another organism that was transmitted by an insect was new to Tonino. All he ever heard about were human afflictions and diseases. Sometimes Tonino's head was sent spinning when he remembered the promise he had made to the Blue Fairy. He would say over and over, *"How can I save everything?"*

The cultural center gives tourists many options. Tonino was interested in seeing the housing and clothing worn by the people from the different Pacific islands. He was also interested in the diverse customs of the islands. The islands of Old Hawai'i, Tahiti, Samoa, Tonga, Fiji, and New Zealand all had cultural centers at this one central facility. Here they presented different aspects of their culture (e.g., music, dancing, food). Tonino liked the Hawai'ian hula dances the best and was intrigued by the *mele oli,* or chants. He liked the sounds of the chants. These two things, hula and chanting, are foundations of the Hawai'ian culture.

While at the cultural center, Susan and Lisa went off to do some shopping; Tonino pulled out Professor Gibbs's book from his backpack. Dennis couldn't help but notice what Tonino was reading. "So you're interested in monarch butterflies?" he asked.

"Oh, yes. It is one of my passions. My cousin Carlo and I followed the monarch migration in an ultralight airplane from Nantucket Island, Massachusetts, to Florida just a few days after Thanksgiving."

Dennis said, "Yes, I remember reading about that. Were you the two boys that crashed into the pelican squadron at Cape Canaveral?"

"That was us," Tonino proudly replied.

"It must have been a great trip," said Dennis.

"It was but it was extremely scary. We were always concerned that we might injure the monarchs, and then when we crashed into the pelicans, I was sure we had killed some. Fortunately, however, none were injured. On the positive side, we were able to see things that no one had ever seen before."

"Give me an example," responded Dennis.

"We could see the position of the antenna while the monarchs are migrating. The antennae are not very rigid and are hardly used while migrating so they are held back over the head. In normal flight, they are held out in front of the head. I have spoken to Lincoln Brower about this, and he has encouraged us to write an article about our flight for the *Monarch Newsletter*." Tonino went on to explain that he spent several days at the Mexican *refugia* in *El Rosario* during his Christmas vacation.

Dennis responded, "I imagine because you have Gibbs's book, you already know the monarch has journeyed from California to inhabit the various Pacific Islands."

"Yes, this book is one of the main reasons why I decided to postpone going to college for one year. Susan and I wanted to follow the path of the monarch from California into the Pacific Islands. Unfortunately, we won't be able to see all the islands."

Their conversation was cut short because Susan and Lisa returned. Dennis said it was time to leave for Honolulu because everyone was very tired.

Meeting the Forensic Entomologist and Learning about White Monarchs

The next day, Dennis took Susan and Tonino to the University of Hawai'i, Manoa campus, to meet Dr. Lee Goff and Dr. John Stimson. During his visit with Dr. Goff, Tonino told him about his cousin Vincenzo, who was planning to be a lawyer, and how he had seen a book on forensic entomology in Dr. Grimaldi's office. "I am also very much involved in using insects, and other arthropods, to solve various crimes," Dr. Goff told them.

Dr. Goff spent about an hour telling them about the latest cases he was working on. Some of these cases are discussed in his book, *A Fly for the Prosecution*. In one case, the police found a dead grasshopper underneath the body of a dead woman; the grasshopper's left hindleg was broken at the femur area. Later, when Dr. Goff examined the clothing of one of the key suspects, he found the perfectly matching piece of the grasshopper's hindleg, which linked the suspect with the dead victim. How else could that piece of leg have gotten into the cuff of the man's pants? "My cousin will just love this story about how the grasshopper's leg solved a murder case," Tonino said.

Tonino stored every bit of information away so he could tell Vincenzo all about it. He also asked Dr. Goff for one of his business cards. Tonino and Susan thanked him for taking time to talk to them. While they were leaving, Tonino looked down at the card. In bold letters, it said FORENSIC ENTOMOLOGY ENTERPRISES: ACAROLOGY, MEDICAL & FORENSIC STUDIES. "Boy, will Vincenzo be surprised when he gets this," he said.

Tonino was beginning to realize the true meaning of friendship. He not only was thinking about things his relatives would like, he had already sent postcards to all his relatives and friends. He was trying to keep his part of the agreement with the Blue Fairy.

On the way to Dr. Stimson's office, Dennis pointed out a display case in the hallway. In it, Tonino saw something he had never seen before. In fact, it is something most people have never seen, including Dr. Brower, who has seen over several million monarchs. In the case was a perfect specimen of a white monarch butterfly, or *lepelepe-o-Hina*. Dennis noticed Tonino looking at the case and said, "Dr. Stimson will tell you all about that."

After Dennis made the introductions Dr. Stimson said, "Please sit down." He told Tonino about the latest aspects of his research on the monarch. Tonino was completely enthralled by what he heard. Stimson and co-workers believed that about 4 percent of the mutant white monarchs in Oahu were experiencing bird predation, especially by two unauthorized, cage-released bulbul species: the red-whiskered bulbul, which came from Asia around 1965, and the red-vented bulbul, which appeared in the mid-1950s. They believed that these two birds, and possibly other birds, were not deterred from eating the monarch by the poisonous cardiac glycosides that usually protected the caterpillars. This may be due to their ability to detoxify the toxins, or they may have avoided the toxins that are mainly stored in the butterfly's wings. The other possibility was that the Hawai'ian milkweed plants contained less of the toxin than some other species.

Dennis pointed out to Tonino that Dr. Brower had written an article for *Scientific American*, "Ecological Chemistry," that might discuss the latter possibility. Dr. Stimson continued, "The birds are visual foragers and selectively feed on the orange forms of the monarch, bypassing the white forms that are not so easily seen against the whitish, Hawai'ian sky."

Tonino was flabbergasted about how much there was to know about one single insect species. As they left, Tonino thanked Dr. Stimson, who gave him two reprints of his articles on white monarchs.

As they departed, Dennis said, "I'll show you the milkweed plant they feed on here in Hawai'i."

Just outside the building were several milkweed plants. Dennis told Tonino, "Here they are called crown flowers, *Pua kalaunu*, and have the scientific name, *Calotropis gigantea*. They appeared in Hawai'i around 1890, but why they were introduced into the islands is not known."

The plant looked so different from the milkweed Tonino had seen with Howie on Nantucket. This plant was big (ten to twelve feet tall), which explained its other common name, giant milkweed; it had seed pods about five to six inches long and about three inches wide. Dennis said that there were several different genera within the cardiotoxic milkweed plants, known as Asclepiadaceae. Just to make sure it really was a milkweed, Tonino snapped off one of the leaves. Sure enough, out poured the milky white latex sap that gives the plant its name. Tonino also made an excellent observation. He asked Dennis, "What are the small, crescent moon-shaped holes in the leaves?"

Dennis pulled the leaf down to get a better look and replied, "That is where the first instar (i.e., the living stage of the insect between different molts) caterpillar cuts the veins of the leaves by making a moon-shaped trench. This trench cuts off the supply of the milky white latex from the rest of the plant. The young caterpillars then feed on that portion of the leaf where the latex has already drained out and dried. If they don't do this, they get trapped in the sticky latex and die."

Getting caught in sticky plant exudates was something Tonino was quite familiar with. He remembered reading how insects fell into the sticky resin of plants during the Tertiary (Oliogocene) period, which formed amber. He also remembered having that terrible nightmare where he jumped to avoid being eaten by the insectivorous dinosaur and ended up becoming caught in the plant resin. What a relief when he realized he had only been dreaming.

They left the university and drove to Dennis and Lisa's apartment.

That evening, Dennis said, "Tomorrow we will leave for the airport about nine o'clock in the morning. You will take Aloha Airlines directly into Hilo, which is on the Big Island, Hawai'i. I have arranged for Dr. Marlene Hapai to meet you at the airport. Some people call her the 'bug lady of Hilo.' She has just written a book called *Bug Play*, which is designed to help teachers teach children about insects."

"That sounds fine," both Susan and Tonino replied.

It was getting late, and Tonino and Susan were tired but anxiously anticipating their flight to the Big Island. The next morning they had breakfast outside and enjoyed fresh mango, papaya, banana, and pineapple. It took Susan a lot of coaxing to get Tonino to at least try the papaya. After a teaspoon of this wonderful, orange-colored fruit of the tropics, Tonino was hooked on papayas. Packed and ready to go, they got into Dennis's car. Dennis had purchased a lei for Tonino and Susan to give to Dr. Hapai.

He explained, "This is the custom here in Hawai'i. Also, be careful not to crush the traditional and fragrant *Maile lei*, which is made by intertwining two different varieties of the same native and fragrant vine."

Meeting the Bug Lady of Hawai'i

When they arrived at the airport, Dennis and Lisa said good-bye. Susan and Tonino said *mahalo* (thank you); taking special care not to crush the special lei, they alternately walked and hopped into the terminal.

The flight was on time, and forty-five minutes after takeoff, they landed at the Hilo International Airport. Dr. Hapai was waiting and holding a sign in the shape of a cricket that read, "Aloha, Tonino and Susan." Tonino whispered to Susan, "Do you think she knows we are really crickets?"

"I doubt it! Remember, Dennis said she is called the 'bug lady of Hilo'; she probably just likes crickets," responded Susan.

Susan took the Maile lei and put it around Dr. Hapai's neck. Once they were in the car and on their way, Tonino wanted to test Dr. Hapai's knowledge of crickets. He asked, "What's the Hawai'ian name for cricket?"

"An adult cricket is called *unia,* while a young cricket whose wings have not developed is called *uhini pua*. The general name for crickets is *uhini.*"

That short response satisfied Tonino, but made him think even more about languages and the origin of words; he was glad that he had the power to speak and understand any language he wanted.

Dr. Hapai took them to Susan's aunt and uncle's farm. Due to their busy schedules at the farm, Aunt Mary and Uncle John couldn't take time off to meet them at the airport. Dr. Hapai was originally born in the area of Puako, and her mother lived in the same town as Aunt Mary and Uncle John, so she volunteered to take them to their farm. "This will give me a chance to stop and see my mother," Dr. Hapai said.

The drive from Hilo was beautiful. "Nothing like Boston," Tonino said as he turned to Susan.

Dr. Hapai stopped at her mother's house before taking the two teenagers to Susan's aunt and uncle's. They only stayed long enough to meet Dr. Hapai's mother. As Susan and the other ladies started talking about Hawai'ian quilts, Tonino slowly eased his way outside. On their way to Dr. Hapai's mother's house, Tonino had seen a yard filled with hundreds of little tents or, more accurately described, little A-frame houses, about four feet high. In front of each one was a beautifully multicolored rooster. Tonino, being extremely curious, investigated these small structures.

Being a city boy, he knew very little about farm animals, especially this type of bird. His conscience warned him that he could be in a dangerous situation. Of course, just like Pinocchio, he ignored his conscience. He was most interested in the A-frame structure, not the rooster, which he had never seen before. In order to prevent the rooster from making a lot of noise in response to an approaching human and possibly alerting the owners, Tonino morphed. Alerting the owners could create problems, and he wanted to avoid this. As you know by now, Tonino is never satisfied with a cursory look. He had to get almost on top of the bird to see the A-frame. As he hopped closer, the beautiful rooster cocked its head to the right, lifted up its left leg, and focused on the edible insect approaching him. These roosters were fed only commercial food; thus, they would prefer anything organically raised (like Tonino!). Before Tonino knew it, the rooster had lunged forward and grabbed him. Tonino instantly felt a sharp pain in his abdomen. He turned quickly and tried to escape. The rooster pecked with another head thrust, this time grabbing the cricket by its left front leg.

Dangling in the rooster's mouth by his left foreleg, Tonino had to act quickly or be swallowed in the next move. Almost instantly, he transformed. You can imagine how surprised the rooster was, holding a young boy by his left shirt sleeve Tonino collected himself, got up, and brushed off the dirt. He was completely embarrassed. In order to check if any damage had occurred in his cricket form, he morphed again. He carefully felt his left foreleg where his tympanum (the membrane located on the inside femur of the front legs of crickets) is located. He only hoped it wasn't damaged; otherwise, he would have problems hearing. He also checked all his abdominal spiracles (openings that exchange gases with the air). Any damage here could interfere with normal air intake. Just before he left, he morphed back, looked the rooster straight in the eyes, and scolded him. He then walked back to the house, arriving just as everyone was coming out the door.

Susan noticed that Tonino kept rubbing his left arm "What's the matter with your arm?" Susan asked.

"I think I just have cramp," he said.

Susan got the umbrella out of the luggage and opened it up for Tonino to lean on. He now felt like Grillo-parlante when Pinocchio threw the hammer at him and was almost killed.

In the car, as they pulled away, Tonino asked Dr. Hapai, "What are those A-frames? I have never seen a chicken farm like that in Massachusetts."

Dr. Hapai laughed and explained what those little A-frames were. "These are individual homes for roosters, or *moa kane*, which are used as fighting birds. Here, they are also called game birds. The cocks, or males, must be kept separate or they will kill one another. It is a common sport of the Filipinos; here in Hawai'i, it is called *hakaka-a-moa*. These birds are being raised mainly for shipment to Manila. There are hundreds of these farms in Hawai'i. It is illegal to fight and gamble on game birds in Hawai'i; however, it remains a very popular underground sport."

Tonino asked, "Did Hawai'ians traditionally fight roosters as a sport?"

"Yes, cockfighting was a sport of the ancient kings."

As they were leaving, Tonino could see the rooster that tried to eat him. He wondered if his encounter with that bird would affect its future as a fighting champion.

Tonino's life was coming together. He was now able to recognize when previous events had some bearing on something that was happening. He had a flashback to his experience with Pedro in Puerto Rico at the cockfight and also the dinner conversation he and his friends had about whether this sport should be banned or not. Tonino decided that he would have to read more about this increasingly popular, ancient, and controversial sport.

Staying at Susan's Aunt and Uncle's Farm

When they got to Aunt Mary and Uncle John's farm, Susan saw her aunt standing at the mailbox. Susan got out of the car and said, "Aloha Auntie!" She presented her with a lei and gave her a great big hug. She then introduced Dr. Hapai and Tonino. Dr. Hapai couldn't stay because she wanted to return and spend more time with her mother. As she left, Susan and Tonino said, *"Mahalo."* Dr. Hapai drove off, and when she looked back, she saw Susan and Tonino walking down the driveway with their backpacks on, each holding one of Aunt Mary's hands. Knowing so much about insect behavior, Dr. Hapai couldn't help but think she really saw three crickets hopping down the driveway. When Dr. Hapai got to her mother's house, her husband, Archie, and son, Keha, had arrived. When she explained what she thought she had seen, everyone laughed.

Keha said, "Mom, you have a better imagination than some of the kids in my class." Archie and Dr. Hapai's mom both nodded in agreement.

Aunt Mary and Uncle John had lived in Hawai'i for fifty years. They didn't have enough money to buy the farm until five years ago. It was a lovely farm located in Honokaa. They grew macadamia nuts and the famous Kona coffee. Susan and Tonino were going to spend about thirty days with them. They settled into their lovely room, discussed family history on Susan's side, and then went to bed. Uncle John had to get up early to do his farm chores, so he always went to bed early. That first day, they made themselves acquainted with the farm, and Susan spent time discussing previous family events with her aunt. That evening, however, they planned to go to Hawi (pronounced "Havi").

Hawi was a town that both Tonino and Susan had read about. It was a cozy little historical town on Highway 270 in North Kohala. It formerly was the home of the Kohala Sugar Company. Now that the sugarcane mills were gone, people found other kinds of work, either within town or at the hotels along the Kona coast. The main street of Hawi had many art shops. It would remind Tonino of Northampton, Massachusetts, which he had visited with Dr. Stoffolano.

Hawi continued to grow and attracted people interested in crafts, music, and the arts. It already had attracted some musicians. One night, Susan and Tonino went to the Bamboo restaurant-bar. Because Susan played the violin, a string instrument, she liked to listen to John Keawe, a local slack key (*ki ho'alu*) guitarist who played at the Bamboo. The

Hawai'ian word *ki ho'alu* literally means to "loosen the key." John Keawe has composed many of his own songs, including *Auhele*, which is about drifting or sailing aimlessly. Tonino's favorite song was *Whale Talk*, which is about a mother humpback whale having a conversation with her calf. John is from North Kohala, and it is interesting to note that the Hawai'ian name for the humpback whale is *kohola*.

The young cricket's interests had grown considerably. Not only was he interested in music, etymology, museums, monarch butterflies, biodiversity, and conservation biology, but because his trip to the American Southwest, he had developed a new love: petroglyphs. Oh, yes, don't forget his love for computers. Computers were a blessing for Tonino. He already had created a folder on his laptop for each of these topics. He laughed when he remembered Joe telling him, "Remember everything because you never know when you will need it." *That was fine for Joe, whose world centered around Italy and the North End, but today there is such an information explosion that computers are essential*, Tonino mumbled to himself.

The best purchase Tonino had made before he left on his trip to the Southwest was a laptop computer. He kept reminding himself, "Having this on my trip will make it easier for me to store all the information I collect." However, he still kept a handwritten diary with pencil sketches. This was for his parents and Joe to read and enjoy, because he knew they did not like computers.

John Keawe and *Whale Talk*

That evening, Susan and Tonino drove to Hawi for dinner at the Bamboo restaurant. Before dinner, they went to browse in the Kohala Koa Gallery, a small gift shop near the restaurant. Here, Susan noticed a book and tape that she knew Tonino would like. She called Tonino over and showed him both items. He read the title of the tape, *Whale Talk,* and then the book title and author, *Na Ki'i Pohaku* by P. F. "Ski" Kwaitkowski. This book was about what the ancient people called "stone images": Hawai'ian petroglyphs, or *Ki'i Pohaku*. Tonino purchased both the book and tape.

They entered the Bamboo restaurant-bar and sat at a small table for two. Following dinner of mahi-mahi (a fish also known as

Dorado) with a coconut curry cream sauce, they sat back and waited for John Keawe to begin playing. Susan really liked him. He was a handsome man with white hair and a white mustache and beard; his dark, penetrating eyes and dark eyebrows were set against a background of brown skin. The crowd really enjoyed John's music, and at the break he took time to walk into the audience to greet and talk with everyone.

Every time he performed, John explained the origin of his string instrument and talked about the songs he played. He began, "Historically, the indigenous Hawai'ians seldom used string instruments. The only one they did use was called the *ukeke*. It is a two- or three-stringed, bow instrument about forty centimeters long that is very similar to the Jew's harp. Today, it is an endangered, or maybe even an extinct, Hawai'ian musical instrument. Hawai'ian music came mainly from percussion instruments, such as the *pahu*, which is a drum made from a section of a coconut tree trunk with either a fish or animal skin covering, and the *ipu*, an instrument made by sewing two dried gourds together. This percussion instrument is pounded against the floor or lifted in the air and slapped with the free hand. The ipu is usually used with chanters."

John went on to explain other things about Hawai'ian culture. "In the early 1800s, cowboys or *vaqueros* from Spanish Mexico, now California, were brought to Hawai'i to teach the Hawai'ians how to become *paniolos* or cowboys. With them they brought the guitar and the tradition of singing in the lonely moonlights to pass the time away." John pointed to the strings on his guitar and continued, "They played with the strings loose in order to get the key they wanted. These *paniolos* learned how to pluck melody on the upper strings and, at the same time, get bass on the lower part of the strings. Thus, the guitar I play is called a slack key or loose string guitar. The Hawai'ian name to describe slack key music is *nahenahe*, which means soft and soothing."

Being Portuguese on his mother's side, John knew the history of the ukulele, whose original name was *caraquinhos*. He explained, "In the late nineteenth century, sailors brought the Portuguese instrument called the *braguinha* into Hawai'i. This small, four-stringed instrument, commonly known as '*machete de braga*,' was to become the prototype for the ukulele; it is still used on the Portuguese island of Madeira."

Tonino loved learning the origins of words. He was surprised to learn that the name *ukulele* literally means "jumping flea." Its origin is from the Hawai'ian language (*uku* = flea and *lele* = to jump). Even after doing his term paper on the importance of crickets in the history of mankind, Tonino was still finding new ways in which insects were part of various cultures.

Before finishing, John always took requests from the audience. When Tonino raised his hand, John asked him, "Where are you from?"

"Massachusetts," Tonino replied.

"Did you know that the Ukulele Hall of Fame Museum is in Duxbury, Massachusetts?"

Tonino couldn't believe there were so many museums in his own state, never mind one on ukuleles.

John asked Tonino, "What do you want to hear?"

Susan knew immediately what it would be, and she was right. "*Whale Talk*," replied Tonino.

So, as John played the song, both Susan and Tonino sat back in their rattan chairs, rested their heads against the high backs, closed their eyes, and imagined they were swimming with the whales.

After the song, Susan and Tonino departed for the farm. It was a full moon, and on the way back, Tonino could see the ocean far below, the waves with their white caps, and the crashing surf. "Let's go to the beach tomorrow," he said.

"That would be great," Susan replied.

A Dream and a Hawai'ian Beach

Before they went to sleep, they discussed how very happy and content they were with their stay so far. For whatever reason, maybe it was because they had just heard John Keawe playing the slack key guitar and saw the beautiful ocean on their way home, Tonino had a wonderful dream that night. He dreamt he was sitting in a small café along the coast of Italy. A young man was playing the accordion, and an older man with a mustache and beard was playing the mandolin (a stringed instrument that was very popular in Italy and was modeled after the short-neck lute, which has eight strings). They were playing "When the moon hits your eye like a big pizza pie, that's amore."

Tonino told Susan about the dream while eating breakfast the next day on the lanai of the farm. After a new and novel breakfast of a *loco moko*, which is a scoop of rice, topped with a fried egg and hamburger covered with gravy, they left to check out the beach in Puoko. It was Sunday and they wanted to avoid the crowds. Susan's aunt and uncle had to work.

Most beaches are places of contrast, and the different natural habitats are usually clearly divided. Walking down the path to the beach, Susan and Tonino could see tall palm trees swaying in the ocean breeze and the milo, a very popular shade tree. On the path were crushed and dried coconut husks. They had turned brown, not the shiny green color of the fresh coconut. The coconut fibers reminded Tonino of baleen. Next they came to a sandy area, which took them to the water's edge. Beyond were some reefs, which slowed down the advancing waves. The contrast on the beach of white sand, green vegetation, blue water, and the white clouds suspended in the blue sky was most striking.

After checking out three beaches, they decided on the one they liked. There were a few surfers riding some of the big waves.

Tonino began to think, and think, until finally Susan said, "What's bothering you?"

"Nothing really, I just have been thinking about waves and surfing. Since so many behaviors have developed independently in various parts of the world having similar habitats, I wonder why surfing didn't develop in other parts of the world."

"Great question, but I have no idea," Susan replied.

Tonino had borrowed a Hawai'ian dictionary from Aunt Mary, because he was trying to learn some new words.

Tonino wanted to know the Hawai'ian word for waves. He looked up *wave* in the dictionary. To his surprise, there were about thirty different Hawai'ian words for wave: high waves, breaking waves, receding waves, and so on. After a while, Tonino realized that words that had numerous meanings, as in many other cultures, played an important part in the lives of the Hawai'ians.

As they sat on the beach, Tonino developed a game he called "pop-up." He explained the rules to Susan and said, "Now! Let the game begin."

Susan was competitive, but not as much as Tonino. He believed his competitive spirit was due to being raised in the North End of Boston. Soon, Tonino shouted, "Over there in the shallows where the waves are being calmed down by the rocks. Do you see it? It just popped up."

"What is it?" Susan politely asked.

"Wait a few minutes and it will come up again. See, over there."

Susan carefully followed where his finger was pointing. Soon up popped a cute little head with large dark eyes, a beak, and two nostrils. "It's a green turtle," he said. "They are feeding on the algae growing on the rocks." Tonino was five points ahead.

A few minutes went by without either of them seeing anything.

Just then, Susan nudged Tonino.

"Look straight out near the horizon and keep your eyes on that spot."

In a few minutes, Tonino could see a round black object appear. It then went under and up came a beautifully structured tail with two fins. "What is it?" Tonino asked.

Being Japanese, Susan knew something about whales. "It's a whale, but I don't know which kind. I believe seeing a whale should count for more points than a small turtle."

"I don't think so," replied Tonino. In fact, he declared, "The game's over, I win."

Always wanting to take front stage, Tonino launched into a discussion about the turtle. "The Hawai'ian green turtle is slightly smaller than its Atlantic coast counterpart. It is a vegetarian that feeds on algae and sea grasses. Unfortunately, it suffers from fibropapilloma tumors (90 percent infection rate in some parts of Hawai'i) and is on the endangered list."

Susan was always amazed at how much Tonino knew. As they reclined on their towels, focusing on the sky instead of the water, they couldn't believe the aerial show that many, many monarchs were putting on right above them.

"They are so beautiful. I love the way they flap, flap, flap their wings and then make a short glide," Susan commented.

Tonino agreed. Tonino's brain switched to his flight with the monarchs from Nantucket Island to Florida and realized he wasn't ready to share all the details of the intimate experience.

Finding Hawai'ian Crickets

"Let's go behind some of those boulders over there," he said, "transform, and see if we can see any insects on the beach."

To his surprise, Tonino found two marine crickets. After they introduced one another, Tonino asked them where they lived. Jim and Hope said they spent most of their lives in the wet-rock zone where the waves splash against the boulders. They both lacked wings and had big, dark colored eyes. The big eyes suggested to Tonino that they spent most of their active time at night and rested during the day.

"I am interested in knowing more about crickets here in Hawai'i. Can you tell me anything about crickets in the culture of the Hawai'ians?" Tonino asked Jim.

"First of all, Tonino," Jim said, "you must remember that Hawai'i, as well as the other Polynesian islands, is inhabited by people who are oceanic; their lives rely on the oceans. They live on an island in the vast Pacific Ocean, which covers one third of the earth's surface. There are thirty major island chains in the Pacific Ocean, sixteen of which are Polynesian. I am sure you are well aware that there are no truly marine insects. This may explain why insects, unlike the turtle or shark, never came to play very important roles in the Polynesian cultures."

"That makes perfect sense," replied Tonino. "I had never really thought about it that way."

"However, there is a story about the singing tree snails on the island of Molokai that involves crickets. The snails live in the rain forests, and the early Europeans associated the beautiful singing they heard with these snails, which are rather plentiful. It took about fifty years for people to find out that it was really the song of a cricket that they heard."

"That's a great story," Susan interjected. "Do you know which cricket it was?"

"I don't, but you can check with Frank Howarth, an entomologist at the Bishop Museum on the island of Oahu. We have seen him before when he came collecting crickets in this same spot. Luckily, we avoided being caught. I can't imagine being killed and put on a pin in some entomologist's Cornell Drawer."

"We'll do that when we get a chance," Tonino replied.

Before long, Tonino was bored being in his cricket form. He often told Susan that the routine of resting, finding food, eating, cleaning one's antenna and palps, hiding from predators, finding a mate, and defending mating territory was not diverse enough for his liking. "On the other hand, when we are in insect form, we don't have stress and all those bills to pay," Tonino would say.

They said good-bye to Jim and Hope and transformed.

Not wanting to get sunburn, they decided to leave. As they departed, they took one last look at the black, rough lava. Many green turtles had used their flippers to pull themselves out of the water and were basking in the sun. "I hope they have suntan lotion on," Tonino said jokingly.

"Yes, and I hope it is at least SPF number 30." She looked at Tonino and said, "I believe the sun has fried your brain."

On the way back to the farm, they discussed many things, and Tonino's mind returned to home and his younger years.

Returning to His Youth

Tonino felt he knew a little bit about whales, but he could not identify them by sight. His interest in museums had taken him to both the Boston Aquarium and the New Bedford Whaling Museum, both in Massachusetts. He had read *Moby-Dick* by Herman Melville and

John G. Stoffolano Jr.

also remembered wanting to visit Melville's home, Arrowhead, in the Berkshire Mountains near Tanglewood. As everyone knows, crickets do not live in the water. In fact, crickets normally don't swim. This is why most of Tonino's life was centered on the land. Tonino, however, remembered reading *The Amber Forest*, by the two Poinars, where they reported the Pygmy mole cricket, of the Tridactylidae family, had front legs for digging while the hindlegs were modified for swimming. These insects live on the banks of ponds and streams and often jump into the water and must swim to get out.

Tonino remembered that pterodactyls were dinosaurs that had fingers (*dactyl*) on their wings (*pteron*). Based on this, he figured out that Tridactylidae crickets must have three paddlelike structures on their hindlegs. This is probably the only cricket group that can swim. He realized he should have asked Jim and Hope if they could swim.

Tonino's thoughts returned to when he was younger. He remembered watching the video of Disney's *Pinocchio* with the Yin family. He liked to tell everyone that he was related to Jiminy Cricket. His human friends would just look at him and say, "You have a great imagination." In other words, they didn't believe him. His animal friends, however, especially the insects, were greatly impressed. Jiminy Cricket was one of their heroes because few animals were fortunate enough to be so well established in the literature of humans. Tonino was impressed that in Disney's film, *Pinocchio* had the brilliant idea of lighting a fire inside the whale, causing him to sneeze, thus permitting them to escape. Tonino wondered what type of whale could stay underwater so long without surfacing for air. He launched into another tidbit of information, and Susan, as usual, listened politely. "After all, whales are voluntary air-breathing mammals. If they were to fall unconscious underwater, they would drown." Tonino, however, had no reason to tell Susan about insect breathing. She already knew.

Entomologists know that insects do not have noses and lungs, thus technically they do not breathe. Instead they use what is called tracheal respiration. The movement of the upper and lower part of the body is called ventilation. This muscular movement helps

212

get air into the tracheal system by compressing the trachea. This forces the air out, and when the muscles relax, the trachea spring back to original size and air enters. The spiracles or openings to the respiratory system are located on each of the abdominal segments and on the last two thoracic segments. These openings lead into a series of flexible tubes called trachea, which are kept open by spirals of chitin called taenidia. Just inside the spiracles are tiny, chitinous hairlike structures that filter out dust, just like the hairs in the nostrils of humans. Finally, these spiracles can be closed or opened by special sets of muscles.

Tonino thought about why he didn't like certain things. Whenever he would say he didn't like something, such as being on the water, his parents would ask, "How do you know you don't like it if you have never tried it?" This was so true. He had always said he didn't like papayas, even though he had never eaten one. Remember, his first opportunity to eat one was at Dennis and Lisa's apartment. He really had no choice but to eat it because Susan was very persistent. Even Susan didn't know he had never eaten a papaya before. After Tonino put his spoon down, he announced to everyone, "Now that was delicious." He enjoyed testing himself by doing things he didn't want to do or trying things he didn't like.

When they got back to Aunt Mary and Uncle John's house, the fresh ocean air had made them tired, so they were not very talkative at dinner.

Tonino Goes Whale Watching

Susan's aunt and uncle purchased tickets for everyone to go on a whale watch. Susan had told them how they had to cancel their whale watching trip in California because of bad weather, so Aunt Mary wanted to surprise them. Uncle John personally knew Captain Dan McSweeney, who owned *Whale Watch Adventures*. That evening at dinner, Uncle John announced to everyone that tomorrow he and Aunt Mary were going to take the day off from work, and they wanted Susan and Tonino to join them on a whale watch. Tonino and Susan could not disappoint them when they had already gone through the trouble of getting the tickets and arranging for extra help to cover their work on the farm.

"Do you get seasick?" they asked both Tonino and Susan at breakfast the next morning.

They both looked at one another as if to say, "How do we know? We have never even been on the water before, and we don't think insects can get seasick."

As insects, they were correct when saying, "We don't think insects can get seasick." Humans have an inner ear apparatus that contains a fluid and tiny hairs called cilia that function as our organ of balance. Basically, insects and humans are very much alike, but there are some differences. Since insects lack cilia, it is highly unlikely that they can get seasick. Being seasick or having motion sickness, however, can also be caused by messages being sent by the eyes to that part of the brain controlling balance. Whether this functions in insects is not known.

Being young and proud, they both answered, "Of course we don't!" Just to make sure they wouldn't get sick, neither of them ate breakfast.

As they approached the marina at Honokohau Harbor on the Kona coast, Susan pointed out the van with a ten-foot, fiberglass humpback whale model on top and large letters on the side saying, "Whale Watching Adventures." Before boarding the boat, they were each given a wonderful brochure, *Whale Watching Guide: Hawai'i's Marine Mammals*, which described almost everything you ever wanted to know about whales and dolphins. Really, Tonino, Susan, Uncle John, and Aunt Mary didn't need this written material since Captain Dan did such a wonderful job of talking the tourists through the lives and habits of whales.

In Captain Dan's words, "There are two kinds of whales, baleen whales and toothed whales. Baleen whales have a horny, tough material, like fingernails, that continuously grows from the roof of the mouth and hangs down like the bristles on a paintbrush or the dried fibers of a crushed coconut. It's called baleen. Baleen whales, which include the humpback, gray, blue, and right, use the baleen to filter out the zooplankton (i.e., krill, and other small organisms from the sea water they take into their mouths). Before swallowing what they have gulped into their mouths, the water is pushed out through the baleen, which acts like a filter keeping the food particles in, and then they swallow."

Captain Dan went on to give them a clearer explanation of how the baleen really worked. He did this by comparing the baleen mechanism with a food that some of the tourists were familiar with. "It is like eating artichokes. You place the bract into your mouth, leaving just enough hanging out to hold onto, close your teeth onto the bract, and you then gradually pull out the bract. As you withdraw the bract, your teeth act like baleen. In both cases, the teeth and the baleen are the structures keeping the food item in the mouth prior to being swallowed."

Tonino's little computer was working, and he instantaneously remembered eating breadfruit with Pedro and his relatives in Puerto Rico. That was the time when he was comparing the flavor of breadfruit with that of artichokes. He remembered how surprised he was to learn that Captain Cook introduced breadfruit, or 'ulu, to Hawai'i and how this became an important food item for all Polynesian inhabitants.

Captain Dan went on with the regular program. "The other group of whales actually use their teeth, thus they are called toothed whales, like Shamu the killer whale; they eat squid, large fish, and sometimes other marine mammals like seals and walruses."

While he was presenting all this information, Captain McSweeney was constantly scanning the ocean for signs of whales. One good sign is the blow, or a stream of air plus water that whales produce by exhaling when they reach the surface of the water. The blow looks just like Old Faithful, the geyser in Yellowstone National Park. Other signs are tail slaps, chin slaps, and breaching. Breaching is probably the most dramatic. This is when the whale propels itself almost completely out of the water, twists its body, rotates, and crashes down with a great loud slap on the water. Sometimes, the whale is able to completely get its body out of water. Dan went on to explain how Pacific Life Insurance Company has a wonderful logo showing a breaching whale.

Just as Captain Dan started another sentence, Tonino interrupted and shouted, "There is one breaching at ten o'clock!"

Everyone quickly got up from their seat and headed for the railings with digital cameras, video recorders, and binoculars in hand.

"It's a humpback (*Megaptera novaeangliae*) calf. Wait just a moment and the mother should surface," Dan announced over the loudspeaker.

Just then, a huge shiny black object began to emerge from underneath the ocean's surface. First Tonino could see the blowhole with all the water vapor from its exhalation (90 percent of air in the lungs is expelled in whales, while humans only exhale about 40 percent), plus some surface water shooting out, then out came the dark region between the blowhole and the dorsal fin, then the dorsal fin, then the long tail, and finally the fluke of the tail. In just a few moments, up came another huge whale.

"This is the escort male," responded Captain Dan. He went on to explain that each female with a calf at her side was guarded by a single male hoping to mate with her. At this point, Tonino's mind left Hawai'i and switched to Boston, where he had read in the library about male sentinel crickets; they don't sing but station themselves near a singing male in hopes of mating with the female that is attracted to the other male's song. These sentinel males avoid being parasitized by flies that are attracted to the male song. They are sort of escort male crickets.

Once Tonino processed this information, he immediately switched back to Hawai'i and listened to Captain Dan talking. Just then, Tonino noticed a huge splash off to the right, only about a hundred feet away. He missed whatever made the splash. He kept his eyes focused on that spot. Soon, up came a huge head, then the long winglike pectoral fins, all of which was followed by a spectacular twist of the body and the whale landing on its back.

Tonino whispered to Susan, "Did you see those crustylike structures on the pectoral fins?"

"What are they?" Susan replied.

"They are barnacles, which are arthropods, just like us."

"They certainly don't look anything like us."

Their eyes returned to the ocean ballet just in time to see the teenager whales practicing their breaching. It was their beginning lessons, and their mother had been showing them how it was done. It was as if all these whales were trying to use their winglike pectoral fins to fly. Tonino could relate to this because he had recently molted from a tenth instar larva or nymph into a young adult. This last larval molt was meaningful for Tonino. Like teenagers, he couldn't wait to become an adult so that he could do all the things they did. He had always been a bit concerned, however, because his parents knew that at room temperature, house crickets have ten instars, while at 86°F they would have only eight. Like most parents, Giovanni and Maria wanted Tonino to be normal and to develop on time. Unfortunately, however, they could not keep their home at a constant warm temperature. Thus, it took Tonino two extra molts to become an adult with fully mature and functional wings. Tonino now had two functional wings, each containing the essential mechanisms for chirping (i.e., scraper, file, and mirror).

Captain Dan had continued talking, and Tonino's attention returned to hear what he was saying. Only male whales sing and only during the mating season. Scientists are not positive about how they produce the sound because whales lack vocal cords. They can travel a hundred miles and, like elephants, can detect frequencies humans can't hear.

Dan switched topics to the whale young. "Each calf requires about 50 to 150 gallons of milk each day, and that's a lot of milk," Dan announced.

Such a wonderful experience I am having, Tonino said to himself.

Captain Dan went on to talk about the migration routes of these whales, the other marine mammals they might see that day, and how endangered the humpback whale was. Tonino noticed that some of the whales had dark tops and white undersides.

Tonino interrupted by raising his hand. "I would like to know if the black top and white bottom is an example of countershading, and what are the predators of the whale?"

"Great question," Dan responded. "Yes, this is an excellent example of countershading; the whale's main predator is the killer whale."

Dan had been taking a lot of black-and-white pictures. While he was explaining how he used his photos to identify each whale, his technician came around with a photo album to show everyone the key characteristics they used to distinguish an individual whale.

As he leafed through the album balanced on his lap, looking at the hundreds of photographs of dorsal fins and tail flukes, Tonino fondly remembered sitting on his mother's lap when he was little. Instead of whale pictures, he could still see the photographs of his parents and relatives. Dan went on to say that he had established a research foundation whose main goal was to help learn more about individual whales, their habits, and migratory routes.

"We hope this information will help us keep the species from going extinct." This comment from Captain Dan was important to Tonino. He was beginning to realize that many people and groups throughout the world were taking up the charge, not only to save the environment, but to save individual species. This removed a lot of stress because he continually remembered his promise to the Blue Fairy.

Dan was linked with the West Coast Whale Research Foundation, while another group in Hawai'i was connected to the Pacific Whale Foundation. The latter group had made over 2,700 individual identifications in the North Pacific using the pigmentation scars and patterns on the underside of the tail flukes. They also set aside marine sanctuaries for endangered whales and dolphins in Australia, New Zealand, and the United States. Tonino was learning so much. This same scenario sounded so much like the monarch story. Deforestation was leading to destruction of habitat and the possible death of millions of overwintering butterflies. Even though Dr. Brower and others were trying to protect the area, it was a very delicate situation.

"I just wonder if we can really save most of these plants and animals from extinction," Tonino said to Susan. "Especially whales, since some countries, like Japan, still kill them for food."

Tonino had hit a nerve, since Susan was Japanese. Susan gave him an awful look of dissatisfaction.

On the way back to the marina, Tonino figured out in his head that if all forty-eight people on the boat had paid $40, that would come to $1,920. With two trips per day, it would be $3,840 per day. *That's a lot of money*, he said to himself.

Captain Dan was now entertaining questions. Someone asked the same question Tonino wanted to ask: "Is this just a business like running a grocery store?"

"No," replied Dan. "It's a lot more. This is a whole new industry, which is known as ecotourism. In addition to giving people jobs, ecotourism helps collect information about plants and animals that may be endangered, it gives the tourists information about both the living things and their habitats, and it informs everyone about the importance of biodiversity and conservation of both habitats and the living organisms."

"Let me tell you a wonderful saying by Baba Dinn, an African ecologist who loved nature: 'In the end, we will conserve only what we love, we will love only what we understand, we will understand only what we are taught.'"

Dan went on to say, "Ecotourism also focuses on getting people to know and understand more about animals and plants. If they don't know anything about them, they will never be interested in saving them or preserving their habitats."

Tonino chuckled to himself. "What's that all about?" Susan asked.

"The saying Dan just gave is one Howie told me when I was in Nantucket."

Dan continued, "By having ecotours of various ecosystems, there is less detrimental impact on both the habitats and organisms. Do you remember what I said when we spotted our first whale? I said we must not get any closer than a hundred feet."

This all made perfect sense to Tonino.

An older man asked, "What kind of whale was Moby-Dick?"

"He was one of the largest toothed whales, the sperm whale. They were hunted, not only for their meat, but for their oil, which was used to light the lamps of the early settlers in New England."

This was an opportune time for Tonino to ask two burning questions he had always had about whales and his great-grandfather, Jiminy Cricket. "I have two questions," he said. "The first is, what kind of whale was Monstro in Disney's *Pinocchio*? Second, how long could a whale of that type stay underwater without breathing?"

"Like Moby-Dick, Monstro was also a sperm whale. Of all the whales, sperm whales can stay underwater the longest: between one to two hours," replied Captain Dan. No one had ever asked Dan these questions before, so he asked Tonino, "Why are you interested in knowing about Pinocchio and how long sperm whales can stay underwater?"

Tonino didn't want to reveal his true identity. "I just wanted to know," replied Tonino.

Tonino's interest in words led to another question he asked Captain Dan. "You said the scientific name of the humpback whale is *Megaptera novaeangliae*. I wonder if the genus name means large wing, and if so, does it refer to the large, long flippers?"

"I don't know, but it is a great question," Dan replied.

Tonino thought to himself about the word *pteron*, which means "wing," but for the whale it must refer to his large pectoral fins. Thus, *apterous* would mean "without wings."

Huh, he said to himself. *I now have some new words.* Tonino also thought about the species name *novaeangliae*, but he couldn't figure it out.

He asked Captain Dan, who responded, "The species name refers to the New England coastal waters where the humpback was once very abundant." Dan announced he would like to use the last ten minutes of the trip to play some recordings he had made of humpback whales over the twenty-three years he had been studying them. He said, "I would like everyone to remain silent and just reflect on this trip and think about how gentle these large, endangered, and elegant marine mammals really are."

As the tape came on, Tonino immediately thought about John Keawe's *Whale Talk*, which he had played at the Bamboo restaurant. Tonino could now put real images to the song, which was about the conversation between a mother humpback and her calf. Tonino would not let go of the fact that the Japanese were still killing whales for food.

Tonino looked at Susan and said, "Why would anyone want to kill these gentle and harmless marine mammals?"

Rather than giving Tonino the pleasure of making her angry, Susan just shrugged her shoulders and refused to answer the question.

Tonino continued to think about the similarity between Kokopeli, the humpback flute player, and the humpback whale, which also used sounds or music to attract a female.

After they left the boat, Tonino stopped at the van with the large whale on top to buy a T-shirt depicting several different kinds of whales. He did this because the money from the sale of these shirts went to support Dan's research on whales. Tonino's appetite had been whetted. He wanted to know more about whales and these wonderful islands in the South Pacific. He told Susan's aunt and uncle about these thoughts while riding back to their farm. Aunt Mary said they had a *National Geographic* video series, *Nomads of the Wind*, which focused on the original discoverers and how they settled the Pacific Islands. "You are welcome to watch it," she said.

Other Polynesian Islands, Different Languages, and Images

Because they were only going to one other island, New Zealand, Tonino felt watching the video series would give him a more complete knowledge about the 20,000 to 30,000 islands in the Pacific Ocean. After dinner, they started the video. Tonino already knew some of the information because he had seen *Polynesian Odyssey* in the IMAX theater on Oahu. It was important for Tonino to integrate information, thus giving him a more meaningful experience. He didn't just like learning isolated facts, he liked to get a complete picture by integrating various facts. It was amazing how things were fitting together. It was as if all the isolated experiences in his life to date were falling into place and were fitting together like pieces of a puzzle. He realized that his life would not be complete until all the pieces were put together, and not a single piece remained. *Only after death will the puzzle of my life be completed*, he said to himself.

Tonino was experiencing an influx of ideas and new information about different cultures. For instance, before whales, petroglyphs, and monarch butterflies were integrated into the fabric of his life, Tonino didn't know anything about them; he didn't even care to know about them. Now, however, they were major components of his life. He asked himself, *Other than seeing some sailors in Boston and some Polynesians at the cultural center, what do I know about tattoos?* Of course, the answer was absolutely nothing.

He had already borrowed Aunt Mary's Hawai'ian dictionary; now he needed her English dictionary. Tonino was impressed that Aunt Mary and Uncle John spoke three different languages: English, Hawai'ian, and Japanese. He was glad the Blue Fairy had extended his wish to be completely fluent in any language he wanted to speak at that moment. He realized that different cultures spoke entirely different languages, and this only enriched life on this sphere we call Mother Earth. It is truly a part of our human biodiversity, which should be preserved. He wondered how many spoken languages in the United States were no longer used. *Have any of the Native American languages gone extinct?* he asked himself.

One problem, however, that Tonino recognized with so many different languages was that having too many often resulted in poor communication, or no communication at all, between groups; it often resulted in misinterpretation of what was being discussed. He was learning, however, that the Hawai'ian language was surviving and not in danger of going extinct.

Tonino looked up *tattoo* in the *Merriam Webster Dictionary*. Here is what it said: "From the Tahitian word *tatau*, which is an indelible figure fixed upon the body especially by the insertion of a pigment under the skin." This tradition of the Polynesians had its origin about 3000 BC and originated with the ancient Lapita culture of Melanesia and Southeast Asia. The manner and incised decoration of the pottery of the Lapita culture is believed to be the precursor of the Austronesian and Polynesian tattoo. This Lapita pointillè or stipple technique was also applied to the pottery as a form of decoration.

Tonino had many questions that remained unanswered: Was there any connection between the Lapita pointillè technique of decorating pottery and the technique he had seen used by the French impressionists in the Boston Museum of Art? What kind of instrument did the tattooer use to puncture the skin? Why did they wear tattoos? Was there any relationship between the designs on petroglyphs and those of tattoos? Tonino later read in the book he purchased on Hawai'ian petroglyphs that there is a petroglyph of a bird figure that was also used in ancient tattoo design.

He asked himself, *I wonder what they use for a pigment?* He had heard that the *moko* or Maori tattoos of the people of New Zealand were considered one of the most extensive of all the Polynesian peoples, possibly with the exception of those of the Marquesas Islands. Between AD 500 and 600, when the Hawai'ian islands were settled by the Marquesans, the custom of tattooing came with them. The Hawai'ian tattoo, however, was much simpler and was limited to small areas of the body. In fact, on his third and last voyage, Captain Cook wrote, "Tattowing [sic tattooing] or staining the skin is practiced here, but not in a high degree, nor does it appear to be directed by any particular mode, but rather by fancy. The figures were straight lines, stars, and circles, and many had the figure of the *Taame* or breast plate of Otahiete, though we saw it not among them."

Tonino now knew that Hawai'ians used tattoos, but to a limited extent compared to the Maoris. He was also excited to learn that the Hawai'ians originally used a bone instrument, *moli*, and the sap of the leadwort, an indigenous plant, to blacken them. Finally, he learned that there were many different names for tattoo in the Hawai'ian language, and each name was dependent on what the tattoo looked like and how it was made (some were made with dots, others with spots).

In his new book on petroglyphs, Tonino learned that the earliest style of human designation was the stick figure. Males are represented by a close-waisted figure and often had long genitalia, while females had an open-waisted figure, which designated the birth canal or uterus. Reading about these stick figures and how they were made in the rock, he wondered why no one had ever done a "stick insect." He then remembered the stick insect design he saw in the American Southwest, even though it wasn't a petroglyph. After learning all he had time for about tattooing, Tonino couldn't wait to get to New Zealand to find out more about this interesting cultural tradition.

Tonino's heritage dates back to the Romans, who had a written language. Even though he loved books and the written word, Tonino was becoming more and more interested in those cultures that lacked a written language; these societies either preserved their cultures in a spoken form that was passed down through the ages or left just a graphic representation of their culture (e.g., zemis, Mimbres bowls, or petroglyphs). Susan remembered Tonino telling her about the petroglyphs he saw during his trips to Puerto Rico, New Mexico, and Arizona. He often spoke about the book by Campbell Grant, which was about the people and rock art of Canyon de Chelly. Of course, Tonino had the book. He couldn't resist buying books that interested him. His room at home had several shelves filled with them. They didn't, however, always remain on the shelves, because once in a while he noticed his parents looking at them.

After looking up information in the dictionary about tattoos and settling into reading his new book on Hawai'ian petroglyphs, Tonino kept visualizing the figures he had seen on his trips to Puerto Rico and the American Southwest. Finding what he was doing so interesting, Tonino called Susan to tell her what he had learned.

"How much the images look alike," he told her. "A good example is the petroglyph symbol for a woman. In Hawai'i it is shown as an open circle, with the opening at the bottom representing the birth canal, and a dot in the center of the circle, while in the American Southwest the circle arrangement and the dot are identical, but the Native Americans have added arms and a head. To my knowledge, these two cultures had no contact and yet they came up with the same symbol for woman. This situation is unlike the Mimbreño designs of birds and various lizards on their pottery, which are

225

similar to some of the Hohokam designs, but here the two peoples had contact. The Hawai'i and Native American situation is like intellectual convergent evolution."

In fact, anthropologists call it independent discovery or invention. It was also striking that the objects or forms depicted in both places were also very similar (i.e., people, daily implements, types of clothing, and animals). At the Puoko Petroglyph Archaeological Preserve near the Mauna Lani Resort, as elsewhere in Hawai'i, the petroglyphs, known as *k'iipohaku,* or images in stone, were done in *pa'hoehoe,* or smooth lava with stone tools. At this site there are about 1,200 petroglyphs. None of the books on petroglyphs he had read, and none of the real petroglyphs he had seen, so far, included insects. Other animals were depicted, especially larger animals, such as deer, fish, birds, whales, and sharks, but not insects. Tonino realized that one must be very careful in interpreting the meaning and significance of various artifacts, such as petroglyphs.

Spirit of Place by Lee and Stasack (1999) takes a more scientific approach to the meaning of Hawai'ian petroglyphs. This book even has a section on kite petroglyphs. It appears that the Polynesians made and flew kites. In fact, they may have been the first flying machines; the authors explain how the Polynesians used kites to power and pull rafts. As usual, specific myths are associated with kite flying in Hawai'i. To Tonino's surprise, the book has a section on petroglyph transformers. These show men taking the form of either fish or turtles and reports that by taking on these forms, humans would be able to cross boundaries between their lives and those of the animal. The idea of transformation is worldwide, has permeated all cultures, and has impacted the lives of many people.

Wondering why no insect petroglyphs exist, Tonino got his laptop out and put in a disc marked "Petroglyphs." One of the file names is "Insects in Southwestern Native American Cultures." He pulled up that topic. Two references stood out. They are Cole's *Legacy on Stone: Rock Art of the Colorado Plateau and Four Corners* and Schaafsma's *Rock Art in New Mexico.* He then remembered the figures of the insects, especially of the cricket, depicted on the Mimbres sherds. Returning to his new book on Hawai'ian petroglyphs, he noticed several stick figures of men. These rock carvings were not only made on exposed rock, one was carved on the sides of a lava tube. Tonino learned that this is a hollow tube formed by molten lava flowing underground in already formed channels or by lava cooling on the sides, forming a channel and then forming a roof over the top. This creates a structure like a straw through which future lava can flow. This reminded him that he and Susan must make a trip to see the volcanoes and flowing lava before they leave this enchanting group of islands.

A Monarch Festival

Time was going so fast that only twelve days remained before they were off to New Zealand. Tonino looked at Susan and said, "What should we do our remaining days?"

"I don't care; why don't you get a newspaper and see what's happening?"

Tonino walked up to the mailbox to get the daily paper. Aunt Mary and Uncle John were gone for two days to buy some new farm equipment in Honolulu. They had left the pickup for them to use. Grabbing the paper out of the mailbox, Tonino opened it and started to read it as he slowly walked back to the house. All of a sudden, he changed his pace and shouted, "Wow!" as he quickly hopped back to the house. Susan could hear him all the way in the house. As he hopped into the house, Susan could see how excited he was.

"What has you so excited?" she asked.

"Look here! It says that tomorrow is the beginning of the Merrie Monarch Festival. We must go!" Tonino shouted enthusiastically.

As you know by now, this was not how Tonino usually planned to go somewhere. Usually he would get some literature about where they were going and possibly even call a few people to make plans for such an event.

Apparently, he was so excited about going to a monarch butterfly festival that he charged ahead with his eyes closed. In cricket form, however, he obviously couldn't have done this. Regardless, when Tonino was like this it was almost impossible to change his mind. Early the next morning, after checking everything they were supposed to on the farm, Tonino and Susan set off for Hilo to see the monarchs.

As they entered Hilo, they couldn't believe the traffic. Even though parking was difficult to find, they parked not too far from the stadium. The three days of events were held in the 5,000-seat Edith Kanakaole Stadium. There were huge buses and many smaller buses bringing people from the hotels to the event. Tonino knew this because he could read the names of the hotels on the sides of the buses. "I can't believe so many people have come just to see a butterfly," he said. "Then again, some people go crazy over insects."

When they arrived at the stadium where all the main events were going to take place, they realized they hadn't reserved tickets. "It will be impossible for us to get tickets this late," said Tonino.

In an instant, and with a blink of the human eye (but not a cricket's compound eye, since insects do not have eyelids and cannot close their eyes), two small crickets paraded, hopped, and weaved in and out between the feet of hundreds of spectators anxiously waiting in line. From behind, it was easy to tell Susan from Tonino because she had a long and beautiful ovipositor at the tip of her abdomen and located between the two cerci. She carried it in such a pretty way. This was one special thing Tonino noticed about her when they first met in Tanglewood. As they hopped their way through the crowd, they almost got stepped on a couple of times.

Finally, they made their way into the stadium and up to a position where they could see the large stage with two side ramps leading up to the platform. They saw a lot of people and beautiful stage settings, they heard loud music, but they saw no signs of any monarchs. Not even a picture of one. Susan was busy looking at all the ladies. They were wearing colorful dresses known as *muumuus* and had beautiful wreath leis around their necks. They even had head leis, beautiful arrangements of flowers in their hair.

She commented on this to Tonino, saying, "Just look at all those beautiful flowers."

"I know," said Tonino. "It must have taken hours to prepare them. Also, did you see the men were also wearing leis around their necks? What a spectacular and colorful event, and just think of it, all to celebrate a butterfly."

Before they knew it, six young boys came out on stage and blew conch shells to start the event. The royal court was introduced, and they paraded in and took their seats.

By this time, Tonino even had Susan convinced. "Such a wonderful ceremony for celebrating a beautiful butterfly," she said.

Frustrated, he said to himself, *This is very odd!* As a cricket, he couldn't hear what they were saying, but he could read what this event was about. He looked up and noticed everyone was reading something. When the Hawai'ian national anthem was being sung, a man near him put down the booklet he was reading. Tonino quickly hopped over. On the front cover was a picture of some man he didn't know. It wasn't Lincoln Brower or Orley Taylor. He quickly read, "Thirty-Second Annual Merrie Monarch Festival." This didn't tell him anything more than before. He then read what it said below the picture of the person: "Hula is the language of the heart & therefore the heartbeat of the Hawai'ian people."

At the end of the anthem, and just before the man reached to retrieve his program, Tonino hopped off to rejoin Susan, who had moved to the center of the bleachers; this was probably the best seat in the house for two crickets. As they would later find out, it was also the place where channel 4 had one of its television cameras.

"What did that brochure say?" Susan said as she poked Tonino with her left foreleg.

Tonino started to tell Susan what he had read; as the announcer was introducing the first *wahine* group (a woman's group) from Koala, Hawai'i, Susan started acting very strange. She ignored Tonino and kept her eyes fixed on the stage while Tonino talked to her. Just when Tonino started to tell her about the saying at the bottom of the program he noticed Susan was completely focused on what was happening on the stage. He realized Susan was no longer listening. As he turned, he could see what Susan was so engrossed in watching. On the stage were forty female dancers. They all wore beautiful dresses made out of some sort of plant. They also had plant material and flowers in their hair. They were all dressed alike but each dancer's face was very different and beautiful. Around their necks were beautiful leis. The dancing was exceptionally beautiful and was done in conjunction with music.

By this time, they realized this was a hula contest and not a celebration of any monarch butterfly. "Why use the words *Merrie Monarch*?" Susan asked Tonino.

"I have no idea."

Since they had come such a long way, and they both loved different cultures, they decided to stay. Besides, this would give them a better insight into another aspect of Hawai'ian culture.

"Let's stay, but we have to leave around ten o'clock in order to get to the farm before it's too late."

There were several short breaks during the program so people could move around instead of sitting in one place for such long periods of time. During the first break, a woman sitting just next to Tonino and Susan removed her crown flower lei and placed it beside them on the bleachers.

Lei Day is celebrated each year in Hawai'i on May 1. Loved ones are given leis of different types. Giving someone a lei is a sign of welcome or congratulations, or it can even mean "I love you." The crown flower, or *pua kalaunu,* has several varieties and makes exceptional leis. One variety has a completely white flower, another has a solid lavender form, while another is mostly white with purple markings on the petals. The lavender variety was introduced into Hawai'i about 1888, while the white form from India and the Far East was introduced in 1920. The Hawai'ians decorate their heads and necks with beautiful things. After all, these two parts of the body are considered sacred by Hawai'ians.

The crown flower is a perfect flower to use for leis. It is regal looking because, when the petals are removed, the remaining part looks like a crown. It also doesn't have an overpowering smell like some flowers. In addition, four different types of leis can be made from this plant. A lei made from just the crown, without the petals, usually has seventy to eighty crowns. A lei made from the whole flower takes about fifty to seventy blossoms, while a crown flower bud lei and crown flower petal lei each take about sixty and a hundred flowers, respectively.

Tonino immediately recognized the flower the lei was made from. He pointed out to Susan, "Look, these are the flowers from the same plant Dennis showed us at the university near Dr. Stimson's office."

Tonino counted how many flowers made up the lei; he was concerned that by removing the flowers to make leis, the plants would not have a chance to be pollinated by insects and wouldn't produce seeds. As he hopped around the lei counting the last flower, which was seventy-five, he saw something no one else noticed, not even the person wearing it. On one of the crown flowers was a recently hatched, first instar monarch caterpillar. Normally caterpillars eat leaves, but it probably was removed when the person making the leis removed the flowers. Having nothing else to eat, it had already made a hole in one of the petals.

Tonino had to act quickly since he knew that if he didn't, he wouldn't be able to save the caterpillar from either being killed by the person wearing the lei or starving to death. With some great persuasion, he convinced the caterpillar to crawl off the flower. He explained to the caterpillar what its fate would be if it didn't join them.

Tonino used the word *its* because it is almost impossible to tell the sex of a caterpillar, especially the first instar. Tonino didn't know if it was a male or female. Unlike the adults, where it is easy to tell the males because of the obvious, black scent pouches on the hindwings, it is impossible to tell the sex of caterpillars.

Tonino was correct. Just as the newly hatched caterpillar left the flower, the woman picked up her lei. While she was putting it on, she noticed the small hole in the petal of the flower.

"I wonder what made that hole?" she asked her friend.

"I have no idea," her friend replied.

Tonino told Susan that they would transform back into humans around ten o'clock; he explained to the caterpillar that they would take the caterpillar back to the farm with them. "Don't be afraid, we won't hurt you," they assured the caterpillar.

At 9:55 p.m., there was a break and no one noticed the two crickets turning into humans. Also, no one noticed Tonino carefully picking up the caterpillar and putting it into an empty Kona coffee cup. As they started to leave, Tonino put the cup into his pocket.

They left the gate to the stadium and finally found their uncle's pickup truck. "Even though we didn't see any adult monarch butterflies," Tonino said, "you must admit we learned a lot about the hula, and hopefully we saved a monarch caterpillar."

They both felt like great conservationists.

"We also heard some beautiful music," Susan said as they started back to Honokaa.

"The historical aspect of the festival interested me the most," said Tonino.

Susan said, "We now know it was King David Kalakaua, the Merrie Monarch, who was on the front of the program. In 1886, at the King's Jubilee, he first used the ukulele to accompany the hula dancers. Just think a moment, if it wasn't for him this aspect of Hawai'ian culture would have been lost, and this wonderful art form depicting both language and culture would have gone extinct."

Tonino said, "It is difficult for me to understand why the missionaries banned the hula. Just think if King Kalakaua didn't establish this festival, an entire aspect of Hawai'ian culture could have been lost forever." Tonino often repeated exactly what Susan just said.

Susan and Tonino were both feeling good about this evening's events. Not only did they learn a lot, they were also going to help save a monarch's life.

When they got to the farm, they got a flashlight and went to the crown flower plant near the old barn. Tonino placed the cup down next to a small new shoot of the giant milkweed, carefully opened it, and tipped it over so the caterpillar could crawl out. In order to communicate with the caterpillar, they changed back to crickets. The caterpillar was just about to crawl out of the cup.

"Wait a minute!" Tonino shouted.

In fact, since caterpillars don't hear well, he had to shout the same message a couple of times, louder and louder each time. The caterpillar stopped in its place. Several of its prolegs stopped in midair as if the caterpillar was trying to avoid stepping on something unpleasant. "What do you want?" the caterpillar asked.

"I just want to make sure you get onto the white crown flower plant before we shut off the flashlight," he said. "What's your name?"

"My name is Faith," the caterpillar responded as she put down her prolegs one at a time, grasping the plant with her hooklike crockets at the terminal of each proleg, and slowly climbed onto the crown plant. "Thank you both for saving my life. Maybe someday I can do something for you. It is not pleasant to die of starvation. By the way, what are your names?"

They each told Faith their names. As soon as she was on the crown flower plant, the two crickets transformed, picked up the flashlight, and started toward the house.

Susan had been thinking about what Faith, the monarch caterpillar, had said to them. "How do you think a monarch caterpillar could ever help us?" she asked Tonino.

"Other than being very beautiful and lifting our spirits, I don't know," Tonino replied.

Susan had never been that close to a caterpillar before. "What are those black, filamentlike structures on her anterior and posterior ends?" she asked.

"I don't really know what their function is, but I believe they are called tentacles."

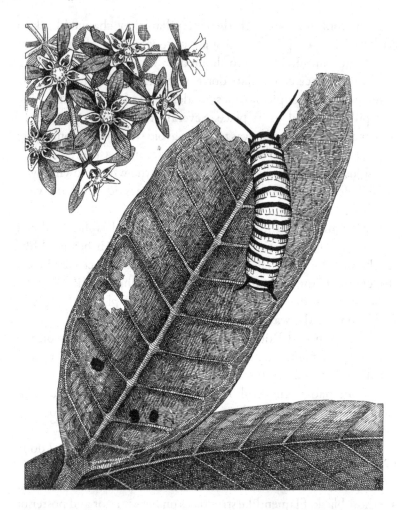

Susan did not have the same passion for animal life that Tonino did. Thus, she was often frightened by their sudden appearance. Just before they arrived at the back door, a large object flew erratically and landed on Susan's arm. She was terrified. "Get it off me! Hurry, Tonino, it's a bat, hurry, get it off me!"

Tonino knew what it was from his experience in Puerto Rico; he put his hand under the moth and lifted it away from Susan. "Don't be afraid, it's not a bat, it's only the black witch moth."

"You mean it really isn't a bat?"

"That's correct. Some people also think it is a nocturnal butterfly, but it's just a moth in the family Noctuiidae. It also migrates like the monarch, and its wingspread can be as much as seven inches. In Mexico it is called the 'butterfly of death,' or *mariposa de la muerte*. Various cultures have developed different myths associated with the moth. Several view it as an omen of death, but the Hawai'ians believe if a moth lands on you, it is the soul of some loved one who has come to say good-bye. I am sure you will like the myth associated with the Bahamans better. There, the moth is known as the money moth."

"Why is that?" asked Susan.

"They believe that you will receive a lot of money if a moth lands on you."

"Well, I hope that it's true. Going to college is going to be very expensive."

That evening, before retiring, both Susan and Tonino discussed how one culture is often invaded by another culture, which usually leads to the loss of the first culture (a.k.a. acculturation). That evening at the Merrie Monarch Festival they had learned that the hula, which was so important in helping tell stories about Hawai'ian history, had been banned by the missionaries but was saved by the Merrie Monarch. Susan, who loved plants, mentioned to Tonino how their trip a few days ago to the Amy Greenwell Ethnobotany Garden, in the village of Captain Cook, was encouraging because now botanists were working with traditional medicine men to help preserve important plants used in ancient times. They learned that "Papa" Henry Auwae, a medicine man from Hilo who had died at the age of ninety-four in 2001, never charged for his services, and his list of herbal medicinal plants included 2,500 different plant species.

"We just don't know what new drugs are out there," Tonino remarked to Susan. He continued by saying, "Again, as we have said before, this is why we must preserve and conserve endangered plants and animals. I also believe that many ancient cultures, such as Native American and Hawai'ian, are beginning to renew their

---

traditional medicine programs, and these should be incorporated into what we know as Western medicine."

They also discussed how they had misunderstood what they had read in the newspaper. They certainly couldn't admit this to Susan's aunt and uncle.

Some evenings, Tonino read until he was tired enough to fall asleep. That night, while he was looking for something to read, he noticed a pamphlet on the coffee table in the living room. He picked it up and started to read the pamphlet, *Rare Animals and Plants of Haleakala National Park.*

Susan, in contrast, liked to watch the news on TV before going to bed. While Tonino sat down to read the pamphlet, Susan turned on channel 4. There was a story about the Merrie Monarch Festival. Susan told Tonino to stop what he was reading and watch. They both clapped as the commentator announced the hula contest winners. The report ended by showing the audience at the festival. The camera moved down and suddenly stopped and focused on three unusual guests. "As you can see," the announcer said, "there were three special insect guests here at the Merrie Monarch Festival. I hope they enjoyed tonight's events as much as we did. *Mahalo* and good night."

Tonino thought to himself, *Little did the commentator know that it was not just any caterpillar but a monarch.*

Susan and Tonino just looked at one another in disbelief.

As she turned off the TV, Susan said to Tonino, "Don't stay up too late reading. We have to get up early to check on Faith."

"Don't worry," he said. "I won't."

Susan knew that if Tonino found something interesting to read, he often wouldn't put it down until he finished.

Late Night Reading; Habitats Threatened

The booklet he was reading discussed how Hawai'i was being threatened by human intervention. Tonino didn't know that islands were more fragile systems than major continents.

He learned that Haleakala National Park is located on the island of Maui. Many of the life forms on Maui, and the other Hawai'ian islands, were results of millions of years of evolution. In fact, it's believed the Hawai'ian archipelago is made up of 8 major and about 124 smaller islands. These islands, estimated to be over forty million years old, are isolated; over two thousand miles separate them from the closest continent. Because of this isolation, and its tremendous variety of habitats, unique life forms have evolved here.

Now, however, the various habitats, plus their living organisms, were being threatened by introduced animals, such as pigs, rats, mongooses, even the mechanical bulldozer, and now the coqui or minuscule tree frog from Puerto Rico. Tonino remembered asking Pedro if he knew what *Eleutherodactylus*, the genus name for the coqui, meant. At the time, neither knew, but now Tonino knew it meant "free toes," which refers to the fact that the toes are not webbed. He remembered how noisy it had been that evening at dinner in Puerto Rico, and now he understood why the Hawai'ians consider the small frog a real pest.

"It's noise pollution at its best," Tonino said out loud. Of course, Susan wasn't there to hear.

Even though the mongoose, for example, was introduced to the islands of Hawai'i for a good cause (to kill the rats that were out of control on the sugar plantations), it had now become a pest and was threatening the island's native bird life.

Tonino thought to himself, *What is a pest?* He went to the dictionary and read, "In nature there is no such thing as a pest. This term only applies to how humans relate to other life forms, and often to themselves. Thus, a pest is something that somehow interferes with our normal lifestyle." Tonino thought about the small tree frog recently introduced into Hawai'i. It was a pest because it was not only eating all the native insects, it was also causing noise pollution. Tonino continued to read the pamphlet and saw a beautiful line drawing of the Hawai'ian cricket, *Prognathogryllus kipahulu* Otte. Tonino had learned in high school biology class that the first part of the scientific name for any living organism is the genus and the second is the species name. He also learned that what follows often designates the person who identified the specimen. Thus, it was natural that he would think that this Hawai'ian cricket had been discovered by Dan Otte. In addition to this genus of crickets, there were three other genera on the island of Maui: *Paratrigonidium*, *Leptogryllus*, and *Thaumatogryllus*.

Further on in the pamphlet it mentioned that even though many of the species of crickets live in a fully protected research sanctuary on Maui, the cricket's survival is being threatened by rats and rodents, which prey upon these rare insects. Tonino was greatly impressed with this pamphlet but was mortified by the thought of being eaten by a rat. Tonino thought of David and Bruce, his mouse friends in Boston and New York, plus Emmaline from Amherst. He was sure that none of them would ever harm him. He recalled Dan Otte's statement that many hundreds of species of crickets still remained undiscovered. "I guess Wilson and Janzen are right," he said. Just as Susan entered the room, he said, "We had better get to the task of describing all these plants and animals before they become extinct."

Because Susan hadn't heard everything he said, she answered with a question, "What are you talking about?"

Tonino, without looking up, said to Susan, "Nothing, just thinking out loud."

Susan and Tonino realized they had done very little to help Aunt Mary and Uncle John around the farm, so they offered to help. They worked very hard at different chores. This made Susan's aunt and uncle very pleased. Not that they needed the help, but it was encouraging to them that these two youngsters knew enough to offer to help their relatives.

Faith's Progress

Every day, Susan and Tonino checked on Faith's progress. She had eaten so much she left huge holes in the leaves of the milkweed plant.

"What are those black things that look like small blackberries on some of the leaves?" asked Susan.

"That's caterpillar poop or, more entomologically correct, frass. I remember Dr. Stoffolano telling me that when he had some researchers from Italy at his home, and they were standing underneath the maple tree in his yard, one of them said, 'It's raining.'

"'Not true,' Dr. Stoffolano had said. 'That's feces or frass from the gypsy moth caterpillars raining down on us.'"

Before they knew it, Faith had turned into a beautiful green and gold chrysalis (the exocuticle of the exoskeleton of the last instar larva, inside of which the adult butterfly is formed). They felt good. Not only had they helped Aunt Mary and Uncle John, but they also helped this monarch, which certainly would have died and now was almost ready to emerge as an adult.

Volcanoes, Lava, and Lava Crickets

The following day, they planned to visit Hawai'i's Volcanoes National Park, which was about an hour and thirty minutes from Honokaa by truck; before they left, they checked on Faith. The sun was shining on the chrysalis, which normally looked like a green jewel with some gold spots. Now, however, it was clear, and they could see the dark black and orange adult butterfly starting to emerge. Faith didn't quite have her wings fully expanded; Tonino asked if they could help her.

"No, I am okay," she said. With that reassurance, Faith continued to swallow air and get her heart rate accelerated so that she could pump hemolymph into the veins of her wings using the wing accessory pulsatile organs. This is how butterflies, moths, and most winged insects unfold their wings.

Once her wings were unfolded, Tonino said, "We are leaving now to see the volcano. Is there anything else we can help you with?"

"No, I'm fine. However, I may not be here when you return, so I want to thank you both for all you have done for me."

"You're welcome," they said, and off they went.

When they arrived at the national park, they first looked at the large, inactive Kilauea crater. After that, they went to the visitor's center. Tonino wanted to learn something about volcanoes and see an active lava flow. Susan convinced him to read the various posters before doing anything. They were able to read the following information about the park: Volcanoes National Park was established in 1916 as the twelfth national park in the United States. The legend has it that Pele, probably the most feared and most revered Hawai'ian goddess, was chased from Niihau, a smaller island, and she came to reside in Halema'uma'u crater, which is at the southern end of the Kilauea Caldera.

Tonino looked at the park on a map. "It makes up 377 square miles of the most diverse habitat and goes from desert to rain forest," Tonino said.

"We had better go and hear the slide show about the park and volcanoes. It's the best way to get a quick overview of the area," Susan said.

Just before the lights went out, they hopped into the last seats at the auditorium. The talk took only twenty minutes, and before they knew it, they had to leave so another group could enter. Tonino thought that, in addition to museums, zoos, nature centers, and ecotourism, the U.S. National Park System, which includes 384 parks, was a great idea; in 1916, President Woodrow Wilson had approved legislation to establish the National Park Service.

After the slide show, Tonino asked Susan, "What did you learn?"

She replied, "That women, like Pele, were considered by several different cultures to have key roles in nature. Many cultures were matriarchal and not patriarchal."

"What do you mean?" asked Tonino, looking bewildered.

She went on to explain. "Remember you told me that for the Native Americans the earth is referred to as Mother Earth? We just learned that one of the most powerful Hawai'ian gods was Pele, often called the 'Woman of the Pit.' They believe she boiled the rocks and sent the torrents of lava down on the land below."

"We probably should leave many worldly or important matters in the hands of women," replied Tonino. He went on to say, "You know, my father would never even consider giving such important matters to women. I guess it depends on your generation, because I have no problem with it."

"That's good," replied Susan. "It was also interesting that the evidence that the god was a woman was based on the two forms or shapes of lava often found after an eruption. These forms looked like strands of hair, referred to as either Pele's hair or Pele's tears."

They also learned there are basically two distinct types of lava, *a'a* (chunky, rough, and spiny) and *pa'hoehoe* (smooth, almost like uncooked cake batter). Based on his prior visit to the Bishop Museum, Tonino was anxious to see the crickets that were in some way associated with lava.

They then went to the gift shop of the lodge. Fortunately for Tonino, he recognized Frank Howarth, whom he had met at the Bishop Museum. Frank and Tonino struck up a conversation. Tonino remembered that Frank received his BS degree in entomology at the University of Massachusetts and knew that he had published a book with William Mull on Hawai'ian insects and their relatives. Frank and Fred Stone also published articles on crickets of the Big Island. Based on the writings of these people, Tonino wanted to see *Caconemodius fori* Gurney and Rentz, a cricket species that lives in the cracks of the lava during the day but comes out at night to feed. He also wanted to see the cave crickets that live in the lava tubes. Tonino and Susan were going to see the active lava flow at night, so he convinced her to see if they could find the lava tube crickets.

It was only a ten-minute drive to the lava tube. After a short time in the lava tube, Tonino turned to Susan and said, "Let's go and see how Mother Nature creates new habitats for living organisms."

"What do you mean?"

"I don't find these lava tubes very exciting. I want to see the real, hot, flowing lava."

They were disappointed they couldn't find any lava-tube crickets. It was getting dark, and they drove down to the ocean near Pahoa to see an active lava flow before returning to the farm. It was about a forty-five-minute drive down the southeast side of the volcano. As they approached the ocean, they could see a thirty-foot cloud of steam rising from the site where the lava was flowing into the water. It was one of the most fascinating, and truly memorable, sights Tonino had ever experienced. Here was hot lava, which looked like red-hot embers of coal except that it was over 2,000°C. Tonino remembered his father telling him about the eruption of Mount Vesuvius in Italy, which had destroyed both Herculaneum and Pompeii.

Tonino told Susan, "You know, the power of natural forces, such as wind, water, fire, and earthquakes, are something we have to learn to live with. As humans, we will never be able to conquer them. As crickets, we take what we get from Mother Nature."

Barriers had been erected along the highway because the lava had recently gone over the road. They stopped, parked the truck, and walked down to an area where the National Park Service had established a temporary office and information booth. They asked about the active lava flow and were told it was best to see it after dark. They were also informed that they would need a flashlight. "Please stay on this side of the roped-off area. It is dangerous to go beyond that point," Matt Stoffolano, the oldest son of Dr. Stoffolano and the ranger in charge, told them emphatically.

Tonino decided that to get a good look at the flowing lava and to see how close the lava crickets live to the active flow, they would have to transform into crickets and go beyond the roped area. "This way," he told Susan, "no one will see us and try to stop us."

"Are you sure we should be doing this?" Susan asked.

Tonino turned around, pulled her close, wrapped his arms around her, gave her a kiss, and said, "Come on! Let's go. You know I wouldn't hurt you."

At that moment, Tonino heard a little voice inside his head saying, *Tonino, you shouldn't be doing this.* Tonino just shook his head and shrugged off his conscience. Before morphing, Tonino noticed an interesting bush near them with many red berries. Tonino asked the ranger if they were edible.

"Yes, but no Hawai'ian would eat them without offering the first berries to Pele. The elders, or *kupuna*, consider not offering the first berry as a serious insult to Pele, who would certainly shower bad luck on those disregarding the ancient custom. Also, these ohelo berries are a favorite food of the nene, Hawai'i's state bird, which is on the endangered list. Where are you folks from?"

Tonino responded, "Massachusetts."

The ranger then said, "Well, you should know that the lowbush blueberry, high bush blueberry, and cranberry, which are all so popular in New England, belong to the same genus as the ohelo berry."

Tonino said, "I read in the Hawai'ian dictionary that the English translation for the 'ohelo berry' is 'cranberry,' but because cranberries only grow in wet bog areas, I don't think this is a good name for the ohelo berry."

This discussion made Tonino wonder about the origin of the word *cranberry*.

Disregarding the warning to stay outside the roped area and to not eat the ohelo berries without first making an offering to Pele, Tonino picked two berries and ate them. "Come on, let's go," he said to Susan. They both transformed and hopped under the yellow roped-off area. No one, not even the ranger, saw the two crickets heading toward the dangerous lava flow. Before they knew it, Susan and Tonino were standing on lava that had solidified and was just a little warm to the touch of their tarsal pads. They crawled down into a lava crack and came upon their first lava cricket. This was the first lava cricket Tonino had seen in Hawai'i, and he was surprised to see he lacked wings. *These crickets are apterous,* he thought to himself. (Tonino wondered how they communicated and why they lacked wings.) He knew it was a male because it just had two cerci at the end of its abdomen and lacked an ovipositor.

Since his parents raised him to be polite, he said, "My name is Tonino."

"My name is Dan," the other cricket responded.

Following their greetings, Tonino and Dan had a long conversation. Tonino told Dan that he and Susan wanted to go to see the active flow. Dan said, "I wouldn't do that if I was you. It is very dangerous, and you can become trapped very easily if the lava flows around you. Then it is like being on an island surrounded, not by water, but by extremely hot lava. It's very dangerous."

Again, Tonino's conscience said, *Tonino, this is the fourth warning: twice by me, once by Matt the ranger, and once by Dan. Don't do it.*

Tonino reassured Susan that nothing would happen if they did this during the day rather than at night. Thus, they decided to spend the night in a well-protected crack and wait until the early morning to get close to the active lava flow. The lava they slept on was just warm enough to prevent them from slowing down too much. The skies were so clear at night that the radiant heat readily escaped from the air, cooling off the ground considerably. The sky above was spectacular. The lack of civilization in this area was excellent for watching the stars, and as Tonino learned later, there are at least nine telescopes for observing the heavens at the Mauna Kea Observatory, which is about 14,000 feet above sea level.

They both had a good night's sleep because the active lava flow wasn't far away and provided a warm haven for these cold-blooded crickets. One might question whether crickets really do roam around on warm lava. Tonino had read in Otte's *Crickets of Hawai'i* that "even before plants grow there, crickets colonize the bare and sometimes still warm lava." The next morning, like so many youngsters, Tonino disregarded everyone's advice and decided to approach the flowing lava.

As they left the crack and hopped onto the top of the cooled-down lava, Tonino and Susan saw what a beautiful day it was. In the distance, they could see the volcano, and when they turned around, they could see the azure blue ocean with steam rising where the hot lava met the cool ocean. Hopping closer to the flow of lava coming down from the volcano, it became much warmer. Also, they now could smell the deadly gases, such as hydrogen sulfide, which when mixed with water produces sulfuric acid. Susan and Tonino had been told by the ranger that these fumes are especially dangerous for older people with heart problems and for females that are pregnant. Tonino figured that this didn't apply to them. They were now close enough to see the hot molten lava. They were both very excited.

"Let's go, now that we have seen it," Susan said nervously.

"Okay. We had a real good look," responded Tonino.

As they turned to leave, something drastic began to happen. The ground underneath them shook, and Tonino heard a voice say, "You shouldn't have eaten those berries without first giving me some."

Tonino looked up toward the top of the volcano, and as the smoke swirled around, he was convinced that he saw a woman with long flowing white hair. Was it Pele? Before he knew it, the main lava flow above them divided and formed another flow. Just like Dan the cricket warned them, Tonino and Susan were now surrounded by lava. Without a doubt, they would not survive being on this small island for very long. Besides, it was hot, very hot.

They were both extremely scared. Susan snuggled close to Tonino, and they just looked at one another. *What do we do now?* they asked themselves. They couldn't transform because they would have gotten into trouble with Ranger Matt for being this close to the real lava. And anyway, the flow of lava on both sides of them was too big to jump over even if they were human size. None of Tonino's magical powers would help them get out of this situation. They already were small, and being invisible wouldn't help. They looked all around them, and the only thing they could see was Dan and several other crickets that had heard about the dilemma and were gathered to assess the situation.

Out of the blue sky came two orange-winged butterflies. "Look," Tonino said to Susan. "Two monarch adults."

As they came closer, one of them hollered, "Hang in there! We will get something for you to hold onto, just be patient." In a few seconds, they were back with long, thin strands of Pele's hair dangling from their four visible legs. It is important here to note that monarch butterflies belong to the family Danaidae. Individuals in this family, as in the family Nymphalidae, hold their forelegs close to the body; they are not visible. Thus, many think they only have four legs.

"When we come within reach, wrap it around your thorax and abdomen and hold tight," the female monarch said.

When the ropelike lava strands from each monarch came within reaching distance, Tonino and Susan each wrapped the strands several times around the junction between their thorax and abdomen. Before taking off, Tonino reached down and made sure he had all his equipment, including his backpack, which housed his computer.

"Hold on!" the monarchs shouted.

Just as Tonino and Susan were lifted off the hot lava, and just below Tonino's hindtarsi and Susan's ovipositor, the two lava flows united, forming one big flow. As they were being carried to safety, both crickets realized how lucky they were.

After flying to safety, the monarchs gently lowered the two crickets to the ground. Tonino immediately unwound the strand of Pele's hair, put all his gear on the ground, and hopped over to antennate Susan and see if she was okay.

"I'm okay," she exclaimed. "We must go and thank the monarchs."

"*Mahalo*," they both said at once.

"Aren't you Tonino and Susan?" one of the monarchs asked.

"Yes, how do you know our names?"

"You probably don't recognize me, but I am Faith, and you saved my life at the Merrie Monarch Festival. This is my mate Gary."

"I surely didn't recognize you. When we last saw you, your wings weren't even unfolded."

"That's right. Gary and I are starting a family, and we were looking around for a good place to settle when we saw what was happening to you. I'm so glad I had a chance to repay the favor. You know, you saved me from starving to death."

Even though it was difficult, they all embraced. This was to most humans a funny embrace: the crickets had one antenna on each of the monarchs and the other one on their mate while the butterflies tried to put their wings around both crickets without rubbing off any scales. It is the scales (*Lepis*) that give butterflies, skippers, and moths their order name, which is Lepidoptera. See if you can figure that one out.

Gary and Faith said, "Aloha," and took off.

Tonino and Susan were still pretty scared but hopped back to safety and transformed when they were on the safe side of the roped-off area, where no one could see them. They then took a position on the cliff that was within the safety zone and sat down to rest after that heated and dangerous ordeal. Sitting on the ocean cliff, they watched several birds fly up to where the hot lava was flowing over the cliff into the ocean.

Tonino asked himself, *I wonder what they're doing?*

As Matt the ranger approached them, Tonino asked him what was going on.

"Those are black noddys, or *noios*, which are endemic along these cliffs. They started nesting on the cliffs before the lava flow began and now can't get back to their nests."

Again, Tonino had to show off his knowledge. "They are terns, aren't they?"

"Yes, they are," Matt replied.

Tonino turned to Susan, "I never realized how often plants and animals are killed or have their habitats destroyed by volcanoes, floods, fire, and other natural causes, such as lightning."

"That's true," Susan replied, "but I still believe that humans are having a far more devastating effect on habitats than Mother Nature is."

"I'm surprised to hear you say that," Tonino said.

Susan didn't reply because she knew what Tonino was talking about. After resting and watching the glowing red lava flow in the darkness, both Tonino's and Susan's thoughts turned to Dan and the other crickets that lived in this rough and barren habitat. By ten o'clock, it was too dark to see anything, and they left the park.

Tonino the Great Traveler

They had now been with Susan's aunt and uncle for what appeared to them a long time. The evening before Susan and Tonino left for New Zealand, Aunt Mary and Uncle John prepared a wonderful dinner of chicken, which Tonino learned was called *moa*. He had also learned the name for female was *wahina* and for male *kahane*, thus he was able to figure out that the males or roosters he saw in Hilo were called *moa kahane*. The conversation that evening, however, wasn't focused on the food, but was centered on the travels of Tonino. Both Susan and her relatives were astonished that, being so young, he had already seen so many different and wonderful places. Susan, being a cricket herself, knew that in general, crickets are not great travelers. Unlike the whales they had just learned about, which migrate between the Pacific waters of Hawai'i and the waters off the coast of Alaska, plus the monarchs, which migrate between the continental United States and Mexico, crickets don't move very far from where they hatch. In fact, no known cricket species migrates, whereas their relatives, the migratory locusts in Africa, do travel great distances.

"Where do you get your traveling spirit from?" Susan asked Tonino.

Tonino thought a moment and replied, "I guess from Grillo-parlante. He took several trips while following Pinocchio around. Certainly, I didn't get it from my father. Once he came to the United States at the age of two, I don't think he ever left the North End of Boston." This was another major difference between Tonino and his father and why he would always say, "I'm nothing like my father."

"Is Newton near Boston?" Uncle John asked Tonino.

"It's not far. Why do you ask?"

He responded, "Only because our conversation reminded me of John Palmer Parker, who lived in the 1800s. He was also from the Boston area and was an adventurous young traveler like you. He came from Newton and jumped ship at the age of nineteen in 1809; in 1816 he married the granddaughter of Kamehameha I and established one of the largest cattle ranches in the world. It's near here, up in Waimea. It's 200,000 acres and has about 35,000 head of cattle. It's a very interesting story, and I thought you might be interested reading about the history of the ranch. In 1950, Billy Bergin wrote an excellent book about the ranch; its title is *Loyal to the Land: The Legendary Parker Ranch*. It was published locally by the University of Hawai'i Press."

"When I return home, I will make sure to read it," responded Tonino. In fact, Tonino decided to find Parker's original homestead in Newton when he returned home.

The question of how Tonino got the travel bug made him think about where he picked up the other behaviors and habits that made up his personality. *It's nice when you can trace these particular things to someone in the family lineage. This is certainly another aspect of not only finding one's roots but knowing one's roots*, he thought to himself.

As usual, Tonino's mind began to wander. He launched into a discussion with everyone at the table about his trip to New York to see Dr. Grimaldi. He told them about Grimaldi's interest in amber from the Dominican Republic. Tonino also brought up the movie *Jurassic Park*.

Uncle John immediately chimed in and said, "You know that most of *Jurassic Park* was filmed in Waimea Canyon of Kaua'i while the scene with the velociraptors running down the hill was filmed in one of the valleys on the east shore of Oahu."

Tonino didn't want Susan's uncle to think he didn't know anything, so he asked if anyone knew what *velociraptor* meant. No one did, they just shrugged their shoulders. "Tell us," Aunt Mary finally begged Tonino.

For Tonino, this was an easy one since he had taken Latin in high school. "It comes from the Latin *velocis*, which means 'swift,' and *raptor*, which means 'robber.' Being one of the fastest dinosaurs, it was able to grasp its prey with its front legs, just like a robber snatching a purse." Even with all that effort and bravado, no one at the table, other than Tonino himself, was impressed.

The next day, Susan and Tonino departed for New Zealand. Susan's aunt and uncle drove them very early to the airport in Kona. They hugged and kissed and said how much they had enjoyed the visit. When they got to the airport, Aunt Mary grabbed Susan gently by the arm. She said, "The traditional greeting and departure gesture in Hawai'i is the *honi*, which is where two individuals gently touch their foreheads together and then touch noses. Each then inhales to exchange breath. This way you share *ha*, the 'breath of life' that is so important to the Hawai'ian people."

Tonino listened in and immediately processed the information in case the same custom existed in New Zealand.

"I wish you had told us sooner," Susan replied.

"I believe that if you learn about too many new customs from a culture too soon, you tend to ignore them. However, after watching you and Tonino, I believe that you are now ready to embrace them."

"Is there anything that you didn't get to see or try?" Uncle John asked.

Tonino responded, "Many things! The next time, I would like to try *poi*, which everyone says is one of Hawai'i's original staple foods from the taro plant."

Aunt Mary and Uncle John watched as Tonino and Susan walked into the departure area of the Kona airport. "*Mahalo*," Susan called.

Saying Good-bye to Pele

Aloha Airlines doesn't fly directly to New Zealand so they had to return to Honolulu for their connecting flight to Auckland. The flight was short, only thirty-nine minutes. Tonino always preferred the window seat so he could see everything possible, even if it was only the different shapes of the clouds below. The plane skirted the Kilauea volcano, where Pele lives. Because it wasn't completely light out, Tonino had a great view down into the Kilauea Caldera. He could see the red-hot, molten lava bubbling—the same lava that trapped them and almost resulted in their death. Pele did not show her face.

As they headed out to sea, Tonino could see an aggregation of sharks. These two images, volcano and sharks, brought to Tonino's mind images of Pele and her elder brother, *Ka-moho-ali'i*. Both could transform into many different forms. Many of the mythological beings or gods in the Hawai'ian culture (about 40,000 in number) can assume several different forms (e.g., animals and humans). *Ka-moho-ali'i* took the form of a shark. As a man, his hands were tattooed, possibly using the sap from the leadwort plant as the dye. It was he who guided the first outrigger, and Pele, to Hawai'i. He is the custodian of the water, and here we see the importance of opposites in Hawai'ian culture. It took both fire and water to make these great islands.

Tonino, however, couldn't let his mind rest. He began to think of the dog shark, *pesce cane*, who swallowed Geppetto in the original Pinocchio story, and how the shark has been maligned and depicted as an object of brutality, especially in the American movie *Jaws*. Yet, in Hawai'ian culture, the shark plays a very important and peaceful role. Tonino already knew about the great white shark, and he was not looking forward to seeing one in New Zealand.

Tonino had a few moments to think before they arrived in Honolulu. He remembered the ceremonial hula at the Merrie Monarch Festival. Now, however, he realized that none of those dancers had been wearing a mask. This seemed odd to him since most cultures he learned about either painted their faces or wore masks of some type. He remembered Sösööpa, the cricket katsina, wore a muddy yellow case mask and learned that Hawai'ian kahunas wore gourd masks for various ceremonies. *Why not for the hula dancers?* he asked himself. Tonino was so intrigued by this observation that he added the topic "Masks" to his list of things to learn more about.

Finally, they landed. Quickly they made their way to Air New Zealand for their flight to Auckland.

Chapter 11.
Tonino's Trip Down Under: New Zealand

Auckland Museum and Maori Culture

Tonino and Susan arrived in Auckland at eight o'clock, checked into their hotel, and decided to go to the Auckland War Museum. They had slept most of the trip so they weren't tired. Tonino was excited to have a new place to explore; he couldn't wait to learn about the indigenous peoples of New Zealand. What intrigued him the most was that the museum sits on top of an extinct volcano. *No Pele to bother us here,* he thought to himself. Little did Tonino know, however, that this island was "alive" and is called the "shaking island" by the local inhabitants.

They entered the museum, picked up a program, and sat down to decide what to do. As he read down the program, something caught Tonino's eye. It was the regular cultural event put on by the Maoris. It said something about a woman doing a traditional dance called the *poi* dance. Because he had just told Susan's uncle that he wanted to try eating poi, the word instantly caught his attention. He showed it to Susan, and she said, "I know what you're thinking! You are thinking about the food poi that is made from the taro plant in Hawai'i. You know, it may not be that at all."

"You may be right," Tonino said, "but you know I love words, and I can't imagine being wrong again. Remember, they are both Polynesian islands. There must be some connection. This dance probably has something to do either with the making of the poi or its religious significance."

"We only have five minutes before it starts; let's go and see it."

They entered a dimly lit room with a circular stage. On the stage were many people, both men and women. There was also a large wooden canoe (*waka*) with paddles sitting on the floor. Before the program began, a man using only the air from his nose was playing a bone flute. The music stopped and a woman introduced the program and welcomed them to *Aotearoa* or New Zealand. "*Aotearoa*" is Maori and means the "land of the long white cloud." She explained that the program would first of all show the poi dance, and then the audience would see something about warriors and their canoes. As soon as she stopped talking, out came eight beautiful Maori women. Each woman was holding in each hand a string connected to a ball, which was about three to four inches in diameter. Traditionally, the balls were made from New Zealand flax fibers, which were also used to make fabric for clothing. Tonino remembered that the shiny ball of the White Mountain Apaches was stuffed with agave fibers, while the indigenous people of the American Southwest often used the fibers of the yucca for making ropes and sandals. Each of these plants belongs to the family Agavacea. Tonino was amazed how different cultures used whatever materials were available for making things, and he learned that if the environments of these cultures were similar, they often ended up using similar materials to make the item, thus independent invention or discovery.

He whispered into Susan's ear, "Materials used by these cultures were biodegradable, but now we use plastics and other synthetic materials that do not decompose. We are heading for a major catastrophe."

Susan whispered back, "I agree."

As the beautiful and relaxing music began, the women starting singing and swinging the balls in regular twirling motions. They did this in perfect unison. Oftentimes they would let the balls bounce off various parts of their bodies. Susan and Tonino noticed how gentle and beautiful everything was, and they noticed that the music sounded a lot like Hawai'ian music. Next, the narrator gave a brief history of the wooden canoe (*koreti*), which was made from the Totara tree. She also explained how important the canoe was to the Maoris. They used the river canoes (*waka tiwai*) for getting fresh water and food, and for navigating the rivers; they used the seagoing canoes (*waka tete*) for navigating along the coast and fishing; and they used the war canoes (*waka taua*) for engaging their enemies. The Maoris, unlike the Hawai'ians, were master carvers of wood, stone, and their own bodies. The Maori *waka taua* was a masterpiece of their carving skills. The narrator then said a few words about the Maoris as warriors, and the men showed how they would use the *waka taua* in battle. Certainly, this beautiful war canoe being propelled by two rows of exquisitely tattooed warriors must have been an awesome, and possibly terrifying, sight to their enemies. When the program was over, the narrator took questions. Tonino was the first to get his hand up. She asked him, "What is your question?"

"Can you tell me something about what the word *poi* means?"

She explained that it had nothing to do with the Hawai'ian word *poi*; in Maori, it meant "ball" or "sphere." She continued, "In the poi dance, each poi, or sphere, is attached at the end of a rope that is then moved in swinging motions around the dancer." After all the questions, the narrator encouraged everyone to visit the wonderful exhibits of the museum.

Tonino loved museums, while Susan had less of a passion for them. "I'll go with you," she said, "but when I feel I've had enough, I will go to the gift shop and meet you there."

"That's fine."

The first exhibit they viewed was accompanied by a short narrative. They pushed the button and sat down. Waiting for the program to start, Tonino briefly closed his eyes. In an appropriate flashback he saw what Joe and Isabella wrote inside the cover of the book on milkweed butterflies they gave him for his birthday: "To our technology boy from the North End. Remember! Before there were computers, there were butterflies. Love, your dear friends, Joe and Isabella."

The narrator sounded like the same person they had just heard. "The Maoris came to a rather harsh land. It was not like Hawai'i. Because of this, the Maoris had to develop various types of clothing and housing to deal with the rainy and cold weather. They possibly developed the first raincoat. Also, food was not as readily available as it was on the other Pacific islands, especially Hawai'i. Their main source of food were the roots of the various bracken fern plants, plus birds (*manu*) of all sorts. They ate the wood pigeon (*kereru*), parrots (*kaka*), bell-bird (*kokomako*), kiwi, and many other birds. They even trained their special breed of dog, which is now extinct, to hunt kiwis. Their faithful and plentiful fern root (*aruhe*) gave them their carbohydrates; the Maori call it '*te tutanga te unuhia*,' which translates to 'the staple, which can never fail.'"

The next part of the narration made Tonino look at Susan with disgust. A lack of protein may have resulted in the practice of cannibalism. The Maoris ate human flesh, mainly of their enemies, either as revenge against them or to obtain the *mana* of those they consumed. (Tonino will learn about a similar practice in China, where emperors gave their own mana to their own cricket warriors via a mosquito.) Unlike the Hawai'ians, who did not like the taste of whale meat, the Maoris actively hunted and ate whales, because they lacked land mammals; whales were a major source of protein. Lacking sophisticated boats and harpoons, they often fed on stranded whales that were believed to be a gift from *Tangaroa*, who was the God of the Oceans. Stranded or beached whales were considered to be sacred, and like the shark for the Hawai'ians, the whale for the Maori served as a guardian during long voyages.

Their harsh environment forced invention. They developed elaborate snares and traps for both birds and rats. They possibly developed the first mousetrap. The Maoris were not agriculturists or aquaculturists, like the Hawai'ians, who cultivated taro and raised fish in ponds. Instead, their main concern was storing food during the cold months. Because of this, they built special storehouses known as *pataka,* where they stored smoked meats and fish. They also used specially designed gourds (*taka hue*) to store meat of various birds in their own fat. The general Maori name for gourd is *hue,* while a gourd used to store something is *taha wai.* A gourd to store water is known as *taha.* According to *Hawaiian and Other Polynesian Gourds* by E. S. Dodge, the gourd rattle used as a musical instrument seems almost universal. The Maoris, with one exception, seldom wore masks, unlike the Hawai'ians, who used gourds to make elaborate helmetlike head covers (really masks) for the chiefs and warriors. Usually only Maoris of high standing wore gourd masks, which were often tattooed. To protect their faces from the sun, they often wore a *matahuna* or face-hider. Tonino realized that since gourds were plant material, they would not have survived as artifacts because of decay.

The exhibit narration continued, "What evidence we have is from written accounts of early travelers. Anyway, why cover their beautiful facial tattoos or *mokos*? It wasn't until Europeans came that they had access to and started to eat pigs, breadfruit, yams, squash (*kamokamo*), and maize or Indian corn (*kanga*). The latter they steeped as unhusked corncobs. They placed them in standing water for several days, removed the husks, and cooked it to form a cereal, known as (*kanga wai*, corn steeped in water), to which they added sugar. We welcome you to this wonderful land of volcanoes, glaciers, deserts, rain forests, and seacoasts. Enjoy the rest of the museum."

"Wow, what a concise and informative narrative about this island and its indigenous peoples," Susan said as she stretched her arms and legs.

Tonino followed suit. Their bodies, especially their legs, were still a little cramped from the airplane.

The Giant Moa

As they moved down the dimly lit corridor, they could hear sounds that turned out to be a re-creation of the sounds of the habitat of the largest land bird ever to live—the giant moa.

Tonino looked at Susan and said, "That's a big bird. It almost looks like Big Bird on *Sesame Street*. Do you remember that program?"

"I heard about it, but my parents wouldn't let me watch TV. Instead, they insisted I use that time to practice my violin."

"Maybe that's good," Tonino replied. "By the way, I forgot to ask you. Hearing about the bracken fern made me think of eating fiddlehead ferns each spring in Boston. Did you ever eat them?"

"No!" Susan replied. "Why do they call them fiddlehead ferns?"

Tonino responded, "If you look at the emerging fern, before its end uncoils and the leaf unfolds, it looks like the head of a fiddle."

This made Susan and Tonino both think about how many children's books show the cricket making its beautiful chirping sound by using a fiddle. "Wow, does that idea or image lead to misconceptions about how crickets really produce sound," Susan said.

They continued looking and reading. They read that there are twelve different extinct species of moa and that they varied in size from the nine-foot giant moa to birds that were about the size of our common turkey. Also, they were surprised to find out that no non-Maori had ever seen a live moa. It was the Maori, and not the white man, who brought the moa to extinction by overhunting. Archeologists determined this based on the large numbers of moa bones found at numerous midden sites.

Tonino looked at Susan and said, "This situation is very similar to that in Hawai'i, where many colorful birds were brought to extinction by the feather hunters who used the feathers to make cloaks, hats, and adornments for musical instruments and helmets."

Information about Maori Warriors and Their Weapons

The next diorama showed Maori warriors and all the diverse weapons they used to kill their enemies. The music playing was that used for the *haka* or war dance. It showed the principal Maori weapons, which were the spear and club. The long spear, or *huata*, was like the spear used by Romans to defend their fortifications. The Maoris were great inventors, and this showed in their development of weapons. The *hoeroa*, made from the lower jaw of the sperm whale, was used like the bola of Argentina. Unlike the bola, it was only attached at one end and would wrap around the legs of the fleeing enemy. The thrower could then pull on the rope to stop the enemy from getting away.

Whether the Europeans introduced the bow and arrow to New Zealand is questionable. What was unique about the Maoris is their diverse development of clubs, both long and short (*patu poto*). They were unusual in shape compared to what most of us think about a club; they were spatulate in shape. They used wood, whalebone, and the famous greenstone. Greenstone is a mineral known as nephrite

258

jade (*pounamu*), and it occurs mainly on the west coast of the South Island. Almost all clubs used as weapons were elaborately carved, including the greenstone.

After they finished reading and looking at everything, Tonino and Susan came to a sign that said, "Push this button before leaving." The narrative was in Maori: "*He wahine, he whenua I mate ai te tangata.*" There was a brief silence and then the narrator said in English, "Women and land are the reasons why men die." Both of them would learn how this directly applied to them as crickets when they visited China.

"Tonino, I think I have had enough," Susan said. "I am going to the gift shop and will meet you there. Please, don't be too long."

"See you in a bit," Tonino said.

Hongi, or "kissing the Maori way," is a form of a handshake where the two individuals touch one side of their nose to that of another and then the other side. As a cricket, Tonino found touching antenna just fine. He couldn't imagine trying to get one's spiracles close to another because the legs would be in the way. This Maori gesture is similar to the Hawai'ian *honi,* except Maoris don't exchange breath.

Maori Body Decoration: The *Moko*

Tonino wandered around looking at several exhibits before stopping at a most interesting exhibit. This was going to be his last stop. It was titled *How the Maoris Decorated Their Bodies.* As Tonino read on, he was amazed that the Maoris painted themselves with a red pigment. He thought tattoos were the only way in which they decorated their bodies. Chiefs sometimes completely covered their bodies with this red ochre, or *kokowai,* which is made by roasting the naturally occurring pigment (really, anhydrous iron oxide mixed with various oils). Tonino was not sure if this ancient custom was still around or whether it had gone extinct. Also highlighted were various types of *tiki,* or pendants worn around the neck. *Tiki* was the first mythological man in New Zealand. *Tiki* pendants were made of wood or jade or greenstone; these items were usually kept in a family and passed down from one generation to the next. Tonino couldn't think of anything like this in his family. In fact, he wasn't really sure if anything was saved of his relatives.

Tonino was surprised to read that another independent invention was the cord drill, which was used to puncture a hole in the *tiki* so that a string could be used to suspend the *tiki* from. The last section of this exhibit displayed information about the *moko,* or Maori tattoo. Tonino decided to wait until they actually visited a Maori community before learning about this unique way of decorating the body. As he started to leave, one other object caught his attention. It was part of an exhibit about how Maori mothers cared for their babies. The object that caught his attention was the model of a baby inside a woven basket surrounded by some type of fiber. He read that to keep the baby warm, the mother would surround the baby with moss or *muka* fiber. *A very interesting way to keep a baby warm,* he thought to himself. *I had better hurry. Susan will get impatient.*

They had spent almost four hours in the museum, two hours of which Susan spent in the gift shop. She told Tonino she was hungry.

"Let's go eat and then see a movie," Tonino replied. "I haven't been to one since we left Boston."

After they finished their meal, they asked the waitress to recommend a good movie to see. "*Once Were Warriors,*" she replied. "It's playing just down the street."

Going to the Movies

Few people ever get up and leave once they go inside a movie theater. Almost instantly, Tonino and Susan were "trapped" by this movie, an exciting and realistic story about Jake, a Maori father who is unemployed, an alcoholic, and a wife beater. After seeing the peaceful dancing of the poi dancers at the Auckland Museum, Susan couldn't wait for the movie to end. On the way back to their hotel, they discussed the film.

"This movie showed that domestic violence can occur anywhere in the world," Susan said.

"I know it, but the thing I found most interesting was when the son, Nig, who had joined a gang, eventually found himself by going back to his roots and the tradition of being a warrior. This is what so many troubled youth should do," Tonino said to Susan.

Within a short period of about six hours, Tonino and Susan had seen the docile and beautiful poi dance and then a hostile and violent movie; they were now ready to plunge into this exciting land of mystery and ancient animals.

New Zealand's Tuatara, Kiwi, and Some Extinct Giants

New Zealand, and a sliver of the ancient southern continent Gondwanaland, was isolated from Australia/Antarctica about seventy million years ago as the Tasmand Sea widened. Like Hawai'i, it was isolated for many years and developed unique flora and fauna. Nowhere else in the world do some of these strange animals and plants occur. Just to name a few: *Peripatus*, a wormlike animal once believed to be a link between segmented worms and insects; the kiwi; and the ancient Tuatara. As a youngster, Tonino remembered seeing a picture of a kiwi on cans of shoe polish at Ben Ricci's shoe repair store in the North End. In fact, he remembered asking Ben where that funny-looking animal lived because he had never seen one, and neither Ben nor his wife, a schoolteacher, knew. Tonino and the rest of the North End inhabitants were city folks, not seafaring people like the Maoris. They saw very few animals, with the exception of ants, occasional cricket, pigeons, sparrows, mice, and cockroaches.

Because of his burning desire to know more about kiwis, Tonino went to the library. He hadn't been to a library since he did his term paper, and he wanted to again experience the wonders of what libraries had to offer. He asked Thelma, the librarian, for help in finding some information. She was extremely knowledgeable and knew how to find things in the library; she showed Tonino the section of the library where he could find books on the kiwi. Tonino, however, was of the generation that relied on the computer and the Internet, not books in the library. He went to his favorite search engine, Google, and entered "Genus and species of kiwi," and up came a site that he clicked on. As he read, Tonino got very excited. There are six species of kiwi. All belong to the bird family Apterygidae, genus *Apteryx*. To him, this sounded like birds without wings. He read on: "This is the family of flightless birds." *Ah ha*, he thought to himself, *I was right*.

He was trying to keep quiet because he knew you are not supposed to talk in the library. He read that other flightless birds occur throughout the world: ostriches in Africa, rheas in South America, and the emu and the moa in New Zealand, the latter of which is now extinct. Immediately he wondered what kind of bird the moa was, since he had just learned in Hawai'i that *moa* meant chicken. Was it like the chickens he had seen at the cockfights in Puerto Rico or the rooster he had encountered standing in front of the A-frame house in Hawai'i? He wasn't sure.

On his way out of the library, Tonino saw a book sitting alone on a table. It was *The Song of the Dodo*. "I wonder what this book is about?" he said. He knew about cricket songs. After all, who should know more about crickets than he? He had learned about whale songs while in Hawai'i from Captain Dan, but he knew nothing about dodos and their song. Again, Tonino's naiveté led him to draw an incorrect first impression. He knew that Susan was waiting for him, but he couldn't resist.

Tonino sat down and scanned the book. To his surprise, Tonino learned that this book was mainly about island biogeography and the impact islands have on extinction, rare species of animals and plants, and some of the important scientists who pioneered this area of research. He had heard about Charles Darwin and Alfred Wallace in his biology course. Tonino had forgotten that Darwin and Wallace made major discoveries by studying plants and animals on different islands, not on major continents.

One of Tonino's favorite things to do with a new book is to quickly look at the references. To his surprise, he saw many books by his friend, Professor E. O. Wilson. Tonino knew him as an ant systematist and the father of modern biodiversity. He was unaware Wilson had co-authored *The Theory of Island Biogeography* with the famous ecologist, Robert MacArthur.

Tonino hopped through the pages and was amazed that most of the book focused on large animals, not insects. *Let me see what it says about crickets*, he said to himself. He read about *Deinacrida megacephala*, the flightless big-headed cricket from New Guinea. He also saw there was something about a giant, flightless cricket of New

Zealand. He noticed that the only Maori word for cricket is *pihareinga*. The definition, however, only makes reference to the black field cricket and not the house cricket.

Because of the climate, and no connection to Africa, where the house cricket reportedly evolved, it makes sense that the house cricket is not found in New Zealand, Tonino thought to himself.

He continued to read. He learned that there was a giant, flightless cockroach in Australia. "I wonder if flightlessness and gigantism is associated with island evolution?" he said out loud. "I must hurry to meet Susan for lunch, but I will make a mental note about this book."

Over lunch, Tonino and Susan discussed going to see how the Maoris actually live. First, Tonino borrowed a pen and a piece of paper to write down the name of *The Song of the Dodo.*

While she was in her purse, Susan remembered picking up a pamphlet. "Here is something you might be interested in." She handed Tonino a pamphlet about the movie, *Whale Rider.* "Do you know anything about this?" she asked.

"No, what is it?"

Susan told Tonino the synopsis. "It's about an eight-year-old girl who wants to become a chieftain, but she can't because it is a patriarchal society; however, she proves her strength to her great-grandfather and courage to everyone by riding the back of a stranded whale that is reunited with the ocean."

Tonino noticed in the photo on the pamphlet that the girl in the movie has a tattoo between her lips and her chin. Tonino's brain was always searching his own Internet files. Susan knew when this was happening because he would get sort of glassy eyed.

Tonino said, "When I was in Silver City, New Mexico, with Sue Sturtevant, she asked Karen if the Mimbres people ever featured a cricket on their pottery. She told me that Fred Kabotie, a Hopi, had written about a chieftain riding a cricket. It is interesting that different cultures have a completely different connection with animals than our Western culture does today. Take for example the role of whales in different cultures."

"Tonino, you are correct, but in the Treaty of Waitangi in 1840, the British agreed that the Maori had the right to hunt whales, but as of 1978, the Marine Mammal Protection Act made it illegal for them to hunt any marine mammal."

"Why haven't the Japanese signed this treaty?"

Susan turned her head away, got up, and went to the ladies' room. When she returned, the conversation returned to travel plans and what to do in the afternoon.

On the Way to Rotorua: Fishing and the Weta

That evening, Tonino had a good meal, took a hot shower, and went to bed early. In order to continue their exploration of the indigenous people, they rented a car and drove to Rotorua. There, Tonino and Susan hoped to learn more about the Maoris. It was only a three-hour drive to Rotorua, but because they were both from the city, they wanted an outdoor and fishing experience. Tonino had checked and this was the best place to camp and fish. Their first night, they stayed in a camp halfway between Auckland and Rotorua. Neither Susan nor Tonino had ever camped, let alone fished, so it created a new kind of excitement. After setting up camp at a site along one of the best trout streams in New Zealand, Tonino wanted to try his luck at fly-fishing. The idea of using insect mimics (or "dry flies," as they are known) to catch fish was very appealing to Tonino. This way, no insect would sacrifice its life for the fisherman.

Tonino saw two other fishermen at the stream. He strolled over, acting as if he knew what he was doing. He fiddled with his fishing box and listened in on their conversation. They were discussing how to tie a good mimic of the insects that were emerging along the stream. The older man had found several newly emerged mayflies, and he showed the other person how to tie a mimic.

"Since it is a mayfly, make sure you have the two cerci and median caudal filament," the older man said.

Tonino left to tie his own mayfly mimic. Using the mayfly mimic, Tonino and Susan tried their luck. Before they knew it, they had caught their limit. This truly was beginner's luck, because the two fishermen didn't catch anything.

Susan and Tonino returned to the campsite to cook the fresh trout. The park rangers had set aside stacks of firewood in the campsite for campers to use. As Susan was pulling out the first piece of wood, out came this huge, brown cricketlike insect. She screamed and dropped the wood.

Tonino had never seen an insect like that before, but he had an idea of what it was. He remembered seeing a *National Geographic* issue that talked about these ancient insects. Tonino called over the two fishermen, who were camping near them. They were curious because they heard Susan scream; however, being polite, they did not want to interfere in their business. Tonino pointed the insect out to them.

"What is it?" Tonino asked, and Susan immediately chimed in, "Will it hurt you?"

The two fishermen were so friendly that Tonino invited them to sit for a while. He then explained to them where he and Susan had traveled and how they were enjoying New Zealand: its people, plants, and animals.

The older man said, "I am Graham Wallis and I am a professor at the University of Otago where I study these insects. It won't hurt you," he told Susan. "It is called a weta. In fact, this is a tree weta, and they are very common in woodpiles. The Maoris call them *wetapunga*, or 'Devils of the Night.'" He picked the insect up so that they could get a better look.

"What does *wetapunga* mean?" Tonino asked.

"*Punga* is the Maoris' word for Goddess of Ugly, thus they were considered ugly animals." He continued, "There are over a hundred different species. Eleven of them are called giant wetas, which can be up to three to four inches long. There are three species of tusked wetas, and they all are protected. The tusked wetas have hornlike mandibles projecting from their heads, which are like large tusks."

Tonino thought that these tusked wetas look just like the *caretas* he had seen in Puerto Rico.

Professor Wallis went on to say, "Wetas are a very old group of insects. Many species of wetas are endangered because of the introduction of a mouse species and three different species of rats. The Polynesian rat, which arrived with the Maoris in their canoes, is used as food throughout Polynesia. The Norway rat, which came with Captain Cook in 1769, is a large and devastating predator on ground-dwelling wetas and birds. The ship rat was introduced in 1862 and has devastated birds, big snails, and insects like the wetas. Wetas date back to the prehistoric times, when the dinosaurs inhabited the earth, also called the Age of Reptiles. In fact, they are even older than another ancient animal, the tuatara, which is a major predator of wetas and can reach two feet in length."

In the meantime, the younger person wanted to say something. Before speaking, the younger individual said, "Let me remove my hat." To both Tonino and Susan's surprise, it was a woman. "My name is Alison Cree. I am a professor at the University of Otago, where I teach about the ecology of our New Zealand monster, better known as the tuatara."

Susan politely said, "Would you tell us more about this local monster?"

Alison said, "Sure! There are two species of tuatara; they look like lizards and are called *tapu*, which is Maori for 'sacred' or 'protected things.' The name 'tuatara' means 'peaks on the back' and is very descriptive of the spinelike structures running down their backbone. The tuataras lived around two hundred million years ago and died out (everywhere except in New Zealand) about one hundred million years ago."

New Zealand tuataras were originally protected from mammals, such as humans (who arrived 1,000 to 2,000 years ago), cats, pigs, and dogs, which were not present until more recently. They now are endangered and live on islands that have been made free of rats.

Tuataras have a third eye, or parietal or pineal eye. This impressed Tonino because, like insects, they also have a simple eyelike structure just underneath the skin, located in the middle of the head. Insects with simple eyes (ocelli) usually have three ocelli, which are generally arranged in a triangular pattern; the one located in the middle of the head is known as the median ocellus. The other two, the lateral ocelli, are located above and just to the side of the compound eyes.

Alison continued, "In young tuataras, this simple eye collects ultraviolet light, thus permitting them to make vitamin D, which is essential for their growth."

Tonino was anxious to jump back into the conversation and said, "Do you know that the simple eyes of insects do not serve the same function? Also, the simple eyes of caterpillars are called stemmata."

Alison continued, "The tuatara, like other living organisms that have ancient origins, such as the coelacanth fish, horseshoe crab, and *Peripatus*, are now endangered and face extinction."

"Can we offer you some tea?" Susan said.

"Sure, but let me continue while you are preparing it," Alison said. "For many endangered organisms, recolonization programs have been put into place to prevent extinction. Habitat preservation is an extremely important component of any attempt to save rare species. One must remember, however, that the impact of natural enemies also takes its toll. What they have done in New Zealand to preserve both the wetas and tuatara is to completely remove one of its major predators, the rat, by intensive elimination programs on specific isolated islands."

Wow! That is great information, Tonino thought to himself. *I am learning so much about many different kinds of animals, especially animals I have never seen before. Also, I am learning a lot of information about the problems facing animals and plants and how humans can help slow down extinction. All this information will help me keep my promise to the Blue Fairy.*

Finally, Susan poured everyone some tea. "I'm sorry we don't have any scones to offer you," she said.

"That's all right," Alison replied.

As soon as they finished their tea, both fishermen (or should I say fisherpersons) got up, put their cups on the table, and said thank you to both Susan and Tonino. It was getting late, and Tonino and Susan decided to retire.

Before going to sleep, Tonino thought about how organisms communicated. He remembered Fred Stone, from Hawai'i, telling him that the cave and lava crickets in Hawai'i didn't produce sound; William Mull, Frank Howarth's coauthor, called them "crickless crickets."

Finally, he went to sleep. The next morning they left their camping gear at the site and looked for a pay phone.

Tonino had promised Dr. John Andrews that he would call him in Wellington when they got established; when he and Susan saw a pay phone, Tonino called him and spent a few minutes telling him about their fishing experience. "We were so surprised to see a woman fishing. She is a biologist studying tuataras."

"Was her name Alison Cree?"

"Yes," Tonino replied. "Do you know her?"

"Yes. You know New Zealand is not that big, and most biologists know one another."

Tonino then asked, "Do wetas communicate by sound?"

It was a poor connection to Dr. Andrews, but Tonino could hear Dr. Andrews saying, "No, both cave and ground wetas don't produce sound; they are silent and lack tympani or ears. Not all wetas are big. The giant weta is considered the heaviest insect in the world, weighing up to seventy grams. The life cycle from egg to adult usually takes about two years. Some are even the size of a cricket. Have you heard about the recent discovery in Kaua'i, Hawai'i, where one cricket species is going silent?"

"No, I hadn't. Please tell me about it when we get together."

"I will."

That's interesting, thought Tonino. He had been learning so much about crickets that he had not realized that most other organisms come in all different sizes, colors, and shapes.

"They even have different languages or ways of communicating with members of their own species," Dr. Andrews said.

Tonino concluded by saying, "Tomorrow we will be in Rotorua, and then we go on to Waitomo. We will call you in a couple of days when we get to Wellington."

"Sounds great to me, see you in Wellington," Dr. Andrews replied.

They returned to their campsite and ate the trout they had caught. They also had made sweet potatoes, or *kumara*. They spent most of the day hiking and were tired and hungry. They had forgotten to eat lunch, so they prepared a meager dinner from leftovers. Regardless, when eating outdoors the food always tastes wonderful. After eating dinner, they sat outside in the dark, listening to the evening sounds and looking at the stars. Tonino noticed how different the stars and moon looked down here south of the equator.

As he looked up, he was surprised to see the crescent moon looking just like a bowl, positioned the same way a bowl would sit on a table. Immediately he remembered how the Mimbres bowls were made round, not flat on the bottom, so they would "snuggle" into the sand when not being held.

"Traveling is so great," said Tonino. "You get to see so many new and different things."

"That's for sure," Susan replied.

They put all their gear away and climbed into their sleeping bags. The one unexpected sound that seemed to predominate in the evening's silence was the bleating of the sheep on the hillside. Tonino was surprised to find out that New Zealand has more sheep than people. Settling in to go to sleep, Tonino commented how good freshwater fish tasted. This was the first time he had eaten fish from a stream. Growing up in Boston, he only ate fish from the ocean, especially *baccala* (salted cod fish used in Italian, Portuguese, and Spanish cooking). Susan was lucky because during his dreams, Tonino slipped into many of his insect traits. One of these was not snoring. Since insects breathe in such a different way than humans, they do not snore.

No alarm clock was needed. At the crack of dawn, the sheep were extremely noisy. Mothers were calling their lambs, and lambs were calling their mothers. Following breakfast, Susan and Tonino headed off to Rotorua to the ground, or *marae,* of the Maori people (*hunga*) to learn about the Maori and their culture.

Rotorua and Maori Culture

They reached Rotorua, which is only a three-hour drive from Auckland, but now they were halfway there. Once they arrived, they immediately went to the information center, where they picked up a map that showed where they would find the tribal meeting or gathering place, known as the *marae*. Here they spent the whole day learning about the Maoris' crafts, housing, clothing, and body decorations. The first thing Tonino wanted to learn about was the *moko*. Inside the museum area were many displays and posters on the wall describing various aspects of Maori life. Tonino called to Susan, who was looking in the basket weaving area, to come and learn something about how they tattooed themselves. Reading carefully, they learned the Maori *moko,* or tattoo, is considered the best known of all the different Polynesian tattoos; it covers more of the body and face than those of any other Polynesian group (with the possible exception of the Marquesan islanders). Some anthropologists believe that the practice of tattooing evolved from painting the face and body. Some Native American tribes only used body and face paint, rather than tattooing. Many tribes, however, did use tattoos, which could be used to distinguish their tribal connection. Inuit women from the Canadian Arctic and Yakut tribes of Siberia, Russia, sew black thread into their faces. Tattooing is an ancient practice. There is evidence that the Egyptians used it before 1300 BC. In some parts of the world where people have skin that is too dark to show the pigment of a tattoo, they use the technique of producing raised scars or keloids.

In addition to learning about decorating the body, Tonino was interested in how different animals, including humans, communicated. None of the Polynesian cultures had a written language. For the Maoris, tattoos revealed a person's position in life (e.g., rank, breeding, and often the person's occupation). Like a fingerprint, no two *mokos* were alike; rather than signing their names to legal documents, Maoris would draw the design of their individual *moko.* Men often had their faces completely covered with a *moko* and also had them on their buttocks and thighs. Women had them on their lips, between the forehead and eyes, and also on the chin, while children and slaves didn't have them. Tattoos were often added on as people accomplished major feats in their lives or took on new status. The first time Europeans saw tattoos was from the drawings recorded by an artist with the expedition of Captain Cook in 1769.

Tonino found all of this very interesting. Most of all, he was interested in the religious aspects of making the *moko.* Only a priest could make a *moko.* This was to protect the spirit of the individual since the head, which was considered sacred, had to be touched, and blood, which also involved the spirit, was shed while making the *moko*. Tonino remembered how the head was also considered important to the Hawai'ians. The Maori did not produce petroglyphs, like the Hawai'ians and Native Americans, but left dendroglyphs, or records on karaka trees.

Tonino remarked to Susan, "None of the *mokos* I have seen, just like the petroglyphs, have depicted insects. You would think that, being as big as the wetas are, the Maoris would depict them in their tattoos."

"I don't think that the Maori tattoos show any identifiable objects, they are more like a design," Susan replied.

Tonino and Susan were surprised to find out the ancient Maori tattoo was made by actually digging into the face with chisellike tools and other instruments. This tattoo produced a ridged effect on the skin, compared to the traditional tattooing process of just making pinpricks for the dye to enter. Tonino realized that neither of these techniques would work with insects, which have a hardened outer cuticle, known as an exoskeleton. Regardless, he knew that many insects, especially butterflies, had very complex and beautiful patterns and colors. In other words, they didn't need to add designs to a body covering that already was beautiful. Tonino often wondered whether it was better to be in the people form or the insect form. When it came to the Maori tattoos, however, he was really glad he was an insect. Having an ornate *moko* was one thing, but getting it would be another. They say it is very painful, and people often get infections; some have died. For some Polynesian cultures, chanting and dancing are integral parts of the ceremony attached with being tattooed. During the process, the person being tattooed is not allowed to touch any food and is fed by other people.

"Would you want a tattoo?" Susan asked.

"No thank you," Tonino said.

"I don't want one either, even though they are fashionable now," Susan replied.

Tonino was surprised to learn about the pigments used to make the moko. Traditionally, the Maori created their *mokos* with the soot or charcoal from burning the gum or resin from the *kauari* and *kahikatea* trees. This was then mixed with shark's oil. Tonino was surprised to learn about a dye that came from roasting and grinding a special insect. Maoris hunt for and dig up the vegetable caterpillar and roast it. This is the larva of the porina moth, which can become infected with a fungus. The fungus completely consumes the caterpillar underground and sends up a vegetative shoot that is often visible above the soil. This vegetative shoot is why the caterpillar is often called the vegetable caterpillar.

The *moko* serves many functions, one of which is to shock the enemies during battle. It was now time to learn something more about these famous and fierce warriors. To do this, Tonino and Susan went to a special area of the *marae* where several completely tattooed warriors were ready to explain and demonstrate their trade.

Once the audience was seated, the chief said, "*Whaka tau,*" which means "Welcome." He then began his narrative. "During battle or dance, the Maoris would only wear the *maru* or apron." He pointed to his. "Prior to battle or dance, they remove their cloaks, which were often made of beautifully colored bird feathers. By removing their cloaks, thus exposing their *moko* to its fullest, they appeared even fiercer. These designs, the rapid movements they made with their weapons and feet, the blowing out of air from either their mouth or nostrils, their feet stomping, and their facial expression, which consisted of opening the eyes so wide that the white around the eye showed, sticking out their tongues as far as they could extend them, and using the muscles of the face to create bizarre facial expressions, all added to the fierce look of these warriors either during the *haka* or war dance or during battle. All this told the enemy, 'I am going to eat you.'"

Tonino realized that many animals use various strategies to intimidate potential predators. The hissing cockroach of Madagascar expels air through its spiracles. Some tropical stick insects raise their wings and pull back the forewings, thus exposing a bright red color that has black lines, making it look like a bull's eye. The *moko*, however, is universally associated with the Maoris of New Zealand.

Today, the *moko* is making a comeback. The instruments and dyes used are much different than traditional methods. Since they had an unwritten language, Maori people today can trace their lineage by knowing something about the distinctive *moko* of their ancestors. At one time, Europeans would remove a native person's head, preserve it, and sell it to collectors or museums. Now the Maoris, like other indigenous people throughout the world, are pressing museums to return these and other items to their rightful descendants.

"That was a lot of information to process," Tonino said, "but it was extremely interesting."

Susan nodded her head in agreement.

"I guess I was lucky," Tonino said. "For me to trace my roots was not so difficult because of our written language and the way the dead were preserved and put into cemeteries. It must be difficult for some people to trace their roots. I believe that in order to really know oneself, one must first of all know their roots."

"I couldn't agree more," she replied.

Following a full day of learning about the Maoris, they found a quiet place to morph and rest before going to the Maori *hangi* or feast at six o'clock.

Completely rested, they entered the tribe's dining hall and could not believe all the food they could select from: lamb, pork, eel, and kumara that was steamed in the hot vents of the geysers. They even had shellfish. After eating all they could, they got into their car and headed southeast to the town of Te Kuiti. There they went north to their overnight accommodations, which were only a few miles from the famous Waitomo Caves.

Waitomo Caves and Glowworms: An Insect Gold Mine

Tonino was excited about this part of the trip because they were going to see some glowworms. Tonino read in a brochure he had that glowworms are not worms at all. They are larva of a fungus gnat, which is a type of fly, order Diptera, which means two wings. The larva produce a blue-green colored light by mixing an enzyme called luciferase with a protein substrate known as luciferin. They do this in special structures called Malpighian tubules, which are really modified excretory organs. The human kidneys are similar in function. Many other animals produce cold light using these same two chemicals. Tonino knew something about fireflies because they were used at Tanglewood as ushers and lampposts, and they even helped produce some of the fireworks.

Tonino also learned that the fireflies he was talking about are adults of a type of beetle found in New England. Tonino now remembered his friends in New England telling him about how they would collect them and put them into jars. Tonino continued reading the brochure about glowworms. He learned that their scientific name is *Arachnocampa luminosa*.

"Doesn't *campa* mean grublike?" Tonino asked Susan; he loved to think about the derivation of words.

"I'll bet *luminosa* refers to their light," Susan replied.

Neither of them, however, could figure out why they also were referred to as arachnoid, since they didn't look like spiders. "Oh, here it is," Susan replied. "On page 4, it says that 'arachnoid' refers to their ability to spin silken tubes and long threads of silk. Once the long, silken thread is produced, they space out small droplets of a sticky mucouslike material. They live in caves where it is dark, use their light to attract small flying insects into the cave, and catch them in their sticky fishing line. When caught, the larva hauls in the fishing line and eats the insect."

As they approached the caves, they couldn't believe how many tourists were there. They have about 380,000 to 400,000 visitors per year. Tonino calculated how much that would be at $10 per person.

"That's about $4 million per year," he said. "That's even more than Captain McSweeney made on his whale tours. This ecotourism was quite a gold mine."

The tour, which included an impressive boat ride, was spectacular. Tonino was seated near the edge of the boat and could see the walls of the cave very clearly. When they stopped to see the glowworms, he looked over and could see two large cricketlike insects. They looked at him, staring through their reduced compound eyes, and then slowly moved into a crack.

After the trip, he asked the tour guide what he had seen. "Those are cave wetas," he said.

Tonino responded, "When we went into the lava tube in Hawai'i, we didn't see a cave cricket. I was really disappointed."

Tonino thought it was interesting that on entirely different continents, or islands, different types of crickets have evolved to live in similar habitats; they even have evolved similar traits like reduced eyes, long antennae, and lack of wings. The tour guide went on to tell them how there are two other species of glowworms, *Arachnocampa richardsae* on the mainland of Australia and *Arachnocampa tasmaniensis* on the Australian island known as Tasmania. Because of their flightlessness, it is unlikely that these two species and the one in New Zealand would have arisen independently without a common ancestor. He explained that once these islands were separated from the main continent of Australia, the glowworms evolved into separate species.

This was extremely exciting to Tonino. He enjoyed hearing about geography, how continents were formed, and how new species evolved. He thought about how the silent crickets in Hawai'i evolved. Because of the selective pressure on male crickets, which sing by rubbing their wings together, any mutation that prevented a male from producing a sound would favor that mutation because it wouldn't attract a parasitic fly. In fact, when examined, the researcher showed that the file on the wings of silent males was greatly reduced and would not produce a sound; thus, the population shifted from males with normal files to ones that lacked the ability to sing.

Having seen only a part of the middle of the North Island, Susan and Tonino were ready to leave for Wellington, which was about a six-hour drive from where they were. Here they would contact Dr. Andrew, return their rental car, and hopefully see Dr. Gibbs.

Meeting Dr. Andrews in Wellington

The teenagers arrived late at night at the home of Dr. Andrews. They had already eaten, so they retired early. The next morning at breakfast, Dr. Andrews explained a very interesting situation in New Zealand that involved the prickly shrub plant or gorse, which had been introduced as a hedge plant on farms and now has become a serious nuisance plant. Attempts were being made to control the shrub, but recently they found a large area where the giant weta had adapted to this plant as both a source of food and shelter. In this area, it is illegal to destroy this plant, which elsewhere is a major pest to sheep and cattle farmers. There is now a law in New Zealand protecting all species of giant weta.

Susan asked Dr. Andrews, "What is your position on this issue?"

He hesitated and then answered after giving it some thought. "Well, the weta was here first and is endangered, so we must first of all protect the weta. I guess, though, it depends on which side of the fence you are on."

Susan gave Tonino a stare, and he got the message. This was one of Tonino's first lessons concerning how one particular living organism could be considered both bad or good.

He responded, "I guess this is one of the major issues facing conservation biologists. The Mexican people in the mountains need firewood and timber, but many more people want the monarch butterfly to have their overwintering habitat."

Tonino and Susan continued to have verbal confrontations about how the Japanese were overharvesting whales, which they claimed they were only gathering for scientific purposes. If he remained committed about his position, he would have to confront her head on.

That evening they went to a restaurant for dinner. Tonino asked Dr. Andrews what a typical New Zealand meal would be.

He replied, "Well, I guess lamb and a special dessert called a Pavlova."

"I guess I will have the lamb," Tonino responded.

When it came time for dessert, Tonino and Dr. Andrews both ordered the Pavlova, but Susan had already told the waiter, "Just bring an extra spoon, I'll have some of Tonino's."

Tonino continued to think about the discussion he and Susan had about extinction and how overhunting and habitat destruction were causing many plants and animals to perish.

Tonino asked Dr. Andrews, "Are any cricket species threatened with extinction?"

Dr. Andrews replied, "Yes. The common house cricket is threatened in many areas because its habitat is being destroyed or removed."

Tonino asked, "How do you know that?"

"I am in contact with Dr. Head in England, and he was telling me about it."

Tonino changed topics, turned to Susan, and said, "What was the name of that giant bird that is now extinct?"

"It was called a moa," she replied.

"Isn't that the same name the Hawai'ians use for chicken?"

"I believe you're correct."

Tonino changed topics again and asked Dr. Andrews if they could meet Dr. Gibbs, the author of the book on the monarch butterfly in New Zealand. Tonino had been waiting for an opportunity to discuss with him some of the things in his monarch book.

"Sure!" Dr. Andrews said. "We will do it tomorrow after we return your rental car."

As they rode back to his house after dinner, Dr. Andrews told them about Wellington.

Wellington is a beautiful city on the North Island of New Zealand and has 166,800 residents. The city forms a cup or is like an amphitheater because of the natural topography of the land. Because of this, the houses are usually on very steep slopes. It is the home of Victoria University, where both Drs. Andrews and Gibbs teach. The university has about 11,000 students and was named after England's Queen Victoria; in 1897, when the University of New Zealand was founded, it was the sixtieth anniversary of her coronation.

Dr. Gibbs and the Monarchs in New Zealand

The next day, Susan and Tonino followed Dr. Andrews to return their rental car, which took only thirty minutes. Piling into Dr. Andrews's car, they headed to the university to meet Dr. Gibbs. When they entered the room they could see Dr. Gibbs, a tall, slender man wearing glasses and seated at a laboratory bench. After the introductions, Dr. Andrews left Tonino and Susan with him while he went to do some errands.

Dr. Gibbs began by saying, "I just received an e-mail from Dr. Stoffolano stating that you would be stopping by to talk about monarch butterflies. We here in New Zealand appreciate the generosity of the North Americans for letting us share the beauty and companionship of this elegant and monarchic butterfly."

Tonino replied, "You know, I don't think that many North Americans know this butterfly can be found outside of their continent."

"Did you know this butterfly belongs to a worldwide group of butterflies known as the milkweed butterflies?" Dr. Gibbs asked.

"Yes, I did," Tonino replied. "I read Ackery and Vane-Wright's book on milkweed butterflies and your book about the monarch." Tonino went on to show Dr. Gibbs he also knew something about this butterfly. "I know that the genus name *Danaus* was taken from one of the kings of Arabia in Greek mythology."

Tonino continued to try to impress Dr. Gibbs. "I recently went to a lecture by Dr. Orley Taylor on monarch migration; he said that the monarchs use the Earth's magnetic field for orientation during migration."

"That's an interesting theory," Dr. Gibbs said. "However, a recent group of scientists claim that monarchs use sun-compass navigation or the ultraviolet pattern of the sky for navigation. That's the environmental cue that bees and desert ants use for getting back to their nests."

"Thanks for bringing me up to date on that," Tonino replied.

Dr. Gibbs now took over the podium. "I would like to tell you something about the monarch's life cycle. The female searches until she finds a milkweed plant to lay an egg. The egg is very small, about 1.2 mm high, is creamy white, and is usually laid on the underside of the leaf. Here in New Zealand, the milkweed plant was introduced by accident and has permitted the monarch to survive. Prior to its arrival, any arriving monarchs were unable to produce new generations. The larva or caterpillar is an eating machine. The adults only take liquid food, mainly in the form of nectar. You may have noticed the first instar of the caterpillar make a trench in the leaf. This keeps the milky latex from engulfing and entrapping the first instars. This would kill them, you know."

Tonino told Dr. Gibbs that he had seen the trenching behavior and was told of its significance when he was in Hawai'i.

"Well, you are learning a lot for a young man," Dr. Gibbs exclaimed.

Dr. Gibbs continued, "While feeding on the leaves of milkweed, the caterpillars are ingesting the plant's toxins, called cardiac glycosides. This is the chemical Dr. Lincoln Brower found to be distasteful to predatory birds. This substance makes birds vomit; thus, they learn not to eat these orange-and-black butterflies again. The orange color, like red, is regarded as a warning color to would-be predators."

Susan raised her hand and asked, "Is that why they use red for stop signs and traffic lights and yellow for school buses?"

"Yes," Dr. Gibbs said. "The warning colors alert one to be careful and to avoid a situation that can be dangerous. It is also called aposematic coloration."

Thinking about his cousin Vincenzo, who loved forensic crime information, Tonino responded, "That must be why police use a yellow tape to seal off crime scenes."

Susan wondered how color-blind people deal with the issues of traffic lights, fire trucks, and fire hydrants. Tonino had a burst of activity at the synapses in the memory section of his brain and mentally returned to Puerto Rico. He remembered discussing the *santos* with Pedro. After recalling the whole experience, he asked himself, *Why are devils always painted red or wear red costumes?* Unfortunately, he was too shy to ask Dr. Gibbs.

Dr. Gibbs continued, "Would you like me to tell you about prolegs?"

Susan replied, "Oh, please do."

"The caterpillar has three pairs of true legs and five extra pairs of fleshy prolegs. On the bottom of the prolegs are structures called crochets. They are tiny, hooklike structures that permit the caterpillar to grasp onto a plant or your hand. If you let a caterpillar crawl on your hand and you gently try to pull it off, you will feel these tiny hooklike crochets, which look like the upper part of a shepherd's crook or a knitting needle, grabbing onto your skin."

Susan made a wincing face.

"It doesn't hurt at all," Gibbs reassured her. "When the caterpillar is fully mature, it spins a small silken button to attach a special structure on its abdomen called a cremaster, which also has hooks to anchor into the silken button. Once anchored, it then molts, and its last larval cuticle forms a beautiful structure called a chrysalis, within which the pupal stage develops. After the pupal stage has molted to the adult, the adult butterfly emerges from the chrysalis. This is probably the most vulnerable stage of the adult butterfly. When it emerges, its wings are soft and folded. It must pump blood, or hemolymph, into them. The internal blood pressure and the accessory pulsatile organs help unfold them before they become rigid. Only after the wings have hardened or become sclerotized can they fly. This whole transformation process, called complete metamorphosis for Lepidoptera, is truly one of the wonders of the natural world."

Susan looked at Tonino and said, "That is exactly what we saw Faith do."

"That's correct," he responded. Of course, Dr. Gibbs had no idea what they were talking about.

No matter how often Tonino heard or read about metamorphosis, he was continually amazed.

Susan had another question. "What's the function of the tentaclelike structures at the anterior and posterior of the caterpillar?"

Dr. Gibbs thought a moment and said, "As far as I know, no one knows."

Another thing that always amazed Tonino was that whenever he read a book or listened to a lecture in a classroom, it appeared that the author or speaker knew everything there was to know, but when he talked to other experts, he would find out that there was so much still to be discovered. Once you realized this, learning really became enjoyable and could be a central part of your life.

"Anything else you want to know?" Dr. Gibbs asked.

"I have two questions," Tonino said. "First, tell us something about the pre-European presence of the monarch in New Zealand, and second, tell us something about the food of the monarch in New Zealand."

"In my book on New Zealand butterflies, I talk about how R. W. Fereday first recorded the presence of a monarch in New Zealand in 1873. I also mention that when a picture of the butterfly was shown to the Maoris, they all agreed that they had seen the butterfly before any white man came. They called it *kakahu*. Because the Maoris lacked a written language, there is nothing to substantiate this."

Tonino wondered whether the oral record was just as reliable as the written record.

"My second question is about the caterpillar's food here in New Zealand. Please tell us something about it," Tonino said.

"The monarch is a very fussy eater, as you may well already know. It will only eat milkweed plants, thus it is monophagous. These plants have a milky latex material and a pod structure that contains thousands of tiny brown seeds with white, silky-looking fluff attached. The fluff permits the seed to be blown and carried in the wind for dispersal. In New Zealand, the swan plant is the food plant. It gets its name because the stalk connecting the seedpod to the plant resembles a swan. On a worldwide basis, there are about 157 species of milkweed. In Mexico, there are about 59 different species, while in the United States, there are about 106. In New Zealand, four species of swan plant are grown; two were introduced from North America and two from South Africa. None grow wild like they do in Australia."

"Can you write down the scientific name of the swan plant for me? I am trying to put together as much information about monarchs as I can in my computer," asked Tonino.

"Sure." Dr. Gibbs took a few minutes to write it down. "The dispersal of the swan plants around the Pacific islands is almost as interesting as the monarch itself," noted Dr. Gibbs. "Because the small seed is so light and is attached to a mass of white fluff, it is easily carried by the wind. On the island of New Caledonia, it is called the 'gendarme's weed' because when the old mattresses that were stuffed with the fluff were emptied outside the barracks of a prison, the seeds landed nearby and germinated. That is how the swan plant came to be spread on the island."

Tonino thought to himself, *The way things work in life, the impact of humans on other life forms, and the cultural implications are so interesting.*

"What would you like to do now?" Dr. Gibbs asked.

"If possible, I would like you to take us out to see the monarchs and some swan plants," Tonino asked politely.

Dr. Gibbs said he was expecting a phone call but told them where to find them.

Before they knew it, they were standing in a garden where swan plants were growing. Tonino pulled off one of the pods and looked at it carefully. Truly, that part of the pod connecting it to the plant did curve, making it look like a swan. Many of the pods had opened, and the seeds were being parachuted all over.

Tonino pulled out a large plastic garbage bag from his backpack and began to collect seedpods. Susan helped him fill the bag.

Returning to Dr. Gibbs's office, they met up again with Dr. Andrews, who was in his office chatting. They thanked Dr. Gibbs for all of his information and Tonino said that he would keep in touch. They exchanged "snail mail" addresses and also e-mail addresses.

That evening after supper at Dr. Andrews's house, Tonino and Susan carefully removed the fluff from all the seeds, because they knew if they wanted to take the fluff back to the United States, they would not be permitted to import any seeds, plants, or animals. They performed this task outside. Even though it was slightly windy, they continued to separate the fluff from the seeds. Because of this, fluff was blowing around everywhere. Before going to bed, Dr. Andrews explained he and his wife were flying the next day to Dunedin, located on the South Island of New Zealand, to visit a friend. They would be gone for three days, and if Tonino and Susan drove them to the airport and picked them up, they could use the car and stay in their house.

What a generous offer, Tonino said to himself. This is fine with them because they had done a similar thing in Hawai'i with Susan's aunt and uncle. The only difference here was the driver sits on the right instead of the left, and everyone drives on the left side of the road rather than the right, like in the United States.

Susan told Tonino, "Just keep thinking, stay to the left and you will be right."

Dr. and Mrs. Andrews had an early flight. After Susan and Tonino dropped them off at the airport, they had all day to do things around Wellington. "Let's just go into town for a while," said Susan.

Cricket Match and Museum

Tonino and Susan decided to spend some time touring Wellington. One of the most impressive sights of downtown Wellington is the government building, more commonly called the "Beehive" because of its shape and small windows that look like individual hexagonal cells of a honeycomb. Tonino thought hard but couldn't think of any other building having an entomologically related name. He thought for another moment. "Susan, maybe you can help me. Were bees ever used by architects to design buildings?"

"Yes, there is a book by, I believe, Juan Antonio Ramirez, who mentions the following architects who designed structures based on beehives: Le Corbusier, Antonio Gaudi, Ludwig Mies van der Rohe, and Frank Lloyd Wright."

"I didn't know that." Tonino searched the computer in his brain and said, "I now remember the world-renowned grasshopper weather vane on top of Faneuil Hall in Boston. My father always pointed it out to me and would say, 'Why didn't they use a cricket?'"

Tonino had a flashback to his trip to the Berkshires with Pedro and Ming Ming when he had pointed out the weather vane to them. The Faneuil Hall weather vane, like all other weather vanes in early America, were extremely important to both farmers and fishermen alike, who needed to know wind direction and force. In 1742, the artisan Deacon Shem Drowne constructed the wonderful orthopteran that now proudly sits on top of Faneuil Hall. Just as one could ask why Collodi had picked a cricket to be the conscience of Pinocchio, one could ask, Why a grasshopper for a weather vane? Tonino recalled reading the following information in *Boston Ways*, by George Weston:

Many reasons have been given: that there was such an insect on the Faneuil coat of arms (which there wasn't); that the farmers who frequented the market liked grasshoppers (which they certainly did not); that chasing locusts was connected with a boyhood romance of the Deacon's (which seems unlikely); and that the design was suggested by a similar one which was on the Royal Exchange in London. You may take your choice, but the last seems the most reasonable.

After touring the downtown area, they decided to go to the botanical gardens. The flowers and trees were truly spectacular. "What a magical place," Susan said as she clutched Tonino's hand and gave him a kiss on his cheek.

"Let's have lunch in the Begonia House," Tonino said.

Of course he was yielding to Susan's affection since he knew she loved to eat in beautiful places. During lunch, Tonino overheard someone say something about a cricket match that afternoon. He excused himself and asked the person where it would be held. The person responded, "Basin Reserve."

Tonino and Susan could hardly contain themselves. "Let's go," they excitedly said to one another. "We haven't been in our cricket form since we were at the Volcano National Park in Hawai'i, and if it's for crickets, we should be welcome," Susan said.

Just about inhaling their lunch, they got the directions and drove to Basin Reserve.

They quickly parked and locked the car, and then they changed into crickets. Already, a huge crowd was queuing up to get in. This was a huge crowd; Tonino and Susan were surprised so many people would go to see crickets. After seeing how many people went to see the whales and glowworms, however, they realized that such a thing was possible.

Susan quietly said to herself, *I just hope Tonino is not disappointed like he was with the Merrie Monarch Festival.*

They entered the stadium and found a small spot on the bleachers. As they looked out over the stadium, all they could see were three postlike things sticking up from the ground. They couldn't see any crickets.

"Let's go onto the grass and see if there are any field crickets out there," Tonino said to Susan.

This time, Tonino didn't hear any warning of danger either by his conscience, the Blue Fairy, or any guard at the stadium. So, off they went, hopping over small obstacles and down the stairs. When they came to the fence, they just hopped between the chain links (another benefit of being a cricket). As they hopped around the field, they couldn't see any crickets.

Susan asked Tonino, "I wonder where all the crickets are?"

"I don't know. Let's go over there so we can climb up on top of those sticks to get a better view."

It would have been a high jump to reach the top so both of them sort of inched their way up one of the three upright sticks. When they reached the top, they had a much better view. They now could see another group of sticks about seventy feet away. Neither of them had ever seen anything like this before.

"Let's see if I can get any response by calling," Tonino said to Susan.

Tonino took the correct stance on top of the horizontal stick, flexed his wings, and began to stridulate. As he pulled one wing's scraper over the file of the other wing, a very distinct sound of a house cricket issued forth.

Immediately, Susan said, "These are probably field crickets, and they won't be able to understand your song. Also, don't forget, it may be even more difficult to communicate with them because they are New Zealand crickets; they probably have a different accent."

Tonino knew he could be multilingual in human form; however, he wasn't quite sure about cricket form. He concentrated and began pulling one wing over the other. He stridulated, producing the song of a male communicating with another male in defense of his territory, and he also tried producing the song of a male communicating with a female in search of a female partner. Susan, of course, was not too happy when he started to produce the latter. He alternated between the two types of songs for about ten minutes.

"My wing muscles are getting tired. I must stop and rest," he told Susan as he lay down on the horizontal stick.

As he lay there, totally exhausted and resting on top of the stick, Susan kept looking around. All of a sudden, she perked up. Her antennae became straight rather than limp, her cerci and ovipositor did the same, and she lifted herself off her six legs. She could see some men in white shoes, white pants, white shirts, and white hats coming toward them. Closer and closer they got. They came so close that she finally said, "Tonino get up, some men are coming."

Tonino perked up also and looked around. Sure enough, there were three men positioning themselves around the three vertically arranged sticks. The one on which they were perched had three upright sticks supporting it. They were each separately standing on the two crosspieces that were also made of wood. One man stood behind the sticks; he was wearing a helmet with a facemask, plus some type of protection attached to each of his legs. Tonino noticed that the helmet was made of plastic and not like the gourd mask of the Hawai'ian chiefs. The man was also wearing a glove on his left hand, while another man stood in front of the sticks with a big stick in his hands. The combination of the mask, the glove, and the white uniform was something Tonino had not seen before. In the distance, about a hundred feet away, was another man with a ball in his right hand. About twenty-two yards past him were sticks just like the one they were standing upon.

A moment of silence occurred followed by music and singing. Tonino and Susan were sure it was the national anthem of New Zealand. This reminded Susan of the beginning of the Merrie Monarch Festival. Tonino, however, was oblivious to everything. He wanted to see crickets and that was that. The next thing they saw was the man with the ball running at them, his right arm cocked behind his head and catapulting forward. They could see this ball coming right at them, striking the ground about three feet in front of them, and then they heard a great crash of sticks.

That's all they remembered.

Luckily, Jack Tobin, a New Zealand black field cricket, had been able to understand Tonino's chirping, despite his Boston accent (even though he had tried to communicate with a New Zealand accent). Jack formerly lived in Nahant, Massachusetts, a small coastal community of about 3,632 just northeast of the city of Boston, with his daughter, Maggie, and his son-in-law, P. J. In fact, Jack spoke with a Boston Irish accent because he spent a lot of time talking to his grandchildren, Amy and Mary Elizabeth. Jack knew all about accents because his family's background was Irish. During the 1845–1852 potato famine in Ireland, the majority of the Tobin family left for New Zealand while P. J.'s grandmother and grandfather settled in Boston.

Tonino was surprised to learn that a fungus that attacks and destroys potato plants could have caused such human destruction. Regardless of this historical event, it was lucky for Tonino and Susan that Jack had emigrated and settled in New Zealand. Susan and Tonino were saved; they would have been killed by players stepping on them without Jack's help. Jack responded to Tonino's territorial call, saw the accident, and immediately sent for help. Without being noticed by any of the players or spectators, Susan and Tonino were individually carried to a safe spot until the emergency cricket team arrived by hummingbird-copter; they used stretchers to fly them off the field to the hummingbird landing deck, which was just adjacent to the field. Apparently, other crickets have been injured on the cricket field, and this emergency system had been installed just a few years ago. Since there were no major injuries, the emergence team took them to the house of Jack and Ruby, two crickets that lived outside the stadium and, just under a big tree on the edge of the parking lot. Surprisingly, it was only a few feet from where Tonino had parked Dr. Andrew's car.

The emergency team did not take their pulse because insects have an open circulatory system, where the blood enters the small openings (a.k.a. ostia) of the heart in the dorsal blood vessel, thus they lack a pulse. Once the blood enters the ostia, it is pumped forward into the aorta and dumped into the head area. For insects, having an open versus a closed circulatory system, as in humans, is an advantage because cholesterol-related problems associated with clogged blood vessels do not occur. Ostia was a port city in the ancient Roman Empire. It was the opening to Rome from the sea.

Insect ostia are thus openings into the heart for the blood to enter (incurrent ostia) and in some cases excurrent ostia.

The emergency team splashed cold water onto Susan and Tonino's faces. As soon as water touched them, they both came to. "Where are we?" they both responded.

"Don't worry, just rest," Jack said.

They put their heads down and took a short nap. When they woke up, they found out that they were in Jack's house.

"How did we get here?" Tonino asked.

Jack explained everything that happened after the ball hit the wicket: the hummingbird ride to his house, and being carried inside by two of Jack's mouse friends. "What were you doing up there on the wicket anyway? You could have been killed," Jack said in a concerned voice. "Also, why were you defending the wicket as a piece of your own territory?"

"It's a long story and too complicated to explain now," Tonino responded.

"Anyway, you are safe and you can stay here with me and my wife Ruby tonight if you wish."

Even though Tonino was very sore and extremely tired, he kept thinking about Dr. Andrews's car in the parking lot. "If possible," he said, "we would like to eat dinner with you and then take off."

"That's fine!" Jack exclaimed.

During dinner, they exchanged addresses and Tonino explained a little about the trip they were taking.

"That's great," Jack replied. "See as much of the world as you can while you're young."

Following dinner and a rest, they were ready to leave. They thanked Ruby and Jack and hopped away, quickly found the parking lot, and morphed. As they drove toward Dr. Andrews's house, Susan looked at Tonino and started to say something. "Don't go there," he said. "I know I should have questioned whether this was really a cricket match, but you know I love crickets. I am a cricket! We both are crickets!"

They reached Dr. Andrews's house; climbing up the stairs and getting into bed was a major task for both of them. They didn't wake up until noon the next day. They felt much better, though a little sore in the joints. Crickets belong to the phylum Arthropoda. *Arthro* is Greek for "jointed," and *poda* means "foot." Thus, arthropods are those animals that have both jointed feet and appendages. At the moment, Tonino and Susan's joints were sore from the accident, not from arthritis (inflammation of the joints).

"I must find out more about this cricket match," Tonino said to Susan. "Look up 'Cricket' in the telephone directory and see what you can find."

"Here's something: Cricket Museum, located at the Old Grandstand Basin Reserve between Sussex and Dufferin Streets. That's where we were yesterday. Try this one number and see if they're open."

Tonino got the automatic voice machine telling him that the museum would be open until 3:30 p.m. and that parking was available in front of the Old Grandstand on nonmatch days. "Before we go, we must eat lunch," Susan said.

"All right, but let's hurry."

Tonino was on another mission. After they finished lunch, they left for the Cricket Museum.

Tonino felt very much at ease as they entered the museum. He already knew that he would come away learning what this cricket match was all about. Also, he knew he would come out uninjured. Inside, there was so much to see and learn. He now knew that cricket was a game. As soon as he learned that, he remembered the time in the Boston library when he saw some references about cricket, the men and the game, something about rules, and something about the history of cricket. It all made sense now.

At the museum, Tonino saw the Addington Bat of 1743, which is one of the oldest cricket bats. It reminded Tonino of the hockey sticks all the kids in the Boston area carried during the winter months. He also recalled the Hopi Cultural Center Museum, where he saw the Hopi throwing stick, which had a curve at the end, just like a hockey stick, but was used for throwing at rabbits and other wild game.

The museum also displayed Dennis Lillee's aluminum bat, which was banned from the test cricket match in Perth in 1979, and other more recent wooden bats; the Addington Bat was curved at one end, while the newer bats were straight. Tonino also liked the cricket ball made of rope that had been used by New Zealand and Australian prisoners of war in northern Italy in 1942. The only thing that Tonino didn't see was something about the origin of the word *cricket*. He asked one of the docents, a guard, and several visitors to the museum. No one knew. He then asked the guard if he could speak to the curator of the museum. The docent returned and told him that someone would be with him in a few minutes.

In a few minutes, Tonino was talking to Stephen Green, the head curator. "How may I help you?" he said as he greeted Susan and Tonino.

"I like to learn about the origins of words, and I also have a great fondness for real crickets. I was wondering how this sport got the name cricket."

Green looked puzzled. He scratched his head, just like Tonino's father always did when trying to figure something out, looked away for a moment, and turned to Tonino as if the answer had come to him.

"You know, I really don't know! Our board of directors, which includes some vintage cricketophiles, is meeting now, and in a few minutes they should be available to answer your question."

As the beautiful wooden doors, made of kauri wood, opened, Green motioned for Tonino and Susan to enter. "Gentlemen, I would like to introduce Tonino and Susan, two young students from the United States who have posed a question that I am unable to answer. Ask them your question," he nodded to Tonino.

Tonino looked at this austere body of twelve elderly and distinguished men sitting around a huge wooden table, also made of kauri wood. As Susan looked around the table, she noticed that they were all men. She wondered if women played cricket. Each man had a teacup and spoon in front of them. Tonino knew they were drinking tea because he could smell it. It smelled just like Ming Ming's house. In front of every other man was a pile of biscuits.

"Well lad, what is your question?" the man sitting at the head of the table asked.

Tonino looked at everyone at the table and said, "I would like to know the origin of the word *cricket* as it applies to this game. Can any of you tell me its origin?"

Certainly such a knowledgeable-looking group of twelve men on the board of the cricket museum would know the answer.

"Please! Sit over here and have some tea and scones," the man said.

They made a spot for Susan and Tonino at their table and asked if they would also like some tea.

"Sure," Susan immediately responded. She loved tea.

It took awhile for them to be seated, to get their spot of tea, and to make a choice of scones.

The waiter asked, "Would you like marmalade, butter, or fresh cream on your scones?"

Susan replied, "I'll take mine plain. You know, I have to watch my weight."

Tonino, on the other hand, said, "Everything please."

As they started eating, Tonino could hear the conversation going on among the twelve men at the table. After about fifteen minutes of loud and active conversation, the room fell to absolute silence. The man at the head of the table looked at Tonino and said, "We don't know!"

Immediately, Green stood up, moved toward the door, and left the room as he said, "Let me try one reference."

While he was gone, Tonino started to explain why he and Susan were in New Zealand. Soon, Green returned with an old book in his hand. "Here it is; I thought I had seen something in *The History of Cricket* by Eric Parker."

"Read it to us," they all said in one voice.

"'How then,'" Green read aloud, "'are we to derive the name? Surely in the same way as other names of other things or creatures are derived, from words of like sounds—a dozen such likenesses of sound and meaning suggest themselves. There are the two languages of Greek and Latin, each spring from a common source, but separating into different results as the two branches of the common stock traveled, one into Greece and one into Italy. The words most often on the lips of the traveling peoples, mother and father, remain the same sound, though the shapes of the written letters become some of them different: mater, pater, μητηρ, πατηρ. Words less commonly used change a little more in sound and shape... And now come to England and the Anglo-Saxon language, or even the Norman. Take the words *crick, creek, cricket, crook, croquet.* All them carry with them the same essential, underlying meaning—something with a twist or curve in it, something out of the straight. A crick in the neck comes from a twist, something irregular. A creek is a winding inlet. A crook is the curved stick used by shepherds. *Croquet* is another form of the word *crochet*, which is the diminutive of the word *croc*, or *croche*, a *crook*—a game played with crooked stick. And so we get two words allied in meaning, *cricket*, a diminutive of the word *crick*, and *crooked*. As to sound, *cricket, crooked*—is there much difference? Cricket is a game played with a crooked stick.'"

Immediately, this made sense to Tonino because he had just seen the crooked bat of Addington. It also made sense that the crochets on the bottom of the prolegs of caterpillars looked just like a small shepherd's crook or the crochet hooks of his mother's knitting needles. He remembered when he hollered at Faith to get her attention, how carefully she put down her prolegs to grasp the stem with the crochets of each proleg.

How wonderful words are, Tonino thought to himself. *There is only one major problem now. Why was the name cricket given to my group of animals?*

"Well, that solves the origin of the word for the game cricket, and I believe we should put an explanation of this in the museum. Young man and young lady, we certainly have enjoyed meeting you," responded Green.

"Thank you for the spot of tea, the scones, and the stimulating conversation," Tonino said as they turned to leave.

"Wait! Just one thing before you leave. What are your last names?"

Susan replied first, "Maki."

Tonino looked around the room, turned to leave, and sort of whispered, "Cricket." Green escorted them out and had the door open.

Tonino was hoping no one would hear his name. He took a couple of steps as if to leave, but when he turned around to see the puzzling look on everyone's face, he knew that they heard.

In fact, Green said, "I am sure they heard you, but hearing 'Cricket' as a person's last name in a cricket museum is sort of unusual. It has never happened before."

As they left the museum, Tonino said to Susan, "I learned a lot. I now know why the game is called cricket, but I have another question."

"What's that?" Susan asked.

"Now I need to know why we are called crickets."

"Tonino, that can wait, we must get to the airport to pick up Dr. and Mrs. Andrews."

On the way to pick them up, Susan read some information about the South Island. She learned something else about this strange land, New Zealand (called *Nukilani* in Hawai'ian).

Susan told Tonino there was a glacier on South Island.

"That sounds great," Tonino said. "We must go there. I have never seen a real glacier."

Dr. Andrews and his wife were waiting at the arrival area when Susan and Tonino got there. They had had a wonderful trip and listened intently as Tonino explained the derivation of the word for the game cricket.

Dr. Andrews responded, "I have lived here all my life and never knew that."

At dinner, Tonino and Susan expressed an interest to see the South Island.

"I believe you should," Dr. Andrews replied. "Tomorrow morning we will make arrangements for you to fly there and rent a car."

They would be flying into the airport in Nelson, which is the fourth largest city in New Zealand. Its population is 44,400, and it would be easy to rent a car. The two youngsters said good-bye to Dr. and Mrs. Andrews, thanked them both for everything, and boarded a small plane for Nelson. When they went to rent their car, they also made arrangements for getting to Stephens Island. It wasn't easy. New Zealand doesn't have railroads, and Stephens Island is only reachable by ferry, so they made reservations, drove to the ferry station, and took the ferry across to the island. Stephens Island is due north of D'Urville Island. It is the home of some of the most unique animals and plants on the planet.

Stephens Island, Conservation Biology, and Tuatara

One of the main things Tonino wanted to see on Stephens Island was the giant weta. Once on the island, they often stopped, took out their binoculars, and looked for birds, identifying them using their *Birds of New Zealand* guidebook. Tonino, coming from the city, only knew about pigeons. He described to Susan how many Italians eat pigeon by roasting them and basting them with olive oil and rosemary.

"Sounds good," Susan replied.

He also told her about how many Italian men still keep homing pigeons on the rooftops of major cities like in New York City.

Tonino started to read aloud to Susan about the extinction of birds in New Zealand. "The Maori hunted lots of birds. Some of them they ate, and others they just used for feathers to make their cloaks." Tonino noted to Susan, "The same customs of making feathered cloaks also occurred in Hawai'i. I don't know if you saw the statues of Kamehameha, but his cloak was made out of bird feathers."

"I do remember seeing the beautiful cloak."

Tonino continued to read, "Someone is reported to have counted the number of feathers in one of the cloaks at the Bishop Museum in one square inch and then multiplied that figure by the total number of square inches in the entire cloak. That figure was 450,000 feathers, and since each bird provided only 6 to 7 desirable feathers, it comes to using 80,000 birds for just this one cloak."

"I didn't know that! How awful," Susan replied.

Tonino changed the topic of bird extinction and asked Susan, "Did you see the skeletons of the moas when we went to the poi dance demonstration? They were in the hallway."

"No, I didn't."

"It was the largest bird that ever lived. There were many different species. Bones were often found in caves that the Maoris probably used as shelters. All these birds, and some others, were hunted to extinction." Tonino remembered reading about how in the United States, massive hunting brought the passenger pigeon to extinction. "Don't think that just modern man helped bring animals to extinction. Both the indigenous Maoris and Hawai'ians overharvested birds just for their feathers. The lesson here is that we now know so much more about species numbers, habitat fragility, and overuse of natural resources that we can avoid putting too much pressure on any one species. That pressure can force a species into extinction."

"I guess if we want to see a giant weta, we should morph and look around."

Susan agreed. Soon they saw a giant weta approaching. They knew it was a weta because they had seen a tree weta while camping. The difference, however, was that this weta was large (about five inches long, while Tonino is less than one inch long).

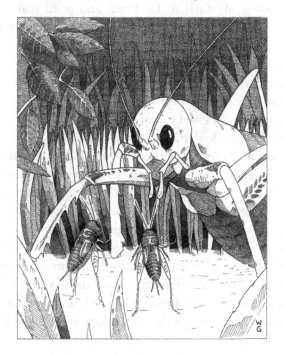

"Greetings," the giant weta said.

"Greetings to you," Tonino responded.

"What is your name?" asked Susan.

He replied, in a beautiful New Zealand accent, "Lawrence H. Field at your service."

"I am Tonino Cricket and this is Susan Maki." Being a male cricket and more vocal, Tonino monopolized the conversation, which didn't bother Susan. "What is it like living on this island?"

"Well, at first it was great. But then the rats arrived, causing major carnage, and almost completely bringing giant wetas to extinction." Susan remained silent, but was aghast at this almost ethnic cleansing. "Things have gotten better since the government instituted the trapping and poisoning program that completely eliminated rats from the island. Now we can move around rather freely without concern of being eaten."

At that moment, something that Tonino thought was a monster lunged out and grabbed Lawrence by the right foreleg. Tonino quickly morphed and grabbed the monster's mouth, preventing it from closing any further. He pried and pried real hard until Lawrence fell out. Then he chased it away. After he morphed back, he asked Lawrence, "Are you okay?"

"Yes, but I am sure I will have a sore right foreleg tomorrow. I have seen a lot of strange things on this island, but I have never seen any animals change into a human."

"It's a special gift given to my family by the Blue Fairy."

"I wish I could do that," Lawrence responded.

Tonino and Lawrence settled into a long conversation about the diversity on Stephens Island, especially the strange animals and plants. When he felt he had enough information, he said good-bye to Lawrence, and both he and Susan transformed.

After one complete day of touring the island and learning about the extinction of so many organisms, Tonino was somewhat depressed. He was unable to think about his major charge in life. The Blue Fairy had said, "I have come here to ask you to become the environmental conscience of the world." To him, this was a very, very heavy responsibility and one that didn't have an easy solution. Susan realized that Tonino was having problems and agreed to get him to their next destination, which she believed is what he really needed (instead of looking at endangered animals and plants).

Tonino on the Franz Joseph Glacier

That evening they packed and planned to leave early the next morning to go to the Franz Joseph Glacier. It was a long drive, but extremely beautiful and worth every moment. *What could be more barren of living things than a glacier?"* Susan asked herself.

Finally, they arrived at the base village, where everyone prepared for either a climbing ascent to the glacier or a plane ride directly onto the top of the glacier. They checked into a hiker's cabin for two nights. That evening, Tonino and Susan shared travel experiences with people from all over the world. There was a large group from Japan, and Susan really enjoyed talking to them. Unfortunately, because of his depressed condition, Tonino became even more confrontational when discussing the Japanese killing whales. Tonino was obnoxious, he knew it, and so did Susan. Finally, he excused himself and went to bed. He was asleep when Susan retired. The next morning, both Susan and Tonino signed up for the plane ride to the top of the glacier, where you actually get to walk on the glacier and see crevasses.

Everyone participating in that event assembled all the necessary gear and boarded the plane. Besides the guide, there were ten people making the tour. They had their spiked shoes on, warm clothes, ropes, and backpacks. In addition to the normal gear, Tonino had a pack full of fluff from the milkweed pods he collected with Dr. Gibbs. Why he still had the fluff in his backpack, even he didn't know. Everyone was advised to wear dark sunglasses and lots of sunscreen lotion. They were told about the hole in the ozone layer in this area of the world and the high incidence of skin cancer here.

The plane flight to the top of the glacier was scary for Susan. Once they landed, she was okay. They were having a great experience. What a thrill to be actually walking on a glacier. They had been shown how to use the ropes and other emergency gear. When they stopped for lunch, their guide, David Daintree, told them that after lunch they would do a little climbing around one of the crevasses.

After resting for about thirty-five minutes after lunch, the group started out; within twenty minutes, they reached one of the crevasses. Before beginning their attack on the crevasse, David gave them a ten-minute talk concerning global warming and its effect on glaciers. David was a scholar of Latin studies and was only doing this part-time, but he felt committed to making his contribution to saving the earth and its resources. He also felt that water, rather than oil, would be the natural resource of importance in the near future. David showed the group the various flags that marked ten-year periods of glacial retreat.

David said to the group, "This effect on glaciers, which are really tied up liquid water in the form of ice, should be of major concern to everyone regardless of where you live."

Tonino looked at Susan and said, "I had no idea this was one of the major impacts of global warming."

David continued, "Now, while we start our climb, remember everything I told you."

The plan was to climb down only about ten feet into the crevasse, make a rope ladder to cross the fifteen-foot expanse, and then climb up the other side. Tonino was the last person in line. Everyone had climbed down and crossed over to the other side, and all but Tonino and the guide were on the other side of the crevasse. Tonino had safely made it down and was getting ready to cross the rope to reach the opposite side. For some reason, and this had never happened to him before, he sort of lapsed mentally and imagined he was a cricket. Even though he never fully became a cricket, the connection between his brain and his eyes had started to become insectlike. As everyone knows, insects can't blink because they lack eyelids. As Tonino lapsed into this strange mode, somewhere "in between" two different life forms, his dark glasses slid off his face and hung down around his neck. The bright light was too much and he couldn't see where he was placing his foot. Down, down, down he went.

No one could believe what was happening. Even David the guide seemed totally surprised. Tonino's weight snapped the safety rope, and he started sliding down for thirty feet.

Being of good sound mind, and also very agile, he kept his cool. He quickly morphed into a cricket. He thought this would allow him to survive the fall much better. The thing that saved him was the pack of milkweed seed fluff. He landed right on it. When he stopped sliding, he quickly changed himself back into people size. He did this because he knew that crickets and other insects are cold-blooded and assume the temperature of the surrounding environment. Well, it was below freezing thirty feet down in the crevasse. He was able, however, to maintain voice contact with everyone on top.

"Are you okay?" David hollered.

Susan held her breath because she was afraid Tonino was gone forever. "Yes," the word came as Tonino's voice echoed off the walls of the icy crevasse.

"Try to keep moving so you don't freeze anything, especially your ears, hands, and feet." They thought they would have him out that afternoon, but they lacked rescue equipment; they informed Tonino he would have to stay there all night. People donated sweaters, which they dropped to Tonino.

"We'll be back after the first sign of light in the morning," David said. He pounded in a bright red, visual marker so they could find him the next day.

Tonino could tell when they had gone because their voices got more and more faint, until finally he couldn't hear them. The last thing he heard was the airplane starting up and taking off. *What should I do now?* he thought to himself. The group had thrown down several extra jackets, sweaters, and even two blankets. Tonino was now in his people form; he could freeze some of his extremities, plus he had no food. He took off the pack with all the milkweed seed fluff. He placed the jackets on top of the blankets and made sort of a nest. He remembered the exhibit at the Auckland Museum, the last one that caught his eye, where the Maori mothers surrounded their babies in moss or *muka* fiber. "I guess I'll try it," he mumbled to himself.

Inside he made a beautiful igloo out of the milkweed fluff. He then made a tunnel out of the sleeve of the jacket so that it reached the center of the fluff igloo. The only way to get into this so-called sleeping bag was to crawl up the sleeve of the jacket. Tonino knew that only the clothes he was wearing changed size when he transformed. Because he had made this shelter out of people-sized things he wasn't wearing, he would be able to enter the sleeve of the jacket and stay quite warm once he was in the interior of the milkweed fluff igloo. Another benefit of transforming was that, as a person, it was very common to freeze one's ears because they stick out and away from the head. Cricket's ears, however, do not stick out from the head; they are not even located on the head, but are found on the foretibia of what are called the "long-horned" grasshoppers and crickets, and the first abdominal segment of the "short-horned" grasshoppers.

He morphed, crawled up the sleeve, and snuggled down for the night. Another advantage of turning into an insect is that many insects can survive short periods of very low temperatures, even freezing. In fact, this is a great way to observe an active insect: put them on ice or in the freezer for a short time. It won't kill them but will slow them down.

As he rested, Tonino tried to keep himself from thinking about his dilemma. He recounted all the ways he could remember how plants or plant materials are used by both humans and insects for shelter, food, and so on. "Oh, and don't forget medicines," he reminded himself. However, his mind was sort of stuck in his current situation. Rather than dwell on it, he thought of similar situations and remembered reading *James and the Giant Peach* when he was little. Crawling into his homemade igloo reminded Tonino of when James crawled into the hole and up the tunnel to get inside the peach. He also remembered a discussion in that book about short- and long-horned grasshoppers and the differences where the tympanum or ear is located.

He remembered Dr. Gibbs explaining how the milkweed fluff had been used for comforters, pillows, and even life jackets. During World War II, when the supply of kapok was cut off from the Philippines, young children in the United States collected the fluff from milkweeds and put it into large burlap sacks. It was sent to factories where lifejackets were made. The fluff, which comes from the seedpods, is also called Java cotton. The kapok tree itself is found in tropical America, Africa, and the East Indies.

Before he went to sleep, Tonino thought about being in Mexico with Dr. Brower, Pedro, and Ming Ming. If the monarchs could survive the cold and even freezing temperatures, plus sometimes snow in their *refugia*, surely he could do it. Just the thought that another insect could do it was enough assurance for him to think, *I will survive until tomorrow.*

The next morning, he heard a tremendous racket above him and even felt a tremendous wind, even though he was quite well insulated. He quickly pulled away the fluff covering, crawled out through the sleeve of the jacket, and transformed. Suddenly, the noise and wind stopped. He then heard David the guide and Susan both calling, "Tonino, are you okay? Can you hear us?"

"Yes, I'm okay."

What a rescue: ropes, ladders, rescue team, and yes, a helicopter. When he reached the surface, Susan ran over and kissed him. She had been crying, and some of the tears looked like Pele's tears except they were frozen and were clear, just like glass.

"We are sorry," David said, "but you will have to go back in the helicopter even though you say you're fine." Susan rode back in the helicopter with him.

As they lifted off, Tonino forgot his brush with death. All he could think about were the helicopters in *Arachnophobia* and *Jurassic Park*. Of course, this accident was big news, and Dr. Andrews and Dr. Gibbs heard about the young boy from Massachusetts who fell into a crevasse. "Boy," Dr. Gibbs said, "this youngster certainly gets his share of international publicity."

Finally, after all that traveling and seeing wetas, glaciers, glowworms, geysers, Maoris, and lots of sheep, they returned to Wellington. Susan and Tonino had such a wonderful experience in the Pacific islands, both culturally and educationally, that it made them reflect on how other people in the United States viewed this part of the world. They both agreed that, in general, most North Americans know very little about the culture and people of the South Pacific.

"How many Americans know that the Pacific Ocean makes up about two thirds of all the oceans put together? How many people know that New Zealand has glaciers, and how many people know that the monarch butterfly has established itself in most of these South Pacific islands?" Tonino asked Susan.

"Not only that, how many know anything about the indigenous peoples of these islands? We have been lucky to see the Maori and Hawai'ian cultures on such an intimate basis," replied Susan.

During breakfast, Tonino and Susan shared most of their experiences with Dr. Andrews and his wife. Tonino, however, didn't tell them about the cricket incident. "We couldn't have done this without your help," Tonino said.

Leaving for China

That evening, Susan and Tonino packed for the next leg of their trip. The next day, they would leave for China. Dr. Andrews took them to the Wellington International Airport. They knew they had to be checked in at least two hours before their international flight. Since they had mailed some books, souvenirs, and clothing back to their respective homes, all they had were their backpacks, CD player and headphones, computer, and of course their umbrellas. It would be a long flight, between twelve to fourteen hours.

They couldn't thank Dr. Andrews enough.

"Don't think anything of it," he said. "I enjoyed having you as my guests. Say hello to Dr. Stoffolano when you see him next."

"I will, and again, *grazie per tutto*" (Italian for "thank you for everything"), Tonino responded with confidence. He knew Dr. Andrews would understand this because he learned Italian when he was on sabbatical in Italy.

Chapter 12.
The Nightmare Montage

A Collection of Tonino's Experiences

During their flight to China, Susan and Tonino both decide to watch the movie, *Medicine Man*, starring Sean Connery as Dr. Robert Campbell and Lorraine Bracco as his assistant. As they got further into the movie, Susan looked at Tonino and could tell that she wouldn't get any sleep for a while after the movie. Whenever Tonino showed so much facial expression during a movie, he always had a lot to discuss following it. Usually Tonino liked to watch the credits at the end of a movie. This time, however, he just about pulled Susan's earplugs off.

"I just can't believe that humans, as a species, are destroying about 96,000 acres of tropical forest each a day!" Tonino exclaimed.

Many of the other passengers heard him and looked over at him. Usually he felt embarrassed over such incidents, but this time, for some reason, it didn't seem to bother him. "The topic of habitat destruction is so important and urgent," he whispered in Susan's ear. Tonino went on to say, "This movie accentuates the importance of prospecting the plants and animals of tropical regions for chemicals that could be used as medicines to treat major afflictions. In this case, the modern medicine man, Dr. Campbell is looking for a drug to treat cancer."

Little did Tonino know, but this major affliction (i.e., cancer) would eventually touch his own personal life.

Tonino continued, "Did you know that a rainforest has over a hundred inches of water each year? Also, it usually has large trees that provide a dense canopy. Studies like those depicted in this movie about the organisms inhabiting the upper canopy of the rainforest are actually being conducted. People like Dr. Meg Lowman, who has studied canopy ecology in Australia, Peru, and Africa, are essential for us to have a complete understanding of how plants and insects interact, and at the same time, they will use this data to try and preserve biodiversity."

"What else did you relate to in the movie?" asked Susan. She knew that Tonino was always seeking ways to integrate information into past experiences.

"I couldn't help but notice that Sean Connery and several of the indigenous people were wearing tattoos."

"What else did you like?" Susan asked.

"I liked the way the producer included two traditional medicine men in the story. It was especially important, I think, that the traditional, indigenous medicine man knew that it was the ants living in the bromeliads that produced the important medicinal effect, and not the bromeliad, as Dr. Campbell thought, that was important to find and isolate the important anticancer compound."

Just before they went to sleep, both agreed that even though chemical prospecting is an important aspect of studying biodiversity and preserving natural habitats, there are many more reasons for saving habitats that don't have a dollar sign attached to them. For these two crickets, destruction of the various habitats throughout the world meant a lot. It meant loss of habitat for members of their own race and their close relatives, the katydids and grasshoppers.

Susan bent and whispered in his ear, "Now that the movie is over, try to go to sleep."

When she was finished, she kissed his ear. She knew that he was really excited, and that it would take some reading to calm him down. "I just have a few more pages of Wilson's book on *Biophilia* and then I will try to sleep," he responded.

After about fifteen minutes, he finished the book; Susan was still awake, so he told her that he had gained an even greater love and respect for all life forms.

Because of all the extinction problems and endangered plants and animals he learned about in New Zealand, Tonino had a tremendous backlog of mental images waiting to spill out. As a consequence, he fell asleep and started to dream; he found himself ready to be figuratively eaten alive. He dreamed that he was reading *Biodiversity*, a newspaper published by one of Mehitabel's relatives (the cockroach in Don Marquis's wonderful book *Archy and Mehitabel*), which has kept the animal world appraised of what animals are endangered and what ones have already gone extinct. It also highlighted cases where the "most wanted" insects or pests of humans are listed. Unlike Wilson's book *Biophilia*, where he paints an amiable relation between humans and other organisms, this newspaper focused on the major clashes that have taken place between humans and other life forms.

It appears that the love-hate relationship that has existed forever between animals and humans had gone beyond the debate stage and reached a climax. Tonino, being both a human and insect, especially a house cricket, was always on the fringe of these debates. Public exposure and mass media abuse was inevitable since he had to be on the forefront of these issues. "Damn that Blue Fairy," he would often say. Unlike Ralph Nader, who is a political animal, Tonino didn't take kindly to politics or to politicians. The only crickets he thought were disliked by humans were the mole crickets.

Tonino had just seen the TV program *Most Wanted Insects*, hosted by the BBC and sponsored by Orkin Pest Control. The first most wanted were the mosquitoes, which are vectors of living organisms that cause human diseases, such as West Nile fever. The second most wanted in the United States were two cousins, the tawny mole cricket and the Southern mole cricket. They were costing the state of Florida about $93 million a year in damages to turf and pastures. They were especially hated in several southeastern states from Florida to North Carolina because they were tunneling under and destroying man's most beloved golf course turf. Some humans, however, liked them because they were causing serious damage to the plant beds of seedling tobacco in North Carolina.

Like Tonino's father, these two crickets had immigrated into the United States. The major difference, however, is that his father entered legally while the above two crickets entered illegally. They came in around 1900 into the seaport of Brunswick, Georgia, without their natural enemies, and have been causing trouble since. These demons were about one and a half inches long, with forelegs modified for digging with the first segment of the front tarsi being spadelike, brownish in color with small beady eyes, and short "hairs" covering the body.

Tonino listened carefully to the description of the mole crickets, which are dangerous and prone to cannibalism. The description, especially the use of the term "hairs," made Tonino upset. During his human form, he had heard about all the misconceptions humans have about many things because of the poor choice of words. He was constantly reminding everyone, including his insect friends, that when they molt, they do not shed their skin but shed their exoskeleton. The terms "skin" and "hair," as used by humans, do not have counterparts in the insect world. Their structure and origin are completely different.

Tonino continued to dream; he decided to go outside. He was in Florida at the Doral Golf Resort and Spa in Miami. It was midafternoon, and the PGA tournament, with a million-dollar purse, was coming to an end. Tiger Woods was one stroke behind the leader, Phil Mickelson. If Tiger could make this putt he would win the tournament. It was a twenty-foot putt, and the crowd was completely silent. Tiger's focus was incredible. He pulled his putter back and then sent it forward, hitting the ball perfectly. It was headed in the right direction. The crowd was ecstatic and so loud that no one could hear anything. About one inch before the cup, the ball suddenly veered to the right. Tiger had lost the match.

Tonino was watching in his cricket form and knew exactly what happened. He quickly transformed and ran to Tiger, shouting, "There was interference, you really won."

"What do you mean?" Tiger said.

"Your ball veered to the right because of a mole cricket. Let's go to the hole and I'll show you."

Tonino bent down and carefully lifted up the grass just three quarters of an inch from the hole. As he did this, it exposed a male mole cricket from its burrow. Immediately Tonino picked up the cricket and said to Tiger, "Let's go and appeal the match." Tonino found a Styrofoam cup and put the mole cricket in it. He knew that the hindlegs of mole crickets are not modified for jumping, thus this cricket would not be able to get out of the cup. The tournament directors met for several hours. Tonino was very nervous because he liked Tiger and wanted to help him. Finally, the door to the official's room opened. Jack Nicklaus read the verdict, which ultimately stated that this was a natural obstacle and that Mickelson remained the winner. Of course, both Tiger and Tonino were disappointed.

"Thank you for all your help," Tiger said. "May I have the cricket?"

"Sure, here it is." Tonino hopped off and found an isolated spot to morph.

Male crickets can be very aggressive, which can include taking bites out of their competitors. Females are not usually aggressive or cannibalistic. As soon as he morphed, Tonino was surrounded by at least twenty male mole crickets. Leading the group was a female named Madonna. Unlike most female crickets, she was a leader, extremely aggressive, and very vocal. They were chanting and shouting, "Kill the house cricket! He betrayed our friend and leader."

"Wait!" Madonna shouted. "Let me be the first to take a bite out of him. I hear that house crickets think their 'singing' is better than ours."

As Madonna's mandibles tore into Tonino's large hind femur, he chirped with pain, so much pain that his labial palps quivered and his mandibles shuttered. The intense pain caused him to wake up. He was in his human form, sitting next to Susan on the airplane; blood was oozing from his left thigh. The dream injury to his left leg reminded him of his great-great-great-grandfather.

"What happened?" Susan asked.

He told her about his dream and how Pinocchio had tried to kill Grillo-parlante with a mallet. "Luckily he survived, otherwise I wouldn't be here today," Tonino said. "The main outcome of that incident left him with a weak left leg, and he had to use a cane the rest of his life."

Tonino wiped the blood away with a Kleenex and noticed that he must have picked off a large scab in his sleep. It took him awhile to recover from the dream; however, it made him wonder, since humans sometimes dream they are animals, did animals dream they are humans? He remembered Lassie, the Yins' dog. When he watched videos at their house, Lassie would be asleep on the floor; sometimes she barked and would move her legs while still dreaming.

Chapter 13.
China and Cricket Warriors

Arriving in Beijing and the Yin Family

Their trip to China started in Beijing, where Ming Ming's family still had relatives. Ming Ming's sister, Lucy, would be flying in from Boston to meet them in Beijing. She had never visited these relatives, and since Susan and Tonino would also be there, her parents agreed to let her go. They liked Tonino so much and also respected him a lot. They knew he would take care of her once she got there. Tonino was always amazed at how different cultures behaved once they settled in the United States. Take the Yin family, for example. They are 100 percent Chinese, yet their children have names like Lucy, Melinda, Felix, and Amy. In order to be even more American they adopted a dog and named her Lassie and gave all of the children American-sounding names, except for Ming Ming.

Tonino remembered when the Yins became American citizens. There was a big party, lots of Chinese food, apple pie and vanilla ice cream, and a small American flag for everyone. What a wonderful event! It was events like this that enriched his life and gave him a better idea of what it was like to be a "citizen of the world," as Tonino's mother would often say. Susan had many of the traits of Tonino's mother, who was such a gentle lady, which is why Tonino liked her. He knew that both of his parents would love Susan when they finally got to meet her. Right now, that seemed very far off, and his mind began to focus on their trip to China.

The captain announced that the flight would be landing in an hour; the lights were turned on, and the stewardesses got ready to serve breakfast. Tonino had ordered hot cereal, toast, and orange juice. Susan ordered yogurt and hot tea. It was cool in the plane because the heat had been turned down while everyone was sleeping.

Tonino received his meal, opened the cereal, and poked Susan. "Notice the steam coming from the cereal!"

"I see it! Look here, you can also see it coming from my hot tea," Susan said. "Remember seeing the hot steam coming from the hot springs in Rotorua?"

"I do. It's like the spout coming from the whale's blowhole and also seeing your breath on a cold day," Tonino said. He mentioned a grasshopper that has special glands at the base of its spiracles. When threatened, it expels air from the spiracles and mixes the secretions from these defensive glands, which form a bubble and repels predators that contact it.

Susan replied, "Can you explain this a little better? I don't see the connection between the grasshopper and steam or water vapor."

"You're correct. I just wanted to make the connection with the 'exhalation' of the grasshopper with our exhalation and how for the grasshopper it could also be used as a defensive mechanism. What we are talking about is water vapor or secretions coming out of a breathing hole. For insects it is the spiracle and for whales it is the blowhole." Tonino then began to giggle.

"What's so funny?" she asked.

"Did you ever watch *Seinfeld* on TV?"

"No; remember, my parents wouldn't let me watch TV."

"There was one program where his friend Kramer is hitting golf balls out over the ocean and he gets a hole in one. The ball lands directly into the blowhole of a whale. If it plugged up the hole, which it could, the whale would suffocate because they are air-breathing mammals. Well, the whale gets close to shore and is having trouble breathing. His other friend, George, is pretending to impress his new girlfriend and he tells her he is a marine biologist. To impress her even further, he goes out, removes the ball from the whale's blowhole, saves the whale, and becomes a hero in the eyes of his new girlfriend."

"That's a great story," Susan said.

"Yeah, but if you ever watched this program, you would see how funny this situation really was."

Breakfast was finished, the plates were cleared, and soon the pilot announced their arrival into Beijing's International Airport. They exited the plane. Waiting for them were Meng Ping and her husband. Since neither Susan nor Tonino knew them, they held a sign that said, "Welcome Susan and Tonino." Of course it was in English because they knew neither of them could read Chinese (they didn't know about Tonino's ability to read or speak any language).

It was around four o'clock when they arrived at the home of Ming Ming's relatives. Tonino and Susan were both surprised to see how small their apartment was. It was located in the heart of Beijing. It was very hot, so Tonino went to the window to get some fresh air. As he looked down from the fifth floor, he was surprised that he couldn't see the street.

He returned and whispered to Susan, "I can't believe how bad the air pollution is."

We all know about Tonino's concerns about Mother Earth and the negative effects so many people were having on the health of this precious sphere.

He told Susan, "This air pollution in China is just another example of man's impact on the environment."

At lunch, Meng told them a little about China and compared it to Western culture.

Arthropods and the Chinese

Both teenagers were interested in knowing that to the Chinese, unlike most Western cultures, insects have always played a more prominent role in their culture than mammals. The Chinese were the first to domesticate the silkworm, which is still used to produce the important fabric. Tonino was amazed to know that at one time this insect united the Eastern and Western parts of the world via the Silk Road. Also, like the silkworm, the cricket became a very special insect to the Chinese. Kia Se-tao, who lived during the first part of the thirteenth century, the period of the Sung dynasty, wrote a book,

Tsu chi king (*Book of Crickets*). Tonino read in the small leaflet that Meng gave him during lunch that there were three major periods in Chinese history relating to crickets; until the T'ang dynasty, Chinese mainly appreciated crickets for their songs; during the T'ang dynasty (618–906), they started to raise them in cages, and during the Sung dynasty (960–1278), they raised crickets as warriors.

After doing the dishes, Meng said, "Take a nap; tonight we will go to the Donghuamen Yeshi night market located near the Forbidden City. We can eat there." Following the nap, everyone left the apartment and embarked on what Tonino would call "a great experience." On the way they came to a huge crowd outside a Chinese pharmacy that was known for its traditional medicine.

It was extremely noisy, with people pushing and shoving. Soon a young British woman began speaking from the back of a truck, standing next to a cage. At first Tonino wasn't interested in what she was saying but wanted to see what was in the cage. As he neared the cage he could see a huge Asiatic black bear (commonly known as moon bears for having a white crescent-shaped mark on their chest) jammed into a small iron cage. The bear smelled terrible and looked extremely unhappy. Almost instantly, Tonino remembered how Shaquille's fingers had closed in on him at the basketball demonstration at the Boston Garden and how it felt to be trapped in a cage. The sight of the bear also jogged his memory and he remembered the Blue Fairy appearing at Smokey the Bear's gravesite telling him about the cruel behavior of some Asian countries toward bears. Tonino turned to Meng and asked, "Why is this happening in front of a pharmacy?"

"It's a long story and extremely controversial. Let me try to summarize what is going on. In traditional Asian medicine, the bile of bears has been shown to be very important in treating specific conditions associated with the human gall bladder and liver. In order to supply the demand by traditional pharmacists, bears—especially the Asiatic black bear—are killed just for its prized gall bladder. This slaughter for a specific organ put great stress on the natural populations. As conservation groups became more vocal, this practice was made illegal. Still, however, there is a great demand for bear gall bladders. I think it was in Korea that someone developed a technique of caging and restricting the bears, putting a catheter into the bile duct and harvesting their bile without killing the bear; bear farming became extremely popular. The most recent estimate is that in China alone there are about 7,000 bears being farmed using this technique. Modern science has shown that a bile salt has been shown to be effective in treating various liver diseases; this is the effective chemical ingredient in bear bile. This chemical is also important in controlling the amount of cholesterol in the blood. Since the chemical can now be synthesized, the cruel and inhumane treatment of bears is unnecessary. I believe bear farming is now illegal in China."

"Wow," Tonino responded. Tonino then noticed someone handing out pamphlets and picked several of them up. They were from the Animals Asia Foundation. Quickly scanning the pamphlet, Tonino remembered the Blue Fairy told him he would deal with the situation when he encountered it. His response was to save the pamphlet and send in a donation to the cause of China's bear rescue when he returned home. He realized that he couldn't personally take on every environmental or inhumane issue and must decide how he would help each cause.

Meng grabbed Susan by the arm and said, "Let's go into the pharmacy." Pushing and shoving, they made their way to the door.

To enter, Tonino had to push extra hard on the door. As it opened, the hinges produced a chirp, just like a cricket. Once inside, Tonino saw numerous shelves behind the counter, filled with jars. Each jar contained all sorts of plants and animals. Meng explained that someone would come in and describe their ailment to the pharmacist, who would then make a mixture of various items to treat the ailment. There were praying mantis egg cases, cicada exuvia, bee propolis, silkworm frass, dried seahorses, and many more interesting items.

Meng explained, "Shen Nung, the founder of Chinese herbal medicine, wrote the definitive book *Shen Nung Pen Tsao Ching* (circa AD 100). In that book he listed twenty-one insects used in medicine, while *Ben Cao Gang Mu* (*Encyclopedia of Chinese Medicine*) by Li Shizheng (1578), listed seventy-three insects of medicinal importance. I am not sure whether the number of insects used in Chinese medicine has increased or decreased."

After seeing as much as they could in the pharmacy, they went to the market. Tonino and Susan were shocked, not only by the enormity of the market, but also by what was being sold. Leaving the food area, they came to several tables that were covered with cricket cages, live crickets, and even utensils for raising and trapping crickets. Susan picked up a small clay pot that was covered with a small lid that had many holes in it.

She asked Meng, "What is this?"

"During the summer months, when it is hot, cricket aficionados would keep their crickets in these pots. The thick pottery walls don't let heat penetrate very well, and the crickets remain cool because heat that does enter readily escapes through the holes in the top of the pot."

She continued, "I am told that the Field Museum in Chicago has a great collection of paraphernalia for raising crickets. Some of the clay pots date back to the Ming dynasty (1368–1643). They also have a collection of fancy gourds for housing crickets. When they are small, the gourds are forced to develop inside clay molds that have elaborate designs on their insides. As the gourd grows, it presses against the relief and assumes the shape and all the intricate designs. These molds are then broken, the gourd is dried, and a hole is cut into the top, which is then fixed with a lid. I believe that this craft is now extinct. Apparently, the gourd and cricket are somehow always connected by the carvings on the lids, which are usually made of ivory or jade."

All Tonino could think about was his terrifying experience in New Mexico when he was shut in the bean pot. He also pondered the statement that in China, the cricket and the gourd were inseparable companions.

"Look!" Susan said excitedly. "See these small, beautiful blue-on-white porcelain dishes. And look here! These tiny beds or sleeping boxes are great."

Tonino was impressed. He asked the merchant if they could ship things back to the United States.

"Certainly, we just did a big shipment to Philadelphia for some professor named Otte."

Tonino purchased a lot of things, gave the man the address of Joe's grocery store, received the receipt, and they continued shopping. As he walked, his mind wandered to the funny incident when Joe received two cases of grasshopper food for Pedro's nutrition experiment. Immediately, he got a big smile on his face.

"Why are you smiling?" Susan asked.

"Oh, nothing, I was just thinking of my friend Pedro."

They stopped for dinner, which consisted of the following: scorpion soup, ant and chicken egg casserole, stir-fried silkworm pupae, and stir-fried cicadas.

"What do you think?" Meng asked Tonino.

"So far, so good. I liked the scorpions, but would have liked them better if they had just molted."

"What do you mean?" Susan asked.

"Well, in Boston we can buy soft-shelled crabs. We often had them stir-fried at Ming Ming's house."

"What do you mean by soft-shelled?" Meng asked.

"In order for arthropods, which have a hard and often tough exoskeleton like we crickets do, to grow, they must first molt. A hormone known as ecdysone for insects and crustecdysone for crustaceans initiates the molt. When the old cuticle or exuvium is shed, it takes awhile for the new cuticle to harden. In the meantime, these newly molted arthropods, which are white, are very vulnerable to predators. Thus, the term soft-shelled is applied to these arthropods. They are much easier to eat and you can enjoy their flavor more. When we were in Arizona, we went to the Heard Museum and saw a white cricket katsina. Once their cuticle hardens, it darkens and becomes yellowish brown."

"How interesting," everyone agreed.

Meng called the waiter over and ordered two more things. When they arrived she explained what they were. "This one is called *Chongcha*. It is a tea made from the frass or excrement of two species of Lepidopterans: *Hydrillodes morosa* and *Aglossa dimidita*."

Immediately Susan looked at Tonino. "Is this what I think it is?"

Tonino responded, "Yes, if you are thinking of the black and hard pelletlike things we saw on the leaves of the milkweed when we checked Faith."

Meng interjected, "This tea is very medicinal. It cures diarrhea and also is believed to treat bleeding hemorrhoids."

Tonino wondered if the last treatment had anything to do with where the frass is finally processed. Being small, most insects tend to lose water. To avoid this, caterpillars produce a very dry fecal pellet in their rectum by removing most water and putting it back into their hemolymph.

"I think I will have to pass on this one," remarked Susan.

Meng continued, "Another tea we could have is caterpillar fungus tea, but it is very expensive."

Tonino asked, "Is this the same type of caterpillar fungus that the Maoris used for making the black coloring for their *moko*?"

"I believe so," Meng responded. "This last drink is called ant wine."

"How do they make it?"

"Well, Tonino, one steeps ants of the genus *Polyrhachis* in rice brandy. The problem is that this ant has been overexploited and faces extinction because of this human use."

Tonino thought about how the passenger pigeon, the dodo, and so many other living organisms were overexploited as food and ultimately became extinct. Tonino thought to himself, *I wonder if Dr. Wilson knows about this ant?* He took out his notebook and wrote the genus name down. Next to it he wrote, "Ask Dr. Wilson about this ant."

"Wow, what a meal. I will never forget this!" Tonino said. Thinking to himself, he wondered why crickets weren't on the menu. He asked Meng, "Why don't the Chinese eat crickets?"

"I believe they consider them sacred and important in other ways, such as harbingers of good luck."

Tonino responded, "We have a similar belief in Western culture; it is most aptly expressed in the Dickens story, *The Cricket on the Hearth*, which was published in 1845. In that story it says, 'To have a cricket on the hearth is the luckiest thing in all the world!'" Tonino continued to talk. "Being near the hearth wasn't such a lucky thing for Grillo-parlante, or the Talking Cricket, in Lorenzini's 1881 book of *Pinocchio*. He lived in the house of Geppetto, and it was near the hearth that Pinocchio tried to kill him." Tonino scratched his head like his father always did when thinking. "I wonder if Lorenzini got the idea about the hearth, the cricket, and the kettle from Dickens? I know Dickens lived in Italy in 1844, before Lorenzini wrote his story." Tonino moved the conversation into a different arena. "Since we have had such unusual things to eat here, can you tell us something about what fighting crickets were fed?"

Cricket Warriors

Meng picked up the conversation, "The procedures and rules for feeding crickets are very elaborate. The Golden Bell cricket, for instance, is fed on wormwood."

Tonino asked, "Isn't the drink absinthe made from wormwood?"

Susan, who had taken a course in art appreciation, replied, "Yes, and many famous impressionist painters, especially Vincent Van Gogh, who drank it in the cafés of Paris. Also, I remember the 1876 painting by Edgar Degas titled the *Absinthe Drinkers*."

Tonino chimed in and said, "Ernest Hemingway also drank absinthe in Spain, just prior to the running of the bulls. He also mentions absinthe in his book, *For Whom the Bell Tolls*."

Because the conversation got sidetracked on absinthe, Meng never did explain what crickets were fed.

Susan interrupted the thread of conversation and asked, "Do cricket handlers do anything special to encourage the crickets to sing?"

"They often used a 'tickler' made from a bone or reed handle that has a fine rat whisker, not a mouse whisker, at the tip. Handlers often used these to incite the crickets to sing."

Tonino then asked, "I wonder if the whisker mimics the antenna of another cricket?"

"I don't know," responded Meng. "Another interesting thing they do is to take an already established good singer and coat the tympanum with a special wax. This way, the cricket has to increase the strength of his stridulating in order for it to get its own sound feedback, thus increasing the volume of the sound. They also apply a tiny drop of wax (tree sap mixed with cinnabar for the red color), a process known as *dian yiao* or *zhan yiao*, to each of the wings. This also results in an amplification of the chirp."

Meng knew the teenagers wanted to know everything about crickets, so she continued speaking. "All this information mainly deals with the regular feeding and maintenance of crickets. For cricket fighting or *douxi-shuai*, special foods were often prepared. They also had a regimented breeding program to produce what they called 'generals' and 'marshals,' and the best fighters came from the southern province of Kwant-tung."

The most interesting thing Meng told them was that the best fighters are pampered like babies, and if the fighter is having "breathing" problems, it was fed a "bamboo butterfly" (possibly *Ypthima savara*, Nymphalidae).

"As the time for fighting drew near, the cricket warriors were fed a special tonic from the root of a specific plant. Also, many were fed female mosquitoes that had just taken a blood meal. An emperor would often do this with the intent and hope to empower his special warrior with his own spirit, or mana. Unlike the Maoris, however, no one had to be eaten to obtain mana. It is said that great fortunes were won and lost at cricket matches. The battles took place in arenas given special names; the special place here is called Autumn Amusements. The name probably stems from the amusement one would receive, mainly in the autumn when the male crickets are mature and begin to chirp and display defensive and aggressive behavior for territory and mates."

Tonino rudely interrupted Meng and asked, "Could we go to a cricket fight?"

Meng hesitated and patiently responded, "I will try to find one that is open."

After their conversation, they headed back to Meng's apartment, where they spent the night. The next morning, before going to the airport to pick up Lucy, they all had a cup of tea and a bun (Chinese are not big breakfast eaters).

Tonino didn't forget what he had asked Meng, so on the way to the airport, he asked again, "Can we go to a cricket match?"

"On our way to the airport, I will ask my husband to arrange for us to go."

At the airport, a huge crowd had gathered to meet their relatives and other arrivals. "There she is!" Meng shouted when she spotted Lucy.

Once they were in arm's reach, Lucy embraced her aunt for a long time. She had only seen her in photographs. "How great to see you," Meng said.

Tonino, who loved culture, noticed that they did not kiss in their greeting. *Nothing like the Hawai'ian* honi, he said to himself, *where individuals touch noses and share one another's breath or like the Italians who kiss on both cheeks.* This didn't seem odd to him since he had noticed the same lack of public display of emotion by Ming Ming's family in Boston.

"Are you tired?" Meng asked Lucy.

"No, I slept most of the way."

"Good," Meng responded. "Because we may go to a cricket match this afternoon."

"That would be wonderful," responded Lucy. "In Philadelphia, near where I live, they have revived the custom of cricket fighting. I have heard that an entomologist named Otte has been instrumental in this revival."

They arrived at the apartment and Meng's husband said there was a cricket match at two o'clock. Lucy had just enough time to freshen up and change her clothes.

On the way out of the apartment, Lucy stopped her aunt and said, "I am so happy to be here. My parents were sorry to miss this visit, so I must make a mental note of everything and tell them about it."

In order to obtain a full appreciation of the fighting match, Meng's husband arranged for Ernie, a close friend and entomologist from Taiwan, to meet them at the Autumn Amusement. Ernie was visiting Meng and said he would be glad to serve as both guide and interpreter for Tonino and Susan. Above the door to the arena was a beautiful drawing of two crickets fighting.

"Here it is. Don't expect anything too fancy," Ernie said.

They walked up two flights of stairs, which was exhausting because of the heat. Finally, they reached the top and entered a small, dimly lit, and rather stuffy room. It was nothing like the Galleria where Tonino had seen the cockfight in the mountains of Puerto Rico. That arena was circular and about thirty feet in diameter. Also, unlike this arena, it was open to the fresh air. In the center of the room was a small table; a video camera was focused on a small, circular arena, eight inches in diameter, that had sides high enough so that the crickets couldn't jump out.

Each cricket was weighed and classified as lightweight, middleweight, or heavyweight; his memory took him back to the Galleria in Puerto Rico and the weighing in of the gamecocks. This time, however, there was no wiping or cleansing of the gladiators. Over against the wall were shelves with small cages, each containing a cricket warrior. A man was sitting at a small table with some sort of balance weighing a cricket. Once he weighed it, he would say something to the man holding the empty cage.

"What did he say?" Susan asked Ernie.

Ernie said, "He said, 'This one is a heavyweight.'" The man put the gladiator into the cage and took it to the section labeled "Heavyweight."

As the crickets were weighed and categorized, Ernie explained several things to Tonino and Susan. While they were talking, more spectators, all male, were coming and going. Susan stood out like a sore tarsus. It was still forty-five minutes before the fights commenced.

Ernie felt that Tonino and Susan should have some background information so he began a conversation. "The best cricket warriors come from Shandong Province," he said.

Tonino rudely interrupted and said, "Meng told us that the best crickets come from the southern province of Kwant-tung."

"That may have been in the past but now it is Shandong." Ernie continued, "During the autumn it is estimated that over 500,000 people from all over the world descend on this region of China. Everyone is in search of the best gladiator. Some estimate that there are 300,000 to 400,000 cricket enthusiasts in Shanghai. It is reported that people have paid $700 to $1,200 for one fighter. Also, it is estimated that this so called 'devotion' to crickets brings $36 million to this province each year."

"Do these cricket warriors have any experience at combat?" Tonino asked.

"It is hard to say. Probably some have had some encounters in nature but this is where the handler comes in," responded Ernie. "The handler will give his fighters special food and training."

Susan asked, "Are any fighters female?"

Meng replied, "In China, the only female cricket ever kept is for singing, the female of the black tree cricket. The black tree cricket is also referred to as the Golden Bell because of the sound of the male. In this species, unlike other crickets, the female must be present for the male to sing, thus they are not fed to birds like other species. The male crickets in China are prized both for their song and as warriors."

Tonino thought to himself how lucky he was to be of Italian descent. Italian males (whether cricket or human) have always prided themselves as being great singers. He remembered being exposed to Italian opera music when he was very little. His father used to listen to it every Sunday. He knew about his great-grandfather Jiminy, who had a great voice and sang *When You Wish Upon a Star* in Disney's version of *Pinocchio*. Also, as far as he knew, Italians or Romans never put crickets into the fighting arena. Unfortunately, however, when Tonino visited Italy, he became aware of the brutal fighting between human gladiators when he visited the Roman Coliseum. They often fought to the death. He even remembered his aunt Anna telling him how the crowd or the emperor sometimes determined the fate of a downed warrior by giving either the thumbs up or thumbs down.

After hearing all about cricket warriors, Tonino tried to recall all the examples where animals were able to transform between their animal form and human form. He recalled the discussion he had about Smokey the Bear. He had forgotten the one transformation story of the supernatural Hawai'ian green sea turtles. These sea turtles came from the eggs of a giant sea turtle. The mother turtle had dug four holes to lay her eggs. As she watched her offspring come out of the nests, she was very happy because they were all well. She thought that all the baby turtles had hatched, but then she noticed one just emerging from the fourth hole. This turtle of hers, however, was nothing like the others. It had a polished brown color, just like the wood of the kauila. Thus, she called her Kauila. Its unique markings also indicated that she had special powers, or mana. Rather than seeing a star in the sky, like Tonino and Jiminy had, the mother turtle heard a voice coming from the ocean telling her that Kauila was a special gift to the children of the islands. Most unique was Kauila's ability to transform from a turtle to human form, especially when children were in danger of drowning. When she returned to the ocean, she resumed her turtle form. Tonino's thoughts returned to the cricket arena when Susan poked him in the ribs.

The first match was delayed so Ernie continued to tell Tonino and Susan about cricket fighting. "There are two major fighting crickets, *Velarifictorus micado* and *Velarifictorus aspersus*. The first is considered an invasive pest in New Zealand and has the common name of Japanese fighting cricket, while both go by the colloquial name *Cu Zhi*, or fighting cricket. I must tell you that very little research has been done to elucidate why animals are aggressive. A recent study on male Mediterranean field crickets, *Gryllus bimaculatus*, however, has given us some insight as to the possible mechanism behind aggression."

Tonino instantly recognized the cricket's name and envisioned being in his aunt's garden in Florence, where he met Tito Schipa, Jr.

"This is a great piece of research," Ernie continued. "Once a male has lost a fight, it refuses to fight again for at least twenty-four hours. Well, owners of cricket warriors can't wait that long for their warrior to regain composure and become aggressive again."

"What do they do then?" Susan asked.

"The handlers would clasp the losing cricket between their two hands and shake it up. Then they would throw it up into the air so that it would fly a little."

Ernie noticed that Tonino was cringing.

"What's the matter?" Ernie asked.

Tonino responded, "Nothing! It's okay. I just remember a similar instance when I was at a basketball game in the Boston Garden and found myself trapped in the big hand of the famous basketball player, Shaquille O'Neal."

Ernie continued, "Dr. Hans Hofmann, a neurobiologist, studied aggression in these crickets. To check out the ancient Chinese belief of cricket gamblers, he decided to see which of the two behaviors restored aggression. He designed a mechanical tumbler, and following a defeat, the loser was placed into the tumbler-cage. What he found out was that tumbling did not restore aggression. He then developed a flight mechanism, attached the cricket by a wire to its thorax, and placed the cricket in a wind tunnel. This made the cricket fly. Everyone knows that for an insect to fly, it must first jump. This removes the tarsal or foot mechanoreceptors that are part of a neural circuit that inhibits the initiation of the wing movement, thus flight is suppressed if tarsi are in contact with the ground. After a ten-second flight, the cricket's aggressiveness was restored. Thus, Hofmann confirmed the age-old technique of restoring aggression in a losing warrior by tossing it into the air.

"He also showed that by cutting the nerves going from the thoracic muscles (which control flight) to the brain, the loser never regained its aggression. Thus, they believe that some neurotransmitter is released by the flight neurons, which somehow 'resets' aggression. If the nerve connecting the flight system and the brain is cut, the neurotransmitter is not released. In fact, Hofmann believes that better understanding the relationship between motor programs and the site controlling aggression in crickets may help humans suffering from depression. It's getting close to the first match," Ernie told everyone.

Ernie handed Tonino a small card showing the various levels of aggression based on behavioral positions of fighting crickets; he said, "Since you have never seen a cricket match before, maybe this card will help you better understand the fight itself."

Tonino looked at it quickly and noticed that the card contained drawings that had been made by Hofmann and his colleague during their study. "I wish I had a card like this when I saw my first cockfight," responded Tonino. "I would have looked for specific aspects of the fight and tried to understand the strategies used by the birds."

Tonino took a few minutes to study the card; however, he stopped when he heard someone rushing up the stairs and slamming the door to the room.

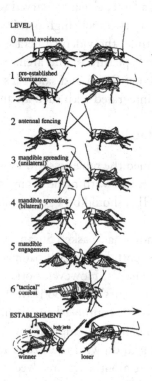

Just then, a man in a great hurry entered the room. He was dressed in traditional Chinese clothing. He had a matching cap and a beautiful full-length, embroidered silken robe that was tied at the waist. At his waist was a silken drawstring bag called a *tao*, which was attached to a golden, silken twisted belt. He untied the tao from his belt and opened it by loosening the drawstring. He carefully pulled out a cricket cage that was handsomely carved with a jade top. He hurried over to the weighing station, carefully took out his warrior, and passed it to the person doing the weighing. As soon as the weight was known, the cricket was put back into its cage and moved to the table containing the fighting arena. The man in the robe sat down at the table. In a few seconds, the other trainer was positioned at the table with his warrior.

"How are we going to be able to see the match?" asked Tonino.

"Just wait and you will see."

On the wall was a large, elegantly carved wooden cabinet. As it opened, they saw a forty-two-inch, high-density, flat-screen television inside. At the same time, the video camera was turned on. In less than a minute, a clear picture of the arena was displayed on the screen. Tonino looked at Susan and said, "It's amazing to see such modern technology integrated with such an ancient custom."

The Real Cricket Match

The TV camera scanned the table to show everyone the warriors of the match. The excitement within the room increased in intensity. Ernie commented, "This should be a great match. Both crickets are champion fighters."

"How do you know that?" asked Susan.

"Notice that they both have very broad backs (i.e., pronotum of the thorax) and large heads. However, notice the one on the right has a gray tinge to the 'hairs' on its body (really, setae)."

Feeling his own head, Tonino asked, "What does having a large head have to do with being a champion?"

"It has something to do with the size of the mandibles, which are the structures of the mouthparts involved in biting and chewing. You will see in a few moments how they use them."

Tonino quickly looked at the diagrams showing some of the "moves" the warriors might use.

The "director of the battle," as he was called, gave a brief history of each warrior's past battles and announced to the crowd the names of the warriors and their trainers. At the command of the referee, or "army commander," at the table, both men lowered their cricket holders into the arena and dumped out their warriors. These two crickets had never met before, so initially they turned their backs on one another and walked to the wall of the clay arena. As he reached the wall, the cricket of the man who came into the room last produced a small chirp.

Immediately, the second cricket turned and ran directly toward him and touched the first cricket with its antenna. Quickly, the first cricket turned, and they both engaged in antenna fencing. This went on for a short while, and the crowd could see the first cricket's mandibles spreading. With its mandibles spread as wide as he could, the first cricket rushed at the other cricket, which opened its mandibles wide also. Mandible engagement ensued, and each cricket tried to flip the other. The first cricket pulled loose and jumped onto the back of his opponent. In this top position, he was able to use his mandibles to grab the opponent's left antenna. Soon, he jumped down with his opponent's antenna in his mandibles. A small droplet of hemolymph (like blood) oozed out of the antenna wound. The now left-antennaless cricket quickly pulled its right antenna between its mouthparts in a cleaning motion. When he tried to do that to his left antenna, he realized it had been ripped off. This seemed to infuriate the wounded cricket. He darted at the first cricket and sank his mandibles into the femur of his opponent's left proleg.

Tonino empathized and felt his own pain as he grabbed his left arm.

"What's wrong?" Susan asked.

Tonino quickly responded, "Oh, nothing."

Tonino was remembering how Pinocchio had thrown the hammer at his great-great-great-grandfather, injuring his left proleg and forcing him to use a cane the rest of his life. He also remembered other leg incidents, such as having his hind legs caught in the gray-breasted jay's mouth. The most embarrassing incident, however, was when the rooster in Hawai'i had grabbed him by the left proleg and how he cleverly escaped by morphing. If only the first cricket could do that now! The most painful memory for Tonino was when he had been dreaming and Madonna took a big bite of his hindleg. *How that hurt!* he said to himself.

The crowd began to cheer for the first cricket. With the precision of a surgeon, the first cricket grabbed his opponent by the neck and began to squeeze with his mandibles. His opponent's legs became limp, and the referee knew that this cricket was seriously wounded.

329

The first cricket's mandibles had injured the ventral nerve cord going to the brain from its motor center, the thoracic ganglia. With a swift movement of his hand, the referee picked up the wounded cricket and handed it to his trainer, who was extremely concerned about his warrior. The first cricket tried to touch his leg wound with his mouthparts but was unable to. He walked to the center of the clay arena and began to chirp, producing a rivalry song of victory.

Everyone was shouting "*Shou lip, shou lip*," which means "Victorious cricket." The robed man gathered up his warrior and proceeded to another table where men were lined up to get their winnings. He waited his turn in line and showed off his winning warrior. When he reached the table, he was given a large amount of money.

No one in Tonino's group had placed a bet. They were there only for the cultural experience. Tonino is very concerned about the losing warrior.

"What will happen to him?" Tonino asked Ernie.

"He will be cared for by his trainer and given special foods. He may never fight again but may be used to father other future warriors."

"Wow! That was certainly exciting. I found cricket fighting more exciting than cockfighting," Tonino responded.

Susan chirped in, "Both were brave warriors."

"Ernie, what happens if a cricket warrior dies?" asked Tonino.

"If he was a *shou lip,* he would be placed in a silver coffin and would get a solemn burial."

Tonino reflected for a moment on being at the gravesite of Grillo-parlante in Florence, Italy. He knew he had not been a cricket warrior. In fact, he had not even been a great singer. Instead, Grillo would always be remembered as the conscience of Pinocchio. Tonino thought, *I wonder if Grillo-parlante was buried in any type of coffin?*

Ernie said, "Let's go; I believe you have seen the best fight of the day."

"Sure, let's go," Susan responded.

On their way home, Ernie gave the two youngsters more to think about.

Crickets and Festivals

Ernie talked about crickets in the Chinese culture. "They are not only important as warriors but also as singers."

Tonino spoke next. "In Italy there is a festival that is very old and is held on Ascension Day. It is called *Feste del Grillo* and is held in Cascine Park in Florence. Children used to be able to buy a cricket cage with a cricket inside and listen to its beautiful music. Dr. Stoffolano told me he had gone to that festival, but because of the animal rights or 'Green' movement, it is now impossible to buy live crickets."

Tonino supported the idea of not killing animals, especially insects, but knew how important it can be for children to raise them. In fact, Dr. Stoffolano didn't even see one live cricket at the festival. Instead, there were only plastic robotic crickets.

Ernie picked up on the discussion. "In China there is a similar festival called *Jiaodeng*, and people go to listen to the crickets chirp. I believe, however, that one can still get live crickets at the festival." Dr. Stoffolano had suggested that Tonino read a book by D. Rudacille, *The Scalpel and the Butterfly*; the Asian view of having live insects at a festival was very different from that of most European countries.

Ernie told Tonino that recently, more emphasis was being placed on conservation of both crickets and katydids in China. "We do not want to overkill or overharvest a natural resource that is so valuable both culturally and economically to the Chinese," he said. "Just think what you Americans did to the passenger pigeon."

Tonino was becoming ever more aware that young children spend less time in the outdoors observing nature. To him, not being connected to nature was a problem. Again, he told everyone they should read the books, *The Last Child in the Woods* and *Geography of Childhood: Why Children Need Wild Places*.

Susan Persuades Tonino to Go to Japan

That evening, Susan engaged Tonino in a serious discussion. "Since we have seen many of the cultural things you wanted to see, why don't we continue our trip and go to Japan? Only then can you get a more complete background about Japanese culture, my heritage, and me. You said how important it was for you to go to Puerto Rico to better understand Pedro."

Tonino leaned back and scratched his head as he thought, *Maybe I can really get at the root of why Japanese still kill and eat whales. This practice has disappeared in most modern countries.* "Sure!" he responded to Susan. "You are correct. I should get to know your culture better, and this certainly will help me understand you better."

The next day, Susan telephoned her uncle Yorimoto, who lives in Taiji. They bought tickets and Susan began to plan the trip.

Gamecock Fighting

Tonino was relentless. He had to keep on going and couldn't miss any cultural event. After the cricket match, Meng had told Tonino that in China, gamecocks are also trained for fighting, human amusement, and betting. Tonino asked Meng to arrange for them to go to a cockfight. Susan wasn't quite sure she wanted to go because she had heard that the loser was often killed and there was a lot of blood. Against her own will, Tonino convinced her to go.

He told her, "I saw my first cockfight in Puerto Rico with Pedro and his mother. They didn't let the birds kill one another because it took such a lot of time and money to train them. It was an investment they couldn't afford to lose."

Meng arranged for them to go to a cockfight late that afternoon. Outside the arena was a beautiful painting of two male roosters fighting. Tonino was surprised to see so many people at the fights, even more than were at the fights in Puerto Rico.

Tonino was also surprised to find out from Meng that owners of gamecocks in China put mustard powder on the birds' feathers. He asked her, "Why do they put mustard on the birds? What kind of mustard is it?"

She only shrugged her shoulders and said, "I don't know."

Tonino turned to the elderly gentlemen sitting to his right. He pulled the man's beautiful red silken robe to get his attention. A dragon was embroidered on the robe. As the worn face of age turned to look at him, Tonino asked, "Why do they put mustard on the feathers of the birds? What kind of mustard is it?"

The elderly gentleman didn't speak English, so Meng translated (even though Tonino was now multilingual and also out of respect). Her translation to Tonino was, "Because the mustard is irritating to taste and gets into the eyes of the opponent, it prevents the opponent from getting a good hold on its opponent's feathers with their beak and also interferes with its vision. The kind of mustard used is very hot."

Tonino mumbled, "This is quite different from the Puerto Rican custom of putting the poison of the forest centipede onto the spurs or feathers."

Tonino believed cricket fighters were more civilized since they did not engage in using poison or metal instruments, such as spurs.

The old man was impressed with Tonino's question and his enthusiasm for the sport; after the fight, he told Meng to explain to Tonino that cockfighting had a great influence on Chinese culture. He then said that cockfighting was a sport in 517 BC, while cricket fighting didn't start until AD 690.

Gift-Giving and Chitin

For the next few days, everyone enjoyed learning more about Chinese culture. Lucy was staying for a week visiting her relatives, while Tonino and Susan would be going on to Japan. Gift-giving in humans, like gift-giving in empidids, or balloon flies, has evolved to different degrees. Initially, a male empid would hunt and catch an insect prey that they would present to the female, and while she was eating it, he would copulate with her. Another species in the evolution of empid behavior began to wrap up the gift in silk. Thus, it would take longer for the female to unravel and get to the dead insect, giving more time for the males to mate. Finally, males would present the females with an empty silken bundle. For Susan and Lucy, gift-giving was a compelling passion and had its origins in capitalism. Also, Susan felt it was easier to buy her uncle a present before they arrived in Japan. Certainly it would be cheaper.

Tonino soon realized that Susan not only liked to shop, she loved to shop. She and Lucy entered Beijing Arts and Crafts World Mansion store at ten o'clock, and four hours later they emerged from their mission. Susan bought her uncle an ivory carving (*yadiao*) of a crane (*tsuru*) because Beijing is known worldwide for bird carvings. She also found a special gift she knew Tonino would love. While Lucy and Susan were shopping, Tonino browsed the markets and adjacent shops.

During the girls' shopping marathon, Tonino kept seeing a product for sale that he knew really well. He had never seen it sold in Boston, but here in China, it was sold everywhere. There were even huge signs on buildings advertising this product. Chitin is the major carbohydrate molecule of the arthropod's cuticle, but it is also found in yeasts, fungi, and even some vertebrates. He also knew that it gives structure to the arthropod cuticle, but not hardness, like many people think. Also, he had learned in biology class that, next to its cousin cellulose, it is the second most numerous, naturally occurring biopolymer.

The more he thought about it, the more Tonino realized that chitin was a major "trash" problem, with tons per year produced in the United States alone. It never occurred to him that just human consumption of lobster, shrimp, crayfish, and crab resulted in a lot of discarded exoskeletons. In fact, he was from New England, one of the world's major lobster centers, where chitin is being produced at a constant rate; where it goes and what happens to it is the responsibility of the buyer.

While the girls were shopping, Tonino found a small restaurant and ordered some tea. This was one of the only moments he had had to himself, time to think and reflect on his travels. He recalled the evening in the cemetery in Italy. He distinctly remembered the Blue Fairy making him the conscience of the world when it comes to environmental issues. Species were becoming extinct, habitats were being lost, and waste products, such as chitin, were polluting the sphere we call home. Tonino knew a little about recycling paper, glass, and aluminum cans; he had never heard of recycling exoskeletons; he wondered if any useable products could be made from that waste.

He asked the waiter, "What do you know about chitin production in China?"

"Well," the waiter said, "all I know is that the Dalian Xindie Chitin Company in Dahan produces chitin products, such as chitosan, and D-glucosamine for all sorts of human and industrial uses."

"How do you know so much about chitin and biochemistry?" Tonino asked.

"I received my bachelor's degree in biochemistry and was unable to find a job. Since my parents own this restaurant, it was natural for the first son to go into the business of his father. As you can see, I am starting from the ground up. Anyway, getting back to chitin, the Chinese stock market reports that Dalian Xindie Chitin Company has an income of over $5 billion annually."

"Wow, that's a lot of money," Tonino responded.

In addition to being socially conscious about environmental issues, Tonino pondered whether he could also become an entrepreneur and sell chitin futures on the stock market. He looked at his watch; it was time to meet the girls.

"What did you buy?" Tonino asked when he saw Susan.

"You will have to wait until we get back to the apartment because I don't want to break it."

"Okay, but you only purchased two items in four hours?"

"That's right."

These buying marathons amazed Tonino, as it did his father and Joe. Tonino was always perplexed by the amount of time women can spend shopping. The apartment was very hot and crowded; luckily for everyone, Susan and Tonino would be leaving tomorrow.

At dinner, Susan showed Tonino the carved ivory crane she purchased for her uncle. "I am sure he will love it," she said.

In some respects, Tonino was shy, unlike the other men in his family, who were very forward and somewhat aggressive. Thus, he often didn't think about himself. This time, however, he couldn't resist.

"Did you buy me anything?" he asked.

Before she spoke, Susan handed Tonino a small gift that was beautifully wrapped in tissue paper; it looked and felt like silk. "Yes, I did," she said. "I was saving this for last."

Tonino liked the feel of the paper in his hands and really loved the bright colors of the wrapping paper. He took special care in unwrapping it because he wanted to save the paper, which contained numerous drawings of insects. Susan was watching every move

Tonino made. She only hoped that he wouldn't like the wrapping paper more than the gift. Tonino unrolled the last layer of paper, and out rolled a beautifully carved wooden gourd. It was made from sandalwood. The top, where the stem would have been, was an attachment for the intricately woven, silken necklace. The gourd was about one inch in height and perfectly shaped. Carefully, Tonino lifted it up to the light and carefully rotated it in his fingers. On the sides were several beautifully carved crickets.

"I love it!" he said. "I really love it!" He reached over and gave Susan a kiss.

"I am so happy that you like it," she said.

"I will wear it forever. Help me put it on."

Following dinner, Susan and Tonino had to pack. The one item that didn't need any packing was the wooden gourd pendant. When they finished packing, everyone was ready to retire. Tonino found it difficult to get to sleep. He was excited about his trip to Japan. Without thinking, he grabbed the gourd pendant and gently rolled it between his fingers. He could feel the raised carvings of the crickets.

His mind recalled all the times a gourd had entered his life. He remembered how various people used gourds to make musical instruments: the *Qüiro* from Puerto Rico; the Hawai'ian *ipu,* a drumlike instrument made by sewing two dried gourds together; and the handheld rattles made by southwestern Indians. He thought of Ron Rivera, the famous southwestern gourd painter; Karen Rossman, from the museum at Western New Mexico University, who specialized in gourds; the Gambel's quails, which looked like flying gourds; the special face masks used by the early Hawai'ians for various ceremonies; the Maoris who used gourds as household utensils; and now Chinese cricket gourds.

His last thought before going to sleep was, *I just wonder how else gourds will enter into my life?* And then Tonino went off to sleep.

When the alarm went off, it took Tonino awhile to awaken because he was dreaming that he was listening to the bell cricket. After a quick breakfast, they were off to the airport. Because of all the congestion at the airport, Lucy and Meng just dropped them off for their flight to Japan.

Tonino left China with a new outlook, not only animal rights in general but also on the idea of becoming an entrepreneur. He was anxious to experience Japan and gain a better insight into Susan's roots. He had personally witnessed the often bloody combat of the gamecocks and the physical maiming and cannibalism of cricket warriors. Even with the long tradition of cockfighting in China, they often have a moralistic objection to it, not based on animal rights, but that it is a frivolous endeavor, a waste of time and money. Eventually, cockfighting in China and many countries has become associated with disreputable characters, and the sport has fallen in disfavor. Regardless, both cricket fighting and cockfighting are not illegal in China. Tonino thought about the Chinese and the various animal-plant associations in their culture; he recently learned that the cricket and the gourd are often combined. He also learned that crickets and birds are the most commonly kept pets and that the Chinese use these animals in their rotating calendar: the rat, ox, tiger, rabbit, dragon, snake, horse, sheep, monkey, rooster, dog, and boar.

Tonino looked at Susan and said, "Why not a cricket? Why not a cricket? With insects representing the majority of animals in the world, it is unbelievable that not a single insect or, in fact, any invertebrate is on this list. I am shocked to know that the cricket is such an important animal to the Chinese for both singing and gaming, yet it has been ignored in their calendar. Totally amazing!" he concluded.

Susan agreed; neither of them could figure out why insects were not used in the Chinese calendar.

Chapter 14.
Japan and Tonino's Conflict

Going to Hokkaidō

Susan and Tonino arrived in Tokyo and had just enough time to transfer to a local airline to catch their flight to Sapporo. Sapporo is the major city on the island of Hokkaidō and gained international recognition in 1972 when it was the home of the Winter Olympics. It is also the home of Hokkaidō University, which has a close association with the University of Massachusetts in Amherst. They arrived late and checked into their hotel.

Their First Evening in Japan

Susan was very tired and wanted to sleep. Tonino, however, drank too much tea during the flight and was "wired." Susan retired and Tonino left to get something to eat.

Tonino found a small restaurant/grocery store and decided to have dinner. The owner seated him and left to serve other customers. Tonino opened the menu at his table and noticed that it contained the following items:

Zaza-mushi, or aquatic caddisfly larvae (Order Trichoptera)
Sangi, or fried silk moth pupae (Lepidoptera)
Semi, or fried cicada (Homoptera)
Hachi-no-ko, or boiled wasp larvae (Hymenoptera)
Inago, or fried rice with field grasshoppers (Orthoptera)

The waitress watched him and tried to anticipate when he was ready to order. She only spoke Japanese, but Tonino relied on the wish given to him by the Blue Fairy. He asked her to suggest a dish. She said that the *zaza-mushi* was the most popular. He explained to her that he was interested in words and asked her to tell him something about the name of this dish. Her reply was that *zaza* refers to the sound of the rushing water where these insects live, while *mushi* means "insect" in Japanese. Tonino ordered a serving of *zaza-mushi* and some green tea to wash it down.

"Boy, my parents and Joe would be amazed at all the things I have eaten," he said out loud. "I never would have imagined I would have eaten insects. I can't wait to tell Pedro about this. After all, it was eating the grasshopper diet from Connecticut Valley Supply House that made him a better jumper."

After eating this wonderful dish, Tonino wandered into the attached grocery section. On the shelf he saw canned *zaza-mushi*, baby bees, and the other insects that were on the menu.

"I think I will buy one can of *inago* to take home," he told the waitress, and she put the can on his bill. He paid the bill and asked her, "How are the canned insects preserved?"

"All canned insect products are preserved in soy sauce or sugar. That should be no problem for customs when you return to the United States."

Tonino left the small restaurant/grocery store and found a quiet park bench to collect his thoughts. It was almost midnight. As usual, Tonino looked for the one star that had helped him so often in the past. No Blue Fairy this time, but focusing on this star had always helped him collect his thoughts. After staring at the star for about five minutes, he knew what he would do while in Japan.

"Since this is such a crucial time for me to really understand my relationship with Susan," he said out loud, "I will not transform to cricket form but will remain in human form. This way I will not avoid any situation and will see if she does the same."

With that solved, he picked up his bag of *inago* and made his way back to the hotel. Susan was asleep so he was careful not to wake her. Soon, even he was asleep.

At breakfast, they decided to go to a museum. Before leaving, Susan noticed the bag on the counter. "What's this?" she asked.

"It's some *inago* I purchased at a restaurant last night. I want Joe to taste fried rice with field grasshoppers."

"Did you try them?"

"No. How could I eat my relatives?"

Susan smiled and grabbed Tonino by the hand. "Let's go so you can learn more about me and my roots."

Ainu and Japanese Culture

Tonino and Susan entered the National Museum of Ethnology and went to the permanent exhibit section of the museum. Even though museums are Tonino's turf, this was the country of Susan's heritage. Thus, Tonino let her handle everything. Susan saw two sections she was interested in: East Asian Ainu Culture and East Asian Japanese Culture.

After they entered the Ainu Culture section, they watched an introductory video about the indigenous peoples of the island known to most of us as Japan (*Nippon,* or the Land of the Rising Sun). The first thing Susan and Tonino learned was to change their idea of "the" island of Japan, because Japan is not one island. Instead, it is an archipelago (a series of islands in a large body of water). This string of islands is located between the Sea of Japan and the western Pacific Ocean. Unlike the Hawai'ian archipelago, which consists of about 19 islands with 6 major islands, Japan consists of more than 3,000 islands, with the following 4 major islands: Hokkaidō, Honshū, Shikoku, and Kyūshū. It extends thirteen hundred miles, while the Hawai'ian archipelago is somewhat longer (fifteen hundred miles).

Tonino looked at Susan and said, "I always thought Japan was just one big island."

Susan was also surprised and responded, "I did too!"

The most surprising part of this introductory video was yet to come. It surprised Susan even more than Tonino.

The remaining indigenous people of the archipelago are known as Ainu, which means "human." These ancient people inhabited the island of Hokkaidō prior to the migration of what we now know as the Japanese people, who immigrated to the islands from the south. The Ainu are Caucasian, not Asian or Mongoloid. Recent research, however, by anthropologist Gary Crawford of the University of Toronto has shed new light on the Ainu, who were once considered hunter-gatherers, to suggest that they might be the descendants of the *Jomon* people, who came from North or Central Asia and may have been involved in agriculture.

The Ainu and the Ryukyuans are the two main minority groups in Japan, a country most people now think of as being homogeneous. The Ainu have suffered the same plight as any of the world's minority and indigenous groups, such as the Native Americans of North America and the Maori of New Zealand. They have been discriminated against and pushed into a northern region of Hokkaidō, which is very similar to being put on a reservation. After seeing the movie *Once Were Warriors* in New Zealand, Tonino and Susan realized that the situations are the same for minority groups everywhere in the world. Like any minority group, these people suffer from alcoholism, unemployment, drug abuse, and many other social problems, including family abuse. Their plight seems uncertain. Hopefully, their culture and language will be preserved. It is depressing to Tonino that less than a hundred pure-blood Ainu remain in Japan.

The Ainu are a proud people, strongly connected to Mother Earth. Like many of the other "people of the earth" Tonino has learned about, the Ainu believe in transformers and the ability of animals to intercede between humans and the gods. In other words, they are animists. The brown bear is considered sacred to the Ainu, while Asiatic black bears are considered endangered because of the overhunting for their gall bladder, which is used in traditional Chinese medicine.

Tonino and Susan learned that there is an Ainu Museum in Shiraio, which is about a hundred kilometers south of Sapporo and can be reached by taking the railway from Sapporo to Hakodate. They also learned that in 1999, the Smithsonian Museum opened an online virtual tour of the exhibit, called "The Ainu: Spirit of a Northern People."

Susan knew how much Tonino liked museums, especially living museums, but she felt in control and said, "We have so many things to do, let's do the online virtual tour later."

"Okay," responded Tonino.

Leaving the video area, Tonino saw a docent and asked, "Who were the *Jomon* people?"

"These people lived from 13,000 BC up to 300 BC and are known as the first settlers in Japan. Also, they are believed to be the first people to develop pottery. In fact, the name *Jomon* means 'cord-impressed pattern,' which refers to the way the pottery was originally made. These people lived in the upper Paleolithic and are believed to be the ancestors of the Ainu. They are said to be of Caucasian stock and not Asian. Based on the sherds of pottery found during this period, it has been estimated that they produced the first ceramics developed by humans, and their pots are believed to predate by about 2,000 years any ceramics found in Mesopotamia."

"Wow, that's amazing!" Tonino responded. He and Susan walked away and Tonino said to her, "Do you remember me telling you about how Dr. Stoffolano wondered whether humans learned how to make pottery from the potter wasp?"

"Yes, I do remember that."

"Well, based on how these early pots are made, I question whether humans learned it from the wasp, but I guess we will never know."

"Let's go to the room on East Asian Japanese Culture," Susan said.

There was a lot of material to look at and information to learn in this room. The major thing they learned, which surprised Susan, was that the Japanese people are believed to be a mix between the indigenous Jomon and the Yayoi. The latter are believed to have emigrated from Korea. Leaving this room, Susan and Tonino went to the café for a cup of tea.

"What did you like the most so far?" Susan asked Tonino.

"I liked the information about the Hokkaidō brown frogs that some say have the patterns and markings of the tattoos the Ainu woman once wore."

"I know. I also liked that." Susan then began to blush and said, without looking Tonino straight in the eyes, "Tattooing one's mouth, arms, or forehead is one thing, but it also said they tattooed their clitoris."

"Well, that is what's wonderful about culture. Just imagine what young people are doing today with tattooing and body piercing. Not that different."

"You're right."

After tea they continued in the museum. "Here is an interesting room," Susan said, "called Culture."

As they entered the room, it reminded Tonino of the Puerto Rican Museum of History, Archeology, and Anthropology and the *caretas* or carved monster masks. He also remembered how he compared the tusked wetas in New Zealand with these wooden masks. Hanging on the wall were many masks. Below each mask was some written information about how they are used in the theater. These masks, of which there are about eighty, are used in the Japanese theater known as *Noh* dramas. Each depicts a different personality, and it is up to the performer to bring out the expression of the character in his performance (only males take part). Because they are worn during the entire performance, they must be light, which is why they are made of cypress wood. They are labor intensive to make, extremely costly, brightly painted, and covered with varnish or lacquer.

Tonino paused and thought about the comparison between these masks and the mud or gourd masks worn by the Hopi; he recalled how the kachina dancer also assumes the personality or spirit of the mask he dons. The topic of masks was something Tonino was becoming more and more interested in. Masks are used by all cultures and are a way to transcend who we are and allow us to transform and assume a different form or being. Tonino felt very lucky because he didn't need a mask to do this.

He said to Susan, "Carnivale, throughout various parts of the world, probably is the time when there is the greatest display of different masks. Since the Hopi have Sösööpa, the cricket kachina, I wonder if there is a cricket Noh mask?"

"We will have to find out," responded Susan. They moved to an adjoining room.

Above the door was a sign that said "Theater in Japan." The room was set up with information on three walls and a stage. In front of the stage were about five rows of seats, each row seating twenty-five people. Since there wasn't a play going on, Susan and Tonino decided to look more closely at the three walls of information. Each wall had information and items displayed about each of the three most common forms of traditional theater. The first wall, as you entered, was labeled "The Noh Theater." Here they learned something more about this type of theater and saw a few more masks than in the previous room.

The wall on the left was labeled *"Bunraku* Theater," and the one on the right, *"Kabuki* Theater."

Tonino said, "Let's start on the left."

They read that *Bunraku* is considered one of the best types of puppet theater in the world. Tonino put his finger on one sentence, "Unlike Italian puppets (a.k.a. marionettes), such as Pinocchio, these Japanese puppets, known as *ningyō,* lack strings." It continued and revealed that these plays usually taught lessons concerning social obligations, and that Chikamatsu Monzaemon, who lived between 1653 and 1724, wrote many of these plays. He is often referred to as the "Shakespeare of Japan."

When they came to the end of the left wall, they crossed in front of the stage to the right wall. The word *Kabuki* is derived from *Ka-bu,* which means "song and dance" and *ki,* which means "skilled person." The performers in this type of theater are known as *onnagata,* and similar to Noh, no female performers are allowed.

Susan turned to Tonino and asked, "I wonder why women can't perform in this type of theater."

"I have no idea," he responded.

The costuming in this type of theater is extravagant. Unfortunately, this once common form of theater is not as popular as it once was; it is now an endangered art form and could face extinction.

It was getting late, and they returned to their hotel.

Tonino and Susan had been in Japan now for several days. Susan, who doesn't have a tattoo, said to Tonino, "I noticed that very few people here have tattoos."

"I have noticed the same thing. I wonder why?"

"Well, according to tradition, the early Ainu women wore them, but because of the influence of religions like Confucianism and Buddhism in Japan, there has been a negative connotation associated with having one. To many Japanese, the tattoo is considered a symbol of the Japanese mafia, or *yakuza,* and also is associated with someone of the lower class trying to be macho. Also, there was a period when having a tattoo showed everyone that they were a criminal."

"Didn't the Nazis make the Jews wear a type of identification tattoo?"

"I believe they did."

"Regardless," Tonino responded, "as insects, we don't need all that extra 'beautification,' since most of us have elegant, natural, and beautiful markings, just like the Hokkaidō frogs mentioned in the museum. I am sure that tattoos, the way of making them, and their symbolism will always be a part of every culture."

Going to Taiji

Tonino and Susan didn't want to spend anytime in Tokyo so they decided to only use it as a jumping-off point. They make plans to visit Susan's uncle in Taiji, which is one of the most southern points of the Japanese archipelago. It is a small fishing village with an altitude of only three feet above sea level. The trip is six hours from Tokyo, and because of its precarious location, it can only be reached by sea or by taking a long coastal road that borders mountains covered with pines extending almost to the sea.

During the trip, Tonino and Susan engaged an elderly man in conversation. "Where are you going?" they asked him.

"I am going to Taiji. Where are you going?"

"We are also going there."

The man saw that Tonino is not Japanese, so he said, "You must be careful."

"What do you mean?" Susan asked.

"Foreigners going to Taiji are looked upon with suspicion. Make sure you don't carry a camera."

"Why is that?" asked Tonino.

"Apparently you don't know anything about what is going on in Taiji."

"No, we don't," Susan said. "I am going to visit my Uncle Yorimoto Wada. Do you know him?"

"Yes, we both were fishermen for years. He is extremely well known and respected in the village; he retired the same year I did."

"Based on what you have said about the danger in Taiji, is he okay?"

"Yes, he is in no danger."

"What then is the problem?" asked Tonino.

"It's a problem that has a long history. People in Taiji have been hunting and killing both dolphins and whales for years."

Immediately, Susan started to get butterflies in her stomach because she knew that this was a major point of conflict between her and Tonino.

"We believe hunting these animals is a cultural thing; without this aspect of our culture, the people in our community wouldn't have any type of employment. All we have is the sea. We are stewards of the sea, and by killing dolphins we are preventing them from eating the fish we are trying to catch, which we need for survival. What has happened now is that the environmentalists throughout the world have condemned the Japanese, especially those of this village, for killing both whales and dolphins. Many people in Japan refuse to yield to the international community when it comes to what they call cultural imperialism."

"But why would anyone want to eat dolphin when it has the highest concentrations of mercury, other heavy metals, PCBs, DDT, and other pollutants?"

"I don't know. I personally don't like dolphin, but I like whale meat."

Tonino found it difficult to sit still. He had a different perspective about whales, especially killing them. Besides, he had to follow through on the charge given to him by the Blue Fairy when he was in Italy.

Meeting Susan's Uncle

Before they could finish their conversation, the bus driver announced they were pulling into the bus station. They had arrived. Susan had never seen her uncle in person or even in a photograph. "How will we recognize him?" she asked Tonino.

"Let's ask the elderly man to take us to him."

"Okay."

As they departed, the elderly man took them over to an old, gray-haired man who was bent over by many years of pulling in fishing nets. The two men greeted one another formally. When they were finished, Susan gave Yorimoto a big hug and introduced Tonino.

"Glad to meet you," Yorimoto responded as he bowed. "Let's go to my house and have some dinner. You must both be very hungry."

"We are."

Tonino was deeply worried that he would have to eat dolphin or whale meat for dinner; however, he was pleasantly surprised. Instead, it was just a stir-fry with vegetables and shrimp, very similar to what he usually ate at the Yins' house. After dinner Susan helped with the dishes, because Uncle Yorimoto lived alone. Tonino remained in the living room, brooding about how he was going to handle this difficult situation: whales or me. Soon everyone gathered in the living room and Susan pulled out her present for Yorimoto.

"Here is a small present from your sister and me and Tonino."

Uncle Yorimoto was so surprised. He had few possessions in his home, and no one had given him a gift in years.

"Be careful opening it," Susan said. "It's fragile."

Uncle Yorimoto carefully removed the wrapping paper and slowly lifted the lid from the paper box. As he opened it and peered in, his eyes opened wide and tears began to flow.

"It's so lovely," he said. "It's a *yadiao* of a *tsuru*. How can I ever thank you? Your mother always knew how I loved cranes."

This one gift elevated the old man to another level of happiness. Little did they realize how much Uncle Yorimoto knew about cranes, their biology, and their history in various cultures. Yorimoto began his crane lesson.

"The crane, or *tsuru,* in Japanese culture signifies eternal youth, happiness, and peace. I am especially fond of the red-crowned crane, which is also called the Japanese crane or Manchurian crane. It is a large bird and is considered the second rarest crane in the world. Maybe there are 900 cranes that remain in the Hokkaidō region. In Japanese mythology, they are called *tancho* (red peak, because of the red on the top of their head) and are supposed to live 1,000 years."

Tonino was desperately trying to break his habit of interrupting people when they are talking, even though he thinks what he has to say is extremely important to the conversation. What he was thinking about was how Grillo-parlante told Pinocchio he was 100 years old, and now these cranes were thought to live 1,000 years.

Yorimoto continued, "This beautiful, red-crowned, Japanese crane was almost hunted to extinction for its feathers, but now is making a come back."

Tonino finally interrupted because he was dying to know the English derivation of the bird's name; he doubted that Yorimoto would know. "What is the derivation of crane?" he asked.

To Tonino's surprise, Yorimoto did respond. "I have read that some believe the name comes from the favorite food of the crane in southern Germany: the *kran-beere,* which in German means 'crane berry.' What happened, as it so often does when one translates from another language or culture, is that mistakes are often made."

"What do you mean?" Susan asked.

"Well, the German crane berry (*Vaccinium oxycoccos*), which the cranes love to eat, is not the same species as that originally found in New England, but because the flowers of the cranberry in North America look like the head of a crane, they called them cranberries."

Tonino remembered how the swan plant in New Zealand got its name, but he wasn't quite so sure about what Yorimoto said.

Tonino asked Yorimoto, "Have you ever seen a cranberry?"

"No, but I have read that a lot are grown in Massachusetts and that the berries are usually cooked with turkey for Thanksgiving."

"That's correct. The Cape Cod Pequot Indians referred to them as *ibimi* (i.e., bitter berry)," Susan replied.

"I never knew that about the Pequots. It makes sense now because I remember everyone at Thanksgiving adding sugar to the cranberries, regardless of how they prepared them," responded Tonino.

Reference to the genus *Vaccinium* reminded Tonino of his encounter with Pele when he was in Hawai'i and when he ate the *ohelo* berries, *Vaccinium reticulatum*, which are a favorite food of the nene. Tonino then thought to himself, *I wonder how the crane fly got its name?* He then remembered Dr. Stoffolano telling him about the famous dipterist, C. P. Alexander. He recalled that this famous taxonomist was at the University of Massachusetts when Dr. Stoffolano first arrived and that Dr. Alexander described more species of crane flies than any other entomologist. Also, Dr. Alexander was born in upstate New York in Gloversville, just around the corner from where Dr. Stoffolano had been born. How coincidental; two people interested in flies who were from the same town.

Uncle Yorimoto continued to tell Susan and Tonino about cranes.

"One of the most spectacular behaviors of the red-crowned crane is its mating dance. These stately birds jump with their long legs, fan out their wings, arch their long necks, bow to one another, raise their heads to the sky, and call out in unison. Well, I guess you two have heard enough about cranes. It's late, so let's go to sleep. Tomorrow is another day."

Susan gave her uncle a big hug and said, "Thank you for everything."

"Well, thank you for the great gift. I will treasure it forever." He placed it on top of one of the only pieces of furniture in the room, the TV.

It's All about Whales: A Last Attempt

In his last attempt to change Susan's position on whaling, Tonino remembered Baba Dinn's statement about changing people's attitudes about Mother Earth and the living organisms that inhabit this great planet: "In the end, we will conserve only what we love, we will love only what we understand, we will understand only what we are taught."

Rather than a direct attack, Tonino thought that maybe teaching Susan about whales would be a better approach.

That evening he asked Susan if they could have some time alone. "I want to tell you some things about whales," he said. "Hopefully, I can make some comparisons with things you might already know. Having a better understanding of whales might help deal with one another's position on whaling."

"Sure," she agreed.

"Mainly I want to focus on the humpback whale, which is the fifth largest of what are called the big whales. The humpback whale, *Megaptera novaeangliae,* is a beautiful creature. You of all insects/humans should be able to figure out what the genus name means. The common name comes from the shape of the dorsal fin when it dives, and the area behind it, called the caudal peduncle, makes it look like a hump. I am sure you have heard of Kokopeli, the humpback flute player of the American Southwest?"

"I have."

"The humpback is found in all oceans at different times of the year. Like the monarch, the humpback is also a migrant species. As with monarchs, it is also sexually dimorphic; females are larger than males. During the winter months, the whales migrate to warmer waters where they mate and give birth to their young. About 4,500 Pacific humpbacks migrate to warmer waters like Hawai'i, while the Northern humpbacks usually go to the Caribbean. Do you have any questions?"

"Yes, how does the humpback know where it is going?"

"It is believed that they use ocean temperatures and currents, and some also believe they use the earth's magnetic field, but this is an area where more research is needed.

"It spends most of the summer season in the polar ice zone region, where it is part of a very short food chain. The humpback feeds on abundant phytoplankton floating on the upper zone of the sea, zooplankton (krill), and small fish (herring and mackerel). It does this by filter feeding. To do this, they use structures known as baleen, which hang down from their upper jaws. Their feeding strategies are unique. When food is abundant they do lunge-feeding, but when scarce or disperse they use what is called the 'bubble net.' To do this, they submerge and surround the fish with a net of bubbles, which are produced by the blowhole; the bubbles rise, forming a 'bubble cage.' This causes everything to concentrate toward the center and remain in this rising bubble arena. Then they rise up into this cage and open their mouth extremely wide. They can expand their mouth opening about four times the normal size."

"How can they do that?" Susan asked.

"You know that insects are able to expand various segments of their body, especially the abdomen, because of the intersegmental membranes, which are flexible, thus providing for expansion. Well, the humpback has a series of ventral folds or pleats, like an accordion or pleated curtain, that go almost from its belly button to the end of its lower jaw."

"Do you have any questions?"

"Being so big, do humpbacks have any enemies?"

"Yes. Killer whales will attack them. Sometimes they will grab onto the flukes of the tail, and the whale is usually able to pull away. This leaves groovelike scars and teeth marks on the flukes where the whale pulled away."

"Doesn't something like that occur with the monarch?"

"Yes, beak marks can often be seen on the wings of the monarch. Do you remember me telling you about Baccio, the adult butterfly at the monarch parade site, and how his wings were so tattered? They also had beak marks."

"Yes, I do remember that. The mark is where the bird grabs onto the adult butterfly, and because of the taste recognition associated with cardiac glycosides, they let go."

"That's correct."

Tonino continued, "During the winters, female humpbacks are ready to mate. Males produce complex songs, which are known to change throughout the mating season and from year to year. This is so uncharacteristic of cricket song, which is hardwired and varies little if any. Unlike humans, whales lack vocal cords; it is uncertain how they produce their sounds. One must remember the breathing system of a whale is through its blowhole, and this is not connected to the mouth; otherwise, when they feed, water would get into the lungs. As with crickets and many other animals, only the males produce a territorial and mating song. These songs are not produced in their summer feeding grounds."

"Are humpback males aggressive like male crickets?"

"Yes. They appear to establish distances between other males using song, and they become aggressive in the presence of a female. Some examples of aggression are head butting, throat distension, head shaking, and head lunges."

"It must be like two huge trucks colliding," Susan said.

"Other types of sound communication occur in their winter feeding grounds. In the summer sites, however, both males and females produce other types of sound communication. This can occur between either of the sexes and between the mother and her calf."

Tonino remembered the wonderful song, *Whale Talk*, by John Keawe, about a mother humpback talking to her calf. It was his favorite. In order to get at one of Susan's weaknesses, Tonino emphasized the social behavior of the whale and how closely connected the mother was with her calf.

Tonino concluded with one startling fact. "During World War II, whales were used for target practice."

Susan remained quiet and then said, "Let's go outside, transform, and take a walk."

Tonino knew she was trying to avoid the issue. He stood firm in his decision to remain human. "I have decided not to transform while we are in Japan."

"But why?" asked Susan.

"That's just what I decided to do."

Susan had never seen Tonino this way, but agreed.

She turned to him and said, "Thanks for the very informative discussion about humpback whales. I will really think about it."

"Good," responded Tonino.

Both were tired and ready to retire. They went to say good night to Susan's uncle, who was sitting in the other room.

"Before you go to bed, I want to briefly discuss one aspect of your conversation. I am sorry to have overheard everything you said, but this is a small house and I couldn't help but overhear you talking about aggression in humpback whales."

"That's no problem. We understand," Susan responded.

Aggression in Japan and Its Great Warriors

Uncle Yorimoto had survived several wars in his lifetime and has thought a lot about aggression. The first thing he said startled both Susan and Tonino. "You know that biologically speaking, aggression is shown mainly by males, not females." Yorimoto had never married and didn't seem at all aggressive in his behavior, nor did he have a situation to study the behavior of a female. "Maybe women bring out this behavior in men!"

Tonino knew a lot about aggression in male crickets and couldn't agree more.

"What is it about aggression that you want to talk about?" Susan asked.

"I want to tell you something about Japanese culture in using animals to fight one another. This is a peculiar behavior of most cultures; however, some cultures that are closely linked to Mother Earth, like the Native Americans, do not involve themselves in this form of entertainment. I also want to mention some of our greatest warriors.

"The most well-known warriors in Japan are not the cricket warriors, but the *Samurai*, better known as *bushi*, which means 'war-man.' These warriors were well educated and literate. They lived by a very strict code known as *bushido*. As things changed in Japan, the last of the Samurai still carried his most prized possession, the Samurai sword. Today, the sword is only used in ceremonial situations. Originally, their name was *saburai*, which meant 'servant' or 'attendant.' Samurai were proud warriors, and the code they lived by was such that under certain situations, shame or some other disgraceful situation resulted in the Samurai committing *seppuku* or suicide (a.k.a. *hara-kiri*). This precise and ritualistic way of killing one's self is a trademark of the Samurai, but every so often modern Japanese men who are disgraced for some reason, such as embezzlement of corporate monies, also use this method of earthly escape. The origin of this type of suicide is not known, but disembowelment was their choice of death because they believe the 'spirit' resides in their stomach.

"The Japanese are a proud people, and for years Japan remained isolated. This way of existence, and its early use by the Samurai, produced what is often called the 'Soul of Yamato,' in Japanese *Yamato-damashi* (or *Yamato-gokoro*), which was an expression used by Japanese soldiers in World War II.

"Samurai often left the profession to pursue more intellectual or sacrificing professions, such as becoming a priest. One of the most famous samurai to do this was Matsuo Bashô, who lived from 1644 to 1694. He is considered by many to be one of the greatest *haiku* composers, and his poems are still well known in Japan and throughout the world. Another Samurai who changed professions was Chikamatsu Monzaemon (a.k.a. Sugimori Nobumori), who at one time was a monk. His intellectual pursuits led him to write the most well-known and loved plays for the *Kabuki* and *Bunraku* Theaters. During his life (1653–1725), Chikamatsu wrote about 160 plays."

Other Great Japanese Warriors

Uncle Yorimoto continued his discussion of fighting and aggression in Japan. "Some animals that one wouldn't expect to be fighters have been pitted against one another in Japan, in addition to a nonanimal warrior that fights in the sky."

Because he knew that only birds, bats, and insects can fly, Tonino said to himself, *I wonder what a nonanimal warrior is?*

Yorimoto continued, "*Tosa Inu*, also known as the canine Sumo wrestler, is considered one of Japan's national treasures. These dogs are bred to fight like Sumo wrestlers. They are forbidden to bite but must knock their opponent off its feet and stand guard over them."

Tonino rudely interrupted to tell both Susan and Yorimoto something he had learned in Hawai'i. "The indigenous Hawai'ians didn't like whale meat but ate a special breed of dog, which they fed only on taro."

"I didn't know that," they both replied.

"I'll bet you can't guess which unusual animal is fought in Japan," Uncle Yorimoto said to Susan.

She responded, "Crickets?"

"No, no! It's the Japanese or Siamese fighting fish. Our culture and the Chinese are probably the only two cultures that fight fish."

Tonino interjected, "I learned that most fish have some sort of visual protection, such as countershading, that makes it difficult for predators to locate them."

Tonino continued, "I often have seen koi, but they are usually brightly colored and lack countershading. It's almost as if they were advertising their unpleasant taste. I am sure you have heard about the aposematic coloration of many organisms, specifically the monarch butterfly."

"Yes, I have," Yorimoto said. "I wish we had the monarch in Japan. You know the Japanese love insects."

Yorimoto continued, "Cockfighting has recently increased in popularity. Last, but not least, is cricket fighting. I am sure I don't need to tell you about that sport and its increase in popularity throughout the world."

Tonino hopped into the conversation. "What we are worried about now in the U.S. is the considerable demand that is developing for live Japanese fighting crickets. People are willing to pay high prices for them. We have no idea what an introduction of the Japanese bell cricket would do to our ecosystems. Just think what the Japanese beetle did to our plant and food industry."

Tonino moved on to another topic. "What is the major sport for men now in Japan?" he asked.

"I believe it is golf, but soccer is quickly approaching it. Japanese, both males and females, pay enormous fees to join country clubs and play golf. In fact, many fly to Hawai'i, where they can play at much lower rates. Also, it's easier to get to play."

Tonino asked, "Do either of you know what insect has benefited most from the construction of golf courses?" Neither one could answer, so Tonino responded, "The mole cricket."

Yorimoto seemed to have finished his conversation so Tonino said, "You were going to tell us something about an unusual, nonanimal warrior that fights in the sky."

"Oh, yes! I almost forgot. Can either of you guess?"

Susan and Tonino looked at one another and then said in unison, "No."

"It's the Samurai warriors of the sky, also know as the *tsuke rokkaku,* or fighting kite warriors. The word *rokkaku* means 'hexagon,' and because of their shape, these kites have great stability and maneuverability."

"How does one fight with a kite?" asked Susan.

"There are special structures on fighting kites and on their strings. The strings can be coated with a paste of rice or other sticky substance containing coarse sand or sharp glass pieces. The handler tries to cut the string, or umbilical cord, of the opponent."

"According to the historical record, which group of people are considered the first to fly kites?" asked Tonino.

"I believe it was the Chinese and not the Japanese."

Tonino responded to Yorimoto's mention of "cutting the umbilical cord" and asked, "Does the Japanese culture have any special tradition concerning the umbilical cord?"

"Yes, the umbilical cord is cleaned and kept dry as a symbol of the bond between the child and the mother. Researchers recently detected cytomegalovirus deoxyribonucleic acid from the dried umbilical cord of a four-year-old who showed various central nervous system disorders, and now, using this technique scientists are able to pinpoint the cause of the problem as congenital cytomegalovirus infection."

"Science is so wonderful," responded Susan. "Sometimes I wish I had more of an interest."

Tonino said, "I am finding, however, that the connections between science and culture are much more interesting than I thought."

Tonino asked Yorimoto, "Would you tell us something about the bell cricket? I am concerned about this cricket getting into the U.S."

"Sure! It is one of our most popular and culturally important crickets. Its common name is *suzumushi*. In Japanese, '*suzu*' means 'sleigh bell,' while you already know '*mushi*' means 'insect.' It is native to western Japan, including Shikoku and Kyushu, and is about two centimeters long. The Japanese language has what are called seasonal words, and *suzumushi* signifies early autumn. I guess this is the season when the males sing and are establishing territory, plus trying to attract a mate. In Japan, *mushi* are very popular. You can buy *mushi* and *mushi*-collecting equipment in the department stores. You will see young children walking around with collecting nets and jars containing *mushi*. Many of them take a gourd, hollow it out, and make a cage out of it for the bell cricket. This way the cricket gets a home, and it can eat its own house."

Susan looked at Tonino and asked, "Why are you concerned about this cricket getting into the U.S.?"

"Well, while doing a term paper in high school, I read that a shipment of cricket-rearing cage kits was shipped from Japan and intercepted in Chicago, and it contained eggs of a cricket, which they believe were of the bell cricket."

Tonino had been thinking about this for a while because he knew it was illegal to bring this cricket into the United States. He was also interested in knowing whether the shipment was going to the Field Museum in Chicago, which has a large collection of cricket accoutrements for cricket fighting.

"You have now listened to an old man talk long enough," Uncle Yorimoto said. "I guess everyone is tired."

"Uncle, please don't think that we don't want to hear what you have to say. You are so knowledgeable about so many things, and we are so young that we haven't had all those life experiences that you have had."

"It is true," Uncle Yorimoto said. "With age comes wisdom. I only wish I was as wise as you two when I was your age. I didn't listen enough to my elders."

Before they went to bed, Susan asked Tonino, "Tell me more about the belly of the whale and how that might fit into Disney's movie where Geppetto was trapped in Monstro's belly. Also, I want to know more about the soul and the spirit."

Tonino attempted to explain to Susan the difference. "The etymology of the English word *spirit* comes from the Latin *spiritus*, which means 'breath.'" Tonino remembered the traditional Hawai'ian greeting and departure gesture, the *honi*, or the "sharing of one's breath" (*ha*). He continued, "The word *spirit* is broadly used and is often given the following meaning: The vital principle or animating force within living beings. Some cultures believe that the *soul* and the *spirit* are the same. If one restricts the use of *soul* to things that are ethical and moral, then the *spirit* is separate because it includes other attributes of a living organism."

"How interesting," Susan responded. "Please tell me more."

"The horse has a great spirit, but does it have a soul? Many cultures use the term to mean a supernatural being (e.g., the Hopi have over five hundred of these spirits, known as kachinas), a place (e.g., the spirit of place, such as locations where Hawai'ian petroglyphs are found), an object (e.g., the Ainu believe in animals as spiritual objects), or a natural phenomenon (the spirit of Mother Earth). Thus, the word *spirit* means different things to different people and cultures." Tonino looked at Susan to make sure she was listening.

"If one thinks of someone (or something) as having a spirit, they use their mind (i.e., the brain), but do we just have one brain? Some people believe that humans have two brains. American culture emphasizes only the one located in our head. The other resides in our stomach; it can't reason, but it does have a major impact over our lives. Think about those times when you say, 'I have butterflies in my stomach.' This is the second brain talking to the first brain via the vagus nerve. People today suffer from stress, which is a manifestation of the second brain 'talking,' probably too much, to the first brain. Clinical conditions, such as ulcers or colitis, result from these stressful situations."

Tonino paused and Susan asked him, "How do you know so much?"

"Well, I read a lot and listen to what people have to say."

"Let me now tell you about the second brain."

"Throughout civilization, people have recognized the second brain (e.g., the Samurai). Joseph Campbell, one of the greatest scholars concerning myths, devoted an entire chapter, titled 'In the Belly of the Whale,' in his 1949 book, *The Hero with a Thousand Faces.*"

"That is so interesting, but tell me about Geppetto and the whale in Disney's movie."

"The idea of being in the belly is emphasized in the Bible, even though the original writings talk about a fish and not a whale. The Mimbres people, living in the desert, depicted a human being swallowed by a fish on one of their bowls. Walt Disney showed

Geppetto being swallowed by a whale. It was in the stomach of the whale that Pinocchio found his father."

"It was during this period, in the belly of a whale, that life-changing decisions are believed to occur. Returning from the belly should result in one's transformation. Certainly it worked for Pinocchio. Tonino knew that even insects had their head brain (or central nervous system) connected to their visceral or stomatogastric nervous system."

"That is so interesting," Susan replied. "Thanks for telling me about it; sleep tight, and don't let the bedbugs bite."

"Good night," Tonino responded. "Thanks again for inviting me to join you on this trip."

Whale Burgers

The next day was their last day before flying home. Uncle Yorimoto took Susan and Tonino to lunch in Taiji. As they approached the waterfront, Tonino saw something that he had to point out to Susan. "Look there! It's a minke whale being unloaded for meat." Susan turned her head away and said she didn't want to look. Tonino insisted. "Just look at that beautiful and majestic animal."

"I can't," she said.

Uncle Yorimoto and Susan hurried along to the restaurant and quickly got a seat. Tonino lagged behind to watch the whale being unloaded. He noticed a sign posted on one of the buildings. It had a photograph of a young woman eating a minke burger. *I wonder if Susan saw this?* he asked himself.

When he joined them in the restaurant, Tonino picked up his menu, and his eyes went directly to one item. "Let's order minke burgers. By the way, did you happen to see the poster advertising them outside the restaurant?"

"Yes," Susan said, "but I didn't focus on it. It is shameful that they used a picture of a young woman rather than a man eating the burger."

"Why is that?" asked Tonino.

"Because more women are vegetarians than males; I believe this is exploitation of females."

"You are correct but don't forget, women are the major consumers everywhere in the world, so this is why advertisements are directed at them. If you don't want that image to continue, you should encourage other women not to be such great consumers. Why do you always change the focus of our conversation?"

"What do you mean?"

"I started talking about the advertisement for minke burgers, and you immediately changed the conversation to exploitation of women."

"Quit arguing," Uncle Yorimoto interrupted.

"We're not arguing," they both remarked.

You see, Yorimoto lived alone, and he was not used to hearing people disagree. Also, it was traditionally not the Japanese custom, especially in public.

Yorimoto continued, "Let me inform you that young people do not like to eat whale meat. Even more, they dislike the flavor of dolphin. I believe that over time, the habit of eating these two animals will vanish."

"I think you are right," Tonino responded. "I remember my father telling me how my grandparents ate *sanguinacci* (i.e., blood sausage) and *zuppa di polmone*, which is lung soup made from a calf. My parents never ate these dishes, nor were they sold in Joe's store."

After they finished eating, Uncle Yorimoto sensed that Tonino and Susan needed some time alone. "You two should take a walk," he told them as he got up to leave. "I will see you for dinner."

Susan paid the bill and they left.

Tonino quickly grabbed Susan and said, "Look here at this advertisement for minke burgers."

Susan turned her head and headed the other way. Before Tonino could say anything else, she transformed. Tonino dropped to his knees and tried to catch her, but she didn't want to be caught. By now, several people had gathered to watch this young boy trying to catch a cricket. Finally, Tonino succeeded. Just like several previous situations in his own life, his fingers made a cage of the captured insect. Tonino looked at everyone watching and said, "I am going to train it as a fighting cricket."

Everyone laughed because they knew it was a female; they thought the young boy was extremely ignorant.

Tonino quickly hurried away from the crowd that had gathered. He held his right hand up to his ear. He could hear Susan, who was really angry and shouting, "Let me go!"

"Be calm," he said, "and don't hurt your antennae or ovipositor by trying to escape."

The longer he contained her, the more angry she became. He could feel her banging her head against his fingers. Finally, she transformed without giving Tonino a warning. His hands popped open as Susan slid to the ground.

"You look funny sitting there on the ground."

"I know," Susan said. "I am sorry."

"You know, you can't avoid this issue forever."

Tonino helped her up, and they went off to enjoy other aspects of life in Taiji.

They had a quiet afternoon and a light dinner. They had to get up early because the bus left for Tokyo at 7:30. Just before they went to bed, Yorimoto left the room but quickly returned with an old box in his hands.

Uncle Yorimoto handed Susan the box. "This is a gift from my mother, your grandmother. It is something I have saved, and I promised her I would give it to a female of the next generation. Since I didn't marry, it is very appropriate for you."

Susan looked at Tonino and then quickly looked back at Uncle Yorimoto. "I am speechless," she said.

Tonino mumbled, "I find that hard to believe."

Susan ignored his comment and carefully lifted the lid. "How beautiful," she said. "It's elegant."

Tonino was unable to see what was inside, so he moved forward and looked in. "It is beautiful," he said when he saw the kimono.

"Take it out and try it on," they said.

"I'll be right back."

As they waited, Yorimoto and Tonino sat down and started talking about Japan's future economy. Ten minutes later, Susan emerged, wearing the lovely kimono. Her beautiful black hair was piled high on her head; it almost looked like a volcano. Holding her hair in place was a striking wooden hairpin. Tonino had never seen her look so beautiful. He circled around her for a better look. The kimono was embroidered with a red silk background. The rest was filled with various insects. It made Tonino think about the wrapping paper Joe and Isabella had given him for his seventeenth birthday. The wooden hairpin was a carved crane with its neck bent over its back.

"I will treasure the kimono forever and will wear it only on special occasions," she said as she hugged Uncle Yorimoto.

"Your mother will be very proud when she sees you wearing it. Off to bed with you both."

Tonino turned and said to Yorimoto, "Sleep tight, don't let the bedbugs bite."

Both youngsters laughed, leaving Susan's uncle with an inquisitive look on his old, worn face.

Leaving Taiji for Tokyo and Then Home

Susan slept well and dreamt that she was a Japanese Geisha wearing her new kimono. Tonino, on the other hand, didn't sleep well. He kept waking up and wondering whether Susan would ever change her position on whaling. They were awakened by the smell of breakfast, which Yorimoto had already started. As soon as breakfast was over, they left for the bus station. Tonino and Susan were surprised to see Yorimoto using a cane, which he hadn't used at all during their visit.

When they got to the bus station, Susan hugged and kissed her uncle and boarded the bus. Just as Tonino was about to climb in, Yorimoto pulled him back and handed him the cane. "Here is a gift for you," he said. "My grandfather gave it to me. Since I do not have any children, I want you to have it. Keep it and use it wisely. It is made from cedar wood, and according to Japanese wood folklore, it will help you reach your goals."

Susan was watching from inside the bus. Tonino bowed graciously to Yorimoto, and in return Yorimoto returned the gesture. Tonino used the cane to get into the bus and joined Susan. Both waved to Yorimoto and immediately focused on looking at this wonderful gift. Tonino told Susan what Yorimoto said about the cane; he noticed that the handle of the cane was carved into a beautiful *tancho*. Unlike the ivory carving Susan had given Uncle Yorimoto, this crane's head was not bent back over its back. The red crown was at the top, was even painted red, and was very smooth from years of wear.

Leaving Tonino at the Airport and an Unexpected Encounter

Tonino checked in with the airline and realized they had time for some shopping—Susan's favorite pastime. They went different ways—Tonino to the book area and Susan to the clothing area. While looking over the different T-shirts, she felt a gentle hand on her shoulder. As she turned, she heard a voice say, "What a pleasure to see you here in Japan."

"Mr. Ozawa!" Susan said. "It's also a pleasure to see you."

"What are you doing here?"

"I came to visit my uncle, who lives in Taiji."

"Are you alone?"

"No, I came with Tonino."

"Ah yes, Tonino. I remember him well. He is the young man who had the brilliant idea of having animals perform our Fourth of July concert at Tanglewood. I remember that well. It wasn't easy to conduct a symphony using amateur musicians and vocalists."

Susan picked up her bag and said, "Let's find him. He is in the bookstore."

On their way to the store, Seiji asked Susan, "Are you still playing the violin?"

"Yes, but I haven't been able to play much while we've been traveling."

"Don't forget, practice makes perfect."

"I know. That's what my parents keep telling me."

Tonino was surprised to see the conductor. "Are you still at Tanglewood?" Tonino asked.

"No, I retired but they have honored me by building the Seiji Ozawa Hall, which seats a thousand people. My spirit lives on at the site now. Andrew Pincus, a reporter for the *Berkshire Eagle*, wrote a book about this modern building and some other changes that have taken place in Tanglewood. His book has a chapter about the problems they had building the hall."

"What's the name of the book?"

"It's called *Tanglewood: The Clash between Tradition and Change.*"

"I'll try to get it when I get back to the States. How wonderful to honor you that way," responded Tonino.

They chatted for about fifteen minutes, and Seiji looked at his watch. Quickly, he shook their hands and said, "I must go now or I will miss my appointment." As he departed, Seiji turned and said to Susan, "Don't forget. Keep practicing."

Tonino turned to Susan and said, "What a treat to see him here."

"He told me that he now lives here permanently."

"Just think how wonderful it must be to have a building named after you," Tonino said. "His spirit will now join other famous people in the Berkshires, such as Melville, Hawthorne, and Edith Wharton.

"Are you ready to go through security?" he asked.

Susan said, "Can you wait just a moment?"

"Sure."

Susan hurried off to the ladies' room with her bag. In a few minutes she returned, wearing her new T-shirt.

"What a surprise. Are you serious?"

"I am," she replied.

Tonino looked at his watch and realized his flight was an hour before Susan's. They gave each other a big hug and a kiss.

"Maybe I will see you when you go to college. Are you still considering Mount Holyoke?"

"Yes, I am."

"Well, I might go to UMass in the spring."

"Anything is possible," Susan replied.

As Tonino left, he continually shook his head. *I can't believe it,* he kept repeating to himself, thinking about the shirt Susan was wearing.

Finding Someone's Conference Program

Every time Tonino flies, he always looks at the magazine provided by the airline. As he began his flight back home to Boston, he pulled a magazine out of the pocket of the chair in front of him; at the same time, out came a program apparently left by a previous traveler. Tonino began to look it over. "Hmmm, it's a program from some entomology meeting," he said out loud. As he scanned it, he read the following abstract:

Title: Inventing Gaichu (Insect Pests): The Emergence of Economic Entomology in Japan, by Akihisa Setoguchi, Economics Department, Osaka City University

Abstract: *This paper addresses how the introduction of modern entomology radically changed the view of insect pests in Japan. As early as the eighth century, outbreaks of insect pests were reported in Japan. In the seventeenth century, whale oil was used as an insecticide, a technique probably learned from China. Although the method of spraying oil was well known by the early nineteenth century, most Japanese farmers did little or nothing to deter insect pests. Most just prayed to the gods or performed a religious ceremony called* Mushi-okuri *(insect expulsion). They believed it was impossible to control insects because they were generated from humid air in a process of spontaneous generation. There was not even a word for* insect pests *before the late nineteenth century. The word* mushi *(insects) was used for harmful insects. After Japan developed into a modern country, the word gaichu (insect pests) became popular. In 1885, the Japanese government passed a law forcing farmers to control insect pests. The government established the Imperial Agricultural Station and introduced economic entomology in the 1890s. Academic entomological laboratories were also established at the Imperial University in Tokyo and Sapporo Agricultural College. However, it was Yasushi Nawa (1857–1926), a nonacademic entomologist, who changed*

367

the Japanese view of insect pests. He established a private entomological laboratory in 1896 and worked strenuously to educate farmers to see insect pests as controllable. As a result, every farmer in Japan began to use scientific methods to control gaichu.

When Tonino finished reading the abstract, he closed the program. He then opened the travel magazine and began to thumb through it. He found an article about Japan and read the following information:

> Area: about 145,870 square miles
> Highest elevation: Mount Fuji (12,388 feet)
> Common name: Nippon
> National bird: Red-crowned crane
> Major natural concerns: Earthquakes and tsunami
> Flag: White background with red disc signifying the sun
> Economy: Second largest next to the United States
> Religions: Shinto and related groups, 51.3%, Buddhism, 38.3%, Christianity, 1.2%
> National sport: Sumo wrestling
> Major export: Automobiles

As he scanned the rest of the article, he was surprised to read how many young Japanese women preferred not to marry Japanese men because of Japan's restrictive marital traditions. *I wonder if that is why Susan likes me?* he thought. *Surely she is a modern woman. It can't be. She was born in the United States, but then again, who knows? Often, it is very difficult to change traditions.*

After finishing the article, he came to an article about automobiles and was taken by surprise. *I thought I knew everything about my relatives, but here it says that the Suzuki Jimny is a mini-SUV that comes in a convertible and a hard top. Its name came from Jiminy Cricket but was misspelled in the advertisements. I wonder if my parents know about this?*

Carefully, and as quietly as he could, Tonino tore out the article, looked around in hopes that no one saw him, and quickly put it into his pocket. He continued reading and found an article about Japanese resources that focused on killing dolphins and whales.

Using Resources

The recent controversy over killing dolphins and whales is a topic unto itself. Are the villagers of Taiji correct in labeling Westerners, especially those from the United States, as cultural imperialists? Has anyone looked at what American whaling did to this resource at the height of the whaling industry? As much as conservationists, and those involved in various environmental movements, condemn Japan for its whaling, the Japanese could certainly turn the question and ask, "Why hasn't the United States signed the Kyoto Treaty of 1997, which is designed to reduce global warming by setting limits on industrial emissions in the developed countries?" After all, in 1990 the United States was reported to produce about 36 percent of the worldwide emissions leading to the greenhouse effect, making it the world's biggest atmospheric polluter. In a letter posted on the Internet (www.furcommission.com/resource/perspect3.htm), the mayor of Taiji sought international support for the loss of jobs in his small village. Unfortunately, Tonino realized that "progress" and development usually result in the disappearance of items that are no longer produced because of better materials or cheaper sources elsewhere. Just think of all the industries (e.g., whaling) in the United States that are no longer producing useful products. Then think of all the thousands of people who have lost jobs associated with these industries.

Tonino began to realize that money, politics, development, and other issues are as intertwined as a spider web. Trying to untangle the threads shows how everything is connected. Tonino was encouraged, however, when he heard about one fisherman from Taiji who had given up whaling and developed a profitable ecotourism business based on whale and dolphin watching. Exploitation of various resources, such as whales and timber, are currently front line topics. Tonino wondered how the world would deal with the overuse of crude oil, but he also focused on water, a resource that is essential to all life forms. To Tonino, this was a critical topic that must be discussed and tackled immediately and at every level.

Tonino began to think about so many useful articles that can be made from a limited resource. An example is baleen, which once was used for the ribs of an umbrella. Tonino wondered if the umbrella his relatives used had ribs made from baleen. Baleen is no longer used for umbrella ribs, thus it is no longer needed. Somehow, however, some items continued to be produced but now have a different function. There is no need to go into examples here because everyone can name many, but one item in Japanese culture "transformed" and became very popular: *netsuke.*

Tiny Japanese Carvings: *Netsuke*

The traditional Japanese robes were known as *kosode* and *kimono.* However, people who wore them, especially men, had a problem: these robes had no pockets. Thus, men had no place to put their money or anything else they needed. To solve this problem, special containers known as *sagemono* were made. These were attached to the sash, or *obi,* of the robe and were hung by cords. The containers could take several different forms: beautiful boxes, pouches, or woven baskets. All these were kept shut by an *ojime,* or sliding beads on the cords. To close the container at the top, they used a carved buttonlike structure. Oftentimes these were very elegant and detailed. They were called *netsuke.* Once they served an important function for dress, but now they were costly objects of art. It is reported that some of them command prices as high as $10,000. They are so popular on a worldwide scale that there is even a website and society devoted to just these elegant carvings.

Tonino wondered if the old Chinese man at the cricket fight in China used a *netsuke* to close the pouch that held his cricket cage. He distinctly remembered the old man undoing something hanging from a sash that was tied around his waist and removing a holder that was like a gourd. When he opened it, he removed his fighting warrior and then handed it to the man weighing the crickets. He then remembered that bag had been called a *tao.*

Tonino was intrigued by the idea that certain objects in various cultures were once produced for one function (e.g., kachina dolls to teach young children lessons) and were now are sold at high prices as art objects. It is similar to ecotourism, where tourists pay to see living organisms in their natural environment, while at the same time the environment is protected and local people receive an income. Instead of the environment and living organisms being saved, cultural objects are preserved in what could be called artisancultural preservation. What a wonderful way to preserve items in our culture that otherwise might be lost or go extinct.

Tonino read on and found an article about *netsuke*. He learned that they can be carved from various materials: wood, amber, pottery, and ivory. Since ivory is almost impossible to obtain legally, he was surprised to learn that the helmeted hornbill produces an ivorylike substance that is used by carvers. He had never seen a hornbill and wondered if they were like the toucan found on the box of Fruit Loop cereal. He read on and learned that these birds have a large protrusion on their upper bill, known as a *casque* (French for "helmet"), and used as a weight in getting food, but more importantly in fighting for a mate. The males use their *casques* to ram one another in an attempt to gain supremacy and assure it is their sperm that fertilizes the female's eggs. Unlike other hornbills, where the *casque* is not solid, the *casque* of the helmeted hornbill is solid, which makes it ideal for carving. Because of the demand for their *casque* and feathers as resources, they are overhunted and, in many areas, face extinction. The indigenous peoples use the feathers, just like the Hawai'ians did, for making cloaks and head-dresses.

Tonino mumbled to himself, *Another example of a limited resource that will be depleted if not protected.*

The amazing thing to Tonino, however, was that this was not really ivory. He learned that the *casque* is really a keratin product, which is similar to the protein found in our skin, hair, or fingernails. Thus, it is somewhat similar to the main constituent of baleen. Ivory, on the other hand, is composed mainly of dentin, which is mostly inorganic matter, some organic matter, and water. It is what makes up the teeth of many animals. Based on this, Tonino believed that the *casque* is not really ivory, whereas the teeth of the sperm whale, which were used by early sailors to produce scrimshaw, really is ivory. After a burst of neurons, Tonino wondered where the expression "living in an ivory tower" came from.

Finally, he came to a section illustrating many of the wonderfully carved pieces. He focused on the carved cricket and thought that this would be a wonderful hobby for his father. *I'll mention it to him when I return*, he thought.

Tonino's Flight to Boston

On his return flight from Japan to Boston, Tonino sat next to a very interesting person, who joined the flight in Tokyo. He was a handsome man with grayish hair, wearing a Native American ribbon shirt. The man introduced himself as Tom Porter. Based on his ribbon shirt, Tonino knew he was Mohawk, which is one of the tribes of the great Iroquois Nation of the Northeast. The others are the Cayuga, Oneida, Onondaga, and Seneca.

Tonino reciprocated and introduced himself, saying, "My name is Tonino Cricket." Tonino recalled visiting the Josephine White Eagle Native American Cultural Center at the University of Massachusetts, and after his trip to New Mexico and Arizona, he had consumed as much information as he could in such a short time about Native American culture. He realized, however, that there was much he still didn't know.

Tonino asked Tom why he was in Japan and Tom relied, "I was giving a paper at Hokkaidō University's anthropology department on how we Mohawks have purchased land and moved back to the Mohawk Valley of New York and established a native community just outside of Fonda, New York."

Tonino responded, "I know Dr. Stoffolano's mother was part Mohawk Indian. Can you tell me more about that tribe?"

"Sure," said Tom.

Tom began to explain to Tonino all about the Mohawk belief concerning the origin of Mother Earth and the universe. This took a long time, and toward the end, Tonino could smell the food that was being served behind them. This made him very hungry. When they got their meals, Tonino noticed the steam emanating from Tom's meal and visually equated it with smoke.

"Can you tell me something about the significance of smoke to Native Americans?" he asked.

Tom said, "It will take a lot of time, so I'd prefer to do it at another time if it's okay with you."

Tonino nodded his head yes.

Because Tom was so well read, he was able to converse about many important ideas that were taken from the literature he had read. Tom told Tonino, "There is a very important quote from D. H. Lawrence that I think is appropriate here and is one for you to remember."

Tonino listened carefully because he remembered Joe and his parents always telling him, "Learn everything you can, especially from your elders."

Tom recited the quote from Lawrence:

> Every continent has its own great spirit of place...
> Different places on the face of the earth have
> different vital effluence, different vibration, different
> chemical exhalation, different polarity with different
> stars: call it what you like. But the spirit of place is
> a great reality.

Once dinner was served, Tonino began to tell Tom about his trip to the Pueblos. He told Tom how important insects and other desert arthropods were to the Southwestern tribes. He asked Tom if the Mohawks, or other members of the Iroquois Nation, included insects in their culture or myths.

Tom said, "What I do know is that many used bear grease to keep biting flies away. More important than the small creatures were the larger animals, such as bears, wolfs, turtles, and deer. In fact, many of the Mohawk clans are named after these animals."

Tonino told Tom that Dr. Stoffolano's mother came from the Mohawk wolf clan. He described the efforts to save the overwintering *refugia* for the monarchs and how legislation had been enacted to preserve these sites in Mexico. Tonino tried to impress Tom with his interest in conservation biology and biodiversity.

Tom, in return, explained to Tonino how many Native American tribes had gone extinct. "How awful," Tonino said. "What about the languages of the existing tribes?"

Tom replied, "Of the Senecas, there are about 1,200 survivors and only 7 still speaking the language."

Tom then mentioned the others: Cayugas with 11,000 survivors and 50 to 60 still speaking the language; Tuscaroras 1,200 (7); Onondagas, 11,000 (14); Oneidas 16,000 (200); and Mohawks 35,000 (4,500 to 5,000).

Tonino rudely interrupted Tom and asked him two questions. He remembered when he and Ming Ming and Pedro had played a trivia game on their trip from Springfield to Tanglewood. Ming Ming had asked him if he knew what the name "Massachusetts" meant.

"Since you are Native American and we're speaking about Native languages, maybe you can answer this question: How did Massachusetts get its name?"

"It comes from the Algonquin word *Massachuset*, which means 'near the great hill or distant blue hills.'"

Tonino then asked another question (Carlo had asked Howie this on Nantucket during lunch): "How did Nantucket get its name?"

"It certainly is an Indian name but I believe it was not a good pronunciation of its original name. I am not sure what it means. You know many of the names in our country are derived from various Native American languages, but most people today have no idea what they mean."

Tonino chimed in, "It's like all the acronyms—CEO, CVS, GOP, DNA, and ISBN, just to name a few. Most people don't know what they really stand for."

Tom nodded his head in agreement and tried to get the conversation back on track, but Tonino continued, "Another thing I am interested in is why certain items that once were used by various indigenous peoples, such as gourds, for practical household uses (drinking and storage vessels) and ceremonial functions (e.g., rattles), are no longer used in those ways. If you check the American Gourd Society's Web page, you will see that the main use of gourds now is decorative; they are also used for bird houses."

"You are correct, Tonino, and acculturation of all peoples occurs at an even faster rate because of mass media, such as television, the Internet, and the movies."

"I guess you are correct; however, I don't like it. Everything today is plastic. I am sure that someday someone will have to dig up all the macadam or black top under the big malls and use the space for growing food. Unfortunately, we know very little about the effects of those nasty chemicals leaching into the soil below. I am not sure we can even call it soil, because that requires living organisms. I can't imagine what can live below that awful stuff."

In order to stop Tonino from preaching, Tom raised his hands as if he is going to pray and said, "Within ten years it is highly possible that all the languages I just told you about would be lost because the only people speaking them fluently are seventy-five years old or older. These tribes will be biologically alive but will become linguistically extinct."

After hearing this awful news, Tonino said to Tom, "These Indian tribes will become like silent crickets."

"What do you mean?"

Tonino went on to tell Tom about silent crickets and what was happening on the Hawai'ian island of Kaua'i.

"First of all, let me tell you the effect introduced organisms can have on a native population. Somewhere between the 1990s and 2003, a parasitic fly invaded Kaua'i from North America. How the parasite got there, no one seems to know. Recently, biologists reported that the male crickets on this island had mutated in less than twenty cricket generations. Originally, when they started their study in the 1990s, it was normal for males to chirp. This permitted the females to locate them for mating. The scientists observed that once the parasite was introduced, more and more male crickets became parasitized and died because they were consumed by the maggots the female fly deposited on the singing males. The female fly parasite located the male cricket hosts by following their song.

"What happened then is an excellent case of evolution. You may not know this, but male crickets produce sound by rubbing the scraper of one wing over the ridges of the other wing. This produces the chirp or sound. Because the singing males were biologically at risk and died, this favored the male mutants with altered wings, such that they could not produce sound. Because of this selective pressure, the population of male crickets went from only a small percentage of males having altered wings (thus silent crickets) to greater than 90 percent. Because of this shift, this cricket in Kaua'i is mainly silent."

"How do the female crickets find the males if they cannot use sound to locate them?" Tom asked Tonino.

"Well, apparently there are enough singing males to attract females. As the female goes to the sound, the silent male intercepts the female and mates with her. Isn't that interesting?"

"It sure is," responded Tom. "You could almost draw an analogy between this situation and what happened with the native populations throughout the world once the white man invaded their land. Most of these populations, just like we were saying, have lost their language and have become linguistically silent."

It was evident, by some of the things he asked, that Tonino hadn't quite mastered all the cultural skills of an adult; for example, he asked Tom how old he was. Rather than answer this personal question by giving him his chronological age, Tom launched into another story. He told Tonino about the "life stick."

Tom said, "Everyone has their own life stick when they are born. Some are very short, while others are exceedingly long."

Tonino rudely yawned and started thinking about the recent article he read on telomeres and longevity. Tom could see that Tonino was getting sleepy and halted the discussion, and they both dozed off.

Everyone was awakened by the smell of breakfast being served. Soon after they ate, they landed at Logan Airport. While leaving the plane, Tom said to Tonino, "I have a niece that I would like you to meet."

Clearing customs, the two new acquaintances were greeted by Tom's niece. "This is Rhodina," Tom said.

Tonino shook her hand and said, "My name is Tonino."

As Tom and Tonino went their separate way, Rhodina hollered to Tonino, "Maybe I'll see you sometime."

"I hope so," Tonino replied.

Chapter 14.
Tonino Returns Home

Giovanni Is Not Well

Tonino returned home just in time; it was just a matter of luck, or maybe fate. You see, his father had become ill. He was diagnosed as having leukemia. Giovanni, according to people standards, was not that young. He was seventy-five. According to cricket time, however, this is exceedingly old. Grillo-parlante only said he had been in the house for a hundred years to aggravate Pinocchio. It is quite possible that Giovanni's transforming between cricket and human somehow delayed the aging process for his cricket lifespan, especially if he spent more time in his human form. Unknowingly, this may be the strategy of all Tonino's relatives. Tonino couldn't help but think about Tom's comment about life sticks. *Humans must have much longer life sticks than crickets*, he thought to himself.

Forming a New Bond with His Father

Regardless, Tonino returned home at the right moment. His father had been retired now for only one year; he didn't want to retire but Maria insisted on it. Having Tonino home was like a spring tonic or a breath of fresh air. It was just what Giovanni needed. He and Tonino would sit for hours on the bench outside the door and discuss everything. Tonino even suggested that he learn how to carve netsuke. Giovanni, however, didn't want to learn anything new. He was very satisfied with his way of life. He showed

Tonino how to play *briscola* and *scopa,* two Italian card games that Giovanni used to play with his father, Rolando.

He would say to Tonino, "Remember, we must preserve our heritage."

Tonino would laugh and say, "You're right, but remember everyone should preserve their heritage."

In turn, Tonino told Giovanni about what he had learned on his travels. One of the topics was about the use of gourds in various cultures. When he finished, Giovanni started to tell Tonino about a special saying and its connection to a gourd. "*Cucuzzi caravazzi* is the favored eating squash in many parts of Italy. It can grow up to six feet and may be curved at the end."

Tonino interrupted, "I remember Dr. Stoffolano telling me that when he was little and did something stupid, his grandfather would slap him on the back of the head and call him a *cocuzza.*"

This may vary in dialect and spelling, but it means *stupid* or sometimes *lazy.* The relationship between the squash itself and the meaning of the word is unknown. It may be related to a squash just laying around and doing nothing. It could also just mean "You're a squash head." When he heard these little sayings or expressions, Tonino really loved being with his father.

Giovanni noticed something new about Tonino: he now carried an umbrella and a small backpack that could also be carried like a satchel. Stuck in the backpack was a cane that Giovanni kept looking at. Giovanni remembered his father had always carried an umbrella and satchel. In fact, the satchel that Giovanni had been using all these years had been his father's. Giovanni's mother told him that the blue cloth satchel had been in the family since Grillo-parlante. Maria had mended it several times in front of Tonino when he was little.

Giovanni would always say, "Now Maria, that satchel is older than you and I put together. Don't ruin it. It is the old things in life that possess the best spirits."

One day, Tonino told his father, "Let me tell you something about umbrellas that I learned during my travels. Do you know what whale baleen is?"

"No," his father responded.

"Well, there are two major suborders of whales that belong to the order Cetaceae. Within this group are whales, porpoises, and dolphins."

His father said, "I know you tell Joe about the origin of a lot of words; why don't you explain them to me?"

"I didn't think you were interested."

"I am always interested in things you do," his father replied.

"Well, the word *cetacean* is derived from the Latin for 'whale' (*cetus*), and this came from the Greek *ketos*, which means 'sea monster.'"

Giovanni was quick to reply, "Maybe this was why Walt Disney called the whale *Monstro*."

"I believe you might be correct."

"Let's continue our discussion about what you learned about umbrellas," his father replied.

"As I was saying, there are two major groups of whales: the odontocetes, which are toothed whales, and the mysticetes, which use baleen for feeding. Baleen is a somewhat flexible but stiff material like your fingernail, both of which are composed of keratin. Baleen is found in the mouth of these whales, which are called gulpers, and is used to strain out the food particles they take in or when they open up their mouths real wide to gulp."

"What's that got to do with umbrellas?"

"Well, during the Victorian era, which was from 1837 to 1901 and named after Queen Victoria of England, umbrellas were fashionable. At that time, more so than now, people did not want to waste anything. It was also the great era of whaling, and some ingenious person had the idea to use the baleen as ribs for umbrellas. Remember, I said they were stiff but flexible, so they were great for what they were designed for, but like everything else, they became hard to get, which made them too expensive to make."

Giovanni put his arm around Tonino and said, "I am real proud of you."

"Thanks, Dad," he replied. "There is one other thing I would like to talk to you about."

"What's that?"

"Have you heard about stem cell research?"

"No, I haven't."

"Well, stem cells are undifferentiated cells that are found in what is called umbilical 'cord blood.' Recently, researchers are combating leukemia by transplanting these cells from donor blood into people with leukemia. They say it works."

"You know, Tonino, your mother and I didn't have much schooling, so I know very little about these things. If I have time, I will contact Dr. Wilson at Harvard and he will tell me more about these new techniques. He is extremely knowledgeable you know."

Tonino responded, "Yes, I know, he is one of the greatest thinkers of our time. But don't wait. Also, our insect friends know that you could accept hemolymph from other donor insects without any complications, but it is almost impossible to get a hemolymph transfusion."

After this wonderful conversation, both retired.

Giovanni said to Tonino, "Sleep tight, don't let the bedbugs bite."

"Good night, Dad, I love you."

Another Museum, a New Friend, and Native Americans

Giovanni read in the *Boston Globe* about a Native American art exhibit at the Peabody Essex Museum in Salem, Massachusetts, and wanted to share something else with his son. He asked Tonino if he would go with him. They had traveled many Sundays to visit different museums, and this was not very far from Boston.

"Sure, Dad, I would like to go with you. I am worried, however, about you walking."

This was an opportune time for Giovanni to say something about the cane he had seen attached to Tonino's backpack. "Could I use the cane you have on your backpack?"

"Of course; I never thought of that. Susan's Uncle Yorimoto gave it to me. He never married and wanted to give it to someone he liked. According to Japanese culture, he said that using it would help me reach my goals."

"Well, I guess you should use it then, because I have just about reached all my goals."

"Don't talk like that," Tonino responded. "Let me get the cane for you."

Giovanni carefully looked it over and commented, "It is real special. Make sure you take care of it when I am gone."

"Don't worry, I will."

They left the house, and Maria looked at her two loved ones. *Giovanni certainly doesn't move like he used to*, she thought to herself.

Reaching the bus stop was just what Giovanni needed. It lifted his spirit because it reminded him of all the wonderful trips he had taken with Tonino. Even with the help of a cane, however, he was tired.

As they approached the museum, they could see a large, colorful banner that said "'Gifts of the Spirit: An Exhibit of Native American Art, Past and Present." Giovanni really didn't know the extent of Tonino's knowledge of Native Americans, but he would soon find out.

They were hungry when they arrived, so they ate brunch in the museum café before going to see the exhibit. During brunch, a lady played the harp. The harp produces beautiful music created by plucking strings, which vibrate at different frequencies, thus producing different sounds based on the different tension of the strings. Having just discussed how baleen was used to make umbrella ribs, Tonino wondered what harp strings were originally made of.

He then began to tell his father about how Native American art was not even considered art by whites until the twentieth century. "These 'savages' or 'cruel beasts,' as they were called by the immigrant whites, were not considered humans. Unlike the art we see in the Boston Museum of Contemporary Art, most early Native American art lacks signatures by the individual artists. The only identification is to the tribe that did it. The only identity many of these pieces of art give us is the spirit of the maker." He went on to explain to his father, "It wasn't until two major art shows in New York—*Exposition of Indian Tribal Art* in 1931 and *Indian Art of the United States* in 1941 at the Museum of Modern Art—that the different things produced by Native Americans were considered art. Just think how far we have come." Tonino continued talking, "American Indian art is now fashionable and highly collectable."

Tonino remembered seeing the beautiful prints of the world-renowned Navaho artist, the late R. C. Gorman, when he had been in New Mexico. In fact, Tonino had a copy of Gorman's print of the Navaho woman and the monarch butterfly on the front of his high school address book. Tonino checked his watch and told his father they had better finish lunch and leave to see the exhibit.

As they entered the museum, they followed their guided pamphlet through the exhibit. The way the organizers juxtaposed an early piece of art with a contemporary one was highly original and creative. They came to one area showing a woven basket by a Chumash artist next to a bowl called *The Drinker* by Diego Romero, a Cochiti Pueblo artist. The bowl reminded Tonino of the wonderful cricket design on the piece of pottery he saw in New Mexico. They were done in the same simple black-and-white style as the Anasazi bowls he had seen at the Museum of Indian Arts & Culture in New Mexico with Pedro, Sue, and Ming Ming.

As they moved to the next station, Tonino was not watching where he was going, bumped into someone intently looking at the beadwork, and almost knocked her over. How surprised he was when he saw it was Rhodina, Tom Porter's niece. Tonino said he was sorry and then politely introduced her to his father. She was alone, so Tonino invited her to see the rest of the exhibits with them; however, his father soon became tired and sat down.

"When you two finish," he said, "come back and get me." Giovanni also knew that the two youngsters would be better off without him.

As Tonino and Rhodina approached the last pieces of art, Tonino had a suspicion that Rhodina was also a transformer and that she was an insect of some type. *Maybe she is a cricket*, Tonino thought to himself. He made the first inference based on how she responded to the art, the questions she asked Tonino, and the way she answered the questions he asked her. The giveaway that she was an insect was when she said that she often viewed objects in the world as a mosaic and not as a single solid object. The cricket giveaway was when they saw an elegant Dakota flute carved like a wooden bird. She said, "Most flutes are presumed to sound like birds; how insulted crickets must feel because crickets also produce such beautiful music."

Both of them now were on a fast-flowing stream of conversation, so they stopped at the café for something to drink and to continue talking. On the table were free red apples, and this made Rhodina think about the book she was currently reading. She loved to read and wanted to share some of her reading and ideas with Tonino. "Have you read *The Piazza Tales and Other Prose Pieces,* 1839– 1860, a collection of Herman Melville's writings?"

"No, I haven't, but I do like Melville."

"Well, there is a wonderful piece, *The Apple-Tree Table,* which is one of the few cases where Melville writes about insects."

"How does the title about an apple-tree table connect with insects?" asked Tonino.

"In the story, the father buys a table that is about a hundred years old and brings it into the house. To everyone's surprise, however, the mother and two daughters believe the table is haunted because they constantly hear a tick, tick, tick coming from the table."

"Well, what made the noise?"

"One day out of a hole in the table comes a beetle grub that molts and becomes a beautiful, iridescent bug. The amazing thing is that one of the daughters questions whether the talking wood, being at least a hundred years old, could really harbor an insect larva for that long."

Tonino again rudely interrupted. This behavior of his certainly didn't sit well with the Blue Fairy, who was keeping notes of this sort of thing. "That reminds me of another incident concerning talking wood, and an insect that lived for a long time. Grillo-parlante, or the Talking Cricket, was the conscience of that naughty marionette/boy named Pinocchio. Do you know the original story?"

"No, I only saw the Disney movie when I was little. Didn't you just love Jiminy Cricket?"

Rhodina was surprised to hear Tonino say, "Jiminy Cricket was my great-grandfather." Tonino continued, as he could see Rhodina was really getting excited, "Remember, Geppetto carved Pinocchio out of a piece of pine, and when he started carving the wood, Geppetto heard the wood talk."

"I remember that part, but what about an insect living for such a long time?"

"Early on in the story, Pinocchio hears a creek, creek, creek, and asks who is there. Grillo responds, 'It is I.' Pinocchio sees the cricket and says, 'Who are you?' 'I am the talking cricket and I have lived here for over a hundred years.' Of course this made Pinocchio mad, since he knew crickets couldn't live that long. Pinocchio got so mad that he threw a hammer at Grillo and injured him. Most people believed he died, but he was really saved and lived on to pass on his genes."

"Wow! What a story. Did I hear you correctly? Did you say Jiminy Cricket was your great-grandfather?"

"That's right, he was," Tonino proudly responded.

Rhodina knew she was getting close to the truth about Tonino, so she pursued her attack with a final question. "But you are a human and not a cricket."

Tonino also had a strong feeling about Rhodina's life. He stared directly into her eyes and told her he was a transformer.

"I knew it!" she responded immediately, jumping with excitement. "I sensed it! So am I! What a coincidence!"

Tonino said, "Now that we really understand one another, let's continue our conversation about your summer reading."

Rhodina told Tonino that she had just read *Crickets and Katydids, Concerts and Solos*, a book by Professor Vincent Dethier.

Tonino again rudely interrupted the trend of the conversation and said to Rhodina, "I have one last question. It is something that has been bothering me for a long time. What is the origin of the name 'cricket' in reference to you and me?" Even though Tonino knew the answer from the book that he used to find out the derivation of the game cricket, he wanted to give Rhodina a chance to express herself and enter more into the conversation.

It didn't take Rhodina long to answer because she knew French very well. "It comes from the French *criquer*, which means 'to creak'; most crickets make some sort of creaking sound."

"I would never have been able to figure that out. Thank you so much. That is just one more thing off my mind." Tonino was learning more about how to carryout successful conversations and give other people a chance to express themselves. In other words, he didn't always have to take center stage.

Before they left the café to find Tonino's father, Tonino and Rhodina exchanged phone numbers and e-mail addresses because she was going to attend UMass at Amherst in the coming spring. They said good-bye, and Tonino and Giovanni boarded the bus to Boston.

Giovanni knew that Tonino had a liking for Rhodina, and this was confirmed when Tonino said to his father, "Originally I was going to enter UMass in the fall, but now I want to enroll for the spring semester."

"That's fine with me," his father said.

On the way home, Giovanni mentioned to Tonino that he suspected that Rhodina was a transformer and a cricket. Tonino didn't want to get his father's hopes up, as he did with Susan, so he didn't tell him the truth. Instead, he just said, "Maybe."

His father then said, "I wonder if she can play the violin like Susan?"

"I don't think so," Tonino responded.

Tonino didn't want to think about that because he was trying desperately to get over Susan. He could still see her wearing the new T-shirt she had purchased at the airport. It had been awhile. Just like he originally did when he saw her wearing the T-shirt, he shook his head in disbelief and said to himself, *I never thought she would change her mind, and wearing that T-shirt with "Save the*

Whales" on it just hasn't convinced me. Well, I'll find out more in the fall if she attends Mount Holyoke.

For the remainder of the trip, Tonino did not speak. In fact, he was like *The Very Quiet Cricket* in Eric Carle's book and any of the other silent satellite crickets—a very quiet cricket because he was not fully mature and a satellite cricket because he used selective silence when he wanted. Remember, Tonino had learned that satellite crickets originally used selective silence to avoid parasitism by the fly parasite. He was thinking about how he identified in so many ways with Rhodina's culture. Being Native American, she valued Mother Earth, the natural elements like water, and all the living things, whether large or small.

The last thought he had was that he would have to wait until the spring to find out whether they were really compatible. In contrast to Susan, however, he did like Rhodina's affinity with all living things. The bus stopped very near his home, and it took more than the usual ten minutes to get there. Giovanni had slowed down considerably.

How happy his mother was to see them. She had a warm meal waiting for them and was ready to hear every detail of their visit to the museum. You can probably guess what they ate. Yes, between two slices of fresh ciabatta bread, they had roasted red peppers and onions cooked in olive oil and garlic. Tonino and Giovanni both sat back to enjoy the flavors and odors. Tonino especially wanted to savor and preserve the wonderful aroma, which was a family tradition that they all shared.

During dinner Tonino told his mother something about the trip and how he had again met Rhodina, a beautiful Native American girl. "She is going to UMass in the spring, and I was telling Dad that I plan to enroll the same time, and not wait until the fall like I originally had planned."

"That's fine with me," his mother said as she looked at Giovanni for approval.

He nodded his head, so she knew it was okay. Tonino then continued to tell her about what he had seen and what he had learned about Native Americans.

"The population of Native Americans was originally about fifty million people and ranged from the Arctic to the tip of South America. Upon arrival of whites, their population was reduced by 90 percent due to diseases and war. Art was not considered art because they were not considered humans. There were no signatures on art in the beginning, but the art pieces were only attributed to a time period and tribe. No individualization, thus the devaluation of the individual persisted even in art form. Nothing they did was considered art until the twentieth century. Native art was believed to emphasize function rather than aesthetic quality. The artists used natural materials, such as hair, quills, bark, and plant fibers. There were twelve million natives in 1492 in the United States; only 200,000 by 1900. Thus, you can see, Mom, that Native Americans, just like other indigenous peoples, have suffered a lot."

"Well," Maria said, "your generation must make amends and try not to continue this type of imperialist behavior."

Following dinner Tonino called Rhodina. They chatted for a long time and discussed getting together before school started.

Crickets of Hawai'i

Tonino tried not to think about his father's frail condition. Instead, he spent a lot of time reading in the library. In his attempt to understand more about Hawai'ian crickets, he read books by Otte and by Howarth and Mull. Professor Otte's book said that 43 percent of the world's known tree cricket species are Hawai'ian. Tonino was surprised to read that there are no native grasshoppers in Hawai'i. Otte suggested that one of the causes of speciation in ground crickets could be due to crickets being isolated in different lava flows.

His thoughts switched to ants, and he could hardly wait to tell Dr. Wilson about the presence of an ant-loving species of cricket. He also remembered he had lots of questions to ask him. Tonino's mind again switched topics from crickets to ants, when he read about a cricket being associated with an ant. He remembered Dr. Howarth talking about how the introduced Argentine ant had pushed the silversword onto the endangered list of plants on the island of Maui. Most interesting to him was what Otte wrote about his own species, *Acheta domesticus* L.: "Though it is widespread over the globe, it is usually only locally distributed; in Hawai'i it is known only from Honolulu and one small patch of desertlike habitat on the extreme west side of Kaua'i."

From this monograph on crickets of Hawai'i, Tonino learned that Otte found the best way to catch ground crickets was to use bottles baited with cheese. This made Tonino remember how Joe had caught his father before Tonino was born and how he came tumbling out of the soda can when Joe hit it with the broom. At the time, his father had told Tonino, he was not after the cheese but needed a drink. It was the Pepsi in that can that gave his father both water and carbohydrates.

Those Last Days of Bocce

These were the best of times for everyone. Maria, Tonino, and Giovanni spent a lot of time reminiscing, looking at family photographs, talking about Tonino's travels, and just enjoying one another's company. Maria had never seen Tonino and his father getting along as well as they had been lately.

Every day, Tonino and Giovanni would leave the house; Tonino would carry the bocce balls, and the two of them would go play bocce. Giovanni always insisted that he be on the left side when walking with Tonino. The "Yorimoto cane," as it was now called, was in his left hand. *He looks just like his great-great-grandfather holding that cane*, Maria would say to herself. Also, he usually had his right hand on Tonino's left shoulder.

After each game, they would stop to see Joe for a short visit. It was sad for Tonino to see his once strong and handsome father hardly able to move. Tonino now realized how important it was to prospect for new chemicals to treat major afflictions and new diseases of each generation, like AIDS and cancer. He remembered his parents telling him about how tuberculosis and polio had been the major afflictions of their generation. The major difference, however, and Tonino realized this, was that the afflictions of his parents' generation were caused by biological organisms that could somehow be controlled, while cancer and AIDS involved the genetic and immune systems of the afflicted. *Much more difficult to control*, Tonino said to himself.

Even one game of bocce seemed too much for Giovanni. He was still a proud, modern cricket warrior who would not quit. Now, rather than bending over each time to retrieve the balls, he used a metal retrieving device that Joe made for him out of an old olive oil can and a broom handle. Giovanni refused to let anyone do anything for him. His face was no longer handsome according to what some people think, but it had a special character that showed elderly wisdom. It was the face of someone who loved his family, loved life, and helped youngsters prepare for and look to the future.

The last few days he was alive, Giovanni could tell that his life was slipping away. He had reached the end of his life stick. He didn't, in any way, let Maria, Tonino, or any of his friends know that he was aware of what was about to happen. Like all true warriors, he grabbed all the strength he could to survive another day and prepare for the inevitable. That day, Giovanni played his last game of bocce.

A Great Warrior Passes

It was an honorable and peaceful death. He just went to sleep one morning after having his espresso in his favorite chair. On his lap was Tonino's diary. It was opened to a page where Tonino had written just about a week before coming home. Maria had never seen the diary before. How Giovanni got it, no one to this day knows. As she read it, she couldn't help but think that the circle of life was now complete. Tonino represented the next generation.

The diary entry started:

> To my father and friend: I have now had an opportunity to travel, to see many different countries, and to observe many diverse cultures. All these countries are great because they have a strong backbone composed of wonderful

parents, parents like you and Mother. Without this backbone and strong fiber of society, cultures won't function properly and people will eventually destroy themselves and their environment. You were always patient with me—firm, yet not too firm. You always let me make my own mistakes. You let me make my own choices and tried not to impose your wishes on me. By doing this, you gave me a chance to become the person I am; yet at the same time I know that as I grow up, I will become more like you. I remember one time when I was younger, I always thought I wasn't anything like you. Mother certainly made a good choice when she picked you. All those years she let you think that you made the choice. Well, that isn't the way it happens with most animals. I have been reading about mate selection. Most scientists agree that it is usually the female that chooses the male. The female usually assesses the major qualities that she believes to be most fit to sire her offspring. When I return from this trip, I look forward to seeing you and talking about many of the things fathers and sons never get to talk about.

Maria was the one who found Giovanni. She sat next to him for a while, held his hand, read the page of Tonino's diary, closed the pages of the book, and put the Navajo blanket Tonino had sent his father from New Mexico around him so he wouldn't get cold.

Saying Good-Bye

The next time Tonino saw his father was at the funeral. He had been away for just two days in Amherst looking for an apartment with Pedro. So many people came to the funeral. Present were Dr. Wilson, Joe and Isabelle, all Tonino's friends, and all Giovanni's North End *pisani*. This was a very difficult day for Tonino. He saw his mother lose a lifelong friend and companion. He knew that he would have to give her all the strength he could until she had accepted her great loss.

After the funeral, Joe and Isabella invited everyone over to the store for something to eat. Joe had done something special that neither Maria nor Tonino knew about. Giovanni had left his bocce ball set at the store only two days before he passed away. On the top shelf, behind the meat counter, Joe had many trophies. These were mostly for youth sports teams he had sponsored, but now there was something new hanging from the shelf. Joe didn't spare anything for his best friend. He and Giovanni had known one another for many years, too many to count. The interesting thing was that after all those years, Joe never realized that Giovanni was really a cricket. Being such a wonderful man that he was, he had accepted Giovanni for what he was: a wonderful individual.

Giovanni's Spirit: Celebrating the Life of a Great Warrior

The celebration of Giovanni's life after the funeral was somewhat similar to Tonino's seventeenth birthday party, except this time Dr. Wilson came to pay his respects. He arrived early and wanted to spend some time with Tonino because he had been getting only sparse reports from Giovanni about his son's adventures. This was also the time for Tonino to ask Dr. Wilson all the questions he had written in his diary and specifically one that has been troubling him for a long time.

"Thank you for answering my questions about ants and the environment," Tonino said. "I have one more question. I know it is complex but maybe you can answer it succinctly."

"I'll try."

"In your book *Consilience* you mention that culturally humans have always and universally had a belief in a soul. Do you really believe that biologists will be able to someday understand how our genes have predisposed us to this belief?"

"Yes," Dr. Wilson said. "I think it is only a matter of time and technology. In his book, *The Astonishing Hypothesis*, Crick notes that if one were to put the idea of a soul in a biological context that it would ultimately lead to the mind. Thus, neuroscience may be the field that will answer the question, 'What is the soul?'"

Tonino responded, "I personally subscribe to that idea and agree with him that the belief in a soul must be a mental process and that when a person dies, like my father, the soul departs from the body. I have read that some cultures do not believe in a soul, so I wonder how universal this concept is. Finally, some people think the soul and the spirit are equal. I personally do not. The soul is somehow tied to the moral or ethical part of a person, while the spirit encompasses much, much more. As I just stated, when a person dies, the soul leaves but the spirit lives on in the minds of those people who knew him, had heard about him, or had read some of his writings. I believe that when you die, your soul will leave your body because your mind is no longer working. However, your spirit will live on forever in the writings you have produced."

"All I can say, Tonino, is that I am very proud of you. Your father certainly was. He always would say, 'I am so proud of that boy.' Keep up your studies and constantly think about ways in which the sciences can connect with the humanities. Unless scientists do this, human civilizations everywhere will not understand or pay attention to their world. As far as your mission to be the conscience of the world when it comes to environmental issues, I believe this may be a little bit overambitious. If you can win a major battle on one environmental arena, you will have accomplished a lot."

Of course Tonino was worried that this would not satisfy the Blue Fairy, but then again, she may be smarter than Tonino thinks. In fact, Tonino wondered where she has been.

With all these questions answered and discussed, Tonino got to ask Dr. Wilson his very last question. "The local flower shop delivered a beautiful arrangement of flowers all in the colors of the Italian flag. The card read, 'With Deepest Sympathy to the Cricket Family.' The card had the Prince Spaghetti logo on it and was signed 'Joseph Pellegrino.' I know the Prince Company sponsored the ultralight plane we flew for our monarch trip, but who is Joseph Pellegrino?"

Dr. Wilson responded, "Joe Pellegrino is the son of Giuseppe Pellegrino, who was involved in building the Prince Company empire. In 1972 Joseph became president of the company, which was purchased in 1987 by Borden for $164 million. A generous donation from the Pellegrino Foundation established the Pellegrino University Professorship at Harvard University, which gave me such a wonderful opportunity to write. I held this position from 1992 to 1996, and currently I am a Pellegrino University Professor Emeritus. Its benefactors, like Joseph Pellegrino, who make it possible for university professors to focus on their research and writing. I am eternally indebted to him and his foundation."

"Wow! What a connection. Did you know how I got my baptism name, Anthony?"

"No. I always knew you as Tonino. How did you get that name?"

"When my mother was pregnant with me, she heard the commercial on Joe's television with the woman coming out on her balcony in the North End and saying, 'Anthony, Anthony, it's Prince Spaghetti day."

"I remember that ad, now that you mention it."

"Well, my mother said to everyone that if she had a boy she definitely would call him Anthony."

"How then did you get the name Tonino?"

"Joe gave it to me. I was unloading a truck of canned goods one day and he handed me a box of canned sardines from Sicily that was too heavy, and I dropped it. Joe laughed, but his wife said to him, 'Joe, that was too heavy for Anthony and he could have gotten hurt. After all, he is just a little Anthony.' Joe continued to laugh and said, 'I like that name, little Anthony. Let's call him "Tonino," which means "little Anthony" in Italian.' From that moment on, everyone always called me Tonino."

"That's a great history you have there," responded Dr. Wilson. You keep on studying, and someday you will be an entomologist."

"Thank you for coming and for all the support you gave my family, especially letting me and my father come to your office to see the ants when I was little."

"It was my pleasure. I love seeing enthusiastic young people enjoying insects as much as I do. By the way, is there any special place where your family wants donations to go in honor of your father?"

"We haven't decided on that, but you know he loved museums; I think a donation in his honor to any museum would be suitable."

"Okay, I'll do that as soon as I get back to the office."

Joe had cooked Giovanni's favorite dish: fried peppers and onions in lots of olive oil and garlic. Arranged on one of the tables were many different wines from various parts of Italy. Joe wanted to celebrate all his Italian friends, so he provided a wide selection of wines. One of them was in honor of Tonino, even though he didn't drink.

Joe called Tonino over and said, "Look at this label."

Tonino held up the bottle and read the label, "*Villa Tonino, nero d'avola, Sicilia.*" He rotated the bottle and read that it was bottled in Marsala, Italy. As Tonino put the bottle down, his eyes immediately focused on a very interesting bottle, sitting next to the Tonino wine. He picked up the bottle and read to himself, *Grillo-parlante, Trapani, Sicilia.* He knew that Joe didn't know anything about his cricket heritage and just assumed that he accidentally picked up the bottle of *Grillo-parlante.* Tonino thought to himself, *Other than the cricket statue of Grillo-parlante in the Pinocchio Park in Collodi, I can't think of any better tribute to crickets.* Having a wine named after his great-great-great-grandfather was a special tribute to any cricket, especially an Italian one. Even though Joe wanted to honor Tonino with the *Villa Tonino* wine, Tonino was not the main celebrant. This time, however, Giovanni was the center of conversation. Everyone shared his or her favorite story about Giovanni.

About an hour after everyone had eaten and shared their intimate stories about Giovanni, Joe grabbed a large metal spoon and banged on one of the large stainless steel pots he made *pasta fagioli* in. When he had everyone's attention, he went behind the meat counter just in front of the shelves. He had the same white apron on that he had on when he knocked Giovanni the cricket out of the Pepsi can about twenty years earlier. In fact, he grabbed the same broomstick he had used then as a pointer. With a glass of red Chianti in his right hand and the broomstick in the other, Joe pointed to the new object on the shelf hanging next to all the trophies. "Let's all drink and pay tribute to one of the best bocce players in the North End. Today we are gathered here to retire his bocce set. No one will ever again use this set. *Saluti!*" Everyone shouted "*Saluti!*" as they raised their glasses to honor Giovanni. Some even said, "*Cent'anni,*" which means "I hope you live to be a hundred." To Tonino, however, it was a reminder of his great-great-great-grandfather and Pinocchio.

Joe again demanded everyone's attention. Giovanni had made almost everyone in the North End take a solemn vow never to tell Tonino what had happened when his father hurt his leg, it is only appropriate to recount this event so that Tonino will have peace of mind. Talking about peace, Joe's family name, "Pace," means "peace" in Italian, and Tonino loved to tell everyone what it meant. Not only that, he also liked to correct their pronunciation. Most people pronounced it as the English pronunciation: "pace," but it really is pronounced "pa che" in Italian. It is amazing how many immigrants have their family names mispronounced. Most people, however, never feel comfortable correcting those who mispronounce them.

Let's return to the story about Giovanni. Joe continued, "We all know Giovanni told Tonino that he slipped and fell on a bocce ball and that's all that happened when he broke his leg. This is the story that Giovanni told everyone and made everyone promise never to tell Tonino the truth. In case you didn't know, I crossed my fingers behind my back when Giovanni made me promise never to tell Tonino the truth. Thus, I feel I can share the truth with him now. Let me now reenact that evening at the finals of the bocce tournament." Joe went on, "It was the final match for the championship of Our Lady of Mount Carmel's annual bocce tournament. Giovanni, Franco, Sam, and I were playing the Circolo Italiano team from Amherst. The Pace team was losing but could win if we got two points. Sam had rolled in a beautiful ball that snuggled up to and kissed the *pallino*. The other team tried a hard shot to knock Sam's ball away. Rather than hitting any balls, it bounced off the backboard and rolled about three feet in front of the Circolo balls clustered around the *pallino*. Everyone for the Pace team began to chant, 'Giovanni, Giovanni!'" Joe had waited a long time to tell this story, so he told it with great gusto. He even acted it out. "You all know what a proud man Giovanni was," Joe said. "Well, he got up off the bench, puffed out his chest, pulled up his pants, wiped the sweat off his brow with his sleeve, and grabbed the last red ball."

You should have seen Joe prancing around behind the counter and telling this wonderful story about his life-long friend, Giovanni. "The crowd quieted down; Giovanni bent over with his head down, slowly pulled his right arm back, lifted his head and made a visual calculation and measurement, and slowly let the ball go." This was truly a difficult shot because he had to bank it off the side board, go between three other balls, knock out one of the opponent's balls, leave Sam's ball next to the *pallino*, and slowly come to lie next to both the *pallino* and Sam's ball. It seemed to take forever for the ball to do what it was supposed to do—a truly remarkable and skillful shot by Giovanni. It did everything it was supposed to, but rather than beat the closest ball from the other team, Giovanni's ball landed nearly the same distance from the *pallino*. This called for a measurement.

"Giovanni was so excited to get to the other end that he didn't even see the ball that was in front of all the others. As he stepped on the ball, his arms went up in the air, his legs went out from under him, and he landed right on top of the other balls. This was a disaster. These balls would have to be rolled again. I can't repeat what Giovanni said in Italian as he was flying through the air. I believe they were some Italian words that Isabella had warned me to never teach Tonino. The ambulance came, Giovanni was taken to the hospital, and Rico had to substitute for Giovanni. After the game, the entire Pace team went to see Giovanni in the hospital.

"Being the great actor he was, Giovanni performed better in the hospital than at any other time in his life. When the team came in, he was groaning and writhing in pain. When he got ready to find out how the team did, however, it seemed as if everything was fine. 'Well?' he asked, curiously. Then there was a long period of silence before anyone answered. Giovanni was anxious and sat up in his bed. 'What happened, who won?' he asked, waving his hands at everyone. 'Unfortunately, we lost,' I replied. Rather than feeling sorry that the team lost, Giovanni flopped onto his back and said, 'Of course you did; how could the team win without me?'"

By this time, everyone was laughing about this humorous story. Even Tonino could hardly contain himself. Now he knew the truth. What an appropriate time to hear how his father happened to be in the wheelchair when he returned from his trip to Italy.

Maria turned to Tonino and said, "It's so wonderful to see all these people telling such wonderful stories about how they remembered your father. He has given us a great spirit to remember."

"I am sure this story will live on forever and will become part of the history of the North End," Tonino said as he hugged and kissed his mother. Tonino helped Joe clean up and returned home to be with his mother.

Tonino Evaluates Transformation

Tonino took time to escape from the problems in his everyday cricket life. This gave him time to reflect on which was better, being a cricket or a human. One thing he noticed was that as humans age, their skin wrinkles and often they get brown spots, often referred to as liver spots. As a cricket, this doesn't happen. The exoskeleton is both a skeleton and a covering, which is similar to human skin, but different in many ways. *If one is real vain,* Tonino thought to himself, *it is better to be a cricket because aging on the outside is minimal.*

Another interesting comparison is which sex does most of the talking. With crickets, like many other animals, the male puts himself out there and expends a lot of energy defending his territory and trying to get a mate. The females remain silent. With humans, however, most males are "silent crickets," while the females do all the talking. What an interesting switch in evolution.

Tonino Becomes Empowered with His Father's Spirit

Tonino grew in strength, both physically and mentally, following his father's death. He had seen his friend Ming Ming lose a father, so he knew how difficult it was. During that period, Tonino had been a good friend, and now he knew that both Ming Ming and Pedro would be there when he needed them. One of the strangest things to Tonino, even with all his travels and exposure to different cultures, was that he never really understood what was meant by someone's spirit. In fact, thinking very carefully, Tonino realized that some of Jiminy's spirit had been passed on to Giovanni, and now that portion of Jiminy was being passed on to his great-grandson. Tonino remembered talking to the spirit of Pierangelo at the grave in Italy, but he didn't feel he really knew his spirit. He could still hear his father saying, "You may die, but your spirit lives on." Tonino now recognized what a spirit was. His father's spirit would always be with him and with those of the Italians in the wonderful North End.

He remembered the things he and his father did together, the things his father said to him, the way he said them, and the things his father told him about the North End and many other things they talked about. All these things made up his father's spirit. Based on the wonderful stories at Joe's Deli, Tonino also could see that his father's spirit would remain in the North End forever. Tonino wondered if there were things his father wanted to tell him but didn't know how to because generational gaps make communication difficult. *I guess I will never know*, he said to himself.

Maria waited for about two months before giving Tonino a sizeable box of things that his father had put away for him. On the top was a note saying, *"To my little Anthony. Some of these things are only for you. Pass the other things on to the next generation at the appropriate time. This is your charge. Love, Dad."*

   Tonino opened the box, removed each item individually, and examined each one very carefully. First there was an old red umbrella. Next, he looked at the little blue satchel.

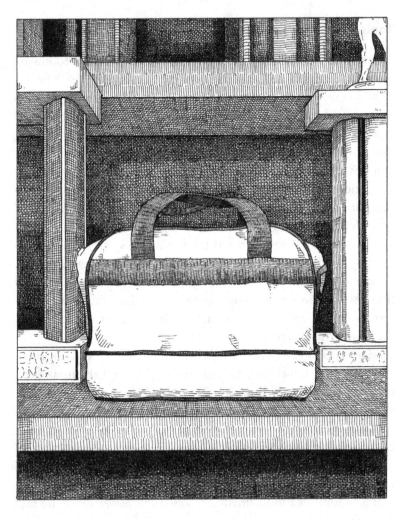

The third item was a sealed envelope that said, *"Inside I discuss topics that will help you in life and some do's and don'ts that every father should tell his son."*

Tonino didn't open the envelope but put it aside for when he was at UMass. The last item was wrapped up. Tonino carefully lifted it out. It felt like a picture, but why would his father give him a picture? Besides, he was sure he had seen every family photo ever taken. There was no way his mother failed to show him every photo in the house. Tonino wondered if she could have missed one. He opened it, only to find the back of the frame facing him. He turned it over. Facing him and looking directly into his eyes was … Yes, it was his great-grandfather Jiminy. Tonino had never seen this picture before. He had only seen pictures of Jiminy after he had become a movie star, those produced by Disney for the movie *Pinocchio,* which showed him as a two-legged, two-handed, upright green cricket with eyes that had eyelids. Here, however, he looked so different; he looked just like a cricket.

Tonino was sure that his mother had never seen this picture either. It was a picture of Jiminy when he was sixteen years old. Tonino found it difficult to take his eyes away from the picture. He felt like he was looking at himself in the mirror. What a strange sensation. At first, Tonino could hardly read the small handwriting at the bottom of the picture. The other reason he was having difficulty in reading it was that it was written in Italian. Being able, however, to translate any language because of the Blue Fairy, Tonino read what it said:

"It is only when you combine the spirit of the person with their physical body that you get a whole being. The only thing left after death is the spirit, the soul is gone. Since this is the only thing we truly leave behind, you must make sure that you live a good life and leave a spirit behind that people will remember as a good spirit. Also, it should be a spirit that you will be proud of leaving behind." It was signed, "Your father, Jiminy."

This brought tears to Tonino's eyes. At this moment, he could only think about what his father once said. "As you get older, you don't need special magic or powers. These are things for young people." Tonino now understood what his father had been saying. Life is real, sometimes even difficult. You get through the hard or difficult times because you deal with them in a real way; all the magic in the world won't solve it for you. You must solve it by yourself.

The Passing on of One's Spirit

One month following Giovanni's death, Maria gave the family Bible to Tonino. "You are now the next male in line of the Cricchetti family. Your father wanted you to take good care of this and to pass it on to your children."

As Tonino took the book from his mother, a folded piece of paper fell out. It was rather old, yellow, and tattered at the edges. Opening it, Tonino saw before him the same lineage of the Cricchetti family that he had seen when in Florence with his aunt Anna and Marino, but this was the original, not a copy.

> *Grillo-parlante Cricchetti* (1881–1921). Hatched in Collodi, Italy, on July 4. Had one son, Pierangelo, in 1899; wife's name Filomena Norelli from Squille, Italy.

> *Pierangelo-parlante Cricket* (1899–1939). Hatched in Collodi and moved to Pavia in 1915. Emigrated to Hollywood, California, in 1917 and changed his name to Cricket. Married Nancy Grimaldi, an Italian American, in 1920 and had a son, Jiminy Cricket, in 1922 who became a movie star in Hollywood. Died in Italy while attending the funeral of his close friend Luigi.

> *Jiminy Cricket* (1922–1963). Hatched in Hollywood, California. In 1940, he became a star in the Disney movie *Pinocchio*. Married Mara Stoffolano in 1945 and in 1946 had a son, Rolando. Jiminy drowned while at sea watching whales off the coast of the Baja Peninsula.

Rolando Cricket (1946–1968). Born in Italy while his pregnant mother Carmella was visiting her aunt in Collodi. Thus, he had dual citizenship. In 1964, he and Carmella had a son named Giovanni.

Giovanni Cricket (1964–   ). Born in Italy, he married Maria in 1982. They had a son, Tonino, in 1982.

Tonino Cricket (1982–). Born in Boston on Columbus Day in the North End or the Italian section of Boston.

Tonino asked his mother for a pen and filled in the date of his father's death. It was so strange for him to realize that he was now the last of the Cricchetti family. At one point in his life, he wanted to change his name back to Cricchetti, but somehow he now felt he wanted to pay tribute to his father by retaining the way his father spelled his name, which was Cricket.

Keeping Busy and Avoiding One's Real Life

Tonino had several months before starting at the University of Massachusetts and wanted to get a lot of things done before he left for Amherst. Susan was in California but would soon be leaving to start her freshman year at Mount Holyoke College in the fall. She would only be about twenty minutes away from Tonino in Amherst. This lovely college is located in South Hadley, Massachusetts. Even though she still loved playing the violin, she was intent at getting a degree in international relations. What would happen to Tonino's new relationship with Rhodina remained to be seen. Regardless, he looked forward to his spring semester with great anticipation.

Tonino spent most of the remaining days working at Joe's. He needed to make as much money as he could for college. Every day after work, Tonino would sidle up to Joe and they would both look up at Giovanni's set of bocce balls. Joe would then say, "He was a great man."

His daily routine after work was to have dinner with his mother and then retire to his room, where he would spend the rest of the evening on the computer. He enjoyed this very much. While sitting at his desk, he would often look up at the world map that his father had given him and see the dots of all the places he had been within the last few years. Pedro and Ming Ming would stop by to see how he was doing; however, he preferred to work at the computer. He didn't even go out with them on Friday evenings. Ming Ming understood and told Pedro this was the same way he felt when his father had passed away. "You have to be patient and understanding with Tonino during this difficult period," he would say to Pedro.

It was almost as if Tonino was escaping the real world and entering a magical world, the world of technology. Not dealing with people certainly created fewer problems, but did it really satisfy his personal needs? He did have one good thing going for him: he could transform into another world.

One evening Tonino worked so late that he fell asleep at the computer. The window had been left open all night. Around eight o'clock in the morning, Tonino was awakened by something tickling his hand. When he woke up, he noticed a beautiful male monarch sitting on his hand. He knew it was a male because of the special pouches on the hind wings. Also, the black vein markings were narrower in the male than in the female. He took a good look at it. It walked around on his hand and extended its proboscis to drink some of the sweat on his hand. It then turned to face him and stayed in that position for several minutes. It was as if he were trying to tell Tonino something.

At that moment, a spontaneous burst of electrical activity took place in Tonino's brain and he recalled the saying that Joe and Isabella had written on his butterfly book: "Remember! Before there were computers there were butterflies." This seemingly unimportant event, plus what Isabella and Joe had written, was enough for Tonino to realize that people, plants, and even insects were more important than the computer. He also was now able to put together the importance of past inventions or discoveries that used similar concepts that are used in modern tools or equipment. An example is the technique of Georges Seurat, the pointillist painter who is often called the "patron saint" of digital imaging. The dots he painted are like the pixels of today's computers.

At that moment, Tonino decided computers were only a tool to make things easier and that he had to spend more time with people and with nature. When he got to Amherst and the Berkshire area, he would have ample time to explore the mountains, the Quabbin Reservoir, and the Connecticut River. Also, Pedro would be there, and he would certainly make new friends.

The next day Tonino started packing. The last thing he packed was his computer. It was the second to the last day that Tonino would be working at Joe's, so everyone came by and wished him well at college. Because of this, Tonino didn't work that hard but spent a lot of time talking to his friends. He kept looking at Joe to see if he was angry, but Joe just waved with a smile. For Tonino, this meant, don't worry, everything is okay.

After work he returned home and told his mother how tired he was. "I can imagine," she replied. "After all, saying good-bye to old friends is very emotional and tiring."

"I guess you are right." Tonino was learning more and more how often his parents were right. Following dinner, he kissed his mother and said good night.

Accepting One's Future

Usually Tonino didn't dream, but he was dreaming that he was sitting on the bench outside their house looking at the stars with his father. Just then, out of the sky came the Blue Fairy. "I didn't ask for you," he responded. "Where were you when I needed you the most?"

"I am sorry I couldn't make it to your father's funeral," the Blue Fairy said, "but I really wanted to see if you could make it on your own. I have some very important things to talk to you about before you go off to college. You know, I haven't pushed your failure to meet your commitment to be the guardian of the world when it comes to environmental issues."

"I know, and I want to thank you for being patient."

"Without knowing it, you have been preparing for this responsibility. You have seen a lot of things in your travels, but now you will be preparing in another way. College will help you by giving you the skills and the knowledge to meet this challenge head on."

"I hope so."

"Take your courses seriously and listen to your professors. Be very selective in choosing your friends. Select a professor you respect and see if you can do an internship with him or her. Use the library and learn all the technology you can."

"I will, I promise."

The Blue Fairy was relentless; she didn't quit. She went on and on. Tonino started to sweat, and his heart began to race. He even got butterflies in his stomach. He tried several times to disengage himself from the situation but couldn't.

Finally, the Blue Fairy said, "Don't forget! I will be watching."

With that, Tonino woke up. *Wow, I must have been dreaming,* he said to himself.

It was early but his mother was up. He dressed and greeted his mom with, "Today is my last day of work."

"Don't believe that," she said.

After breakfast, he left and hopped up the curb. Transforming with no one around, he skipped over to Joe's for his last day of work.

Final Days at Joe's

The last day Tonino worked for Joe was a very busy day. There were many customers and tourists all over the place, and several trucks to unload. Isabella watched as Joe and Tonino unloaded the truck.

As Tonino took each case from the truck, he would always say to Joe, "If this is too heavy, I'll do it myself."

After work, Joe paid Tonino and told him that Pedro was coming over. Pedro arrived about six thirty. Joe had to unlock the door to let him in. The three of them went into the back room. Joe pointed to two boxes.

"These are just a few rations for you 'North End boys' while you are at UMass. We don't want you to starve."

They both hugged Joe and picked up their boxes. Joe opened the door. On their way out, he individually patted each one on the shoulder. "Pedro, don't forget. Even though you are not Italian, you are one of the boys. Don't let the North End down. This is now your sophomore year, and we expect you to score a lot of points. Give Calipari one of those salamis."

As Joe patted Tonino, he felt like his own son was heading off to college. Since Tonino had taken a year off from college to travel, he would be a year behind Pedro. Pedro liked this, because now he got to show Tonino around the Amherst area. "Don't forget," Joe said, "we expect great things from the 'technology kid' from the North End. Give Stoffolano the package of dried *baccala*. This is my gift to him for keeping me informed on how you are doing."

Leaving for College

It was ten o'clock in the morning and Tonino and Pedro were getting ready to leave for Amherst. "Here, don't forget the things you need for registration," Tonino's mom said. "Also, here is a letter that came just yesterday."

Tonino opened the letter.

"What does it say?" his mom asked.

"Oh, it's just something from the Massachusetts Student Public Interest Research Group (a.k.a. MASSPIRG) saying that I should get involved with this group because they are an environmental organization run by the students; it will give me experience in dealing with various environmental groups in solving local and national environmental problems of concern."

Tonino started to throw it away, but his conscience said, *Don't take this so lightly. It may be a way for you to learn more about solving some of the world's environmental problems.* Carefully he put it with the rest of the important UMass material.

The truck was loaded and they were anxious to leave. While they were checking things out, Joe came over carrying two more boxes. He didn't say anything to the boys, but slid them onto the truck. As he left, he just said, "I hope this food helps you both at UMass."

Tonino went over to see what it was. As he turned the cases to see the labels, he saw that it was grasshopper food for Pedro. Tonino had a great imagination, but really believed this grasshopper food might help Calipari with his team. He even called Pedro over and said, "Our next experiment will be a bigger one."

Maria was sitting on the bench that her husband had made. With her husband gone, and now Tonino going off to college, it had become her bench. She couldn't help but feel alone. Not only was her only son leaving, but also much of her husband's spirit was leaving with him. *How can you separate the spirit of a parent from that of the son or daughter?* she silently asked herself.

Both boys were excited. They had a rental truck and lots of clothes, household things, and bedding. They would need these because they were renting an apartment on campus.

Maria waved good-bye and shouted, "Don't forget to write."

Tonino looked back momentarily and thought he saw his father sitting on the little bench. Instead, it was now his mother's bench. His mother was sitting there, not his father. As she waved, she thought about what new experiences and opportunities awaited her little Tonino.

Tonino's Last Words to You

Before leaving, Tonino wrote a few parting words of his own:

> *It is hard to imagine the life of my great-great-great-grandfather, Grillo-parlante. He didn't know what an automobile was. He viewed the moon knowing only superstitions about it at the time. Was it really made of cheese?*
>
> *The origin of one's world is ultimately bound to his/her environment. That is the belief of most indigenous*

peoples. *Does this mean that today's generation, which is not connected to the environment, will find their origin in television or computers? What myths will they have? And, will they have a soul?*

Sincerely,
Tonino

Bibliography

Ackery, P. R. and R. I. Vane-Wright. 1984. *Milkweed butterflies: Their cladistics and biology.* London: British Museum of Natural History Publication No. 893.

Adams, E. C. 1991. *The origin and development of the Pueblo katsina cult.* Tucson: University of Arizona Press.

Anonymous. *Traditional Maori arts and crafts of New Zealand.* Rotorua, New Zealand: New Zealand Maori Arts & Crafts Institute.

Baccetti, B. 1991. "Notulae Orthopterologicae." *Osservazioni corologiche su alcuni ortotteri del centro Italia. Redia* 74(2):525–532.

Baccetti, B., ed. 1987. *Evolutionary biology of Orthopteroid insects.* New York: Halsted Press, a division of John Wiley & Sons.

Batchelor, J. 1901. *The Ainu and their folklore.* London: Religious Tract Society.

Berger, A. J. 1972. *Hawai'ian birdlife.* Honolulu: University of Hawaii Press.

Bisignani, J. D. 1994. *Big Island of Hawai'i handbook.* Chico, CA: Moon Publications.

Bostwick, K. S. and R. O. Prum. 2005. Courting bird sings with stridulating wing feathers. *Science* 309:736.

Brody, J. J. 1983. *Mimbres pottery: Ancient art of the American Southwest.* New York: Hudson Hills Press.

Brody, J. J. 1991. *Anasazi and pueblo painting.* Albuquerque: University of New Mexico Press.

Bush, L. 1959. *Japanalia.* New York: David McKay.

Campbell, J. 1949. *The hero with a thousand faces.* Princeton, NJ: Princeton University Press.

Caplan, J., ed. 2000. *Written on the body: The tattoo in European and American history.* Princeton, NJ: Princeton University Press.

Carle, E. 1990. *The very quiet cricket.* New York: Philomel Books.

Carlquist, S. 1992. *Hawai'i: A natural history.* Laawai, HI: National Tropical Botanical Garden.

Cashdan, S. 1999. *The witch must die: How fairy tales shape our lives.* New York: Basic Books.

Clark, S. R. L. 1977. *The moral status of animals.* Oxford: Clarendon Press.

Cloudsley-Thompson, J. L. 1976. *Insects and history.* London: Weidenfeld and Nicholson.

Cole, S. J. 1990. *Legacy on stone: Rock art of the Colorado plateau and Four Corners.* Boulder, CO: Johnson Books.

Colton, H. S. 1959. *Hopi kachina dolls with a key to their identification.* Albuquerque: University of New Mexico Press.

Cox, J. H. 1970. *Hawai'ian petroglyphs*. Honolulu: Bishop Museum Press.

Crosby, H. 1975. *The cave paintings of Baja California: The great murals of an unknown people*. La Jolla, CA: Copley Books.

Cutter, R. J. 1989. *Brush and the spur: Chinese culture and the cockfight*. Hong Kong: Chinese University Press.

Danielle, R. 1994. *Bocce: A sport for everyone*. Bloomington, IN: Author House.

Daugherty, C. and A. Cree. 1990. Tuatara: A survivor from the dinosaur age. *New Zealand Geographic Magazine* 6: 66-86.

Dethier, V. G. 1992. *Crickets and katydids, concerts and solos*. Cambridge, MA: Harvard University Press.

Dickens, C. 1845. *The cricket on the hearth*. London: Frederick Warne & Co.

Dickens, C. 1846. *Pictures from Italy*. New York: Wm. H. Colyer.

Dickinson, E. 1986. *My cricket: A poem*. Claremont, CA: Old Town Press.

Dodge, E. S. 1995. *Hawai'ian and other Polynesian gourds*. Honolulu: Ku Pa'a Publishing.

Dundes, A., ed. 1994. *The cockfight: A casebook*. Madison: University of Wisconsin Press.

Dunn, M. 1972. *Maori rock art*. Wellington, New Zealand: A. H. & A. W. Reed.

Emory, K. P. 1946. *Hawai'ian tattooing*. Honolulu: Bishop Museum Press.

Etheredge, J. A., S. M. Perez, O. R. Taylor, and R. Jander. 1999. Monarch butterflies (*Danaus plexippus* L.) use a magnetic compass for navigation. *Proc. Natl. Acad. Sci.* 96(24):13854–13846.

Field, L. H., ed. 2001. *The biology of wetas, king crickets and their allies.* Cambridge: CAB International.

Fitzhugh, W. 2004. *Ainu: Spirit of a northern people.* Seattle: University of Washington Press.

Fox, J. G. 1996. Playing with power: Ball courts and political ritual in Southern Mesoamerica. *Current Anthropology* 37(3 June):483–509.

Friedman, T. 2005. *The world is flat: A brief history of the twenty-first century.* New York: Farrar, Straus and Giroux.

Gibbs, G. 1994. *The monarch butterfly.* Auckland, New Zealand: Reed Books.

Gibbs, G. 1994. The demon grasshoppers. *New Zealand Geographic Magazine* 21: 90–117.

Gibson, D. 2001. Among the pueblo homelands of Northern New Mexico. *Native Peoples Magazine* XIV (5):70–77.

Graham, P. 1994. *Discover New Zealand. Maori moko or tattoo.* Auckland, New Zealand: The Bush Press of Auckland.

Grant, C. 1978. *Canyon de Chelly, its people and rock art.* Tucson: University of Arizona Press.

Grimaldi, D. A. 1996. *Amber: Window to the past.* New York: H. N. Abrams.

Grimaldi, D. and M. S. Engel. 2005. *Evolution of insects.* New York: Cambridge University Press.

Hambley, W. 1925. *The history of tattooing and its significance.* London: Witherby.

Hammond, C. 1983. The courtly crickets. *Arts of Asia* 13(2):81–86.

Hapai, M. N. and L. H. Burton. 1990. *Bug play: Activities with insects for young children.* Reading, MA: Addison-Wesley.

Harrison, K. D. 2007. *When languages die: The extinction of the world's languages and the erosion of human knowledge.* New York: Oxford University Press.

Hearn, L. 1905. *Exotics and retrospectives.* Boston: Little, Brown, and Company.

Howarth, F. G. and W. P. Mull. 1992. *Hawai'ian insects and their kin.* Honolulu: University of Hawaii Press.

Jacoby, E. F. 1994. Smokey turns 50. *Conservationist* 40, 64.

Jin, X.-B. and A. L. Yen. 1998. Conservation and the cricket culture in China. *Jour. Insect Conservation* 2:211–216.

Jones, Jenny. 1994. *Giant weta.* Auckland, New Zealand: Heinemann Education.

Joya, M. 1965. Quaint customs and manners of Japan. Vols. I & III. Tokyo: Tokyo News Service.

Judge, K. A. and V. L. Bonanno. 2008. Male weaponry in a fighting cricket. *PLoS ONE* 3(12):e3980, 1–10.

Kabotie, F. 1949. *Designs from the ancient Mimbreñoes with a Hopi interpretation.* San Francisco: Grabhorn Press.

Kaye, G. 1990. *Hawai'i volcanoes: The story behind the scenery.* Las Vegas: K. C. Publications.

Kwiatkowski, P. F. 1991. *Na Ki'i Pohaku: A Hawai'ian petroglyph primer.* Honolulu: Ku Pa'a Publishing.

La Moy, W. T., ed. 1996. *Gifts of the spirit. Works by nineteenth-century & contemporary Native American artists.* Vol. 132. Salem, MA: Peabody Essex Museum Collections.

Langreth, R. 1994. The world according to Dan Janzen. *Popular Science* (December): 78–82, 112–115.

Lattimore, D. N. 1993. *Punga: The goddess of ugly.* New York: Harcourt Brace.

Laufer, B. 1927. Insect-musicians and cricket champions of China. Chicago: Field Museum of Natural History. Anthropology leaflet no. 22.

Laurent, E. L. 2001. Mushi. *Natural History* 110(2):70–75.

Lawrence, D. H. 1964. *Studies in classic American literature.* London: Heinemann.

Leach, M., ed. 1972. *Dictionary of folklore, mythology and legend.* Volume one. New York: Funk & Wagnalls. A Division of Reader's Digest Books.

Lee, G. and E. Stasack. 1999. *Spirit of place. Petroglyphs of Hawai'i.* Los Osos, CA: Bearsville and Cloud Mountain Presses.

Lekson, S. H. 2001. Flight of the Anasazi. *Archaeology* September/October. 54(5): 44-47.

Litowinsky, O. 1992. Writing and publishing books for children in the 1990s. New York: Walker and Company.

MacArthur, R. H. and E. O. Wilson. 1967. *The theory of island biogeography.* Princeton, NJ: Princeton University Press.

McDonald, M. A. 1985. *Ka lei: The leis of Hawai'i.* Honolulu: Ku Pa'a Publishing.

McGinnis, S. 1997. "Zemi three-pointed stones." In *Taíno. Pre-Columbian art and culture from the Caribbean* (edited by F.

Bercht, E. Brodsky, J. A. Farmer, and D. Taylor). New York: The Monacelli Press.

Mack, J., ed. 1994. *Masks. The art of expression.* London: British Museum Press.

McKeown, K. C. 1944. *Insect wonders of Australia.* Sydney: Angus and Robertson.

Mackerras, C. 1975. *The Japanese theatre in modern times.* Amherst: University of Massachusetts Press.

Marquis, D. 1927. *Archy and Mehitabel.* New York: Doubleday Press.

Medeiros, A. C. and L. L. Loope. 1994. *Rare animals and plants of Haleakala National Park.* Hawai'i Natural History Association.

Meyer-Rochow, V. B. 1990. *The New Zealand glowworm.* Waitomo Caves Museum Society.

Moffett, M. W. 1991. Wetas: New Zealand's insect giants. *National Geographic* 180(5):101–105.

Morton, W. S. and J. K. Olenik. 2005. *Japan. Its history and culture,* 4th ed. New York: McGraw-Hill.

Mrantz, M. 1976. *Hawai'i's whaling days.* Honolulu: Aloha Publishers.

Olson, S. 2003. *Mapping human history: Genes, race, and our common origins.* Boston: Mariner Books Pub. a Division of Houghton Mifflin Harcourt.

Otte, D. 1989. "Speciation in Hawai'ian crickets." In *Speciation and its consequences* (edited by D. Otte and J. A. Endler). Sunderland, MA: Sinauer Associates.

Otte, D. 1994. *The crickets of Hawai'i*. Philadelphia: The Orthopterists' Society at the Academy of Natural Sciences of Philadelphia.

Palmer, C. B. 1953. Crickets, nature's expert fiddlers. *National Geographic* 104(3):385–394.

Parker, E. 1870. *The history of cricket*. London: Seeley Service & Co.

Patterson, A. 1992. *Rock art symbols of the greater Southwest: A field guide*. Boulder, CO: Johnson Books.

Pearson, G. A. 1996. Insect tattoos on humans: A "dermagraphic" study. *American Entomologist* 42(2)(Summer issue):99–105.

Pennisi, E. 1993. Chitin craze: Some scientists remain positively charged about chitin. *Science News* 144:72–74.

Perella, N. 1991. *The adventures of Pinocchio by Carlo Collodi*. The complete text in a bilingual edition with the original illustrations. Berkeley: University of California Press.

Phillipps, W. J. 1969. *Maori life and customs*. Auckland, New Zealand: A. H. & A. W. Reed.

Poinar, G., Jr. and R. Poinar. 1999. *The amber forest: A reconstruction of a vanished world*. Princeton, NJ: Princeton University Press.

Pyle, R. M. 1999. *Chasing monarchs: Migrating with the butterflies of passage*. Boston: Houghton Mifflin.

Quammen, D. 1997. *The song of the dodo: Island biogeography in an age of extinction*. New York: Simon & Schuster.

Ravenel, R. 1994. Where there's Smokey, there's never any fire. *Smithsonian* 24, 59.

Reed, A. W. 1970. *An illustrated encyclopedia of Maori life*. Auckland, New Zealand: A. H. & A. W. Reed.

Riccio, A. 1998. *Portrait of an Italian-American neighborhood: The North End of Boston.* Staten Island, NY: Center for Migration Studies.

Robotti, F. D. 1962. *Whaling and Old Salem.* New York: Bonanza Books.

Rodari, G. 1993. "Tonino l'invisibile." In *Favole al Telefono.* Italy: Einaudi Ragazzi.

Romoser, W. S. and J. G. Stoffolano, Jr. 1998. *The science of entomology.* New York: McGraw-Hill.

Rouse, I. 1992. *The Taínos: Rise and decline of the people who greeted Columbus.* New Haven, CT: Yale University Press.

Rudacille, D. 2000. *The scalpel and the butterfly: The war between animal research and animal protection.* New York: Farrar, Straus and Giroux.

Rundell, M. 1995. *The dictionary of cricket.* New York: Oxford University Press.

Rust, J. A., A. Stumpner, and J. Gottwald. 1999. Singing and hearing in a Tertiary bushcricket. *Nature* 399:650.

Schaafsma, P. 1992. *Rock art in New Mexico.* Santa Fe, NM: Museum of New Mexico Press.

Segel, H. B. 1995. *Pinocchio's progeny.* Baltimore: Johns Hopkins University Press.

Selden, G. 1970. *The cricket in Times Square.* New York: Dell.

Shadrake, S. 2005. *The world of the gladiator.* Stroud, Gloucestershire, UK: Tempus Publishing.

Sharell, R. 1966. *The tuatara, lizards, and frogs of New Zealand.* London: Collins.

Slifer, D. and J. Duffield. 1994. *Kokopeli.* Santa Fe, NM: Ancient City Press.

Smith, W. 1952. Kiva mural decorations at Awatovi and Kawaika-a. *Papers of the Peabody Museum of Archeology and Ethnology* 37. Cambridge, MA: Harvard University Press.

Soulé M. E., ed. 1986. *Conservation biology: The science of scarcity and diversity.* Sunderland, MA: Sinauer Associates.

Spires, E. 1999. *The mouse of Amherst.* New York: Frances Foster Books.

Stella, M. 2000. "Pip and Pinocchio: Dickensian motifs in Carlo Collodi." In *Dickens: The craft of fiction and the challenges of reading,* edited by R. Bonadel, C. de Stasio, C. Pagetti, and A. Vescovi. Milan, Italy: Edizioni Unicopli.

Stiling, P. 2000. A worm that turned. *Natural History* 109(5):40–43.

Stimson, J. and M. Berman. 1990. Predator induced colour polymorphism in *Danaus plexippus* L. (Lepidoptera: Nymphalidae) in Hawai'i. *Heredity* 65:401–406.

Stimson, J. and L. Meyers. 1984. Inheritance and frequency of a color polymorphism in *Danaus plexippus* (Lepidoptera: Danaidae). *Journal of Research on the Lepidoptera* 23(2):153–160.

Swinburne, R. 1997. *The evolution of the soul.* Oxford: Oxford University Press.

Taylor, A. 1981. *Polynesian tattooing.* Laie, Hawai'i: Institute for Polynesian Studies, Brigham Young University, Hawai'i campus.

Teiwes, H. 1987. *Western Apache material culture: The Goodwin and Guenther Collection.* Tucson: University of Arizona Press.

Urquhart, F. A. 1960. *The monarch butterfly*. Toronto, Canada: University of Toronto Press.

Urquhart, F. A. 1987. *The monarch butterfly: International traveller.* Chicago: Nelson-Hall.

Venanzetti, F., D. Cesaroni, P. Mariottini, and V. Sbordoni. 1993. Molecular phylogenies in Dolichopoda cave crickets and mtDNA rate calibration. *Molecular Phylogenetics and Evolution* 2:275–280.

Vickery, V. R. and G. O. Poinar, Jr. 1994. Crickets (Grilloptera: Grilloidea) in Dominican amber. *Canad. Entomol.* 126: 13–22.

Vietmeyer, N. 1987. How a bug made the world see red. *International Wildlife* March-April 42–47.

Vittum, P. J., M. G. Villani, and H. Tashiro. 1999. *Turfgrass insects of the United States and Canada*. 2nd ed. Ithaca, NY: Cornell University Press.

Walker, S. E., J. A. Roberts, I. Adame, C. J. Collins, and D. Lim. 2008. Heads up: Sexual dimorphism in house crickets (*Acheta domesticus*). *Can. J. Zoology* 86:253–259.

Weston, G. F., Jr. (updated by C. C. Raymond). 1957. *Boston ways: High, by and folk*. Boston: Beacon Press.

Whittington, E. M., ed. 2001. *The sport of life and death: The Mesoamerican ballgame*. New York: Thames and Hudson.

Wilson, E. O. 1984. *Biophilia*. Cambridge, MA: Harvard University Press.

Wilson, E. O. 1992. *The diversity of life*. New York: W. W. Norton.

Wilson, E. O. 1994. *Naturalist*. Washington D.C.: Island Press/ Shearwater Books.

Wolkomir, R. 1995. Without garlic life would be just plain tasteless. *Smithsonian* 26(9):70–78.

Wood, M. 1992. "The woman and the butterflies." In *Spirits, heroes & hunters from North American Indian mythology.* New York: Peter Bedrick Books.

Wood, M. 1992. "Why the opossum's tail is bare." In *Spirits, heroes & hunters from North American Indian mythology.* New York: Peter Bedrick Books.

Zuk, M., J. T. Rotenberry, and R. M. Tinghitella. 2006. Silent night: Adaptive disappearance of a sexual signal in a parasitized population of field crickets. *Biology Letters* 2: 521–524.

Acknowledgments

Thanks to Dr. William Cooley for giving the author the idea about using the name Tonino rather than Anthony for the main character. This came about as a result of Dr. Cooley reading the Italian short story *Tonino l'Invisibile*, which is about a young boy who can become invisible. Constant encouragement to even get started on this story came from my good friend Nancy Fritz. Professor of geology David Alexander put me on the track of the Festival of the Ascension, or *Calendimaggio,* and the use of crickets as a possible reason why Lorenzini chose the cricket to be the conscience of Pinocchio. It is called *Feste da Grillo* and is held in Cascine Park in Florence. Thanks to Dr. Baccio Baccetti, who provided information about *Calendimaggio* and *Acheta domesticus* L. in Italy. Thanks to Dr. Tremblay, head of the Department of Entomology in Naples, for providing me with information about crickets in Italy. Appreciation to Isabella Bellacari of the *Fondazione Nazionale* Carlo Collodi and Charity Hope, reference librarian at the University of Massachusetts' Du Bois Library, for providing me with detailed information when needed. Appreciation to all those individuals who read different versions of the manuscript and who also may have provided important details. Thanks to the following for translating various documents, etc., from Italian to English: Roland Sarti, Elena Giorgi, and Arturo Figlioli.

Without my wife, Susan, much of the detail, names of places, and sequence of events would probably be incorrect. Her constant attention to detail when we are traveling is unparalleled. I would like to thank all those individuals I have been close to during my life and whose inclusion in this story have helped give the characters their interesting traits and personalities.

Finally, I would like to thank all the readers (New Zealand: Drs. George Gibbs and John Andrews; Hawai'i: Marlene Hapai; Southwest: Sue Sturtevant; final read by Angela d'Errico) for taking time to read this story, which was designed to give a sense of multiculturalism and a sense of the urgency for all of us to help conserve and preserve, not only cultures, but the organisms that share this wonderful Mother Earth with us. Thanks to Kathy Horton, Dr. Wilson's assistant, for sending me pertinent information concerning the Pellegrino University Professorship at Harvard. I am especially indebted to William Griffin for taking on the daunting task of illustrating this book. Finally, a great deal of appreciation goes to Joseph Fatton, who did a remarkable job of editing this book. To him, Tonino and I express our appreciation.

Notes

1. Collodi, C. 2007. *The adventures of Pinocchio*. Translated by C. D. Chiesa with illustrations by C. Chiostri. Firenze, Milan, Italy: Giunti Editore.
2. Ibid.
3. Perella, N. 1991. *The adventures of Pinocchio by Carlo Collodi*. The complete text in a bilingual edition with the original illustrations. Berkeley: University of California Press, p. 197.
4. Spires, E. 1999. *The mouse of Amherst. New York:* Frances Foster Books.
5. Mercatante, S. A. 1983. *The Facts on File Encyclopedia of World Mythology and Legend*. New York: Facts on File.
6. Reid, J. and S. Whittlesey. 1999. *Grasshopper Pueblo: A story of archaeology and ancient life*. Tucson: University of Arizona Press.